DOG'S BREAKFAST

Between the Lines Publishing
1769 Lexington Ave N, Ste 286
Roseville MN 55113
btwnthelines.com

First Published: January 2025

ISBN: Paperback 978-1-965059-04-3

ISBN: Ebook 978-1-965059-05-0

Library of Congress: 2024941882

The United States Department of State reviewed the manuscript of *Dog's Breakfast*, offered no objection to its release in full, and requested the following disclaimer:

> *The opinions and characterizations in this book are those of the author, and do not necessarily represent official positions of the United States Government.*

DOG'S BREAKFAST

Tom Navratil

Acclaim for *Dog's Breakfast*

"I was captivated." –Helen of Troy

"Hoped for something more formulaic." –Marie Curie

"If I had read this book, I never would have invaded Russia." –Napoleon Bonaparte

"The how-to for ambitious diplomats I should have penned!" –Nicolo Machiavelli

"All novels are read before they are ever written." –Sun Tzu

"Looking for a grand epic that captures the sweep of history in its magnificent fullness? Try War and Peace." –Leo Tolstoy

"A terrific airplane read." –Amelia Earhart

"Had Bonaparte not attacked, I would have composed a different grand epic, but equally magisterial." –Leo Tolstoy

For America's diplomats,
among whom I was proud to serve

Part I

Five Days in August

Chapter 1

Just do your duty. Hovering in the living room of the ambassador's residence in the wrong dress, Tara Zadani shifted her weight from one ill-chosen red pump to the other. She needed more than her father's musty motto. Clustered with her new colleagues, waiting for the Vodanian guests to begin arriving, she doubted she would do well in her vague supporting role. In the foyer, the ambassador and his wife flanked the senator from Nebraska, whose visit provided the occasion for the gala reception. Next to them, as if saving his place in line, stood the embassy's number two, the deputy chief of mission, with a cheerful expression and a strange gleam in his eyes.

At parties in Kingston, Jamaica, her first post, there was nothing unusual about bare shoulders and backs. She looked around the room again for a kindred spirit, but none of the embassy women wore anything remotely festive, despite Vodania's infamous August heat. She didn't want to say frumpy, exactly, but they all looked like they came straight from their offices. Which they had, Tara realized, noticing access badges dangling from several necks. What is with these people? In her three weeks in Shizl, Vodania's capital, she had met pretty much all the Americans in the embassy and many of the local staff. They seemed cordial enough, for the most part, but with an air of remoteness, as if she had arrived under the shadow of a giant question mark.

Tara didn't know quite where to position herself. Her only guidance had come from a brief exchange with the head of the political section. Pull guests off the receiving line, he told her, make them feel welcome, get them circulating. Tara had nodded solemnly, despite thinking it sounded like the job description for a friendly sheepdog.

She found herself in a semicircle around the senator's aide, an earnest, ginger-haired young man about her height who talked Big Ten football with a guy from the economic section. The aide kept glancing her way, as if he wanted to engage with her but didn't quite have the nerve. One of the household staff, in a waitress uniform, approached with a tray of hors d'oeuvres. Tara selected a miniature quiche the size of a half-dollar. Everyone else declined with terse smiles. Tara quickly popped the blunder into her mouth. As she started to chew, the aide turned toward her.

"It's gonna be a great year for the Cornhuskers," he said, as if daring her to disagree.

Mouth full, Tara could only lift her shoulders and try to make a supportive sound through clamped lips. At Ohio State, she had gone to one home game. An entertaining spectacle, with the bands and cheerleaders and crazy fans, but when it came to men in tights, she preferred ballet.

"Who else has a defense like that?" the aide demanded, shifting his attention back to the econ guy.

Tara swallowed and edged closer to the foyer, ready to show her teeth when the sheep arrived. She flinched when a large actual dog charged out of the kitchen and bounded across the foyer, tail whipping and paws clicking on the marble, and careened into the guest book stand. A housekeeper in a starchy tunic, stationed near the front door on hat check duty, steadied the stand and straightened the gold-laminated pen in its holder.

As the sound of slamming car doors heralded the arrival of the first guests, the chocolate Lab lunged toward the senator, but the ambassador bent to grasp his collar.

The senator didn't flinch. "Who do we have here?"

The ambassador steadied the rambunctious animal with both arms. "Davos is my trusty sidekick. Aren't you, boy?"

With the dog still straining toward the newcomer, the ambassador looked to his wife, who took custody. The ambassador stood, brushing dog hair off his sleeves and pant legs.

"He's a wonderful companion," the ambassador told the senator. "His only flaw is the shedding. Not something I need to worry about with my deputy here."

They both smirked at the dazzling, freshly shaved head of the deputy chief of mission, or DCM for short.

As the front door opened with the arrival of a stout man in a resplendent suit and matching hat, the senator put his hand on the DCM's dome and said, "How about we gather up some of that dog fur and make you a nice hairpiece?"

The ambassador laughed, but the defense attaché and the political counselor looked straight ahead toward the door. The DCM maintained a steady, tight-lipped smile, but Tara noticed his eyebrows quivering like a pair of rattlesnake tails. Angry embarrassment flashed across his face as his glare burned into Tara. Her insides twisted, like when you tag along with your best friend to her boyfriend's dorm room, and she opens the door and he's getting a blowjob from a girl from down the hall. Something in the DCM's expression reminded Tara of that friend, who soon afterwards lashed back, saying she envied Tara because she never had a serious long-term relationship. Now, starting afresh in a strange new country, Tara suppressed the thought that she was alone once more.

Aah, the joys of being second fiddle. Andy Pulano, deputy chief of mission at the U.S. embassy in Shizl, Vodania, felt something unusual at the outset of yet another evening function. He needed to summon an effort to display the hearty good cheer he considered a hallmark of diplomatic proficiency. Second fiddle, hah. Fourth fiddle was more like it, right below the ambassador's standoffish wife and undisciplined dog.

Andy's eyebrows sagged, rather than their customary romping across the expanse of his forehead. Why, suddenly, was it a strain to project congeniality? Granted, his current assignment offered scant prospects for distinguishing himself. Vodania, a craggy highland wedged in the butt crack between the landmasses of Europe and Asia, a splinter of a fragment of a nation so remote and inconsequential many people in neighboring countries had never even heard of the place. This dust heap was no one's idea of a steppingstone for advancement up the State Department ranks.

And deep in Andy's bones, something else gnawed. The dog.

That pampered, sloppy mutt enjoyed the respect and affection of their mutual master, whereas Andy got less-than-gushing performance reviews. Instead of award nominations, he got fed one too many juvenile taunts in front of half the staff. The look of pity on the face of the new junior officer in the management section, that stung. He would have to counterbalance it, set her straight. But above all else, being abased relative to the ambassadorial pet—whose name pointed to his owner's longing for membership in the global elite who celebrate their fabulousness at the annual World Economic Forum in Davos, Switzerland—heightened Andy's awareness that his own precious career had somehow slid onto a trajectory to nowhere.

When the front door opened, Andy, in protocol order alongside the ambassador's wife, snapped on a smile. On his left, the jovial political counselor did his best to taper his belly so it wouldn't jut out across the line of scrimmage. The defense attaché completed the gantlet in his dress blues, medals clinking together like miniature wind chimes.

The senior local employee in the political section, smoothing his ample mustache downward with forefinger and thumb, stepped into position behind the ambassador's right ear. Glancing at the arriving guest, he leaned closer and pronounced the name of the mayor of Ratovich, a leading member of the New Kleptocracy Party. The mayor handed his hat to the housekeeper, impressed his signature onto the guest book with a flourish, and pocketed the golden pen.

"Mister Mayor, so delighted you could join us tonight," exclaimed the ambassador. "And I look forward to visiting your fair city soon."

Andy added the ambassador's promise to the running tally he kept in his mind of things to follow up on.

The mayor clasped the ambassador's hand in both of his own. "You are always welcome, Excellency."

"Let me introduce you to our guest of honor, who started his own political career as a mayor, in the city of Oatsdale, Nebraska."

"Pleased ta meetcha," the senator boomed, clapping the mayor on the shoulder with his left hand while shaking with the right. "Hardest damn job I ever had. Especially during snowplow season."

Andy brightened his expression as more of Vodania's luminaries, such as they were, streamed in, checking hats if they wore them, signing the guest book if they felt like it and happened to have brought a pen. One by one they shuffled forward to shake hands with the ambassador, the senator, and the rest of the lineup. Andy got into his groove, personalizing each greeting with references to shared experiences, fresh news and rumors, mentions of spouses, children, even sports if he had to. Whatever furthered a connection.

By the time a couple dozen eminent citizens of Vodania had passed through, Andy savored a sense of professional superiority over the senator and his assembly-line repetition. The politician from Nebraska operated with speed and uniformity, except for the extra enthusiasm he bestowed on the more daringly attired 'assistants' to prominent male guests. The senator kept his grin steady, and with a rote handshake told each new arrival, "You have a lovely little country." The Turkish ambassador, when his turn came to receive this compliment, responded in his usual clipped fashion, "Thank you. Our economy is currently the seventeenth largest in the world."

Without reacting, the senator reached for the next in line and said, "You have a lovely little country."

Davos burst back in from the living room, and the ambassador's wife squatted to catch him around the chest. She knuckle-rubbed the animal's head, pressed her cheek to his muzzle, and cooed, "So many important people to meet! So, so many, isn't that right, my little ambassador?"

With a flicker of glee, Andy registered her minor transgression and its subtle whiff of impropriety. There can be but one ambassador.

Currying the benevolence of superiors had earned Andy steady promotions up the career ladder. But what if that path only took him so far? Could there be another route to the glorious, sublime, transcendent pinnacle from which one was exalted into the ambassadorial firmament? Andy knew, in his heart and soul and in every conniving fiber of his mind, that he should, and must, become an ambassador. But how could he transform his position as assistant zookeeper at the U.S. embassy in dreary Shizl, dog-infested capital of the Republic of Vodania, into a vessel for advancement? Marooned on the lumpy back end of nowhere, with his prospects for the ultimate promotion mired in gloom, Andy found himself casting around for a beacon, a ray of light. A sign.

As the first few guests reached the end of the receiving line, Tara Zadani stood frozen in place while various colleagues stepped forward to initiate conversations, seemingly with people they already knew. Receptions such as this were among the few places where ethnic Vodanians and ethnic Pazaris intermingled. Pazaris, the country's second most populous group, were also called Pazari-Vodanians, as well as a variety of pungent epithets and slurs. Tara hadn't expected how striking many of the men looked, if you didn't mind beefy mustaches. And the younger women, good gracious. Overflowing bodices, miniskirts like loin cloths. Displaying their bounty for all to see. Tough competition. But at least she no longer felt quite so exposed in her backless party dress.

Maybe Vodania would not be as drab as it first seemed. In any case, this was what she signed up for. Squaring her bare shoulders, she flashed her game smile at a rumpled older man and extended her hand, ready to test how far six months of language training could take her. She promptly found herself submerged in a flood of grievances pouring forth from one of the local politicians. Tara listened with intense focus, trying to determine if he was Vodanian or Pazari. She was not yet adept at distinguishing the members of one group from the other. Outdoors it was easier, as the Pazaris always wore hats.

Although the Vodanians and Pazaris spoke essentially the same language, Tara had been warned about certain nuances of difference. For instance, the word for food in one language meant poop in the other, and vice versa. Same for mother and dog. Ethnic Pazaris couldn't or wouldn't pronounce the letter V. And the phrase for good morning in Vodanian meant "I have an erection" in Pazari. Whenever Pazaris heard Vodanians saying good morning, they responded "good for you" or "no you don't," depending on the speaker's gender.

When the ambassador deemed that the receiving line had fulfilled its purpose, Andy followed him and his wife and the senator into the main room to work the crowd. With appraising eyes and a friendly expression, Andy noted the presence of at least one member of parliament from each of the country's seven significant political parties. He knew the ambassador would take that as a good sign, especially with nationwide parliamentary elections just over a month away. Prior to the reception, the embassy's political section had worried that the Vodanian politicians would make themselves scarce, for two reasons. First, the ethnic Vodanians knew that hordes of Pazaris would attend, reflecting the minority's excessively exuberant embrace of America. The second reason was the current media kerfuffle. Once again, the vocal U.S. ambassador in neighboring Pazaria had found an occasion to proclaim the strength of the U.S.-Pazaria alliance against all comers, and such pronouncements affronted the Vodanians whenever they felt like being affronted.

Andy's gaze took in the notables, from government, business, media, the arts, and of course politics, clumping together, forming conversational clots that persisted in some cases and promptly dissolved in others. Davos cavorted among the guests, sniffing and drooling, his hard tail swinging and slapping the unwary. To a novice, the swirl of meetings and greetings might look random, chaotic, but Andy studied the patterns, measuring degrees of subservience and respect, collaboration and rivalry. He had long mastered the ritual of the evening cocktail reception. The whirling dance of connecting, cajoling, probing, and parrying normally amused him. To match wits with worthy and not so worthy competitors, to charm and threaten with hints of rewards and punishments, costs and benefits. Enthralling. But somewhere in his mind a shrill whine built, a nagging awareness that his enjoyment of the whole exercise had always hinged on a shaky premise. What if, in the end, devotion and subservience did not pay off?

He moved through the room emitting steady energy, giving attention where attention was due. In another part of his mind, he examined the scene unfolding in the ambassador's residence as if it offered a clue to guide him out of the obscure backwater into which his career had drifted.

The whir of conversations, arguments, jokes, and introductions built a noise vortex, a hurricane of chatter. Tara met a painter who wanted to say something to the guest of honor, so she led her toward the center of the room, where the senator stood alongside the Cornhusker guy. As Tara and the artist got within range, the senator peeked at his watch, elbowed his aide, and pointed toward the DCM with his chin.

"Look at this guy, Andy Pulano. Seems pretty ordinary, right? At first? Another schlumpy bureaucrat. But notice how he watches the whole field. He's a natural quarterback. He's dealing with the linebackers coming at him but he's also reading the dynamics of the entire gridiron and adjusting accordingly. He could run for office, swear to God."

It occurred to Tara that the DCM could be a good person to learn from. If he were willing to share his knowledge. As she was about to interrupt the senator and make the introduction, a tall woman in her forties shouldered past.

"Someone's in a hurry," Tara commented to the artist.

"That's the interior minister, Lenora Xotari. Very close to our president. One of only two women in his cabinet."

The interior minister pushed into the circle around the ambassador, whose expression radiated calm enjoyment. She leaned close and spoke into his ear, and the two of them pivoted into an open space closer to where Tara stood.

"It's very important that we know in advance," the interior minister hissed, "how Vodania will come out in this year's Trafficking in Persons report."

The ambassador inhaled through his confident smile. "Well, as you know, it's a fact-based report. We send in the facts about the performance of your government in combating human trafficking, and Washington puts the information together and decides on the ranking. I know you've been working on the, uh, areas for improvement."

"Oy!" the minister yelped, drawing away.

The ambassador paused, momentarily befuddled until he noticed Davos thrusting his snout up toward his guest's crotch. The interior minister fended him off with a raised knee but still ended up with a large splotch of slobber on the front of her beige wool suit. The ambassador looked around and spotted Tara.

"Can you please help Minister Xotari, get her some towels?"

"Certainly sir."

He aimed the slightest of bows at the interior minister and said, "I am so very sorry."

The interior minister waved off the apology and followed Tara to the kitchen. Tara moistened a handful of paper towels, and one of the kitchen staff came forward with salt.

The Vodanian official maintained an edgy humor. "To be honest this is not even the worst indignity I've experienced today."

"I wish there was something more we could do," Tara said.

"Someone could do something about that dog."

"Well, he's already been neutered, so what's left?"

The interior minister snorted. As she strode back to the party, she seemed to consider the question.

Tara was rinsing her hands in the kitchen sink when she heard an explosive crackle of static, indicating that a microphone had been switched on for the formal toasts. She squeezed into the side of the crowd in the living room to listen to the ambassador's spiel about U.S.-Vodania relations and the vital leadership role the evening's guest of honor had long played in the United States Senate and on a global level.

The ambassador wrapped up. "We are honored and excited to have such a distinguished senator here with us for this very special evening. It's a long way to come, so let's give him the warmest possible welcome to show our appreciation."

The guests clapped, whether from enthusiasm or courtesy Tara couldn't tell, and took photos with their phones. The DCM, positioned in the forefront of the gathering before the ambassador and senator, applauded with vigor before taking out his phone. The ambassador extended the microphone toward the senator, who transferred his wine glass to his left hand and reached over to grab the mic and pull the cord in front of him. At that moment Davos pounced from behind and began humping the senator's right calf. The senator reached down with his right hand to pry the dog away, but Davos locked a firm grip on his thigh with both front paws. The microphone near Davos's dripping jaws amplified his panting grunts of pleasure.

The senator, pivoting to try to shake off the dog, tripped over the microphone cord and fell to his hands and knees, somehow managing to keep his wine glass aloft. Davos seized the opportunity to wrap his front paws around his target's waist and rub his package against the senator's rump. The chocolate Lab managed three or four excited thrusts before the ambassador, straddling from behind, pulled him clear.

Andy Pulano gazed upon the spectacle in wonderment. A message from on high, a wink from the career gods, a new path revealing itself. The first step would be a pair of phone calls.

Chapter 2

Near the end of the reception, her brain buzzing from immersion in the local language and the scrap heap of tidbits and impressions she piled up, Tara met two foreign women who had been in Shizl awhile. Karolina, a cheerful lawyer from Warsaw in her early thirties, promoted democratic election systems on behalf of the Organization for Security and Cooperation in Europe. Monique, a French diplomat of similar vintage, had an assignment to the European Union's diplomatic mission to Vodania. They struck Tara as seasoned, confident, and sassy. And they invited her to join them for a nightcap.

By local standards it was early at Club Boom Shaka-laka, on the edge of Shizl's central plaza. Seated at an outdoor table, with a bottle of red wine and a plate of oddly dainty meat-filled pastries, Tara felt like a nomad who had at last come across fellow wanderers. For a while the three of them observed passers-by as well as the clientele of the club. The men, looking menacing or artsy, and the women, super dolled-up or future matrons on their way to near-Soviet levels of stodginess, all shared a passion for cigarettes.

Monique took out her phone and gestured toward Tara with it. "Was that really necessary, at the end? A bit heavy-handed I thought."

Tara had the same reaction to the scrubbing of each guest's phone by the embassy security and IT people, with the DCM overseeing the process, to erase all photos of Davos having his way with the senator. Reluctant to criticize her side, she lifted her glass and sipped.

"I mean, what if they found dick pics on my phone?" Monique demanded.

Tara snorted wine out onto the cobblestones.

"You have dick pics?" Karolina asked.

"Not at the moment, unfortunately." Monique looked back to Tara. "When the dancing starts up after midnight, with that outfit you'll have plenty to choose from."

Tara glanced around. "These are my options?"

At that moment, four guys in jeans and leather jackets pushed past the table on their way into the club. Tara overheard a gruff Vodanian voice ask, "If you were a dog, who would you rather ride, the interior minister or a U.S. senator?"

Tara raised her eyebrows at her companions.

"Word gets around," said Karolina.

"Very true," Monique agreed. "But the main thing you want to learn tonight, apart from which Vodanian wines are drinkable, is don't wear wool around that dog."

"Sounds like the voice of experience," Tara replied, reaching for a pastry. "How long have you been here?"

"Bit over a year I think. Feels like forever, and like I just arrived yesterday."

"I remember when you came to your first FEW meeting," said Karolina. "So very proper and polite."

"Not like the bitch I am now."

Tara asked, "What's FEW?"

"Foreign Executive Women," Karolina explained. "You should join. We meet for lunch once a month, it's nice. The next one's on Saturday."

"I'm not really an executive. Is two out of three good enough?" asked Tara.

"Actually, one out of three is enough in most cases," responded Monique. "It's not all snooty and selective. Quite a few local women come. They're great fun. The only rule is, No Penises."

Tara snorted. "Too bad it's not No Balls. Then my boss Chuck could come and have more things to hesitate about."

Andy's instincts kicked in before Ambassador Lamkin even finished dragging his unsavory animal off the senator. Display loyalty, control information. He beckoned to a security officer and a communications technician who were among the staff in attendance and installed them in the foyer with clear instructions. In a low voice he told the ambassador what he was doing, receiving a curt nod in response. High praise indeed.

When all the guests had departed, their phones inspected and sanitized, Andy burned to call Shariz and Farao, although the thought of what he was about to do sent his eyebrows skittering. The Pazari crime boss and Vodania's top cop and most dominant criminal. Only the reckless would seek either of their company. But both together? A desperate move for the sake of his desperately needed new promotion strategy.

Andy had ideas on how he would pitch them, entice them, convince them to become co-conspirators without understanding the true objective of their cooperation. But there were factors and angles to consider, many scenarios to game out. About to gamble with the one thing that mattered, his career, he needed to concentrate his deviousness.

Against this priority, taking the senator's aide on a nighttime tour of Shizl held even less appeal than it would normally. But Andy Pulano was never one to pass up an opportunity to expand his network. And he knew that behaving as he habitually did would be essential to controlling risk. Therefore, off they went, their first destination a drop-by at an art exhibit opening.

A narrow downtown street, an unlit, oil-stained parking ramp, and a glum series of basement passageways with low ceilings and a profusion of overhead pipes led toward the Green Zone. Andy supposed that impacting an art gallery deep in the bowels of the former planning ministry building, most of which had been converted to apartments and political party offices, fed the artists' tenuous claims of innovation and cultural rebellion.

No signs pointed the way. The entrance, for those who could find it, was a plain steel door, distinguishable only by a small outline of Vodania's jagged borders rendered in dull green industrial paint.

Inside, under dazzling track lighting, the curators strove for an edgy, in-the-know vibe. Submerged under eight floors of boxy ordinariness, Shizl's hipsters and art makers, steeped in their own stylishness, ignored the gawking mix of journalists, diplomats, and aid workers who crowded into their lair. Political fixers and social entrepreneurs, Andy's kindred spirits, slithered among the attendees. He made sure they included the senator's aide in their smiles and shoulder grabs.

Heavy industrial bolts locked bulky unframed canvasses to the walls. The paintings consisted of blazes and twists of bright colors, overlaid by thick horizontal swaths of black paint. In the corners of each room stood small arrangements of concrete rubble, each mound topped with a litter of note cards identifying the demolished buildings they used to be parts of. After a sufficient quantity of civilized commentary and bonhomie, Andy figured the aide was ripe for the shock of menace the Vodania Forever beer garden would provide.

Strategically situated on the central plaza at an angle across from Club Boom Shaka-laka, Vodania Forever served as a gathering point for thirsty patriots as well as partisans of a local soccer team, the Kalladar Conquerors. Pazaris were well advised to keep clear. Andy and the aide found a table, a square of wood jammed onto iron legs, just inside the portable chain-link fencing that demarcated the beer hall's territorial claims. It was a relatively safe spot for soaking up the atmosphere of hostility and imminent violence on which Vodania Forever prided itself. Dark humid clouds hovered over the plaza like sweat stains on the fabric of the sky.

A band belted out amped-up folk songs on the stage inside. The merciless repetition of thumping percussion and guttural vocals battered the outdoor patrons and invaded much of the public plaza. A handful of national police in track suits occupied a table near the gap in the fencing that served as an exit. Their elbows jostled bottles and ashtrays, or swung out behind them as they reared back to bellow with toxic laughter that sounded like rage. They took up as much space as they wanted.

"Look around," Andy advised. "These are the guys we'll be writing about in our election violence reporting."

Partway through their second beer, Andy concocted a rumor that Ambassador Lamkin was under consideration for the ambassadorship in Kyiv. "And frankly, his talents are wasted here, as U.S. interests are quite minor compared to what's at stake in Ukraine."

To nurture the seed he just planted, Andy confided that Vodanian President Chilik is becoming pricklier and testier.

"It may be just as well for the ambassador to get elevated to a more important post so someone else can make a fresh start with the ruler here."

The aide nodded, and Andy added, "Watch the body language tomorrow, you'll see what I'm talking about."

Andy knew that President Chilik worked out with his personal trainer every Thursday afternoon, and thus could be counted on to be stiff and sore on Friday mornings.

To seal the evening, Andy conducted his young visitor to a vast warehouse on the fringe of the city center. Ignoring the aide's apprehensive look, he led the way across a dark expanse of empty concrete floor. At the far end, a curtain of heavy fabric reached almost to the roof. Soft blue light floated over the top, and soothing melodies in an unknown tongue beckoned from behind it.

They entered the screened-off space. Beyond a scattering of dining tables, a semicircular bar protruded from the back wall. The two Americans took seats near the middle of the curve.

Andy let his guest acclimate to the smooth after-hours ambiance before recommending the brandy. As they waited for their drinks, Andy leaned closer and said, "I shouldn't tell you this, but the Department thinks the ambassador may have trouble getting confirmed for Kyiv."

"Why?"

"For some reason they seem to think the senior senator from Wyoming has qualms, and might put a hold on him."

"That's odd, since she's not interested in foreign policy, at all. Or anything else that doesn't bring bucks to her state," the aide commented.

"I know, right? It strains credulity. I don't know where P staff gets their information." Andy had developed the habit of flattering congressional staffers by using insider lingo, such as P to refer to the under secretary for political affairs.

Andy glanced around the cavernous space and the sparsely-populated tables, each with its own dim candle. "You know," he said in a lowered voice, "it'd be great if you could check it out and have your boss let P know that Ambassador Lamkin would sail through. You'd be doing the ambassador a huge favor, and frankly, a tremendous service for Embassy Kyiv."

"Sure thing," the aide agreed.

If this sideshow succeeded in getting a senator who just visited Vodania to lobby the under secretary for a more prominent embassy for Ambassador Lamkin, the ensuing ripple of irritation through the upper levels of the State Department would make it an evening well spent. Anything that shook, however slightly, the ambassador's standing back home would help. But this was just background music. Mood lighting for what was to come, Andy mused, if his skills proved up to the task.

"From what my colleagues in Kyiv tell me," Andy continued, "they need the kind of experience and leadership he'd bring. And please, don't mention that I broached this. The ambassador did not put me up to it. He would be mortified at the thought of any special pleading. The man has integrity. He just wants to serve. He's not a shameless hustler like yours truly."

"Hey, that's what the process needs sometimes."

"We all have our roles I suppose. I help any way I can."

Andy leaned back against the plush cushion of his barstool. He had made the most of the excursion. But one final touch would make it unforgettable. Their waitress placed a brandy in front of the senatorial aide and a cognac in front of Andy.

"You want cinnamon?" she asked.

The aide looked uncertain.

Andy answered for him, "Yes, he wants cinnamon."

"Cinnamon!" called out the waitress, which set off a wave of cheers and clapping around the space. After a few moments, the sound system switched to a loud, over-produced Arabian pastiche, and a spotlight lit up a door in the wall between the two ends of the bar's semicircle. The door slid open to reveal a young woman in harem pants and a tight-fitting halter dripping with bangles. With the aid of an upright cinder block, she climbed up onto the far end of the counter.

As the music blared, she belly-danced around the curve past ashtrays, glasses, and bottles. When she reached the senator's aide, she planted one bare foot on each side of his brandy glass and undulated the rest of her body. The aide stared at the rings on her toes, evidently uncertain about acknowledging the rest of her moving above him. The music accelerated and she swiveled and gyrated, faster and faster. Andy, and then the aide, craned their necks back as far as they would go.

The belly dancer unclasped and removed her halter, letting her breasts swing with her movements. Andy glanced at the aide, who sat transfixed but discomfited. The young visitor knew better but couldn't help staring. Andy tried not to smirk, knowing the aide would soon have something more to squirm about. An indelible memory was about to form, one that would rise up every time he encountered cinnamon.

From her waistband, the dancer plucked a cylindrical silver vial with a sieve lid and fitted it into her cleavage, where she secured it by pressing her breasts together with both hands. At that point two well-oiled bodybuilders, wearing only gym shoes and gold-colored briefs, strode atop the bar from opposite directions of the semicircle. Each one's mustache curled up on one side and down on the other. When they reached the dancer, one held her at the waist and the other squatted to grasp her ankles. With a smooth lift they turned her upside down, her hair cascading over the counter and into the aide's lap as she arched her neck backwards. After she adjusted the angle of her grip to point the vial at the customer's glass, the body builders jiggled her three times, dusting the brandy with fragrant brown powder.

Chapter 3

Tara Zadani walked into her kitchen, naked except for a towel around her wet hair. Morning came way too early, though at least it was a Friday. The semi-darkness outside let her catch her reflection in the glass door to her tiny balcony. She tsked about the late-night pastry gorging. Don't want to make a habit of that. She turned sideways to the glass and tried to see whether her recent gym outings were doing anything for her butt. Not that anything needed to be done for it. Not yet.

Standing by the stove, she poured a mug of coffee and stirred a clump of golden raisins into a saucepan of boiled barley, a local breakfast staple she had begun experimenting with. She didn't feel all that hungry but knew she would be later. She put a spoonful of the mush into her mouth and frowned. It still needed something. On the counter, her phone went off. At that hour, it wouldn't be good news. Caller ID showed Robert Akes, head of the management section, her boss's boss.

"Tara, good morning, listen, situation over at the residence. Mrs. Lamkin just called to say one of your crew kicked her dog. She's none too happy about it. Get over there right away and fix it."

So, I'm a veterinarian now? Tara took a breath. "Is the dog okay?"

"I don't know, but she's definitely not. Which is why you need to be there, like, now."

"On my way."

Tara took a gulp of coffee and another spoonful of barley. Still bland. Although it was not the local custom for some reason, next time she'd add a sprinkle of cinnamon.

Tara lived in a riverside apartment building in the wide basin that contained the city center. On switchback roads slick with dew, she drove a motor pool sedan up the slope toward the northern bluff, more impatient than ever for her Jeep baby to clear customs already. A stream of traffic rushed toward her, Mercedes and Beemers careening down the mountain to their urgently important offices. Tara swerved and dodged and shifted gears on the steeper rises, glad in a way she didn't have time to bring her coffee. As the road climbed, the houses and grounds steadily improved, and the number of security guards increased.

The sun had barely cleared the ambassador's high front hedge when she arrived. She had heard that the United States government acquired the stately stone chalet under ideal conditions: civil unrest, capital flight, and political panic. During the first few months after Vodania emerged as an independent nation, the State Department snapped up the property to serve as its ambassadorial residence, acting swiftly before the Europeans could swarm in and drive up prices. The chalet offered a number of advantages, most notably its superior location on the northern bluff above the capital. The area had long been Shizl's prime residential neighborhood, where the most established families, the emergent oligarch class, and the majority of other ambassadors clustered together. Up near the peak of the same ridge, commanding a view over the entire valley, stood Vodania's presidential compound.

Tara parked behind a truck from the general services office. The three-man GSO crew, her crew now, was supposed to dismantle the canopy tent, tables, grills, and tiki torches set up for the previous night's reception. Be professional, she reminded herself. As a woman, young and unmarried, her supervisory role upended the authority structures that normally prevailed in Vodania. And her look and complexion didn't help. She would be firm but careful.

Upon entry onto the residence grounds, she stopped the crew's work, gathered them in a quiet corner of the yard, and asked for their version of events. They resented having to contend with Davos while they worked. Like most people in Vodania, the notion of a dog living inside a house, like a person, baffled them. To explain what happened, they reenacted the scene. Two of them hoisted one of the main support pillars for the tent, pointing it skyward at a forty-five-degree angle, Iwo Jima style. The other one, Stimche, the most muscular, was maneuvering a large canister of kerosene onto a dolly.

"Okay now," said Stimche. "You be the dog, and run out from that door, barking like crazy."

Tara looked at him hard, and back to the other two straining to hold up the tent pole. "In your dreams."

"What?"

"Just tell me what happened. Don't make it worse for yourself."

Stimche looked pained. "I'm trying to show you." Veins on his arms bulged from holding the metal canister on its edge. "But okay. Then the dog, with his teeth out, runs toward these guys, who are like frozen. And instead, it comes at me while I'm holding the kerosene, which I'm not supposed to drop. So, I lifted my foot like this."

Tara stepped back as the outside of his boot swung past her knee.

"And the dog was right there?"

"Yes, of course, so I pushed him away with my foot and then Mrs. Ambassador came outside."

"And then what?"

"She said what did you do and I said sorry ma'am we are just trying to do our work."

One of the Iwo Jima guys added, "And she got the dog and went back inside and slammed the door."

"You can set that stuff down," Tara told them. "I understand the situation. Davos presents a challenge and I'll do what I can to minimize the impact. But this kind of thing can't happen again, ever." Turning toward Stimche, she added, "You can't kick the ambassador's pet."

"It wasn't really a kick."

She told Stimche she would drive him back to the embassy after she spoke with Mrs. Lamkin. The other two could finish up. "And I need all of you to promise me there will be no repeat of anything like this."

The men nodded, but it was clear what they meant was fuck that dog.

No matter how close to the top, how crucial your role, an embassy consists of an ambassador and everyone else. Andy Pulano sat among the everyone else in Embassy Shizl's secure conference room, bantering with the heads of the various sections, bestowing praise, probing, keeping tabs. Acting normal, as if he were not about to launch a one-man conspiracy.

All chatter ceased and the members of the country team rose to their feet as the fortified steel door opened with a whoosh. The ambassador led the Nebraska senator, with his aide close on his heels, to their seats at the head of the conference table.

As the first order of business, Ambassador Lamkin introduced his country team. Andy had witnessed this performance many times, and he admired the ambassador's ability to convey gravitas and flair. Invariably, Andy got introduced first, as the ambassador's irreplaceable deputy. The flattery continued in the presentation of the always astute political counselor. Next, the economic counselor, a tireless promoter of American businesses. The mission director for the U.S. Agency for International Development, USAID for short. The station chief, ever keeping a watchful eye. The consul general, protector of American citizens and issuer of visas.

And our real general, ably representing the U.S. military as the defense attaché.

"How big a crew we got working the Vodania account?" asked the senator.

"We're a mid-size embassy," the ambassador responded. "Seventy-two Americans and two hundred and—"

"twelve," Andy filled in, in response to the ambassador's glance.

"—local staff."

"Mid-size," repeated the senator, deadpan. Then he smiled, "Okay, let's get on with all the vital stuff this mid-size is dealing with."

The normal briefing ensued, with the ambassador doing most of the talking, but calling on each of the section heads present to make a point or two. A sleek, polished production. Summing up, he told the senator there were three main points to make to President Chilik.

"The United States wants a constructive relationship with Vodania," the ambassador pronounced, "and that means genuine elections, free of violence and intimidation. Two, Vodania needs to ratify the border demarcation agreement with Pazaria that the U.S., and especially this embassy, has worked so hard to broker. And three, we must see improvements in governance to enable Vodania to modernize and to develop its fullest potential. The United States is willing to help in all these areas and more, but we need a responsible partner to do so."

"Sounds to me like our Mr. Chilik needs a strong clear message, am I right?" the senator asked.

"Yes sir."

"Good. 'Cause it's never been my habit to pull my punches."

The senator then nodded, put his hands on the table, paused, and made eye contact all the way around the room. This should be good, Andy thought.

The senator straightened in his chair and said, "I want to thank each and every one of you in this embassy for what you do for our country. And for those wearing the uniform, thank you for your service and your patriotism. God bless."

"One final point," the ambassador announced, delaying the break-up of the meeting. "I simply want to reiterate in the clearest and firmest terms that it is my order, as chief of mission, that there will be no further mention of allegations of any untoward incident at last night's reception. The DCM saw to the deletion of any and all photographs that could be subject to misinterpretation. If by some remote chance a camera from one of our staff or a guest has escaped his detection, you are to bring it to his attention immediately so he can have it properly sanitized. Am I perfectly clear?"

Andy nodded, his expression full of purpose. *A naughty doggie pic would certainly be a problem. But no longer your biggest problem. Sir.*

When Tara arrived inside the general services office's warren of cubicles, after finishing her task at the ambassador's residence, she reminded herself not to say 'good morning' to any of the Pazari staff. Once was more than enough for that mistake. Instead, she smiled her greetings, satisfied that most of the local employees, Vodanians as well as Pazaris, had their coffees in hand and were progressing from settling-in mode to full productivity. Tara plopped her bag on the chair in her cubicle, and went straight to Chuck's office.

"You missed the eight o'clock."

"Good morning to you too. Didn't Robert tell you he dispatched me to the residence?"

Chuck shook his head, so Tara briefed her boss on the morning's festivities.

"Mrs. Lamkin was okay in the end," she assured him.

Back in her own cubicle, waiting for her government computer to do its morning security calisthenics, Tara reflected on her conversation with the ambassador's wife. Tara had gone into the meeting knowing little beyond the dust jacket version of her story. Years ago, Lithia, a Finnish woman now in her early fifties, gave up her life as an assistant curator in Helsinki's leading fine arts museum to join David Lamkin and his diplomatic career. To postings across Europe and Central Asia she brought her blend of sturdy optimism and traditional northern reserve, collecting paintings and friends along the way. With her stately posture and evident self-assurance, and David's energy and drive, they made a formidable pair. Along the way, evidently, it had never been quite the right time for children.

In the sitting room at the ambassador's residence, Mrs. Lamkin received Tara's apology gracefully. She smiled as Tara sought out Davos to make amends. Tara promised there would not be a recurrence, and said she would ensure better coordination with the household staff to make sure Davos was safe while work was underway.

"This is *his* yard; he *better* be safe."

"I meant, safe from any accident while the work crews are moving heavy or flammable stuff."

Mollified by Tara's point, Mrs. Lamkin said, "I understand Davos can come on a little strong. Even the household staff, as wonderful as they are . . ." She shook her head gently. "They become exasperated with him sometimes. I get it, I really do."

Mrs. Lamkin faced Tara directly, and added, "It's not always so easy being me."

True for us all I suppose, Tara thought, coming back to the present and the accumulation of paperwork on her cubicle's built-in work surface. Then she read an email from Katie Nichols, a friend from A-100 training who was wrapping up her first tour. In Barbados. It would be very easy being Katie, with her thick blond hair and striking silhouette capturing the attention of every ambitious man within pheromone range. During A-100, the multi-week orientation course that all entering foreign service officers go through, Katie stood out for her energy and friendliness. In her breezy email message, Katie detailed her latest crazy adventures, on and off the island, with the new surf school director, a pair of hotel tennis pros who couldn't handle her backhand, and a New York film crew making a hip-hop video.

Tara glanced at her own to-do list for the morning. Prepare the motor pool schedule; approve or deny overtime requests; develop the transportation plan for the embassy's upcoming election monitoring effort. And then gagging down lunch with a senior Vodanian customs official who has long played a crucial role in arrangements for the diplomatic pouch, embassy mail, getting furniture and other procurements in and out of the country. Plus, the big one, household effects shipments. Including, ahem, vehicles. On her introductory visit to his office, the official told Tara he was accustomed to doing business with real Americans, not with some young gypsy. She did not react well. Back in Kingston, when she worked the visa line, she tried not to seethe when applicants complained they wanted to be interviewed by a real American. She had expected better from a senior government official in Vodania. Hence this was to be a peacemaking meal, with the embassy's expeditor and all-around fixer acting as go-between and chaperone. The expeditor, one of the embassy's most senior local staff, had known the crusty official since childhood. They were rumored to be second or third cousins. Good times.

In the seating area of his ornately over-decorated office, President Chilik massaged his own thighs while conferring with aides, backers, and cronies about a potential natural gas pipeline project that would pass through Vodanian territory.

"One of the problems is there's no way to tell if a portion of the gas is coming from Iran," pointed out the finance minister.

"Who cares?" asked the president, rolling his shoulders and arching his back.

"The Americans."

"They always find something to care about." He lifted his teacup and flung the dregs over his shoulder, in the direction of a potted fig tree.

Andy rode in a Chevy Trailblazer filled with fellow members of the everyone else, including the senator's aide, the political counselor, a notetaker, a local employee to serve as interpreter, and the assistant security officer riding shotgun. Led by a police sedan with lights whirling and siren blaring, the motorcade raced toward the Presidentorium, a colossal office-fortress that occupied a promontory above a sharp bend in the Druzhba River. Through the Trailblazer's windshield, Andy caught glimpses of the American flags flapping on their little poles on the hood of Ambassador Lamkin's official limousine, waving at him mockingly. He wondered whether the ambassador and the senator were conferring on how to play the meeting with President Chilik. Or did they showcase their confidence by indulging in small talk or Washington gossip?

The motorcade slowed through the arched gateway that served as the official entrance to Vodania's power center, at the eastern terminus of Shizl's main boulevard, and stopped at the apex of a grand circular driveway. Vodanian security personnel opened the arriving vehicles like packages and escorted their contents past a gaggle of reporters and TV news crews. Andy noticed the senator measuring his pace so as to be able to make meaningful eye contact with each and every camera lens.

A presidential attendant greeted the guests and escorted them to a spacious lounge, decorated with national art and artifacts, for the customary power wait. The ambassador and senator remained quiet. After a suitable interval, an assistant beckoned the American delegation into the president's office, where the leather couches bore indentations from the previous occupants' bottoms.

President Chilik's welcome seemed even more effusive than usual. By Andy's count, he used the phrase 'your highly distinguished excellencies' five times. Not a good sign. As Chilik was gushing along, Andy noticed a puddle near the base of an urn, and wondered whether the president also had a dog problem. After Chilik finally finished, Andy studied the faces of the ambassador and the president as the senator praised Vodania's natural beauty and proud hard-working people and assured President Chilik that America's close ties with Pazaria in no way precluded a warm and friendly relationship with Vodania.

"In Washington, we recognize the importance of your lovely country. But we also have a few concerns."

Andy took in the senator's stern expression. He could see how people found him convincing. He was eager to see him confront Chilik, which would diminish the ambassador's standing. But the senator spoke no further, and instead turned to the ambassador. Punt.

"Well," the ambassador began after a slight pause, "President Chilik and I talk with some frequency. He and his government know exactly where we stand on the main issues that are impeding Vodania's path to fuller development of its potential as a leader in this region, and to fuller integration into the international community."

Addressing Chilik directly, the ambassador said, "Mr. President, I would just like to take this opportunity to ask you to give us an update on where your government is in the process of ratifying the provisional border demarcation agreement with Pazaria and moving ahead to normalize relations."

"Have you been following the news?" the president asked, hands gripping his thighs. "Did you hear about the parade that . . . that . . . that prime minister of our northern neighbor threw to celebrate this so-called agreement? With the American ambassador by his side and a flyover by U.S. fighter jets stationed in his country. He's acting like he just won a war."

"Don't let that distract you," the ambassador advised. "Prime Minister Prismar faces a number of tough domestic challenges. He's just . . . it's fair to say he's trying to make the most of this, to claim his moment in the sun."

The senator leaned forward. "In America, we have an expression: every dog has his day."

President Chilik sat up straight and faced Ambassador Lamkin. "I heard yours had his last night."

Chapter 4

Afternoon sun cooked the tarmac. With two hours to go before the senator's flight was scheduled to take off, Tara waited in the special departure lounge inside Shizl's makeover-ready airport. Along with the expediter and another local employee, it was her responsibility to babysit the baggage and passports belonging to the senator and his aide.

At least she had gotten through lunch with the senior customs official. Gross chunks of charred meat doused with a greasy sauce. And that was the good part. With the embassy's expediter serving as referee, they went back and forth and round and round about how her parents immigrated from India before she was born, how she lived in Ohio her whole life until graduate school, how, yet again, yes, she was and always had been an American citizen. Towards the end, perhaps worn down, perhaps concerned about the way Tara was gripping her steak knife, he sat back and grinned and said he loved India, Taj Mahal, Kama Sutra, maybe they could have dinner together. That stopped her from asking when her Jeep Wrangler would clear customs.

In the special departure lounge, Tara glanced at her two subordinates, who had probably done this routine a hundred times. And it wasn't complicated. Why her presence was nonetheless indispensable remained a mystery. Fortunately, she was not left on her own to ponder the intricacies of international diplomacy, as Robert, the head of the embassy's management section, called or texted for an update every twenty minutes or so.

Friday evening, after a series of nerve-wracking text exchanges with Shariz and Farao to finalize arrangements for a late-night rendezvous, Andy drove away from the embassy down the mountainside toward the Marine house. He had not wanted to stay in his office much later than usual, even with the ambassador safely out enjoying a symphony with Vodania's A-list.

It was that time of the month again. Pretty regularly, the Marine guard detachment hosted a happy hour for the whole American embassy community. Many of the staff seemed to enjoy these events, which raised funds for the annual Marine Corps Ball extravaganza. In the present instance, the happy hour also served as a wheels-up party to celebrate the departure of the 'co-del' from Nebraska. Although this congressional delegation consisted of just one senator and an aide, and lasted less than eighteen hours, most of the embassy had gotten involved one way or another in the over-preparation. And, as with any co-del, pretty much everyone was happy to see them gone.

Judging by the profusion of parked cars with diplomatic plates and the din emanating from the open windows, Andy judged he timed his arrival well. He wanted to stroll in with the party well launched but still at an early phase. His role as DCM was to show up before people got too tipsy, greet everyone and congratulate and thank them for their part in the successful visit, drink a beer like a regular guy. And then, most critically, get out of the way so the troops can relax and have some fun.

As soon as he passed through the entrance, Andy greeted a collection of consular assistants, several off-duty guards, and the expediter. He noted a strong turnout from among the embassy's local employees, including quite a few Pazaris, who usually ceded Marine House happy hours to the ethnic Vodanians. Everyone together, one big happy embassy family. What if this kind of grudging co-existence were to take hold throughout the country? What would be so terrible about that? He would have to explain the problem convincingly to Shariz and Farao if his underhanded plans were to stand any chance of getting anywhere.

Eyebrows dancing a jig, Andy bestowed sunshine upon a gaggle of junior officers from the political and economic sections and a couple of their spouses. He cast a jaunty thumbs-up toward the living room, where one of the information management guys played pool with the station chief's husband as a bunch of motor pool and GSO workers drank beers and watched. Most of the guests crowded around the kitchen and bar area, where the Marines in their tight t-shirts, revealing gym-built chests and biceps, kept busy pouring vodka and tonics and pulling beers from a cooler. Nearby hovered several of their girlfriends, young local women wearing little more than leotards and jewelry.

Approaching the bar, Andy reached his hand up to the shoulder of Colonel Mesko, an Army officer serving as the deputy defense attaché. "Got any pull in this place? I could use a beer."

Mesko half turned his six-foot-two frame, saw it was the DCM, and said "Absolutely, sir." Then, "Budweiser okay sir?"

"Long as it's cold."

"Hoo-aa." Mesko reached forward over the heads of the women in front of the bar to get a marine's attention.

Once he had a bottle in hand, Andy clinked it against everyone's glass within reach. Then he moved toward the living room, exchanging greetings and toasts along the way. Robert Akes, still in management counselor mode, asked if he'd like to make a few remarks. Wrong move, Andy knew, waving off the suggestion. The kind of thing the ambassador did, accentuating the gulf between himself and everyone else.

Andy rationed his beer for forty-five minutes, its minimal flavor depleting as it warmed. He listened to R&R plans, talked up his Boston Red

Sox to the other baseball fans, asked parents how their kids were doing. At last, duty complete, he headed toward the exit and the real work of the evening. Perhaps the real work of his life.

Tara had been to a few Marine House happy hours in Kingston. Reggae and rum. She didn't know what to expect in a place as small as Shizl. Hopefully there would be some interesting local people.

The parking lot was jammed, a positive sign, so she eased her motor pool sedan halfway into a ditch. Worst case scenario, she'd have a glass of wine and move along. She pulled open the building's front door and almost collided with Victor Manchego, a mid-level officer from the consular section. Victor, a grin splitting his face, put a hand against the front of her shoulder to halt her momentum.

"Whoa, slow down."

Tara paused and he wiggled his beer bottle near her face, apparently offering her a swig.

She pulled back, trying not to grimace. "I'm in more of a wine mood."

Tara was about to continue on her way when the DCM emerged from among the guests, aiming for the door. He paused at the two of them and blinked.

"Good night folks, have a nice weekend. And Tara, nice job with the co-del. I appreciate it."

"Thank you."

After the DCM departed and the door closed, Victor touched Tara's shoulder again. "We should go catch a drink sometime."

"What would your wife think about that?"

"Mei-Lin?" After mockingly pretending to concentrate on such a dumb question, he leaned closer to confide, "I probably wouldn't mention it to her. Besides, she's pregnant again."

Despite his Budweiser breath, Victor was kind of cute, and in some ways maybe not a bad guy. But yuck.

Corridor One, Vodania's main east-west artery, took Andy through a broad steppe most of the way to Kharbam, one of the larger towns in the Pazari swath of western Vodania. Squinting into the darkness, he found the turn-off for the formerly paved two-laner that led up into the highlands. He wrestled his Range Rover for fifteen kilometers through and around ruts and hairpin turns, climbing the foothills of the Asich mountain range, his high beams bouncing crazily off the rocks and dry vegetation. At the main intersection and sole traffic light in Kharbam, men on the street assessed him with a brazen mix of testiness and suspicion.

Andy made two more quick turns and approached the Camel Club, a blocky, sprawling one-story structure with darkened windows. A cement perimeter wall topped with razor wire protected the building and its deeply pockmarked gravel parking lot. A narrow gap in the steel gate in front indicated the premises were currently open for business, at the same time signaling that it would be better not to go in.

Patrons could enjoy authentic local cuisine and strong coffee. But those did not constitute the primary reasons for visiting the Camel Club. The establishment offered one-stop shopping for a selection of vices: drinking, hashish, gambling, and prostitution.

Andy eased his front bumper close to the steel gate. After a minute or so, a surly-looking attendant came out, glared at the Range Rover, glared at Andy, glared at the Range Rover again, and opened the gate. Andy bounced his vehicle through a series of craters that looked like the aftermath of aerial bombardment and parked in the shadow of the building. He folded his suit jacket and placed it on the passenger seat next to him, with his rolled-up necktie centered on top of it. He got out and scuffed through the dirty gravel, keeping an eye on a pair of dogs lurking underneath a truck.

A dangerous-looking bouncer standing outside the building's front doorway watched his approach. Andy nodded and said "peace" in the Pazari manner but continued around the outside of the club. Near the back of the building, he tapped a metal door twice with his toe. After a moment a young man with dark hair and darker eyes opened it partway.

"Peace. I am Pulano, I am expected."

The man nodded, gestured with his palm to wait, and closed the door.

Andy used the time to consider how he could justify himself if the ambassador ever found out about his initiative. He couldn't come up with anything better than a posture of affronted denial. After nearly five minutes, the door opened all the way. The same man, now with a broad smile.

"Please, welcome."

Andy followed him along a narrow passageway to an inner lounge dim with smoke. A dozen men occupied leather-upholstered couches, watching soccer on an oversized flat screen. Seated in their midst was the club's owner and one of the region's most notorious crime bosses, Shariz.

"Who's playing?" Andy asked.

Shariz, wearing boxer shorts and a tank top, got to his feet to welcome his guest with a traditional one-armed embrace. "France against Iran. I hope they both lose."

Shariz, a solid man whose mustache tips curled upward in traditional Pazari fashion, headed a thriving consortium in the smuggling and extortion sector. This position arguably made him the leading power-broker among the Pazari-Vodanians. And argue they did, which kept things interesting for anyone in the vicinity, including watchful diplomats. Shariz remained banned from travelling to the U.S., due to credible allegations about certain ill-tempered past actions, particularly during the war for Pazaria's independence from Vodania a decade earlier.

Andy concealed his eagerness to get Shariz into his Range Rover for the long drive back to Shizl. He knew the only way to keep the hospitality to a minimum was to act so comfortable, so at home, that Shariz might begin to wonder if he planned to stay for the weekend. The diplomat flopped into an open spot on one of the couches, smirked companionably at the scowling, smoking members of the smuggling community on either side, and turned his avid gaze to the television screen.

"Don't let me interrupt the game," Andy said over his shoulder to Shariz.

"You want rakia," Shariz said, referring to the local firewater. He didn't bother to phrase it as a question.

After a sufficient interlude of strong beverages and weak pleasantries, Shariz selected a group to trail behind in one of his vehicles. They put on their hats and filed out through the same rear door, and Shariz accompanied Andy to his Range Rover. He waited while Andy flung his carefully folded jacket and tie onto the back seat in a show of respect for his passenger.

Andy drove hunched forward over the steering wheel, peering through the windshield. Even during daylight, the descent from Kharbam was heart-stopping. It was worse at night, especially with the high beams from the follow car making it almost impossible to see the remnants of the roadbed and the edges of the precipices.

When they reached the smoothness of Corridor One and pointed toward Shizl, Andy got Shariz chatting about the latest inter-family jostlings among the Pazaris, including how the seats were likely to divide up in the upcoming parliamentary elections. He also thanked Shariz for his interventions to facilitate the safe passage of the border demarcation teams in recent weeks.

"Is Chilik going to sign the agreement?" Shariz demanded, radiating a thick aura of impatience which spouted from his pores like last night's garlic.

"We're working on him. Our visiting senator pressed him hard this morning."

Shariz emitted a sound somewhere between a scoff and a sigh. Ethnic Pazaris on both sides of the border yearned for international recognition of

Pazaria's territory, but Andy might not have guessed it meant quite so much to Shariz. Good to know.

When the lights of Shizl came into view, Andy pulled over, with Shariz's guys close behind. Andy touched a few buttons on his cell phone and spoke into it, "Ten minutes."

They resumed the drive. When the highway split, Andy took the bypass that followed the plateau along the southern flank of the capital. The route provided an overview of the grid of Shizl's major streets extending all the way to the Presidentorium.

At a crossroads in the still mostly agricultural land surrounding Vodania's largest city, Andy stopped again and switched off the engine. Shariz opened the passenger window and motioned for his follow car to park on the other side of the intersection.

About fifteen minutes later, two hulking black Toyota Land Cruisers pulled up behind the Range Rover. The lead flashed its high beams. Shariz sat a little taller and inflated his chest. Andy twisted the ignition key and drove toward home, the Land Cruisers following tightly.

Andy took out his phone again and pressed the speed dial key for the embassy guard booth in front of his residence.

"Good evening, sir," answered a male voice.

"Hello Mika," said Andy, pleased with himself for having memorized the guards' names and shift schedules. "I need your help with something. It's urgent."

"Yes, sir." He could hear Mika coming to attention. "Something wrong?"

"Meet me outside the back gate. I'm on my way now. I need you to wait for me there. Understood?"

At the ornate gate in front of his residence, Andy braked with his headlights illuminating the driveway and the empty guard booth. After pausing a moment to make sure the guard was out of sight, he pressed the fob affixed to his dashboard and the gate swung open. Andy's Range Rover and one of the Land Cruisers passed through and stopped in front of the portico. From the front passenger seat of the Land Cruiser a tall bodyguard popped out and scanned the area while watching the gate close.

Andy emerged from his vehicle and said "Okay?"

The bodyguard nodded. Andy went up the three granite steps and opened the front door of his residence. Shariz eased himself out of the Range Rover. His boxers and tank top glowed white under the portico light as he ambled up the steps and into the house.

Then the Land Cruiser's driver stepped out and opened his vehicle's side door. After a moment, long legs in dark tailored slacks extended from the back seat. A beige wool jacket followed, and then a stern face topped with black slicked-back hair.

Farao.

Chief of Vodania's border police and in charge of customs and domestic intelligence. Also, President Chilik's uncle. Farao stroked his mustache tips downward, emanating authority and menace, his impact enhanced by assault-level cologne.

In the dark entryway of the house, Farao stared at Shariz, who tried to display indifference by scratching pensively at a dark brown mole on the inside of his right thigh. Without turning on any lights, Andy asked both men to please place their electronics on the side tables. Farao groped through his pockets and took out two phones and a government blackberry. Shariz had no pockets, but he produced a pager from his shoe and two phones from his hat.

"What about our guns?" asked Farao.

Andy shrugged and Shariz smirked and Farao looked like he regretted the question. Obviously, it wasn't that kind of party. Andy led the way across the living room to a side hallway and the basement staircase. At the bottom of the stairs, he paused to pick up the television remote and switch it on. CNN, perfect. He raised the volume, then pointed toward a door in the far corner of the basement.

The three men entered a windowless cement cell lit by florescent tubes hung from the ceiling. The space contained a washer and a dryer and wire shelves full of extra plates, stemware, coffee cups, and saucers. Andy closed the door behind him, twisted the dryer's timer to thirty minutes, and pressed start.

Chapter 5

With no chairs in the small space, Farao hoisted himself onto the washing machine. Shariz responded by sitting on top of the rumbling dryer, ignoring the jiggling of his bare thighs caused by its vibrations. Andy Pulano stood before them, taking in their glaring frowns. This was it.

"You both have a problem," he began. "The approaching election is generating no international interest. Zip. Why? Because there is nothing newsworthy about it."

Shariz and Farao said nothing.

"Hotel revenues are down, restaurants are in trouble," Andy pointed out. "Even the Camel Club."

Shariz made a tight grimace.

"The Organization for Security and Cooperation in Europe is drawing up plans for downsizing, and the European Union is running out of projects to fund. Vodania is in danger of becoming Slovenia too quickly. Too much peace and stability will cost you.

"I need you to understand that Ambassador Lamkin will continue to praise restraint and to speak out forcefully against any violence or intimidation. He has to be able to report to Washington that he consistently takes this stance with President Chilik and the Pazari-Vodanian leadership. That's our way," Andy explained.

"However," he continued, "the U.S. would understand if tensions erupted here and there, renewing the international community's sense of mission. Not killing of course, not terrorism. That would backfire badly. Vodania needs just enough conflict and risk to keep itself interesting, to excite journalists and concerned statesmen and entice them to visit."

Andy paused to let them absorb his suggestion. During the Pazaria-Vodania war, both men made names for themselves. Not good ones.

"You are professionals," he told them. "You know how to manage these things. Let's figure out the next steps. Hit campaign offices when no one's in them. Report beatings on both sides. Again, managed and coordinated, please. Set up the ground rules."

Farao stroked down on his mustache. "Those mother bitches always complain about stuff like this, even when there's nothing."

Shariz flared his nostrils. "We like to keep our air clean. We can't have more Wodanians coming around."

Andy stayed silent while they traded insults back and forth. Let them get it out of their systems.

When they began to repeat themselves, and with the smog of Farao's cologne starting to impede visibility, Andy intervened. "You can keep having slap-fights until you run out of money. Or you can do something to bring people here. They'll come for the gunfire and stay for the scenery."

Shariz's mustache tips twitched, as if a smile got caught trying to escape.

A sour look crossed Farao's face. "It's not a stupid idea."

Shariz nodded once.

Farao glared fire at Andy. "This is really America's policy? Unofficially?"

"Look at me," Andy told him, turning his face to include Shariz. "Really. Do I look like I have the balls to make this up on my own?"

A guffaw broke through Shariz's frown, and even Farao almost smiled.

On Saturday morning, Tara parked on the periphery of the Roma district in southwest Shizl, an impoverished area known unaffectionately as Gypsy Town to most of the city. Aiming to set a good example by arriving on time for her class, she hurried through a gap in the wall that separated the jumble of makeshift buildings and rutted mud alleyways from the rest of the capital. Underfed dogs and children milled about, gazing at her with tepid curiosity as she picked her way through prickly weeds, deposits of drying dog droppings, and everyday debris. Except for the tireless elderly women who always seemed bent on one chore or another, very few adults were in evidence.

When Tara arrived at the supplemental Saturday school, Jovina, the assistant director, stood chatting with two girl pupils. They called it a school, but it was just a shed made of scrap wood with a blue plastic tarp on top, furnished with several low plank tables and benches. A few bulbs strung on wires overhead gave off weak light. With no windows or fans, it got stuffy inside. The conditions these children and their families lived in never failed to tear up Tara inside. In this part of the world there wasn't much to go around, and if there was one thing the Vodanians and Pazaris agreed on, it was keeping the Roma down and, especially, out.

Three boys and another girl arrived. Tara tried not to show her heartbreak at the slim chances any of them had. She started the class, which focused on English and arithmetic, hoping more students would show up. This was her third time volunteering at the Saturday school, and she looked for some indication she was making an impact. The children's attention had a tendency to wander, and at times she struggled to keep them engaged. She had learned a couple of basic moves. Having them repeat words and phrases aloud helped. Calling them up to the chalkboard, which actually was a board, seemed to improve their focus on arithmetic problems.

Such a mismatch between their needs and what she could provide. But she couldn't do nothing. Tara felt the urgency of reaching these young minds, and she strived to become more effective. To connect better, she had started picking up a few Roma words, mainly numbers and basic phrases and greetings. On the way to class that morning, Tara bought a bag of apricots from her favorite vendor at the daily produce market. She had intended to use them to illustrate basic addition. Instead, the pupils demonstrated their command of subtraction.

The solitude of a Saturday morning in the front office presented Andy Pulano the opportunity to work on certain matters without attracting notice. He could operate free from the watchful attentions of his assistant Charlene, as well as from the uninterrupted stream of interruptions that a normal embassy workday poured onto the forehead of the second-in-command. The blessed stillness let him concentrate on improving his prospects in the never-ending struggle for professional advancement.

He decided to start the morning by catching up on the training file. One of his managerial innovations at Embassy Shizl was to require section heads to furnish quarterly reports recording all training their people received, including online classes from the Foreign Service Institute, the State Department's primary training center. With an irresistible combination of charm and open threats, he had finally persuaded the conscientious Charlene to put those incoming reports straight into a folder in the secure file cabinet, bypassing his inbox. Such cavalier dereliction scandalized Charlene, and he knew she wouldn't be able to keep her outrage to herself.

Andy considered it advantageous for word to get around that he did not even glance at the training reports. It would not further his purposes for the staff to realize just how watchful he was. So, alone on the first Saturday in August, he reviewed the ones that had accumulated over the past several weeks, valuing the information as yet another set of data for keeping tabs on his subordinates' preparations and aspirations, on who was up to what. Such data often proved essential for successful mentoring.

After returning the training file to Charlene's safe, Andy fired off a slew of breezy personal messages, by email or text according to each recipient's preference, to half a dozen patrons and friends throughout the U.S. foreign affairs community. He flavored these missives with nuggets of current developments in and around Vodania and offered jocular commentary on the recipients' areas of focus.

He took particular care with messages to the embassy's two main overseers in the State Department's Bureau of European and Eurasian Affairs, commonly abbreviated to EUR. Vonda Vance, the deputy assistant secretary responsible for managing U.S. relations with this corner of the Eurasian landmass, had completed her assignment as ambassador to Bosnia about a year earlier. She still couldn't help but see a Bosnian parallel to every noteworthy personality and event in Vodania and throughout the region. Therefore, Andy found it necessary to master the details of internal Bosnian politics in order to communicate with her effectively. The other message, to her immediate superior, required even more finesse. Geoff Bentwood, the principal deputy assistant secretary, EUR's number two, right below the assistant secretary, said "keep in touch" as often as he reminded the entire bureau to maintain appropriate communications channels.

The fundamental problem, of course, was that both Geoff and Vonda considered Ambassador Lamkin to be their point of contact in Embassy Shizl. And rightfully so. The country desk could and should talk to everyone else. In addition to the risk of appearing uppity, for Andy to correspond directly with these senior officials could be viewed as going behind the ambassador's back, since that was precisely what it was. Seeking a defensible rationale, the DCM crafted his message to Vonda Vance in the guise of an informal request for lessons learned and best practices regarding the launch of community sports programs across ethnic lines, knowing that Embassy Sarajevo had undertaken a number of such projects during her time there. And he wrote to Geoff Bentwood to gush about the assistant secretary's recent message to all EUR bureau personnel about respecting diversity, knowing that Geoff had initiated the missive as part of his ongoing effort to develop a proactive reputation in that area.

In the messages to both Geoff and Vonda, Andy slipped in a mention of his personal sense of a worrisome increase in inter-ethnic tensions boiling below the surface in Vodania. He intimated that this would likely produce an uptick in violence. He took care to emphasize that this concern stemmed from the quivering of his own antennae and did not reflect the official mission view. By suggesting that Ambassador Lamkin did not want to put such gloom in reports back to Washington, Andy stroked Geoff and Vonda by trusting them with raw, insider dish. In the process, he also set up a favorable contrast with the ambassador, which would pay off once his back-channel warnings proved accurate.

Before switching off his computers, Andy checked the cable traffic for relevant developments, threats, and opportunities. He found a couple of items to forward to the ambassador, adding his own comments about possible implications for Vodania. A loyal DCM never lost sight of the importance of showing he was on the job, continuously watching out for the boss. A posture even more essential for a disloyal one.

Andy reflected on the previous night's unorthodox meeting. Despite all the precautions, including his subtle suggestions that Ambassador Lamkin would get spooked if anyone brought up the plan with him, he was exposed in a way he had never been before. The ambassador, should he ever learn the contents of the conversation with Shariz and Farao, would be justifiably furious at his deputy for, among other things, turning him into a hypocrite in the eyes of Washington as well as the most powerful leaders in Vodania. Not to mention the risk that the manufactured incidents could take on a momentum of their own. Instigating a civil war never looked good on a diplomat's resume.

If the ambassador ever did get wind of the initiative, and doubted his deputy's denials, Andy figured he could point out that Ambassador

Lamkin also stood to benefit from being at a post with significant problems, the kinds of dangerous difficulties that receive high-level attention from Washington. After we turn things around and Vodania calms down again, the ambassador could and would do his utmost to bask in the credit. Andy could argue he set him up with an opportunity. What may at first appear to be an act of betrayal could turn out to be more beneficial than conventional loyalty. But in the end, should any unpleasantness with the ambassador reach a crisis point, one small source of solace remained. Despite all of Andy's diligence in deleting photos of the intimate encounter between the senator and the ambassador's dog, one phone somehow eluded inspection. He tapped his front trouser pocket, taking comfort from its presence.

Andy knew he would make an effective ambassador, far more so than most of the plodders currently occupying those commanding heights. But performing the job came secondary. What truly, deeply mattered above all else was achieving the fulfillment of being an ambassador. Reaching the supreme point of existence. Getting there would require distinguishing himself from his colleagues in America's other embassies around the world. To advance to that ultimate level of prestige, Andy Pulano needed a record of solving vital, difficult problems. And how could he build a reputation as a trouble-shooter if there wasn't any trouble?

Tara entered Hotel Apex filled with curiosity about the Foreign Executive Women's club. The lure of new friends and new insights quickened her steps. She had not found a similar networking group in Kingston.

The luncheon took place in the Camellia Room, an elegant, professional setting. Tara spotted Monique, the French EU diplomat, and joined her table. When the Hotel Apex waitresses began clearing away the remnants of the beet and goat cheese salad, the chairwoman rose and stepped to the lectern in the corner of the event room. With only a couple dozen members in attendance, the microphone served mainly to enhance the gravitas of the occasion. The chairwoman riffled through a series of administrative and upcoming event announcements before introducing the luncheon speaker, Mrs. Lotte Wuyts, head of the social responsibility and civic engagement committee.

"Her hubby runs the consular section of the EU mission," Monique hissed in her elegant accent. "They're Belgian," she added, accusingly.

Mrs. Wuyts made an ardent presentation on the minor progress and the vast challenges in the campaign to neuter stray dogs in Shizl. Her descriptions veered into the graphic on certain points, causing those who had not yet finished their coconut flan to put down their spoons. On the positive side, she announced that the EU had agreed to contribute financial resources and to host an event to raise additional funds and attention.

"That is welcome, certainly, but we simply have to do much, much more to drive attention to this problem," Mrs. Wuyts declared.

The speaker glared at her audience. "Conditions are desperate! We all see these poor animals every day, struggling to survive. They roam the streets in packs because no one is taking care of them. It's terrible how many dogs get poisoned here. People just put toxic chemicals in a piece of meat, and problem solved. A horrible death, full of suffering."

Mrs. Wuyts paused to wipe her eyes.

"With the shelter, I have made arrangements, and we are taking another two carloads of puppies to Bulgaria next week. But we can't export our way to a solution. We must evolve the government's and the citizens' thinking here about these innocent animals. Simple talk is not enough, we need action. Direct action!"

She seemed to be focusing directly at Tara.

"We need to find a way to get to those in power, to get their attention and make them *see* and make them *care* about the animals in this country. *All* the animals."

The speaker came out from behind the lectern, still gripping the microphone, and took a few steps toward Tara's table.

"If *one* dog is in danger, *all* dogs are in danger!"

Mrs. Wuyts brandished her index finger at Tara like a mighty sword of justice. "From the alleys of the poor to the houses of the most powerful."

Her voice strained higher and higher.

Tara glanced around at the other attendees, most of whom were intently examining the contents of their coffee cups, and realized she wasn't the only one who found Mrs. Wuyts barking mad.

In the office on Monday morning, Andy pretended to listen to Charlene complain about her weekend as he started in on his inbox. The ambassador's secretary interrupted to inform him that the ambassador was calling an urgent meeting related to security. Ten minutes, in the secure conference room. Uh-oh.

When the ambassador arrived, stomping through the embassy's executive suite, Andy followed at his heels. The ambassador skipped the usual Monday morning bonhomie about his weekend diversions. At the outer door to the conference room, Andy punched in the code and pulled open the door for the ambassador, then darted ahead down the short narrow corridor to yank down on the lever to release the fortified inner door. His palm slipped and he strained at the effort. Andy accentuated the difficulty of the task because he judged it expedient to perpetuate the ambassador's view of his own physical superiority. The ambassador's exceptional terseness that morning signaled major unhappiness.

The defense attaché, the station chief, the political counselor, and the regional security officer stood up at the ambassador's entrance. Normally the ambassador would smile and say "Sit, sit, please," as he made his way to his customary spot. But not this morning.

Andy's eyebrows tightened like Marine security guards at attention. Could the ambassador have gotten wind of his back-channel messages to Vonda Vance and Geoff Bentwood? Or worse, learned of the meeting with Shariz and Farao, despite all his precautions?

After the ambassador lowered himself into his seat, everyone else did the same. The ambassador, flushed and grim-faced, hitched his chair forward until the armrests bumped the conference table. In a voice resonant with anger he announced, "Davos has been poisoned."

Part II

Five More Days in August

Chapter 6

Ambassador Lamkin's announcement about Davos jolted the embassy's national security team.

Ken Dewitt, the regional security officer, commonly referred to as the RSO, broke the stunned silence. "There was nothing in our overnight sit reps or alerts."

General Elfersen, the defense attaché, spoke at almost the same time. "Was it terrorism? Any VIPs among the casualties?"

Station chief Phyllis Snicklehimer jumped in. "We'll check the traffic for claims of responsibility."

DCM Andy Pulano detected the misunderstanding almost before it happened. No surprise that his straight-thinking, by-the-book colleagues would hear 'Davos' and think city in Switzerland, World Economic Forum, all that. But before the ambassador even spoke, Andy could read on his features the bitter, wounded anger of a personal affront. The ambassador's clenched facial muscles gave no sign of the righteous patriotic excitement that a major international security incident would bring out. Therefore, he could not be talking about an assault on Davos, Switzerland.

Over many years, Andy had forged into reflex his habit of divining the motivations and veiled agendas of others. Especially superiors. Perception of the mismatch between what the ambassador meant, and what the embassy's national security team thought he meant, flashed across Andy's mind. The only thing to ponder was whether to let them make further fools of themselves. He calculated not.

The DCM lifted his palm to quell any further embarrassing outbursts from the team.

"I believe the ambassador is referring to his Labrador retriever. This is quite a serious matter."

He turned to the ambassador in listening mode.

"Indeed," responded the ambassador. "An attack on the household pet of the American ambassador is a hostile act and one to which we will respond very appropriately. Someone is sending us—me—a message. Which fits with the mentality in this region. I have a very good idea where this is emanating from, but the first step is to get all the facts. Then we will decide on our response."

Solemn silence ensued as the country team members recalibrated.

"I will rely on the DCM to put together an action plan to coordinate our resources and assets."

"Yes sir." Keep it crisp, Andy reminded himself.

"If we need additional resources or capabilities, I am very willing to reach back to Washington," the ambassador intoned. "You just let me know who I need to call."

He looked around the table before continuing. "The victim is a dog. But not just any dog. And not at just any random time, but at a particularly critical juncture in the power dynamics here. Our local 'friends' will be gauging our reactions, and we cannot signal in any way that we will tolerate this. Bottom line: there will be consequences."

Love it when you talk tough, Big Daddy, Andy chortled to himself. His relief that the ambassador's seething fury was not directed at him instantly got bumped aside by the realization he could channel it for his own purposes. He would need to figure out the best way to induce the ambassador, under the influence of wounded emotions, to make a mistake. Or to make one for him.

"I won't share my theories at this point," the ambassador resumed. "But I will expect you to coordinate your efforts through the DCM. Am I perfectly clear?"

Yessirs all around. Then the RSO put up his hand and said, "Sir, very sorry about your loss. Could you give us details about the killing?"

"Davos is not dead," the ambassador banged back. "He's a tough hunting dog and I have no doubt he will recover. Lithia has him at the vet's now. He was severely ill this morning. He struggled up the stairs to our room and didn't even have the strength to jump up onto the bed. Without going into all the particulars, he ruined a pair of hand-crafted loafers and stained the carpeting in several places."

Tilting toward the DCM, the ambassador added, "You might mention to Robert to have that looked at."

After the meeting broke up, Andy followed the ambassador back to his office. He waited as his boss shuffle-stepped around the mahogany expanse of desk and plopped into his ergonomic executive chair, facing away. The ambassador kicked a gleaming wingtip oxford against the carpet to swivel around. Andy stood in a posture of solicitous attention two paces inside the room.

"I expect you to fix this. It's a priority. We also need to keep it close hold. I told my detail of course."

So much for close hold. The local police bodyguards on the ambassador's security detail gossiped like eighth-grade girls on an endless field trip. They dined out on ambassador stories all the time.

Andy met the ambassador's stern stare and said, "I think your instinct to keep this on a need-to-know basis is exactly right. In that regard, do you think we should get Washington involved at this stage, as we investigate? I'm concerned that . . ."

He paused as if collecting his thoughts before continuing.

"You know how the Department and the rest of the players back there tend to focus on their inter-agency games and all the inside-the-Beltway preoccupations. They lack a nuanced appreciation of the realities we face in the field. Until we get a better handle on who or what is behind this—"

"Who's behind this is not a mystery, at least not to me," the ambassador interrupted. "Chilik and his circle. Profiles in corruption. They're threatened by me talking to the opposition, engaging with the Pazaris, speaking out in public. So, they lash out, send a message. That's the psychology we're dealing with. But you have a point about Washington."

An opening. To widen it, Andy said, "The last thing we want is invidious comparisons between civilian casualties in Ukraine, tensions with China, famines, mass migrations—and a sick pet in Vodania. They'll miss the context here completely."

He figured the ambassador could picture the snickering in the assistant secretary's office during senior staff meetings and took a half step closer. "Not the kind of thing we'd want to see in the *Scorcher*."

"Definitely not." The ambassador shuddered. "I'll look to you to keep that from happening."

The ambassador issued another commanding glare.

"Understood," Andy replied. "With your concurrence, I'll have the team keep this local. If they put it into their channels there's no telling where it'll end up."

The ambassador grimaced. "I'm counting on you."

Please do.

Tara emerged from Chuck's office after the eight o'clock, rolling her eyes and using her lower lip to blow a strand of hair off her face. It was still practically first thing Monday morning, but the weekend's upbeat mood had been thoroughly demolished. Happy hour at the Marine House turned out to be pretty fun, once she got beyond the entrance. Saturday was full, Sunday quiet. A bit lonely, admittedly. She called her parents to catch up.

Her father wondered what sort of impact she was making. Her mother asked, more than once, if she was safe.

If things kept up like this, the question was whether Chuck would be safe. The meeting ran long because she made a perfectly reasonable proposal to look at several new rental properties to assess whether they would be good candidates for the embassy housing stock. Having more options would provide leverage to renegotiate the more overpriced leases. After asking every worrywart question he could come up with, he said let me think about it. What was there to think about?

Tara had barely settled at her cubicle when her veteran assistant said there was an American spouse on the phone. "She sounds upset."

It was Connie Mitchell, wife of the assistant public affairs officer. The Mitchell family had arrived in Shizl in July, during the same week as Tara.

Tara picked up the line. "Hi Connie, are those stair gates working okay?"

"Hi Tara. Yes, they're fine, thank you. Sorry to call again, but I wanted to follow up on a request I made to the crew when they were out here doing the installation. You know the play room in the basement of our house?"

"Yeah?"

"The floor is really hard. It's bare cement. Yesterday, Irena, our youngest, fell again and banged her head. She's only got one tooth and I'm really afraid she's going to break it one of these times. Can we get some kind of padding or something to put down there?"

"Hmmm. Sorry to hear about Irena. Is she okay?"

"I think so, yes. But I feel like I'm taking a chance every time the kids play down there."

"I'll double-check but I'm pretty sure the regs don't provide for floor coverings. Those are considered the employee's responsibility, I believe."

"Yeah, that's what your assistant just told me."

After an awkward pause, Connie spoke again. "Is there any leeway, any consideration for special circumstances?"

I'm guessing probably not, Tara thought. "Let me look into it, talk to Chuck. I honestly don't know if there's anything we can do."

"I'm really trying to make this work." She sounded on the verge of tears.

"I understand. Hey listen, I'm going to be in your neighborhood later this afternoon. How about if I stop by to take a look?"

After finishing with the ambassador, Andy stopped in front of Charlene's desk, the fortress that controlled access to his own office. "I need fifteen minutes each with the RSO and the defense attaché, at their earliest convenience. This morning."

He entered his own sanctum and crossed to the window to peer out across the broad expanse of pastures and farm plots between the embassy and downtown Shizl. The land sloped in irregular gradations down to clusters of apartment buildings closer to the city center. In the distance, the Presidentorium commanded the bluff over the slow-flowing Druzhba. If this tasty new crisis actually originated in the smoky chambers of Vodania's power center, he offered his deepest gratitude. Thank you, President Chilik and minions, for presenting another problem to exploit.

Andy's mind spun with possibilities, as if a substantial inheritance had just materialized. This misdeed, or misfortune, and the ambassador's anger, offered plenty to work with. And it was a situation that, handled with skill and delicacy, could improve one's standing with Lithia Lamkin, a tough customer, seemingly impervious to charm. After all, everyone loves troubleshooters. He craved that title, although he never applied the term to himself. Why shoot something as precious as trouble? In any event, he reasoned, any progress into Lithia's good graces could only help in the overall effort to manage his relationship with the ambassador. That was critical, at least for as long as David Lamkin held the position. But back to the poisoning. Whatever its source, what a wonderful, bountiful treasure, full of potential.

During a mandatory leadership training class Andy attended many years back, the earnest facilitator shared the insight that a stranger is just a friend you haven't met yet. This nugget inspired Pulano's mantra that trouble is just an opportunity in disguise. Usually several opportunities. After years of operating by this code he barely noticed any disguises, instead approaching each fresh problem the way a pickpocket works a parade. Except that now, rather than seeking opportunities to win favor by bolstering his boss's interests, he would gnaw Lamkin's foundations like a colony of famished termites.

Regarding Davos, the first move must be to instruct the eager-to-be-of-service regional security officer and defense attaché to refrain from reporting anything back to their respective Washington chains of command. And to issue the instruction in such a way as to ensure they do the opposite. This would cause them to divert their reporting into less formal channels, which would inevitably highlight it. As for the station chief, he assessed that Phyllis was more likely to send something back to CIA headquarters if he didn't try to manipulate her into doing so. Everyone craves secret, insider info, especially the gossipy stuff. Soft State Department types, i.e. Ambassador Lamkin, overreacting to a sick dog will make quite a delicious morsel of Washington scuttlebutt. And it should foster a useful contrast between the ambassador's emotional flakiness and the steadfast reliability of the DCM.

After calling off the dogs, so to speak, there was the question of who to enlist as confidential assistant and fall guy in waiting. In any kind of crisis, a wise manager develops a distinctive and circumspect supplier of information, a source who is both discrete and discreet. Andy paused to savor his wordplay before completing the thought: as well as a surrogate who can shoulder blame if the problem worsens or remains unresolved. In this case Andy needed someone controllable, with plausible grounds for involvement, and scant likelihood of prematurely, or ever, ruining the mystery, this precious gift.

He turned away from the window to face the open door of his office.

Dog's Breakfast

"Charlene, could you please set up fifteen minutes tomorrow with Tara Zadani."

Chapter 7

Later on Monday morning, the ambassador's limo, ponderous with the weight of its special protective armor, labored eastward through the bumps and curves of the road out to the National Police Academy training facility. Seated behind the chauffeur, Doug Watanabe struggled to maintain his posture on the slick black leather upholstery, his torso twisted to the right toward the ambassador. Doug had spent twenty years and a day with the Los Angeles Police Department, about half of it in the training division. His early career, on patrol in the Valley Bureau, provided most of his supply of cop stories. After he retired from LAPD, the Department of Justice hired him as a contractor to help implement law enforcement capacity building programs in Afghanistan. There, during daily workouts in the embassy gym, he bonded with the consul general, David Lamkin. When Lamkin got the ambassadorship he'd been promised for running the Embassy Kabul consular section for two tedious war-torn years, he arranged for Doug to get the Drug Enforcement Agency liaison slot in Vodania.

"I really appreciate you doing this event," said the DEA rep. "As you know better'n anyone, it wasn't easy getting the service chiefs to agree to joint training. This first class of graduates will face a lot of scrutiny. But we'll get there. And your remarks at this graduation will buy us a lot of goodwill with the leadership, as well as with the force."

"Will Farao be there?"

"No, but Minister Xotari will, along with Chief Stavroski."

"Interesting timing."

"How do you mean?"

"Has the DCM brought you in on the Davos situation?"

"No sir."

The ambassador frowned.

"Someone evidently gave Davos a dose of something toxic. I have my suspicions as to who."

The ambassador paused, glancing at the back of the chauffeur's head. "But we won't go into that now. The point being, I think we need a more active, aggressive investigation. By someone with real criminal investigation skills."

"Absolutely," Doug responded. "After all, it's entirely possible Davos was poisoned with a controlled substance."

"Exactly. I would think DEA would be interested in that angle."

"I'm on it, soon as we get back."

Andy sat still behind his desk, in an attentive posture, as Ken Dewitt presented his plan of action. As the RSO, the head of the embassy's security team, investigating the poisoning incident was Ken's job. Zeal lit up his eyes. A real actual case to work. Andy could tell that Ken was this close to strapping on his flak jacket and tactical helmet.

"And we'll review the footage from all the security cameras for the past forty-eight hours," the RSO continued at full tilt. "Kerry-Anne is there now interviewing the guards. We'll do the night shift this afternoon. And the police on station at the corner. We'll be looking for anything suspicious, anyone or anything that could have breached the perimeter. I'm going straight over after this meeting. We'll check for footprints by the hedge and in the grass, and collect any and all evidence present at the crime scene."

Ken leaned forward, his fists on the edge of the DCM's desk. "Phase two is to interview the neighbors, both the Alambro family and the German ambassador, and ask them both to check their cameras."

"Ken," Andy interrupted. "Those all sound like the proper, normal steps. But we also need to keep this as unobtrusive as possible."

The RSO straightened his posture. "This matter falls under Diplomatic Security responsibility and authority. We have to follow the full procedures for a possible terrorist attack investigation."

"What I'm telling you is we want to keep this local and low key. So be thorough, yes, but don't make a big scene. I'll remind you that everything we do here is under chief of mission authority. As you heard, he has directed me to coordinate our efforts. At this point, it is a local investigation."

To emphasize the instruction, Andy asked, "Do you anticipate any reason to brief or seek any guidance, support, or resources from DS?" referring to the Diplomatic Security bureau in the State Department.

"Not at this time."

"I want to preview anything and everything you send back on this matter. Is that clear?"

Ken's reluctant nod satisfied Andy that he had just flung open the back-channel floodgates.

Not long after Ken hurried off to his detective work, defense attaché General Elfersen appeared in Andy's doorway.

"I assume this has to do with the poisoning incident," he growled, lowering his sizable frame into one of the chairs around the DCM's coffee table.

Andy came out from behind his desk and took the chair opposite. He extended his left leg and flopped a tasseled loafer onto the coffee table, the bottom of his foot angled so it faced just past the defense attaché. The general, over-vigilant about the fact that technically he reported directly to the ambassador, tended to view the DCM as, at best, a peer. So, to set the mood, Andy figured he would remind him of one or two matters.

"That's one of several items," Andy confirmed. "First I'd like an update on planning for the Minnesota National Guard visit."

After badgering General Elfersen about the proposed guest list for the reception the ambassador agreed to host for the Minnesota delegation, haggling over the amount of representation funds the defense attaché's office would contribute for the event, and going over the points that needed to be included in the ambassador's welcoming toast, Andy picked up another instrument of torment: the weapons sale issue.

"As you know," he reminded the defense attaché, "the pol-mil bureau in State has raised a series of questions about the need and end use of several items on the Vodanians' foreign military sales wish-list."

"You're referring to the minimum interoperability requirements, sir?"

Andy loathed military gibberish, their habit of deploying overengineered terms like *interoperability* when they just mean compatibility. But he quieted his inner editor and piled on, laying out his sense of the level of detail and explanation necessary to get Washington approval for each of the FMS items under scrutiny. "We need to work with our Vodanian friends to provide the proper assurances and accountability."

Andy knew the phrase 'Vodanian friends' grated on the defense attaché's hard-nosed sensibilities, given that the U.S. had important military bases in Pazaria, Vodania's rival. He figured he had Elfersen on enough of a tilt. Primed to do things the proper military way, not hamstrung by civilian hand-wringing and fuzzy sentiments. Andy lifted his leg off the coffee table and sat up straight. He looked into the general's eyes.

"Now, about the dog incident. We have to keep this low-key and local for now. We don't want to get our Vodanian friends spun up about this until we know what we're dealing with. So, I, and the ambassador, want you and your team to keep your ears open. But don't pulse your whole network at this point, because word will get around fast and muddy the waters."

"Understood."

"At the same time, to help us determine whether this may have been a probe by a hostile, organized force, we need an expert military assessment of the capabilities required to pull off something like this, undetected."

General Elfersen nodded. "We can do a capabilities assessment."

"Great. But don't let it occupy too much of your time or your team's. We have no indication as yet that this is a military matter. Main thing is to keep in listening mode."

"Don't worry sir, we won't overstaff it. We can walk and chew gum."

Floodgate number two open and gushing.

After the Police Academy ceremony, by the time the limousine approached the residence, Doug Watanabe had run out of ways to praise the ambassador's speech to the graduates of the first training program that included members from each of Vodania's police forces. A very, very, highly super-successful event. Senior officials from the customs, border, national, tax, and capital police all put in a good word for Doug in expressing their appreciation to the ambassador for America's financial and organizational support. Doug would have wanted to be helpful in investigating the dog poisoning anyway, but now felt extra motivated.

The limo drove past the grassy strip outside the residence's perimeter fence, where the brash young RSO, his even younger assistant RSO, and their senior local investigator walked shoulder-to-shoulder, taking baby steps, their heads bent low. They had almost reached the end of the property line without appearing to detect anything significant. Including the presence of the photographer across the street. Expect to see a photo in one of the tabloids in the morning, Doug chuckled to himself, with a smartass caption like 'Someone lose an earring?' Not likely to win points with the ambassador.

With a heavy click, the driveway gate unlocked and began swinging open. The guard stood at attention as the limo rolled through. The RSO stopped his search to observe the ambassador and Doug emerge from the vehicle and proceed into the residence.

In the kitchen, Doug explained his task to the residence staff and asked the cook for a few ziplock bags. The plumper of the two housekeepers led him out the side door into the garden area. She pointed to a spot under a flowering bush. Doug squatted, careful not to stress his knees. With a soup spoon, also courtesy of the ambassador's kitchen, he scraped yellowish goop into the clear plastic bag, careful to avoid getting any soil in the mix. It smelled sickening.

"What the hell are you doing?" demanded Ken, from somewhere above and behind him.

"Collecting."

Doug turned his face away from the mess, took a breath, and scooped up more samples of Davos's earlier misfortune.

"On whose authority?"

"The ambassador's."

"This crime scene is under RSO jurisdiction."

"Tell it to the ambassador."

Doug sealed the ziplock and stood up. Gesturing with the dirty spoon, he added, "Listen Ken, I'm not trying to get in your way. The ambassador wants to know if any controlled substances were used in the poisoning. I'm helping him out. And helping you out too, if you care to look at it that way."

"You're not getting away with this."

Doug turned and walked back toward the side door of the residence.

"I'm confiscating that vomit," Ken declared, but stayed where he was. Punk.

Upstairs, in the master bedroom, the housekeeper showed Doug where the fluids had seeped into the carpet, next to the bed. The carpet was gold-colored, thick and plush, and the household staff had done a thorough job in cleaning up the mess. Still, there was a good likelihood that testable material remained in the deepest recesses. Doug knelt, took out his multi-purpose tool, opened a sharp blade, and sliced into the carpet. Pressing firmly and shifting his weight around as necessary, he cut out two crude circles, leaving holes the size of California grapefruits.

Sun baked the streets of Harabad, the preeminent ethnic Pazari city in Vodania. No breeze stirred the dust and litter that collected against the crumbling curbs and weathered storefronts of the main thoroughfare. At a table under the awning in front of the Highland Café, Eftin Zabor, a city council member from the Pazari People's Party, enjoyed a cup of tea with an attractive constituent. Why shouldn't politics be pleasurable?

A black sedan with tinted windows sped toward them and pulled up close to the curb, its exhaust heat engulfing Eftin and his companion.

After a moment, the rear passenger door opened and a thickset man in a dark suit clambered out. His cousin Anton. His father's half-cousin, technically. Anton got hired by the city police department shortly after the Pazari Homeland Party candidate won the mayor's office. To do what, exactly, was never said, but it wasn't too hard to figure out.

"Eftin, greetings." His cousin also nodded and smirked at the young woman, who made no response.

Eftin flung his nearly-depleted cigarette toward the car, bouncing it off the rear tire.

"Tea?"

"No, no time," Anton replied. "I only came to tell you something." He glanced at the woman again.

"You can speak."

Anton shrugged. "We're going to visit your campaign office tonight, late."

"Which one?"

"The uglier one. By the stadium."

"Again? You goat-vaginas just hit it last week."

"This time we're going inside, smashing things. That's why I'm telling you, Excellency."

After his cousin's car roared off, Eftin said, "Ass pipes. Now I have to go to my mother's house to get her computer."

The woman tilted her head and raised an eyebrow.

"It's so old, it probably doesn't work anymore. We need something in the office for the Homelanders to smash. Then we can get USAID to replace it. And get another new one from the EU."

Tara leaned against the doorframe to Chuck's office, waiting for him to look up.

"I've got an unhappy spouse. Can I get your advice?"

"I usually recommend a glass or two of wine. Wait a minute, I thought you were single?"

"Hah hah. It's Connie Mitchell. She wants a pad or something for her basement floor. It's her kids' playroom and apparently it's a hard concrete floor."

Chuck stared at her, waiting.

"Anything we can do?" Tara asked.

"Floor coverings for non-rep spaces are not in the housing plan nor are they in the budget. You could give her the names of the vendors we've used. But we can't order for her."

Inside his office, during an interlude between afternoon meetings, Andy congratulated himself for his handling of the RSO and defense attaché. Although he couldn't know for certain they would get word circulating in Washington about the supposed attack on the ambassador's pet, the odds were favorable. Every termite helped.

Heavy footsteps and a terse exchange outside his door pulled Andy out of his scheming. The RSO stomped in and planted himself in front of the DCM's desk, barely able to contain himself. Color radiated from his cheeks and neck. His body was clenched rigid with stress as he spurted his outrage about Doug Watanabe collecting evidence at the residence.

"And he's planning to fly the samples to Incirlik tomorrow! I can't believe he's got the budget for international flights to hand-carry stuff!"

"I can set your mind at ease on that point, Ken," Andy replied, leaning back in his swivel chair. "There's a regional DEA conference at the base. He was going there anyway."

"You need to order him to return the evidence to DS custody."

"The ambassador evidently wants DEA testing, which I'll confirm. That's within his prerogatives."

Getting DEA involved. Brilliant. Why didn't I think of that? Pretty soon half of Washington will be tittering about this.

"It's interference with a criminal investigation. I'm the only authorized law enforcement officer in this embassy."

"Ken, you have to let it go. The ambassador is ultimately responsible for security at this embassy. And he has full authority to proceed as he judges best. Besides, when we discussed your plan of action this morning, you didn't say anything about testing any vomit."

Late Monday afternoon, Tara parked across the street from the Mitchells' house, a property which the embassy added to its inventory via a long-term lease several months earlier. It was close to Hotel Apex, in a newish neighborhood north of the Druzhba River that connected to the old city by a four-lane bridge. Tara mounted the steps.

Connie, in casual workout attire and a scrunchie, opened the door before Tara reached it. "It's so nice of you to come out."

"No problem."

Tara followed her inside. A foldable baby chair stood next to the dining room table, facing a plastic bowl smeared with remnants of mushed pumpkin or squash. All the dining chairs had crayon drawings taped to their backs. A sprinkling of picture books and toys littered the couches and the floor. They're living in a kindergarten, Tara thought, but she kept a bland smile on her face.

Before kids, Connie did market research for a company in Chicago. Now she and her husband had a boy in kindergarten, a three-year old girl, and another daughter, who was eighteen months old. On the way toward the stairs, Connie scooped up their youngest without breaking stride.

"Say hi, Irena."

The toddler gave Tara a wide-eyed stare and buried her face in Connie's shoulder. Connie unlatched the baby gate at the top of the stairs and led the way down. At the bottom she said, "Welcome to the toy pit."

Indeed. It would be unfair to say the basement looked like a tornado hit Santa's workshop. But not that unfair. A jumble of cars, dolls, stuffed animals, building blocks and lots of other brightly colored stuff covered much of the floor. An easel and a chalkboard stood in one corner; a pile of cushions occupied another. Sheets of white paper with water-color drawings adorned the concrete walls. The two older children were taking turns jumping from the armchair, the only piece of furniture in the room, onto the cushions.

"It's quite a gallery," Tara offered.

Connie looked at her as if to say, you see what I mean? You see what I'm dealing with here? What she actually said was, "We really like this house. The neighbors are friendly, the street is nice."

Tara nodded.

Connie continued, "It's just this basement play room, this concrete floor. It's not safe, for Irena especially."

They chatted about other aspects of life in Shizl, and Tara repeated that she didn't have an immediate fix but would help if she could.

"Seeing the room helps me visualize what you need. The housing regs are pretty clear, unfortunately, but I'll keep searching for a creative solution." She reached out and patted the child in Connie's arms.

Tara took in the joyful shrieks of the older children vying for Connie's attention, the sweet cuddliness of the toddler, the air of walled-in domesticity, of family. In leaving, fascinated and horrified, she wondered whether she had just glimpsed one version of her own future.

Chapter 8

On Monday evening, the heads of the diplomatic corps gathered at the Samarkand Inn, a landmark in Shizl's old city, for one of their periodic meetings with the foreign minister. U.S. ambassador David Lamkin considered boycotting the event, but decided it was best at this stage not to show the Vodanian government that the attack on Davos had gotten to him. Let them wonder. Let them imagine the repercussions. By the time he entered the oak-paneled, tobacco-scented Samarkand, dignitaries in muttering clumps nearly filled the special events room. The atmosphere seemed more animated than usual. Things were happening. With elections approaching and signs of tension rising, Lamkin knew his counterparts were snapping up any tidbits they could feed their foreign ministries back home.

Taking turns to avoid an unseemly hubbub, the other ambassadors approached the American to seek his views about how dire the situation really was and how much more dire it would become. Almost all of them considered him a more reliable and authoritative source of information than any Vodanian official. Not due to his penetrating political acumen, he knew, although it was penetrating enough, but because they believed he exerted decisive influence over key Vodanian government decisions. Lamkin was careful never to admit to playing such a role, nor to deny it.

German ambassador Monika Basch, a judicious and competent peer, drew him into an empty corner of the room, near the door to the kitchen. They bent their heads together, oblivious to the restaurant staff sidestepping them with large trays of salads and appetizers. She placed her hand lightly on his forearm.

"I heard you had an incident at your residence. Your security people asked us to check our cameras for anything suspicious."

"My dog was poisoned this morning. I think it's pretty obvious who's behind it." He shot her a meaningful look. "But we're looking for proof."

"Anything we can do to help, we will."

"Thank you, Monika."

"Is your dog okay now?"

"I think he'll recover. He was quite copiously ill this morning. A real mess. We're testing the, you know . . ." He pantomimed throwing up. "To find out what they used."

Lamkin noticed other ambassadors speculating about the meaning of his gesture. Fine. Maybe they'll think he was making an overly candid commentary on President Chilik's latest press release on the importance of fair elections.

Ambassador Basch lowered her voice even further. "We can help with the testing too, if you want another analysis. In Berlin we have a veterinary laboratory that can detect over one hundred toxins."

After leaving the Mitchells' house, Tara drove to the fitness center on the lower level of Hotel Apex. She was a little early for the Zumba class Karolina had persuaded her to sign up for. After changing into workout gear, which felt like a nun's habit compared to the outfits on some of the other women, she wandered around to check out the facility, known as Vodania's trendiest exercise spot. In the free weights area, she stopped to watch a super-ripped guy, naked except for a pair of shorts, slamming a body bag strung up in the corner. With skin glistening and hair flowing down to his shoulders, he delivered a percussive flurry of kicks and punches in a beautiful, frightening dance. Tara had never seen a body with that much definition.

After Zumba, Karolina took Tara to her favorite local hangout. The Locust Bar, located along a narrow lane in the heart of old Shizl, had rough stone walls and dim lighting. Hard-looking older workmen and laughing university students occupied about half the tables. A bit scruffy, Tara thought, especially after Hotel Apex. Karolina led the way to an open table and they sat facing each other.

"Okay, who was that stud?" said Tara.

Karolina looked puzzled and turned to look toward the entrance.

"At the gym."

Karolina leaned forward and spoke in a low voice. "Oh. Vlado. He's the top personal trainer in Vodania. Used to be an Olympic wrestler. He trains President Chilik."

"Olympics, I can totally believe," Tara responded. "His muscles were about to pop right out of his skin." She glanced around the room before whispering, "He looks like he'd be good at having things pop out."

Karolina shook her head, but a chime from her cell phone stopped her from responding further. While she took the call, Tara stood up to find the restroom.

Through the cave-like atmosphere, Tara made her way back toward the bar, peering into the other seating areas and dark passageways trying to guess the likeliest spot for the ladies', when something hit her shoulder, hard.

"Oooff!" said a male voice.

Tara turned.

"My apologies. I am very sorry," said a man with a bristle of light brown hair and a quick flash of a grin.

He held a dripping beer stein in one hand and reached for a cocktail napkin with the other.

"My bad, I wasn't paying attention," Tara replied.

He dabbed at his half-zipped workout shirt and the left thigh of his loose cotton trousers. Tall, maybe thirtyish. Cute.

"I spilled your beer."

"No, it's my fault, I was telling this ruffian here about my trip. This is Stefano. And I am Mads."

"Don't be *mad*," she smiled. "I'll buy you another beer."

He laughed and tipped his glass toward Tara as if to toast, then stopped. "It looks like I should buy you a beer."

"I'm not really a beer girl."

"Something else then. Wine?"

"They make great mojitos here," Stefano added.

Karolina came up and said, "You abandoned me."

"I'm just being hassled by Mads and Stefano here." Tara turned toward them and said, "My friend Karolina."

After introductions and further banter, they moved to Karolina and Tara's table. Mads explained he was in the early weeks of a half-year sabbatical from his teaching job in Copenhagen.

"What's your goal?" Tara asked.

"Travel and exploration."

"Do you have a particular destination in mind, or will you know it when you find it?" Karolina asked.

"I'd like to make it to Goa."

"He's searching for the land route to India," Stefano explained.

Mads patted the backpack wedged between his chair and the wall. "With this, I can go anywhere."

He turned toward Tara. "And now, thanks to you, it will have a pleasant smell of beer for the rest of the journey."

"Speaking of journeys," said Tara, pushing back her chair, "I better resume my quest for the washroom, unless you want it to smell like pee."

When Tara returned, she learned that Stefano and Mads had become friends during their grad school years in the UK. Stefano then returned to

Vodania to help start a software company. He also played drums in a semi-serious jazz quartet that performed occasional gigs, mainly in Shizl.

"I'm new here," Tara said to Stephano. "Tell me about the fun stuff in Vodania. What's cool about this place?"

Stefano talked about the nightlife scene and Karolina mentioned a couple of beautiful mountain hikes not far from the capital.

"What about you?" Mads asked Tara.

"Oh, so far it's pretty much non-stop fun." She told them about dealing with Connie and the concrete floor issue.

"You are such a mean one," said Mads. "Why can't she have a pad for the children? No, wait. Please don't tell me."

When Tara opened her mouth to protest, he raised his index finger and held it against her lips.

A combination of surprise, affront, and amusement silenced Tara. The sensation of his brief touch lingered.

Early on Tuesday morning, in the kitchen of the U.S. ambassador's residence, the taller of the two housekeepers slammed down the cleaver she was using to chop cabbage.

"How can we collect the dog's vomit?" she asked. "I already cleaned everything, and then you let that idiot cut holes in the rug."

"He just took out his knife and started cutting. How was I supposed to stop him?" the plumper housekeeper argued.

"Did they notice the rug yet?"

"The ambassador didn't say anything about that. He just said the German embassy is sending someone over around eight o'clock to pick up the vomit for testing."

The taller housekeeper looked at the wall clock. 7:50. "Okay, then we give them vomit."

She opened the refrigerator door and bent forward to peer inside. After a moment she pulled out a plate of uncooked sausages left over from a recent event, a bottle of ranch-style salad dressing, and a lemon.

"For the acid," she informed her colleague.

Working efficiently, she put half a sausage, a cup of dressing, and all the juice from the lemon into the food processor. She added a scoop of dry dog food and held down the pulse button. It turned into a thick, lumpy mixture, orangish in color. She removed the lid and sniffed.

"It needs something."

The plumper housekeeper just stared.

"Go outside and get a piece of dog shit," the taller one ordered.

"Are you crazy?"

"It has to smell a little bit bad."

The plumper housekeeper went outside, muttering and shaking her head. She returned, grimacing, a plastic bag at arm's length.

The taller housekeeper squeezed most of the turd into the food processor and pressed pulse again. Then she poured half a cup of the concoction into a ziplock bag and sealed it carefully. She loaded the rest into a second bag and put both samples into a larger ziplock.

The doorbell chimed.

At Incirlik Air Base in south central Turkey, Doug Watanabe settled into an empty row midway back in the amphitheater-style hall, patting his belly after a filling mess hall breakfast. The seat was roomy, comfortable, and even tilted back slightly. A person could absorb a lot of information in a seat like that. He checked again to make sure the briefcase at his feet was locked. Not that anyone besides Ken Dewitt, the try-hard RSO, would want the contents.

At precisely eight o'clock, an Air Force one-star in full dress blues took the stage. Bless the military, they do like an early start. On the giant projection screen that dominated the stage, a slide came up.

WELCOME

JOINT TACTICAL COMMAND STRATEGIC BRIEFING CENTER

INCIRLIK AIR BASE

"Welcome to the Joint Tactical Command Strategic Briefing Center, Incirlik Air Base," announced the one-star. He stood behind a lectern, facing about eighty conference participants, of whom maybe fifty were uniformed military. The one-star clicked the remote, bringing up the next slide.

UNITED STATES AIR FORCE BRIGADIER GENERAL RICHARD HAYES
FIRST DEPUTY ASSISTANT COMMANDER
JOINT COMBAT SUPPORT PLANNING CELL
EUCOM-CENTCOM JOINT PLANNING ACTIVITY COMMAND

"I am Brigadier General Richard Hayes, United States Air Force, first deputy assistant commander, Joint Combat Support Planning Cell, EUCOM-CENTCOM Joint Planning Activity Command. And I thank you for your service."

The slide also included his official photograph, with part of the stars & stripes visible in the background. He brought up a new slide, which featured the elaborate emblems of European Command and Central Command overlapping like a Venn diagram, plus four words of text:

EUCOM + CENTCOM
COOPERATION = TEAMWORK

"With EUCOM and CENTCOM together, our cooperation equals teamwork," the general recited.

Doug took a deep breath, ready to absorb. He settled more deeply into his chair and stretched out a leg. It rubbed against his briefcase, interrupting his relaxation with the reminder that he needed to find someone to carry the samples back to Washington for testing.

In the defense attaché's office in U.S. Embassy Shizl, General Elfersen squeezed into the secure communications vault, where his oversized deputy, Colonel Mesko, hunched forward facing a computer screen. After the general levered the door shut, the colonel read aloud from a draft tasking request.

"Non-permissive environment. Armed security force inside perimeter fence, external police presence twenty-four seven. Continuous-feed security cameras. Residential area with approximately thirty percent canopy coverage, mainly deciduous. Steep terrain, gradient range seventy-five to one-hundred percent. No road access from north."

"Let me look over the objective one more time," said Elfersen.

He leaned forward to read from the screen. "Force requirements, skill sets, and equipment to neutralize . . . let's change that to incapacitate . . . medium-sized dog . . . let's make it guard dog . . . with zero detection."

"Yes sir." Mesko tapped in the changes.

"You've double checked the budget codes and routing tags for a counterterrorism countersurveillance assessment?"

"Yes sir."

As Elfersen continued scrutinizing the tasking request on the screen, Mesko said, "Sir, gut check?"

"Yes?"

"Just wondering whether we need a special tasking for this, vice doing our own assessment. Seems like a lot of firepower for a fairly low-level incident."

General Elfersen stiffened. "The ambassador doesn't consider himself low-level."

He stared at Mesko for a moment. "In purely military terms, you may have a point. But the ambassador is very spun up on this, believe me, and we need to keep him on our side on a whole range of issues. Meanwhile, Watanabe is digging up the yard, the RSO is pulling out all the stops, who knows what the station is up to. We can't be in passive mode, you understand?"

Mesko nodded.

"Besides the politics," Elfersen continued, "neither you nor I are special forces. With an expert assessment, we're covered if this turns out to be something real."

"Got it."

"Let's check the geo-cords."

They switched places, and Mesko read from the screen as Elfersen looked at the latitude and longitude numbers for the ambassador's residence from their most recent survey of key embassy properties.

"N43.1854217."

"Check."

"E36.3940696."

"Send it."

Chapter 9

Tara arrived at the embassy on Tuesday morning with her mind whirling on two very different tracks. Mads and the DCM. The Danish traveler's lively curiosity and low-key confidence intrigued her. Plus, gorgeous. It was almost enough to make her forget the call from the DCM's secretary. Why did he want a meeting all of a sudden? As she took a seat in the waiting area of the executive suite a few minutes before eleven, she twisted her brains yet again but couldn't think of anything she'd done seriously wrong or especially noticeable. How much harm, or good, could she have done in a month? When Charlotte waved for her to go on in to the DCM's office, Tara stepped forward with what she hoped looked like self-assurance. If there's a problem, fix it. If there's not a problem, keep it that way.

"Sit please," the DCM greeted her. Without looking up from his computer screen, he pointed toward the coffee table and chairs in the corner.

Tara sat and watched his eyes track back and forth across the screen. His eyebrows, so animated every previous time she'd seen him, remained still. But they looked dangerous somehow. Like they could pounce. After a while he stood, came around from behind his desk, closed the office door, and instead of sitting across from her, eased into the chair next to Tara's. With an effort, she stopped herself from shifting away or shrinking into herself.

"You know how I like to periodically check in with the first and second tour officers, mentor, see if I can help or guide in any way?"

Tara nodded.

His eyebrows vibrated as if trying to break free. "This isn't one of those. I have a special, confidential matter for you. Just for you. It's unusual and very sensitive. Super close hold."

Almost sounds like he's about to pull down his pants, Tara thought. That would be so weird and embarrassing.

"The ambassador's dog was poisoned yesterday."

Tara pictured the chocolate Lab collapsed on the back lawn.

The DCM shook his head. "Not fatally. Listen, I'm telling you this in confidence. Very few people know about it. We're treating it as a possible security threat. That is also not to be shared. The ambassador has put me in charge of the embassy's response. And I need your help."

He paused, as if she needed time to process.

"Poor Davos. Is he going to be okay?"

"The ambassador is hopeful. But keep this quiet. You are to report only to me," he continued. "Not to Robert or Chuck or the ambassador or anyone. I don't want lines of communication tangled."

This is even weirder, Tara thought. "What would you like me to do?"

"Find out what happened. Talk to the household staff, the guards, and the groundskeepers. But subtly, in the course of normal business. Don't interrogate them. This is a delicate task and a difficult one. Frankly, I don't know if you're up to it, but it's possible you might be. We'll see. You're well-positioned."

"You want me to find out who poisoned Davos?"

"Yes."

"Is there a deadline?"

"Mostly we want to make sure there's not a dead dog." He flicked a tight smile and bounced his eyebrows. "For now, tighten up the procedures. Have the household staff keep the dog on a leash whenever he's in the yard."

"I'm pretty sure they're not supposed to be doing pet care."

"That's part of what makes this delicate."

They sat for another moment, side by side, until the DCM tilted his head and said, "Indulge me in something, please. An old habit of mine."

Tara looked at him, unsure what he was asking.

"I'd like you to summarize your instructions."

"Find out what happened to Davos."

The DCM's entire face drooped in disappointment.

"Discreetly," she added. "And discuss it with no one but you,"

"For your sake as well as mine." He smiled, a bit creepily.

That seemed to be the final word. As Tara stood to leave, the DCM remained seated. She had to go around the coffee table and cross in front of him. Before she reached the door, he spoke again.

"I'm counting on you."

Tara nodded and grasped the doorknob. A confidential assignment from the front office could be considered an honor. A vote of confidence. So why did it feel so odd? She opened the door and stepped back into the waiting area, where the lurking, smirking presence of Victor Manchego did not lift her spirits. She walked back toward the general services office, back toward her regular workload. Although she could think of no reason for the DCM to have anything against her, it occurred to her she may be getting set up to fail.

If so, he just invited the wrong girl to the prom.

Andy gazed toward his window after the new junior officer left. He felt like she got it. Not that she was too likely to discover what happened. But if she did, he needed to be the first to know. And if she didn't, at least he could show he tried everything.

He returned to his desk. On his computer screen, a fresh email from management counselor Robert Akes set forth possible courses of action to deal with the problem of people leaving their belongings in the embassy gym lockers overnight. Before he could contemplate the intricacies of the locker room issue, Charlene tapped once on his open door.

"Victor is here when you're ready."

"Great, send him in."

Consular officer Victor Manchego, unit chief for American citizens' services, had a well-deserved reputation as a management challenge. Andy figured he'd pull him off-balance by bringing him into the office right away, rather than imposing the normal hierarchical wait. Moreover, it was not likely that an extended opportunity to review the freshest editions of embassy and State Department publications and pronouncements, neatly displayed in the reception area, would have much impact in this case.

"Hello Victor. I'm glad you came to see me." Andy gestured to the chair at the side of his desk. By positioning his guest so close to himself, he could convey intimacy or intimidation, as the situation warranted.

"My door is open and you're wise to confer. What's on your mind?"

Victor clasped a manila folder in his left hand, and he waved it around as he proceeded to unburden himself of complaints about the public affairs section, the management section, and especially about his supervisor Barbara Hertz, head of the consular section.

"Overall, my experience at this embassy has been a pattern of discrimination, creating a hostile work environment."

"Are there documents in that folder you would like to share with me?"

Victor twisted sideways to place the folder on the DCM's desk. He carefully lifted open the top with a swooping semicircular motion like an aide at a treaty signing ceremony. He then arranged three sheets of paper on the surface of the desk. A curtailment request. An extension request. And a grievance.

The curtailment option beckoned. Andy's Montblanc Boheme Marron lay within reach. A muscle twitched in his right hand, creating a slight but perceptible movement of his index finger. He could extend his arm, grasp the fountain pen, sign the form. In two seconds, this problem would be solved.

However, there were downsides. A considerable staffing gap would undoubtedly ensue, straining the consular section, making Barbara even more cantankerous. This gap would necessarily drag Andy into an unseemly plea to the State Department for a replacement. And from a vulnerable position. Embassy Shizl would have to take whoever was available off-cycle, which tended not to be the pick of the litter, as it were. A further drawback was that a curtailment would deprive Andy of a valuable data point for demonstrating managerial prowess. On his watch there had been no curtailment requests from Embassy Shizl, and a small but growing number of extensions.

Having Victor extend would boost that total, but it would expose Andy to justifiable criticism by his eventual successor. Recognizing that in the best of circumstances, in which he has guided the selection process to ensure Shizl's next DCM is someone with whom he is on favorable terms, Andy knew that the future inhabitant of the office would nevertheless inevitably succumb to the temptation to blame him for whatever may go wrong during their time. A standard maneuver. Providing his successor with incontrovertible documentary evidence of poor judgment, by approving the extension of someone like Victor Manchego, would be handing out ammunition to his competitors. Allowing Victor to stay in Shizl a day longer than his normal assignment would risk cracking an essential load-bearing pillar in the reputational edifice Andy Pulano had devoted years to constructing.

"Let's discuss your concerns," he said to Victor. "I understand and appreciate your interest in taking on another public speaking opportunity. There is a wider context, however. The public affairs people, along with myself and the ambassador, have dedicated considerable energy and resources to dampening the firestorm that ensued after your talk at the

American Voices series back in April. References to your comments are finally beginning to fade in the electronic and print media."

"Some of those references, such as from the press in Pazaria, have been very positive."

"Which further enflames the Vodanians, who we are sent here to deal with on a variety of issues. I've listened to the tape of your talk."

"Which I never agreed to."

"Please understand that PA routinely keeps a tape of each speaking event to protect against false claims about what any of us say. Unfortunately, the tapes don't help against true claims. Among quite a few other things, you declared that Vodanians are lazy lying litterbugs."

Andy paused before resuming. "Lazy lying litterbugs. While I allow a bit of alliteration every now and then, this is explosive. Dangerous dynamite, if you like. Which is why I have taken extraordinary measures to control the tape of your presentation. But imagine for a moment if it were to nevertheless slip out into the hands of the media. I can pretty well promise you we would receive a persona non grata notice the same day. The Vodanian government won't be dilatory about sending you packing."

"Dilatory?" asked Victor.

"Sluggish. Lazy, you might say."

Andy paused again to let Victor think about the tape, and who controlled it, and what the consequences of release would be.

"Now, with regard to your contemplation or consideration of filing a grievance against Barbara in connection with the reprimand she gave you. According to her, you told several U.S. servicemen you could make their reports of birth abroad forms 'go away' if that's what they wanted. Why would you offer to disenfranchise our newest citizens?"

"Well, the overall basis of my grievance is that Barbara, and this post more broadly, is anti-Hispanic."

"Anti-Hispanic?"

"Yes sir. As far as I can tell I'm the only Hispanic officer at this post."

"Is that right?"

The DCM clasped his chin thoughtfully and looked at his display wall. Three meritorious honor awards hung in dark frames. Four superior honor awards. And the centerpiece: the director general's award for originality and impact in reporting. All of them bore his full name, in bold calligraphy. Fernando Oscar Pulano.

After a full minute of silence, his eyes never leaving the wall, Andy made a gesture with his left hand, inviting Victor to follow his gaze.

He allowed Victor more quiet time to figure it out, and then said, "If, upon further reflection, you feel this post is somehow anti-Hispanic, I'll be happy to put you in touch with Laura Martin, current chair of State's Hispanic Employees Council. She and I were A-100 classmates and we teamed up to form a committee to get the Department to broaden its outreach and recruitment in the community."

Victor finished reading the plaques, and he looked down at his lap.

Andy sat still for another moment, then leaned forward just a degree or two.

"If, on the other hand, you decide against calling further attention to your ill-advised and illegal idea for supporting the troops, you should think about the evaluation report you'll get at the end of this rating period."

He paused for a beat. "Keep in mind that I'll be writing your review statement, and I have the ability to cast your actions in a more positive light. For example, just to brainstorm for a moment, we could refer to the American Voices episode by noting that your public speaking generated exceptionally widespread interest and resulted in you becoming one of the most prominent and widely recognized officers in Embassy Shizl. As for telling military personnel you could help them evade paternity claims, we could describe that as repeatedly offering services to the troops that went above and beyond. You see what I'm getting at? I've been writing EERs for quite a while and have developed a knack, if I may say so."

Victor looked up and managed a smile.

"But I need to know you're on board, you're on this team and will take direction from your manager. I know Barbara has challenging aspects to her personality, but she's a first-rate consular officer, and you can learn from her. You need to think about what's in this for you, and what you get out of this tour. Barbara is well regarded in the Consular Affairs bureau, and if you can get her in your corner that's a real asset. I can help you while you're here, but not being a member of the consular family, I may not have the same long-term influence she does. And the ambassador, of course, also came up through consular."

Awash in advice, Victor nodded and sat, absorbing.

"Victor, I think we understand each other. It's in my interest, as well as my scope of responsibility, to help each of our officers succeed. Your best course is to withdraw all three of these forms and complete your tour without further incident. And keep in mind that if there is to be a change in the timing of your departure, it may not be up to you or me. It may be decided by outside forces at a moment that's not especially convenient to you or to the embassy."

Victor looked like he got it. Andy gave him a final nod. Victor rose to his feet and walked slowly toward the door.

"In the utility room," said the DCM, "on the left as you exit, you'll find the shredder."

In the Joint Tactical Command Strategic Briefing Center at Incirlik Air Base, Doug Watanabe rolled his shoulders and pressed his lower back deeper into the seat. Good lumbar support. The conference, underway for several hours, liberated his mind, much like a classical symphony. By the time DEA division chief Ellis Caffrey took the stage to bring a Washington counternarcotics perspective to the EUCOM-CENTCOM event, Doug had achieved deep, full-body relaxation. Although his eyes remained open throughout the presentations, his thoughts roamed, from the dog poisoning case to his son finishing up college next year, his ex and her new life in San Diego, the possibility of becoming a grandfather before too many more years, and back to the question of who he could get to carry the evidence samples to the DEA lab in Washington.

Caffrey, well-tailored, fit-looking, launched into his presentation. He gripped the sides of the podium with both hands and leaned forward with so much assertive determination his chin extended past the microphone. Although Caffrey spoke with eloquent force, Doug strained to hear.

"Our numbers have flat-lined," Caffrey declared. "Seizure levels for heroin, cocaine, and fentanyl are actually down from last year. And surveys indicate no supply constraints in major markets."

The slide on the screen showed a complex graph of seizure levels and price fluctuations for four types of narcotics.

"In this part of the world," he continued, "for most controlled substances, we are dealing with transit countries, not source countries." He clicked to bring up a map of the region with arrows of varying thickness depicting major transit routes.

"In certain quarters in Washington there are efforts, misguided in my view, to shift law enforcement resources away from transit countries and toward source countries. Therefore, in order to be able to effectively make the case for a comprehensive, all-of-the-above counternarcotics regime, we need to show results. To do this we have to go after the emerging smuggling networks in ungoverned areas such as the Asich mountain range between Vodania and Pazaria, the tribal regions of Tajikistan, and Greece."

Doug sat up straighter at the mention of the Asich Mountains. He glanced across the auditorium at Paul Giardis, who headed the regional DEA office in Embassy Zagovor in Pazaria. Giardis's turf included several neighboring countries, including Vodania. Total prick.

"We know where the challenges are," Caffrey declared. "We need to take these trafficking outfits down before they grow and metastasize into narco-terror organizations. Work with your national police and customs. Don't be passive. Reach out and touch someone. Use probing tactics to set up bigger operations. Every DEA field agent in this room has authorization for controlled buys of up to ten thousand dollars. You can do cash-flashes anytime. You don't need a mother-may-I from HQ or from the State Department."

In western Vodania, hoisting a book bag and a heap of adolescent exhaustion through the dusty Tuesday afternoon heat, a boy named Kimel meandered home from Harabad Central, the city's older, more dilapidated high school. Rather than taking off his sweaty cap and inserting himself into any of the soccer games that always sprang up after classes ended, he kicked a small rock step by step from the other side of Gotze Avenue all the way to the alley behind his house. Crossing his family's small, walled-in garden, he noticed a cardboard box under the back steps. He lifted the lid to find seven or eight canisters of spray paint. His eyes widened. So that's what Kurst and his friends were up to last night. For the past several years, his older brother had been active in politics.

Kimel peered into the box, at the canisters in their various colors. He selected a red one and slipped it into his school bag.

Tara was reviewing purchase orders mid-afternoon Tuesday when Robert called to give his approval for her streamlining of the motor pool request process. When Tara first arrived at Embassy Shizl, the procedure for embassy staff to arrange motor pool transportation resembled a scavenger hunt inside a labyrinth. It involved paper forms in duplicate and a sequencing of signatures from two different offices—with different, and varying, hours of operation—at both the requesting and approval stages. She thought her staff was joking when they explained the system to her, complete with an elaborate flowchart diagramming the required choreography. For the customers in the various sections of the embassy, completing this clerical obstacle course in a timely fashion could never be taken for granted. The task fell primarily to office assistants, for whom being able to consistently navigate the maze merited effusive, well-deserved praise in annual evaluation reports.

Tara decided to replace the eighteenth-century procedures with a simple online system. It took multiple rounds of determined conversations to bring her local employees on board. Then there was Chuck, who despite his misgivings finally agreed to let her present the idea to Robert. Now that the management counselor had given the go-ahead, Tara should feel happy about this triumph for efficiency. But she wondered whether she should have brought it up during her meeting with the DCM. She shook off the thought. Don't second-guess. She opened her draft email announcement to the whole embassy describing the new procedure and read it over one more time. She pressed send and slumped back into her desk chair and exhaled. She didn't know what exactly to expect. She hoped her colleagues would appreciate the simplification, if they paid any attention at all.

Over the ensuing several hours, her email inbox filled up with messages laden with hearts and smiley faces. On behalf of the consular section, Barbara Hertz sent one of her staff with a bouquet of wildflowers. Gary Hambert, the head of the political section, called to tell her the embassy had never been so unified on anything. Near the end of the day, General Elfersen appeared at the entrance to her cubicle, in full uniform, and saluted.

Inside the auditorium at Incirlik, the last speaker showed his last slide. But before Doug could belly up to the bar at the O club, one obligation stood in the way. Division director Caffrey wanted a huddle on the situation in the Asich Mountains. The usual pep talk, probably. Well, no such thing as a free trip. Doug expected to hear the word 'proactive' more than once, and perhaps even use it himself. But on the bright side, maybe there would be an opportunity to unload the evidence samples.

Doug navigated the building's corridors until he found the small conference room Caffrey had been assigned as a makeshift office. A piece of paper with DEA printed in large letters was taped to the door. He knocked.

Caffrey's executive assistant opened the door just wide enough to squeeze out. His white dress shirt, bulging over his belt, scraped against the door jamb. Too many per diem meals.

"He's gotta make a couple calls to Washington, won't be long," the exec explained, guiding the door closed behind himself.

Doug looked at the exec, a civil service careerist named Hal Passer, who had come across as reasonably collegial at previous DEA conferences, and figured this was the guy, this was the moment. He launched into an explanation about the poisoning of Ambassador Lamkin's dog and the urgent need to get the samples to the DEA lab to test for possible narcotics.

Passer raised his palms. "You want me to take dog puke in my carry-on?"

"We need to maintain chain of custody," Doug responded.

The executive assistant stared, and Doug added, "It's in a sealed plastic evidence bag."

"Sure Doug, that sounds great! And what am I gonna tell Customs when they ask am I carrying narcotics?"

"Tell 'em we won't know until we test."

"Forget it. I'm not a courier. Or a moron."

Doug and the exec stared at each other in silence, until the thumps of approaching footsteps caused them to look down the hallway.

Giardis marched up to them, glaring at Doug. "What are you doing here?"

"Hey Paul, great to see you too."

To the executive assistant, Giardis said, "I thought this was an operational meeting."

"Caffrey wants him in. He is the liaison to the Vodanians."

"Yeah, capacity building, training, equipment, all the warm and fuzzy. But he's not a field agent and has no authority to be involved in law enforcement operations." To Doug he added, "No offense," with a sneering smile.

The conference room door opened behind them. It was Caffrey, jacket off, sleeves carefully folded back to expose his forearms.

"Here they are, my Asich mountain men, ready to fight."

On Tuesday evening, after darkness had fallen in Harabad, Kimel stirred a few pomegranate seeds around his bowl, waiting for his father to conclude the family meal with bowed head and an expression of appreciation for the family's well-being. The fact that just about all the Pazari teenagers endured the same ritual before they were at liberty to go out did not make the wait any shorter.

For most youths in Harabad, there was a single nighttime destination: the park off the city's main plaza. But Kimel had a different idea beyond standing around, smoking, watching the skateboarders and the girls.

When he was finally released from the dinner table, he found his friend Azi in the park and told him about the cylinder in the side pocket of his cargo pants.

"We have to make it count," said Kimel.

Kimel and Azi, fifteen-year-olds who had known each other half their lives, meandered around Harabad's irregularly lit streets, chatting and considering where to strike first. They stopped in the shadows in front of the municipal building. An iron gate blocked the walkway to the main entrance. Gripping the paint canister, Kimel reached his arm through the bars, then pulled it back, remembering he needed to shake the paint first. He put the canister back through and sprayed onto the cement walk the outline of a goat in profile: head, horns, torso, tail, legs, penis. Above it he wrote Marko.

"Who is Marko?" asked Azi.

"That is the question." With a thumb and forefinger, he stroked upward on either side of his mouth, where his future mustache would grow.

Kimel sprayed another Marko goat drawing on the wall in front of the radio station, and Azi did one on the side of an apartment building. The paint was running out as Azi finished adding the name Marko, and he tossed the canister into a bush.

"What are you doing? I need that." Kimel complained.

"It's empty."

"That's why I'm trading it in."

Chapter 10

When Tara arrived at her workstation Wednesday morning, coffee in hand, she bent forward over the vase of wildflowers and inhaled. The mix of fragrances made her think of a mountain meadow. She had barely switched on her computer when Chuck bellowed from his office that he needed to see her right away. Tara figured it was her supervisor's gruff way of calling her in for a word of thanks and praise for the motor pool initiative. She walked across the corridor to his office and stood in the doorway.

Chuck looked up from the paperwork on his desk. "You need to order new carpet for the master bedroom at the ambassador's residence." His expression was deadpan, as usual.

"I thought the place was just refurbished last year."

"It was. But the bedroom carpet is no longer viable."

"What happened?"

"I'm not at liberty to say. But when you take a look, you won't have any trouble spotting the problem."

In the Defense Intelligence Agency in Washington, D.C., an operations support officer turned her head at the sound of a footstep. She glanced at the photo of her husband and daughters smiling from the wall of her regulation-sized cube. Then she winked at her visitor.

"Hey bud, thanks for coming over to see me. My guys in Vodania are hot to get this capabilities assessment done. We can cover it from our regional ops budget, it's only fifty K."

Her visitor, a lanky civilian from DIA's center for combating terrorism, leaned his torso across the threshold. "Fifty K for an assessment, no operational phase?" he asked.

"Correct."

"Not gonna fly, darlin'. Not in this budget environment. There's not enough time to spend it all, so they're only processing bigger stuff that needs to be carried out."

"So, can we tack on a phase two for implementation, and then down the line we go 'Whoopsie', changed our mind, and decide not to go operational?"

"At this point that's pretty much standard procedure."

From the front passenger seat, Tara stared into the thick hedge enclosing the ambassador's residence as the motor pool driver eased the sedan to a stop near the side gate. She puzzled over the DCM's odd request. Command, actually. Find out what happened to Davos, and make sure it doesn't happen again, but don't talk to anyone about it. Sure.

"Is here okay, ma'am?" the driver asked.

Tara turned to face him.

"Do you want to go to the front?"

Tara shook her head. "This is fine. Thank you."

She exited the car into the mid-afternoon heat and the residence guard opened the gate. She walked along the path between the pool area and the main lawn, her eyes swiveling side to side. Flowerbeds moist and mulched, gazebo furniture clean and orderly. Vines climbing the far wall. Nothing unusual. When she reached the garden entrance of the residence, the housekeeper on duty opened the door and said, "Mrs. Lamkin would like to see you."

Tara's mind churned. Another complaint about her work crew? When Tara arranged with the residence staff for a convenient time to come over, she assumed the ambassador's wife would not be home. Was she becoming Mrs. Lamkin's new best friend? Or was this about Davos? As if on cue, the chocolate Lab sprang out from the kitchen to startle Tara with a moist sloppy greeting. She pivoted and steadied him with her hands.

"Great," Tara replied, following the housekeeper up the staircase to the private area of the house, with Davos trotting close behind. They stopped at the door of the Lamkins' study.

Mrs. Lamkin looked up from her computer and said, "I'll be right with you."

After a moment or two she stood and walked toward them.

"Thank you for coming over, Tara. Before we do anything else you have to see this carpet."

"Yes ma'am."

"Please, call me Lithia." She held Tara's gaze to convey she meant it.

"Okay," Tara smiled, keeping pace as they strode down the hallway toward the master bedroom. Davos brushed past them and raced ahead.

Lithia walked to the far side of the king bed, its duvet and pillows perfectly in place, and gestured toward the floor. Tara flinched at the sight of the holes.

"My gosh! What happened?"

"No one told you?"

"Chuck just said the carpet needed to be replaced and that I would see why when I got here." Tara peered closer at the large circles hacked from the luxurious carpet, shaking her head slowly.

"Evidently," said Lithia, "one of the investigators looking into whatever happened to our poor companion here the other day thought it would be a brilliant idea to collect carpet samples. I don't know who exactly. And it's probably for the best that I don't."

"What a shame," Tara commented.

Lithia just nodded.

"We'll get it replaced as quickly as we can," Tara promised.

"I feel like I should offer you a cup of tea or something."

"Well, thank you, but that's okay. I wanted to look around the garden to see if there's anything we can do to protect Davos better."

Lithia smiled her appreciation.

"Maybe you'd like to join me? If you have time," Tara offered.

They walked out into the grounds, with the housekeeper availing herself of the opportunity to tag along. Davos followed as well. Tara reached down to stroke his head, and she asked if anything like this had happened to him before.

"No, he's always been a very healthy, active dog."

Tara led the way toward the rear of the property, where the vines reached up an expanse of twenty-foot-high reinforced concrete. The wall served as a berm against the higher elevation of the adjacent estate, which belonged to the head of the venerable Alambro family. Over the course of centuries, armies and empires came and went, conquering and losing Vodania, but the Alambro dynasty remained rooted and powerful, whether openly or behind the scenes. One of their sons currently served as the deputy finance minister.

Tara peered up at the three lines of barbed wire stretched along the top of the wall at a forty-five-degree angle. As far as she could tell, they did not look like they had been damaged or tampered with. But of course, it would be simple to toss something from the Alambro grounds over the wall. From the street might be riskier, because of the guards, but still not that difficult. If that was what happened, how did the DCM expect her to find out who did it and why? And prevent a repeat? Scanning downward, she noted a narrow space between that high wall and the back of the garage, and a similar one at the other end of the grounds, where the pool utility building squatted in the far corner of the property.

"We'll get these openings fenced off right away to make sure Davos doesn't go sneaking in there and finding any trouble," Tara told Lithia. "Meanwhile, until we know what happened, it might be a good idea to keep a close eye on him when he's outside, and even keep him on a leash, to make sure he's not chewing on something he shouldn't. We want to keep this big boy healthy," she added, patting Davos's flank and winning another smile from Lithia.

Tara left the ambassador's residence wondering what else she could do to address the DCM's order. But with the end of the workday in sight, her thoughts turned more and more toward the somewhat mysterious dinner invitation she and Karolina had accepted from Stefano and Mads for that evening. Following up on their encounter at the Locust Bar on Monday, Stefano had contacted Karolina to propose they all meet in the parking lot of the Kosmo, the trendy grocery store across the river from the Presidentorium. He wouldn't say more, except not to wear fancy shoes.

Shortly after Tara arrived back at her cube in the general services office, the expediter showed up, a serious look on his face.

"Some news for you."

Of course. "Alright, let me have it."

He reached into his pocket and slowly withdrew a set of keys. Car keys. Jeep keys. Attached to a black, gold, and green key ring. The colors of the Jamaican flag.

She jumped to her feet. "It's here?"

He nodded, hiding a grin behind his mustache.

She felt an impulse to hug him. Instead, she accepted the keys with both hands. Looking up into his eyes, she said, "Well done."

Don't wear fancy shoes. Not the most helpful guidance, Tara thought, standing in her panties in front of her closet. After some deliberation she chose close-fitting casual pants, a fairly daring white sleeveless top over a dark bra, and a lightweight shawl to cover up. She didn't want to look like she was trying too much. She added a pink coral necklace she picked up one getaway weekend in Montego Bay. Now for shoes. Something not fancy. Soft leather flats seemed like the best bet.

She descended to the parking lot, where the presence of her lipstick-red Jeep Wrangler convertible, her baby, gave the evening ahead an extra boost. Colleagues had questioned whether it was an appropriate vehicle for Shizl, and Chuck had even sent her an email in Kingston strongly suggesting she sell it there and bring something more suitable.

But what could be more suitable for an intriguing adventure, Tara wondered. She put the Wrangler's top down and rolled along National Boulevard through downtown Shizl with her hair swirling in the warm evening air. A thumping Jimmy Cliff tune created a reggae trail in her wake. Singing along, she swung past the Presidentorium and over the bridge to the Kosmo. Karolina stood near the gleaming arched entryway of the store and stepped forward when Tara pulled up. Karolina paused next to the Wrangler, smiling and shaking her head.

"Wow, girl!"

Tara laughed. "Any sign of those boys?"

She got out and sat on the hood, her feet on the front bumper, inviting Karolina to join her. After a few minutes, a distressed-looking Audi sedan pulled up, with Stefano at the wheel. Mads sprawled in the front seat, grinning.

Stefano stopped alongside the Wrangler. "Follow me."

Karolina dismounted from the hood, but Tara stayed put and shook her head.

"What's the problem?"

"I want a navigator," Tara replied, pointing at Mads.

"He doesn't know anything," Stefano answered.

"I want a navigator," she repeated. "He'll do."

Mads made a show of squeezing into the back seat of the Wrangler, and Tara followed the Audi out of the parking lot. Stefano led them east along Corridor One for about twenty minutes, then turned south to cross the Druzhba over a distressed two-lane bridge. They passed among barley fields, vineyards, and orchards as the sun dipped below the foothills. Stefano turned onto a dirt road, and as they bounced along Tara yelled over her shoulder to Mads to let her know if it got too rough. He responded with a thumbs-up.

Deeper into the Vodanian heartland, Stefano's Audi left the road and labored up the gentle slope of a meadow. Tara tracked behind, grasses and flowers brushing the sides of the Wrangler. At the top of the ridge Stefano parked next to several other cars and a panel van, and Tara pulled in alongside.

Below them lay a smooth blue lake. On the near shore, two cooking fires blazed and a dozen people moved about, chatting and setting out food.

As they walked downhill toward the rustic feast taking shape in the valley, Tara exchanged a look with Mads. Two newcomers crossing paths in an ancient land.

"Here come Stefano and his foreigners," a woman called out as they approached.

A lamb roasted over one of the fires, juices dripping into a pan of peppers and onions. Bowls heaped with shredded cabbage and cucumber slices crowded together on a rough wooden table. Several dozen people clustered around the fires or sat on blankets pressed into the tall grass. Stefano's sister welcomed them with small bowls of wine, while Stefano made introductions to friends from Shizl and to relatives and neighbors from the nearby town where his parents lived.

The conversations were all in Vodanian. Tara said to Mads, "Let me know if you want me to try to translate anything. Not that my grasp on the language is all that firm."

"You know more than I do, that's for certain."

A middle-aged woman displaying a fair swath of cleavage approached, and asked Mads if all Danes were so tall.

"She said your face looks like a fish," Tara told Mads.

"A fish?"

"Like a trout," Tara confirmed.

The woman said something else that Tara didn't understand, and she translated to Mads, "Trout is okay but not as tasty as lamb."

Mads assumed an affronted expression. "I was trying for goat," he huffed, stroking his chin stubble.

Tara translated this for the woman as, "He's getting drunk."

"Good idea," she responded in Vodanian, raising her bowl.

More people arrived, including a trio of local musicians. The ripe glowing moon softened the darkness. Tara met an architect, a couple of teachers, and a cousin of Stefano's who worked in a food processing business.

With the opening notes of the first song, everyone gathered together, hand in hand, to form a wide circle in the pasture. The dance began, and the circle rotated step by step to the right. Tara and Mads shuffled side by side, her left hand electric in his right. She pulled him along as they tried to mimic the intricate steps of the Vodanians. The melodies sounded to Tara as if they had sprung from the surrounding mountains, shifting and repeating, interwoven with the drummer's propulsive rhythms. Mesmerized, and a little giddy, she mostly focused forward or down at her feet, not trusting herself to look too long at Mads, as the party trampled a path through the flowers and grasses.

Chapter 11

At sunrise in the Asich Mountains, survey teams on either side of the Odorian River gorge set out from their base camps. The Organization for Security and Cooperation in Europe had divided its international demarcation experts into two groups, augmented by professional mountaineers and local guides, to place the final markers needed to officially delineate the border between Vodania and Pazaria. Both teams had to climb into the chilly air above the tree line and up over the highest peaks in the range to reach the narrow mesa where the river split the land. On either side, limestone cliffs faced each other across a tight crevasse, far above the surface of the Odorian.

The gorge, a stark cleft in the earth's crust that stretched for fifteen miles, had been carved through the northeastern sector of the Asich mountain range over the span of eons. Along most of its length, the walls of the resulting valley stood sheer and smooth, close to vertical. In its deepest section, the gorge plunged five hundred to a thousand feet below the cliff edge. The river and its dramatic chasms formed a natural barrier that had separated the Vodanian and Pazari peoples for centuries. The steep jagged peaks on both sides made that part of the border uninhabitable and close to impenetrable.

In the embassy's secure conference room shortly after nine on Thursday morning, Andy occupied his usual spot at the ambassador's weekly country team meeting, assessing his position. Overall, not especially favorable. He was on the hook to coordinate the embassy's actions and recommend a response on the dog thing. But the chances of anyone actually determining what happened appeared close to nil, which meant that any response would be unfounded guesswork, a shot in the dark, and therefore not something he would want his name on. What was worse, the incident had not produced any embarrassing ripples in Washington that he could detect. To the contrary, with border demarcation progressing, the ambassador's stock was rising. The one bright spot was that, in less than a week since their laundry room meeting, Shariz and Farao had come up with a creative array of incidents. He had to admire their energy. All they had needed was a little encouragement.

Between progress on the border and regress in all parties' behavior in the election campaign, the action at the embassy's weekly country team meeting belonged to the political section. As usual, but more so. Political counselor Gary Hambert, swelling from the attention, occupied additional space along the side of the table.

"The OSCE team expects to install the last remaining markers on both sides of the border today, weather conditions permitting," Gary announced, addressing the ambassador while simultaneously managing to include everyone in the room.

"How are they getting those granite marker stones up to the peaks?" asked General Elfersen.

"They're not," Gary replied. "Per mutual agreement of both countries' commissioners, they're placing metal spikes at agreed intervals along the Odorian."

"We might be able to help them with helicopter lift if they want the stones up there."

"Not a bad idea," the ambassador agreed. "Let's hold that option as a sweetener for the right moment."

Andy hadn't seen that one coming. Accelerating the process would be unhelpful to his efforts to undermine the ambassador's standing. But he well knew how hungrily the ambassador craved this border deal. It would be the signature accomplishment of his tenure in Vodania. Andy needed to display loyalty while getting in the way.

"It would be a very well-intentioned gesture of support for our friends in both countries," Andy said. "At the same time, we should keep in mind there are still quite a few Vodanians unhappy with Pazaria's independence and with the U.S. role in the war. Having the U.S. military placing boundary stones could play into the hands of those who want to claim that the border itself was made in the USA."

The ambassador frowned. "Of course we'll consider the context carefully before making the offer."

General Elfersen just frowned.

"Once the demarcation phase is complete," the ambassador continued, "let's revisit our action plan for ratification. This is the moment for bringing in Washington and sweetening the pot. I'll work the phones too, but I want a front-channel message with our proposals for senior-level engagement, including by the secretary, and for whatever specific, tangible assistance we can offer."

The ambassador's eyes scoured the room to locate the USAID mission director. Once he had her in his sights he added, "I want USAID to continue to be a full partner in this endeavor, so have your team work closely with Gary's to get our message right."

"Absolutely sir."

In the brief silence that ensued, Andy made a mental note to make sure the Vodanians knew they could drive up the price of cooperation. With proper coaching, they could be counted on to overreach and gum things up.

Gary, evidently assessing that the border topic had run its course, placed his pen on the conference table just firmly enough to be audible. Speaking to the ambassador, he said, "Our other major area of focus is the upcoming parliamentary election. Frankly, it's not going as well as we would like. So far this week there have been further incidents in Harabad, Kharbam, Pritzi, and in the capital."

"And it's only Thursday," interjected Andy, eliciting rueful nods and a few snickers.

Gary picked up where he left off. "The Social Democrats are screaming about harassment and intimidation. And the OSCE is going to issue a statement today or tomorrow about the media environment and government pressure. But of course, the main fault lines are ethnic, and all the Pazari parties are outraged. Violence levels are rising, and becoming comparable to the last election cycle. No fatalities so far, thank goodness."

"This comes from the top," the ambassador declared.

"Sir, I suggest getting in front of President Chilik early and often with our concerns. Establish a record," Andy advised.

"What about doing some meetings jointly with the EU?" suggested Gary.

"Excellent idea," said Andy, nodding.

The ambassador considered. Andy understood that he viewed partnering with the EU as a mixed blessing. If the Europeans would step up more resolutely to link market access benefits and their support funds to current Vodanian government behaviors, then suffering the officiousness of their local rep, High Commissioner Cauchon, might be worth it. At the same time, the ambassador could see as well as anyone that unless the U.S. and EU marched in lockstep, the international community would get nowhere with Chilik and his crowd.

"I think that's probably right," the ambassador assented. "Chilik is going to continue to use the political tensions, especially the inter-ethnic dimension, as an excuse not to sign and ratify the border agreement. And these elections are crucial in their own right for the future of democracy in this country."

For a moment, Andy pondered whether the ambassador actually believed the talking points that poured forth from his lips like a mountain spring, or whether he expected that his endless flow of regurgitation would, over time, carve a channel of good governance through Vodanian rock.

In the Eastern Carpet Kings showroom office, the vice-president eased his teacup down onto his desk and peered at Tara and her procurement assistant.

"For two thousand five hundred, if that is your budget, we could only provide a carpet less plush," he said, in a sad voice. "It is very nice, very very beautiful. But not so thick and soft on the feet. For the one you are talking about, the natural wool plush, the price is four thousand dollars."

"That's way more than we paid last year," Tara objected.

"That's because the bedroom carpet was part of an overall deal."

"But there are two separate invoices, two separate purchases."

"Yes, that was the request of your predecessor, Mr. Franklin. He wanted a discount price for the bedroom, and we made up for it with a premium for the living room and dining room."

He paused for another sip of tea. "But this is the real price for this carpet. Highest quality."

Tara studied the two invoices. There was a fifty-dollar price difference per square meter, for the same product. That's how Franklin got the premium carpet to fit the budget cap for residential space. But it was not a trick that could be repeated, unless someone went knife-happy on one of the downstairs carpets.

Tara recalled a legend she had heard during her A-100 orientation training about a long-ago management counselor in Embassy Rome. It was the Fourth of July reception, the event of the year, and after months of planning and preparations, the great day had arrived. The spacious grounds of the ambassadorial palazzo were laid out with catering stations, beverage stations, tents for shade and seating. A U.S. Navy swing band, deployed from the Sixth Fleet at Naples, warmed up on the bandstand. And that was the problem. With guests due to arrive in less than an hour, the ambassador's wife, who was even more demanding than her industrialist husband, declared that the bandstand was a little too close to the house and needed to be moved three feet toward the pool. The staff, in consternation at this impossible command, found the management counselor. Don't worry, I'll take care of it, he told them. Do you want us to start breaking it down, they asked. Even though there's no time, they added in panicked voices. Don't do anything, he told them. Just make sure everything else is ready. After forty-five minutes, with the bandstand still in its original position, the management chief entered the residence and found the hostess. Ma'am, he said, thank you for catching the problem with the bandstand. May I show you what we've done? He led her out onto the balcony and she took in the entire grand scene. Perfect, she beamed.

Tara looked at the carpet VP. "I assume you carry a selection of thick padding."

In downtown Washington, Vonda Vance, deputy assistant secretary of state for European and Eurasian Affairs, entered Room 212 in the Eisenhower Executive Office Building. Coffee-breath hung in the air and the leather seats were still butt-temperature from the previous meeting. The tight windowless cubby had once stored typewriter ribbons and forms in triplicate. But space inside the White House complex, always at a premium, had grown tighter, so it had become a conference room. The usual interagency gaggle squeezed in around the table: Treasury, Justice, DoD, CIA, DIA, Joint Chiefs of Staff, Homeland Security. Last to enter was Winston Bryce, national security council senior director for Europe, and at thirty-one the youngest person in the room by at least a decade. The little snot, who had no on-the-ground experience in places like Bosnia, used these weekly regional roundups to coordinate messaging, keep tabs on developments, and tee up decisions for cabinet deputies, preening all the while.

When they reached the agenda item on the Pazaria-Vodania border agreement, Winston said, "Before I ask dear Vonda to bring us up to speed on the latest, let me just emphasize again the strong White House interest in getting this glued. Ratifying the border, then normalizing relations between Pazaria and Vodania, is a majorly significant achievement for this administration. POTUS wants to be kept briefed on progress," he fibbed, using the bureaucratic abbreviation for president of the United States.

Vonda had the impression that Winston reserved uttering the title 'the president' for those rare occasions when the young pup had actually been in the same room with him. Otherwise, Winston was representing an acronym. 'POTUS said this' and 'POTUS wants that' meant Winston was referring to the office of the president as a whole, or to his own boss in the national security council, or to himself.

Winston directed his bright gaze across the table. "Vonda?"

"Well, one step at a time," she began. "The OSCE demarcation team finished their work yesterday, so the border is fully marked, for the first time ever. The provisional agreement now needs to be ratified by both sides' parliaments, and then signed by Prime Minister Prismar and President Chilik. The Pazarians can't wait to sign; the question mark is on the Vodanian side."

"What's the problem," demanded Winston. "And how do we solve it?"

"I was on the phone with Ambassador Lamkin this morning. The immediate stumbling block is that they're in the middle of an election campaign, and David's assessment is that Chilik is reluctant to risk angering his base. Especially as ethnic tensions mount with the Pazari-Vodanians."

"When's the election?"

"September eighth. But the new parliament doesn't get sworn in until October first."

"That's too long to wait," Winston declared.

Bill Padden, deputy assistant secretary of defense, leaned forward. "How about we increase the pressure to help motivate this guy? We could beef up the visibility of our force presence in Pazaria, announce a joint training exercise, do more fly-bys along the border."

"I like the idea of incentivizing Chilik," Winston replied. "Vonda, your take?"

From long experience, Vonda knew the optimal response to a bad idea, or to any new idea really, was to defer. "I'll talk to the ambassador again and with my building. We'll want to be careful not to cause Chilik to dig in his heels."

"Well, here's another thought," Winston beamed. "I don't have many of these to dole out, but we could consider offering him a photo-op with POTUS at UNGA."

He used the standard government pronunciation of the acronym for the opening of the United Nations General Assembly. UNGA, rhymes with cowabunga. The annual heads of state conclave in New York offered the most pizzazz and glitter of any international political gathering.

Winston radiated pleasure at his power to produce a solution. "That's after the election so it should work, right?"

Vonda smiled to show her appreciation at the prospect of presidential attention to one of her clients. But there was a problem.

"I don't know if Chilik is coming to New York this year," she said. "Usually, he sends his foreign minister to UNGA."

"Well, we'd certainly expect him to come for a photo with the president, right?"

Europa Brauhaus in the Tysons Corner mall was among Travis's favorite spots for entertaining clients. Amid the Friday happy hour din, he lifted his beer stein.

"Dortmunder!" enthused the young business development exec. "Classic English ale."

As long as Harrimore Services was footing the bill, Travis enjoyed client relations, even with schleppy guys like Lt. Col. Hensrath, a bureaucrat-warrior from DIA's counterterrorism procurement office. Chatting up customers for Harrimore was not that different from shooting the shit at Theta Phi after a game.

Travis clinked beer steins first with Hensrath and then with Julia, the new hire in his unit at Harrimore he brought along to lighten things up. He took a moment to admire their departing waitress and her Oktoberfest mini-dress. Beers at college were never delivered like that. And Hensrath was basically alright, tolerable. A little downbeat maybe, but not in all that annoying of a way.

Lt. Col. Hensrath turned to Julia and inquired, "What were you doing before you joined Harrimore?"

"Getting my master's at GW." Julia's voice sounded a bit strained, as if she were nervous.

The three of them talked sports and TV shows and flagged down Helga, as Travis referred to her, for a plate of shrimp nachos. Lt. Col. Hensrath was still active-duty Army, and when Travis brought up a recent movie about Navy SEALs, Hensrath said, "I've known guys like that. Inspiring."

"Damn straight," Travis agreed. "We're proud to have an awesome team of combat vets at Harrimore. The question is how do we keep 'em all productively occupied." He looked at the DIA officer.

"Well, I don't know about that," said Hensrath, taking a swig of the Dortmunder. "But a small requirements analysis job came in today. It's only fifty thousand for the assessment, and we're looking for a quick turnaround, like two or three weeks. Sound like something you'd be interested in? We'd do it no-bid, on a contract amendment basis."

"Fifty K," Travis smiled. "The paperwork'd probably cost us half a that. We're looking for bigger stuff, sir, real actions where we can put our full capabilities to use."

"So are we," Hensrath replied. "With Congress shoveling money at us, these tiny projects get overlooked. I'll understand if you don't want to bother. It's just that our defense attaché in Shizl's got something cooking and I'd like to help him out."

"I'm sorry, where's Shizl again?" Travis asked.

"Vodania," Julia piped in.

Lt. Col. Hensrath nodded confirmation in her direction.

"You said requirements analysis. Is there follow-on potential? Anything operational?" Travis studied the officer's expression.

"Could be, but it's not defined and that'd be a separate funding decision. Part of the purpose of the assessment is to develop a range of options."

Travis picked up a shrimp and brandished it like a pointer. "Tell you what. You think it's important, we'll take a look at it. I'll talk to our planners and logistics guys on Monday and make sure they can fit in another project."

Travis raised his stein and they all clinked again.

High above the Odorian River, an amber effusion of late afternoon sun warmed the rock face at the top of the Pazaria side of the gorge. In the shadows below, runoff from lingering pockets of snow soaked into the cliff, making its surface damp and slick. A tiny rivulet, one of the many thousands that flowed every spring and summer as the temperatures rose, undermined a deposit of snow before seeping into the rock.

The snow dislodged a piece of slate. Sliding down a chute, the slate loosened stones, gathering force. The rockslide dislodged boulders, expanding its width, obliterating snow deposits in its path. For a full minute, the mass plummeted toward the floor of the gorge, carving another scratch into the ancient cheekbones of the cliff. The barrage of rocks and ice poured crashing into the Odorian River, damming its low summer flow.

A silent dust cloud ballooned skyward, then gradually settled. The water further upstream kept coming until it reached the new barrier, where the river paused, gathered strength, and slowly rose, its dark little fingers feeling their way up over the rocks and around the lower part of the barrier—on the Vodanian side.

Part III

The Dog Days of Summer

Chapter 12

August tightened its grip. Above the Roma enclave in southwest Shizl, pure blue heat seethed from the still, cloudless sky. Almost nine o'clock on Saturday morning, and Tara, perspiring, hurried through the mostly quiet alleyways. She sensed something going on. Up ahead, excited kids spied her and ran shrieking forward. She heard a clamor as she approached the street corner near the Saturday school. The volume increased when she came into sight. Children crowded around the doorway of the ramshackle shed that served as a classroom. Jovina, the assistant director, tried to settle them down. Inside, thirty kids squeezed together instead of the usual handful. They filled all the seats and stood pressed against the walls.

"Hi Jovina. What's going on?"

Jovina smiled at the sight of Tara. "Many students today."

Tara weaved to the front of the room, and many of the children began calling out the word *kai-she*. It turned into a chant. *Kai-she! Kai-she! Kai-she!* The children clapped and smiled.

Tara looked at Jovina. "What are they saying?"

Jovina hesitated, looking embarrassed. "*Kai-she* means apricot."

"*Kai-she! Kai-she! Kai-she!*" The chanting rose, the clapping grew louder.

What have I done, Tara thought? These poor kids. She held up her hands and smiled.

"Good morning girls and boys." She greeted them in Romani before switching to English. "I am here to teach English and math. That's what we learn on Saturday mornings."

There were still several kids calling, "*Kai-she*."

Tara patted down the pockets of her shorts, fingered the leather clutch hanging over her shoulder, and extended her hands palms up.

"Sorry, I didn't bring *kai-she* today. If you want to stay for English and math, you are welcome."

Jovina spoke to the group at some length in Romani, and most of the children filed out, smiles fading, a few still murmuring the word *kai-she*. Six girls and four boys stayed for the whole lesson, and when it ended Tara and Jovina encouraged them to return the next Saturday.

As Tara was about to leave, Jovina touched her arm. She was a slim woman in her early twenties, and she tilted her face upward to fix a dramatic gaze on Tara's eyes.

"I don't know if you will have time, but I want to invite you to my brother's wedding. In September, at the equinox."

Tara felt touched, but she wondered about the propriety, whether she actually belonged at such an event.

"That's so sweet! Are you sure? I don't think I've met him."

"It's okay, you are my friend. It would be a big honor to our family. Please."

In Shizl's National Concert Hall on Saturday evening, the European Union sponsored a gala, a fundraiser to promote a visual arts literacy project—their latest brainstorm. Squeezed in among the thick crowd in the vast atrium, Monique, a French diplomat seconded to the EU mission, shook her head.

"Pointless. Clueless. Feckless. Classic EU," she groused to one of her colleagues, making no attempt to present any semblance of institutional loyalty. "Just what Vodania needs."

Thanks to this noble endeavor, Monique mused, future generations of Vodania's citizens would be able to enjoy fiercely abstract sculptures rusting placidly in their parks and squares. Cultural programming funds from EU headquarters in Brussels paid for this ungainly collection of twisted, tortured slabs of metal. The kick-off event aimed at publicizing the program and raising funds to offset installation costs, which mostly consisted of official and unofficial fees for obtaining site permits. Inviting mayors and city council members from around the country to the gala was a nice touch, though, letting them help pay their own bribes.

Regardless of one's views on charity art, the event offered a diversion, a reason to don festive attire. Respectful, even warm, conversations took place across ethnic lines. Monique's boss, EU High Commissioner Cauchon, glowed, basking in the success of it all. But for the most part, people came to dance. After a glass or two of wine, in many cases. The eight-piece Roma band found its groove. Monique swayed a little to the music too, despite herself.

A handsome man approached and introduced himself as Eftin Zabor, a member of the city council in Harabad. A Pazari, presumably. They were usually not as bold as the ethnic Vodanians about approaching foreign women. Monique hadn't planned on dancing, but why not?

"I wonder if we could meet somewhere else," he spoke close to her ear.

Feeling affronted but also marginally intrigued, she gave him a look intended to convey poise and curiosity. She felt debonair.

"Our party's campaign offices got attacked last week," he added. "With the election so soon, we must replace computers and furniture that were destroyed."

His dark eyes smoldered and he put a warm hand on her forearm. "It's urgent."

So much for romantic intrigue, thought Monique. Another would-be adventure that fizzled before it started. After promising Eftin to have someone call him, Monique wandered closer to the dance floor. She noticed Vodania's former president Kimi Borzinski, the tall, craggy-faced leader of the Nationalist Party. Without warning or warm-up, he strode right up close to Chandra Chilik, the current president's current wife, and stood blocking her way. A thin silk evening gown hugged Chandra's lithe body. She tilted her wineglass and sipped, staring up at Borzinski, her expression deadpan except for a sparkle in her light brown eyes.

Her husband's rival reached forward and tugged the wineglass from her lips and from her grasp. Without moving his gaze from Chandra's, he thrust the glass to the side, in the expectation someone would relieve him of it. With his right hand he took her right hand and pivoted behind her. With the fingertips of his left touching the small of her back, he guided her to the center of the dance floor. The other dancers shifted to make space.

On stage, the musicians stomped their feet and slashed at their fiddles with renewed intensity. While President Chilik engaged in matters of importance elsewhere, Kimi and Chandra spun each other around the ballroom with graceful passion, grinding their pelvises together at one moment, flinging each other away the next, their eyes locked and burning.

At sunrise Sunday morning, sticky paint glistened on the corrugated steel that formed the back wall of the covered market in the mountain village of Upper Sheff. The dawning light revealed the name Marko scrawled in large red letters, with rivulets of excess color trickling down, merging with the sketch of a goat. On a school wall in Pisk, a public bus in Kurtoff, on the pavement in the middle of the main intersection of Lupovo, more red goat drawings appeared overnight. Like ancient cave paintings, the goats always appeared in profile, and for some reason always facing left. Across western Vodania the goats proliferated as if alive, escaped and rampant on a tropical island with no predators. They all carried the name Marko. Drawn by many different hands on widely varying scales and surfaces, from miniatures on stop signs to massive renderings on the sides of buildings, the goats shared roughly similar proportions. Heads proud and upright, torsos lean, legs straight, horns and penises large and wickedly curved.

Thus spread the Marko phenomenon, going viral across Vodania and into Pazaria. The motivations of the perpetrators remained mysterious. Were they imitators? Supporters? Speculation online and in the media, as well as in the schools and markets and cafés, covered many possibilities. A political movement. A gang. Or simply a passing summer craze. Was Marko a religious figure, an emerging prophet? Was he a renegade American commando, leading a separatist movement from strongholds in the Asich Mountains? Cynics suggested all the Marko-ing was merely a promotional campaign for an as-yet-undisclosed product, perhaps condoms or a new brand of yogurt. Others saw it as a rite of passage by young men celebrating their escape from virginity.

As the days passed, Kimel and Azi kept their role to themselves. Naturally, they wanted to avoid getting into trouble, even though they doubted anyone would believe they started something that became so big. But mainly they wanted to keep the mystery alive. Although they no longer added more goats to the graffiti population themselves, they watched their creation grow and multiply, an unbelievable ripple that never reached the edge of the pond because the pond kept expanding.

Grigor Khalamente, President Chilik's chief of staff, itchy and sweaty in a blazer over an open-collared shirt, paused in front of the door to his boss's personal bedroom and study. Clutching a copy of the Sunday morning edition of the Vodanian Sun, a nationalist-leaning tabloid, he rapped twice. Hearing an assenting grunt from within, he opened the door to find Chilik plopped on a generously proportioned armchair, in exercise attire, watching a soccer match on his new home entertainment system.

Grigor approached and handed him the paper. The front-page headline read EU Promotes Political Reconciliation. A large color photo showed Kimi Borzinski and Chandra Chilik on the dance floor, clasping each other tight.

Chilik scowled at the paper and shoved it back at Grigor.

"Tax audit. And arrest a couple of campaign organizers."

Tara piloted her red Wrangler along the spine of hills that stretched east from Shizl halfway to the border. Coniferous trees and low brush in muted hues of green and brown covered the semi-arid landscape in irregular patches. In the valleys she glimpsed tile roofs and stone walls and the thatched coverings of animal shelters. Here and there sticks and branches planted in tight lines formed sheepfolds and goat pens.

In the passenger seat, Karolina said, "This is probably just how it looked two hundred years ago."

Tara nodded. Two thousand, probably.

Every Sunday, from April through October, the Shizl Hiking Club gathered at a different location to wander across the Vodanian landscape. Tara understood from Karolina it would be mostly ex-pats, along with a few friendly locals expanding their horizons. There was only one person whose horizon interested Tara. From a conversation on Friday night, Mads knew she was going. But he didn't commit.

Not that there was much hope of anything developing between them. He was exploring the world and had already spent a week in Vodania. So not likely to be around much longer. For all she knew, he could already be on his way to his next destination. Well, it was a nice day for a walk, and the mountain air offered a respite from the unrelenting heat and tobacco smoke of the capital.

At the rendezvous point, eight or ten hikers in colorful moisture-wicking garb clustered near their parked cars. No Mads. Karolina made introductions. While they were chatting about the quality of the weather and the benefits of exercise, another car arrived. Tara kept her back to it.

She heard a door open and saw Karolina's face light up. "Didn't expect to see you here, Love."

Tara spun around. It was Monique, among a clutch of European women with their hair tied back sensibly or tucked under visors.

"First time for everything," Monique replied. "I wanted to see what all the hoopla was for."

More minutes passed, and in a silent language of gestures and glances the group determined it was time to get underway. The expedition, a pageant of lavender, lime, and fuchsia, began marching up the road, past thistles and tall-stemmed grasses. Tara filled her lungs and exhaled slowly. Come on, girl, enjoy that fresh air.

Movement at the crossroads café down the slope caught her eye, and she turned to see three men emerge. One of her hands flew up to her mouth. He was among them, his good cheer visible from afar.

When the trio caught up to the main body of hikers, Tara turned to face Mads.

"Who invited you?"

He smiled and lifted his palms.

"Are you a member of this group?" Tara challenged him again.

"Just a guest," he replied.

"Of whom?"

Mads savored a deep inhalation, taking in the scene.

"You're a glommer," Tara continued. "You overhear a conversation about something and you just glom right on."

"There are worse things than glommers."

"Like what?"

"Imperialists."

"Who's an imperialist?"

Mads looked like he was trying to keep a straight face. "Are you up here planning the next assault?"

"I'm on the give-peace-a-chance side of the house. Not the invasion side."

"Same house though."

At least he sees me as American, Tara thought. Mads kept smiling and walking. The two cousins of Stefano's he came with strolled alongside, as the road ascended toward higher ground.

"We have nothing like this in Denmark," Mads remarked. "It's all flat and low, with the sea all around." He addressed Stefano's cousins. "You're lucky to have all these mountains."

"These are not the real mountains," one of them responded.

"What's your thing about mountains anyway?" Karolina asked, joining in.

"You can elevate, you can rise up," Mads responded. "When you are higher you see more clearly, you think more clearly, you feel more deeply. At least, I think so."

Understanding that proper hiking club behavior called for making sure to intermingle with everyone, Tara and Karolina moved ahead to catch up with Monique, who walked among an assortment of Dutch, Belgian, and German women. Lotte Wuyts, the animal activist, was among them. The European ladies were talking about exercise again, or still. One mentioned she was considering hiring a personal trainer.

"There's a real cute one who works out at the Apex," Tara ventured. "Vlado, right?" she said, turning to Monique for confirmation.

"Don't ask me. I'm not the sort to go stuffing myself in spandex and leaping about."

"I know who you mean," said a Dutch woman. "Yes, Vlado, I think. The one who trains President Chilik."

"Alright, yes, I've heard of him," Monique acknowledged. "From what I understand it's very personal training indeed."

This produced a soft round of knowing snickers. Monique patted Tara's arm in mock sympathy.

At a curve in the road, the whole ensemble filed onto a footpath leading up into a stand of tall pines. The fragrance reminded Tara of summer camp. And canoeing and belt-making and having to explain she wasn't that kind of Indian.

When she found herself alongside Lotte Wuyts, she ventured, "I heard you speak at FEW last weekend. You were very passionate. Have you been doing animal rights advocacy a long time?"

"No, I never was involved until I came to Shizl and saw those poor dogs everywhere. In our first week here, a dog died right on our street, from poisoning."

"What kind of poison do they use?" Tara asked.

Lotte paused for several seconds before replying.

"I hope you're not going to ask me about your ambassador's dog. I was already thoroughly interrogated by your security man. The fact is, if someone truly wanted to harm that dog it would be dead, like so many dogs every day in this country. I hope it is okay, and that you Americans will support this cause. For the rest of us it is so difficult to get the authorities here to pay attention."

She appealed to Tara with a fervent, demanding stare.

"It's an interesting idea," Tara replied. "I'm pretty new, but as far as I know the U.S. hasn't made animal rights a foreign policy issue."

"Well, you should. Even if it's just locally, informally. It would make a huge difference."

For the next several minutes, as the trail exited the shade of the pine trees and wound through a boulder field, Lotte lectured about the dog problem, reprising her luncheon speech. Mads caught up from behind and matched his steps with Tara's. Lotte understood the signal and dropped back, parting with "Please talk to your ambassador about this!"

Tara appreciated the rescue, and also felt grateful in a way to Lotte Wuyts for creating the need for a rescue. For a while she and Mads walked side by side in silence. He occasionally offered her a hand on the steeper, more precarious parts of the path, in a natural way. Not condescending or superior.

He talked about why he chose to become a teacher, and he told stories about his students, their struggles, their progress. His blue eyes radiant, he shared again how mountains make him feel.

"Do you think that's strange," he asked, "since Denmark has none?"

"Neither does Ohio," Tara pointed out. "At least, not the part I grew up in."

She watched his stride, the way his boots stroked the earth as he moved. Such a shame he was only passing through. Still looking down, she asked, "What are your plans? What's next for you?"

"Hard to say. I'm enjoying the moment."

"You have a wife back in Denmark? A girlfriend?"

She raised her glance to see Mads shake his head.

"Then what are you running away from?"

He laughed. "Why can't I be running toward something?"

They continued side by side, a hiking party of two. She sensed she could say anything, share anything. His way of listening conveyed a curiosity and open heartedness she had never experienced, not in this way. He was an adventurer at heart, she decided. In the privacy of the open air, she found herself confiding in him. Across the rough terrain, she shared her hopes and doubts about the foreign service and its mixture of high purpose and the mundane. She believed in diplomacy but so far hadn't experienced much of it. She told Mads her parents were proud of her but had their doubts too. Especially her father, whom she quoted, "If I wanted my children to work for the government I could simply have stayed in India."

Mads laughed at her impersonation. Then he touched her back, his hand filling the space between her shoulder blades, and said, "I'm glad he didn't."

Tara pressed into his hint of an embrace and let the meaning behind his words course through her.

Chapter 13

On Monday morning, one week since the ambassador's startling announcement about Davos's poisoning, DCM Andy Pulano convened the embassy's national security team. He knew the ambassador expected answers and options. There would have to be a price to pay, for someone. However, with the dog apparently recovered and the press of major priorities such as a decent election process and a border agreement with Pazaria, Andy worried that the ambassador's righteous anger might begin to cool. He needed to keep the pressure on and show the ambassador he was doing so. Fan his smoldering outrage without getting singed.

From his customary off-center position at the head of the table, Andy stiffened his eyebrows and looked around the secure conference room. Defense attaché General Elfersen, regional security officer Ken Dewitt, station chief Phyllis Snicklehimer, Drug Enforcement Agency liaison Doug Watanabe, and political counselor Gary Hambert, all in their places. To Andy's left, the ambassador's seat remained empty. Nobody ever sat there, even when there was no expectation he would appear.

"We'll start with the RSO," Andy announced, all business.

Regional security officer Ken Dewitt briefed at considerable length on his team's thorough procedures. He described the many steps involved in conducting the investigation in and around the grounds of the ambassador's residence. He disclosed that their diligent searches uncovered no signs of any intruders or mechanisms for delivering poison to the dog. No unexplained footprints, food scraps, shell casings, or noticeable wounds on the animal. The security cameras at the residence, as well as those at the neighboring Alambro family compound and the German ambassador's house, showed no unauthorized persons at any of the premises during the forty-eight hours prior to the incident on Monday morning, one week ago. There were no claims of responsibility, nor any credible street chatter about the attack. Although the investigation could not rule out a penetration of the security perimeter, the lack of evidence either meant there was no penetration, or the perpetrators were so skilled they left no trace.

"Or," the RSO warned, "it was an insider."

"We're following up on that possibility I presume," Andy responded, borrowing from the ambassador's rhetorical style.

He called on General Elfersen next. With no apparent movement, the defense attaché somehow managed to sit up even straighter.

"I appreciate the RSO's expert investigation and I thank him for his service," Elfersen began. "From a Defense Department standpoint, we have commenced engagement on a requirements and capabilities assessment, to determine the level of capabilities, the skill set, that a hostile force would require to accomplish the mission under the specific circumstances and conditions prevailing in the location at that particular point in time."

He delivered his spiel in a single breath, Andy noted. Impressive lung capacity.

Elfersen paused a regulation one-point-five seconds before continuing. "Our objective analysis will determine if Vodania's military forces, particularly their special operations units, which have received U.S. anti-terrorism training, have the tactical and operational capabilities to complete a mission of this complexity with complete stealth. Our analysis will also enable us to assess other national and sub-national forces to identify potential hostiles who could have conducted the attack."

Andy, well-versed in this vernacular, understood the defense attaché to mean that a study was underway. In all likelihood, a variety of offices in the Pentagon would participate in, or become aware of this assessment. All to the good. He made sure not to show any recognition that the defense attaché had contravened his explicit directions to keep this matter local.

Doug Watanabe, when it was his turn to speak, focused on the DCM. Trying hard to contain his glee at his own involvement in the case, he reported that the evidence samples he gathered at the ambassador's request were on their way to a DEA lab in Washington for testing. He noted that he asked for priority handling but was not in a position to estimate how long it would take.

At the conclusion of his presentation, Watanabe added, "The Vodanian cops are still joking about Davos sniffing at their minister and rejecting her in favor of Senator Mifton. Juvenile stuff, not threatening."

Ken Dewitt's face and scalp reddened. Ever vigilant about any encroachment on his role as official liaison with the Vodanian police, he shot back with, "I haven't heard anything like that. But I try to keep things professional."

Watanabe shifted his gaze to the RSO, who in deference to imminent baldness kept his crew cut at a quarter inch. "For the sake of relationship building, once in a while it helps to let your hair down."

Tara Zadani had to get up early on Tuesday morning for a meeting with the DCM before the start of the normal work day. She figured he chose the timing so she wouldn't have to explain her whereabouts to her immediate supervisor Chuck or to section chief Robert Akes, since they were not supposed to know about her investigation of the Davos poisoning. The secrecy felt odder and odder to her.

She drove with the Wrangler's top down, before the day's heat arrived in full, out of the valley of downtown Shizl and up the slope to the embassy.

In the executive office, greenlighted by Charlene's nod, Tara poked her head through the DCM's doorway and tapped once on the open door. He looked up over his reading glasses and waved her in. She took two steps forward.

"You wanted an update on the Davos situation?"

"Yes indeed. What have you got?"

The DCM made no move from his desk chair, nor invited Tara to sit, so she remained on her feet.

"Two precautionary measures. I inspected the garden carefully and found two places where Davos could get into trouble, potentially. At either end of the high back wall there are spaces to squeeze into, behind the garage and behind the pool house. So, we've fenced those off. And I suggested to Mrs. Lamkin and to the housekeepers that they keep Davos under constant observation when he's outside."

"Good." His focus felt intense. "What's in those spaces?"

"Just shrubbery behind the pool house. A drainage pipe next to the garage."

"Are there signs the dog has gone back in there?"

"Nothing conclusive, but he certainly could have."

"Any theories of the case?"

She recalled the vengeful look on Interior Minister Xotari's face after Davos slobbered on her at the reception. And twice Tara had been subjected to the fanaticism of Lotte Wuyts. But there wasn't enough to make either one into a convincing theory.

"Not yet," she admitted.

The DCM smiled, as if that was what he expected. "Keep me—and only me—posted."

Tara left, carrying the DCM's apparently low expectations like a load of fuel.

After reassuring himself that the new general services officer was not in any danger of closing in on the poisoning mystery, and before the start of the morning intel briefing, Andy managed to send a couple of carefully phrased emails to people in Washington, probing for any ripples from the incident. He worried that it might go to waste as a source of embarrassment.

Of more immediate concern, as he took a seat on the couch in the ambassador's office for the intel brief, was the risk that the station's sources might reveal that certain incidents provoking tension in the election campaign were actually hoaxes. Such a disclosure would lead to all sorts of uncomfortable questions, with the potential to reveal his instigating role. In which case, game over.

"Today I offer a modern twist on an ancient philosophical question," began Erika, one of the station's young analysts. She beamed at her small audience around the coffee table: ambassador, DCM, political counselor, defense attaché, station chief. She was one of those analysts who always tried to make her presentations entertaining.

"If a few tons of rock fell into a deep remote gorge," she continued, "and no one was there to hear the sound, does that mean it wasn't seen?"

Erika opened her binder and took out a sealed envelope. "Thanks to our geospatial mapping capabilities, we can now say the answer is no."

She tore open the envelope with a flourish and passed the ambassador a sheaf of aerial imagery of the Vodania-Pazaria border.

"These are close-ups of an area in the Odorian River gorge," she explained. "They show there was an event in the last four to five days, probably a small avalanche, that blocked a short stretch of the river and diverted its flow."

"How extensive is the diversion?" asked the ambassador.

"Approximately ten meters long. With the result that around a hundred square meters of land is now on the Pazaria side of the river."

"The whole border is two hundred and seventy-three kilometers, around a hundred and sixty miles," political counselor Gary Hambert pointed out. "A hundred square meters is about the size of our cafeteria."

"This is nothing," asserted the ambassador, looking up from the photographs. "Although it's more than I've gotten on the Davos poisoning." He cast a look at Andy.

Andy nodded in solidarity, as if he were not the target of the ambassador's impatience. You're right, Skipper, let's keep that ball in play.

"Well, to be fair," interjected station chief Phyllis Snicklehimer, "Knowing the Pazarians, on a lot that size, they could squeeze in five or six Roma shacks."

"Don't give them any ideas," Gary joined in. "They might start another resettlement program."

"We do share these feeds with the OSCE," Erika pointed out. "Therefore, both sides potentially know about the anomaly. Their software can pick it up. If they're checking."

Andy could hardly contain his delight. Another gift from the heavens. With an effort, he frowned and said, "No need to call it to anyone's attention."

"Certainly not," the ambassador agreed.

From his study, Ambassador Lamkin heard two careful taps on the front door knocker. His German counterpart and next-door neighbor, Monika Basch, had requested a private meeting, and the interlude before lunch was a mutually convenient time. Ambassador Lamkin heard Davos sprinting through the foyer, ready to give their guest a proper screening. The housekeeper's steady footsteps followed. When the front door swung open, there was a sharp gasp and the housekeeper said "No" a bit harshly. After a moment of shuffling, the door to the study opened, and Ambassador Basch stepped in, composed and dignified in a tailored suit. Behind her the housekeeper kept a grip on Davos's collar.

Ambassador Lamkin stood up to welcome his visitor. They shook hands, both of them cupping their left hands around the clasp to intensify the greeting.

While they stood in close proximity, Ambassador Basch said, "I wanted to see you because I felt it best to share this in person. Not good news, I'm afraid."

Ambassador Lamkin motioned for her to sit on the couch, and he positioned himself in an adjacent armchair. On the bookshelf behind him stood recent memoirs by several former U.S. presidents and secretaries of state and defense. All in pristine condition.

Ambassador Basch studied her nails for a moment, then made eye contact. "We received back the results from the testing for your dog. They did not find any poisons or drugs."

"However." She swallowed and appeared reluctant to continue. "What the laboratory report said is that the mixture they tested is most likely the consequence of severe, systemic gastro-intestinal dysfunction. The digestive system appears to be completely compromised."

Ambassador Basch looked sadly at Ambassador Lamkin as he listened.

She added, "The veterinary technicians concluded that the most probable diagnosis is advanced cancer or a serious injury. Something which has eroded or ruptured the barrier between the stomach and the intestines, mixing up the contents and the flow."

She paused once more. "They advised that if the animal is still alive it is most likely in severe distress and should probably be put to rest."

Ambassador Lamkin stiffened and frowned.

"Though I have to say he seems very healthy to me," Ambassador Basch added with a curt, dry laugh. She glanced at the study door the housekeeper closed after dragging Davos away.

"We'll keep a close eye on him," Ambassador Lamkin replied. "I'm going to get a second opinion. Eventually."

They sat in silence for a moment. Ambassador Lamkin filled the void by mentioning the landslide in the Odorian River gorge.

"Oh dear," said the German ambassador, furrowing her brows. "I hope this won't cause more problems between the two countries."

"I really don't see why it should," Ambassador Lamkin replied.

Her mouth dropped open for a moment, but she did not challenge his view. Instead, after a brief silence, she said, "David, may I take this opportunity to remind you that we have resumed Sunday evening performances at the conservatory?"

Ambassador Basch's pet project was bringing German and local musicians to the stage together under the sponsorship of Germany's cultural arts council. Very worthy and harmless.

Her face lit up with enthusiasm. "This Sunday we will have a very talented young Vodanian vocalist performing selections from La Boheme. I know Puccini is among your favorites."

"Indeed. Lithia and I are planning a quick excursion in early September for a production of Tosca at the Vienna State Opera House."

"How delightful!"

At lunchtime on Tuesday, in the corporate offices of Harrimore Services, in Chrystal City, Virginia, a reeking pile of shame protruded out over the edge of Julia's work station, in the form of a take-out container holding half a tuna salad. A thick corporate brochure pinned open the container's clear plastic lid, and a disposable plastic fork rose up out of the grey-beige mound at the same angle as the Leaning Tower of Pisa. At Harrimore Services, lunch was supposed to be for networking, also known as business development. Instead, Julia had stayed in to concentrate on assembling the documentation for a new contract, the first one she had been assigned to put together.

Her eyes flew back and forth between her computer screen and a printout of a previous contract she was using as a model. The new contract had a tight deadline. At fifty thousand dollars, it was apparently considered tiny, but her boss Travis said it was a toe in the door and maybe they could grow it. DIA wanted detailed operational planning for something called stealth reconnaissance and security countermeasures, against a specific target in Vodania.

As Julia was typing in the geo-coordinates of the location, her desk phone rang. She continued typing in the numbers, but she recognized from the extension that it was human resources calling. Julia had been trying to figure out Harrimore's corporate policy on student loan support, which sounded really generous, but was turning out to be more complicated. Before picking up the phone, she finished inputting the latitude, N43.1854217.

But she transposed the 1 and the 7 at the end of the number sequence, so it came out N43.1854271.

After listening to a lengthy explanation of how to use her timesheets to calculate how much of her loans may be eligible, Julia pulled up the target location on the global satellite mapping software. It pinpointed a spot on the ridge north of Shizl, Vodania. There was a sizable complex nearby, which further research revealed to be the official residence of the president of Vodania. That would explain why the DIA tasking order only identified it as a guarded compound.

At mid-morning on a Wednesday in the middle of August, President Chilik sat stiffly on one of the leather couches in his Presidentorium office. Facing him from the opposite couch, with clenched smiles, were two powerful foreigners.

"Your country is at a crossroads," Ambassador Lamkin proclaimed, after the preliminaries had concluded. EU High Commissioner Cauchon, of earnest posture and elegant attire, did not allow his own face to mirror the Vodanian leader's scowl.

On the periphery of the conversational arena, three aides perched in a row of straight-backed chairs pulled away from the conference table. The president's chief of staff sat closest to him; Gary from the American embassy's political section had taken the middle position; Monique from the EU mission sat at the other end. Fragile wisps of steam rose off the cups of tea that everyone ignored.

"In today's interconnected democratic world, more than ever before, reputations matter, elections matter, and positive relations matter," Ambassador Lamkin pressed on. "Vodania's future depends on democratic standards and universal values, the whole range of civilizational norms. If Vodania, as a young country, wants to fully join the community of nations, it must embrace these values and norms. As president, and as the leader of the majority party of Vodania's largest population group, you have leadership responsibility."

Ambassador Lamkin paused, and High Commissioner Cauchon seized the baton. In a silky, coaxing voice, the top representative of the European Union began his pitch, "With full respect for Vodania's sovereignty and autonomy, the international community has profoundly deep concerns in a number of areas about the current conditions of this election campaign. These include voter registration, state control over the media, and the prevailing atmosphere in the country, which many feel contains elements of intimidation and violence," extending the final syllable into a gentle sigh, gazing at President Chilik almost imploringly.

In nuanced contrast with the undertone of anger in Ambassador Lamkin's spiel, Cauchon seemed to be going for sorrowful.

President Chilik spoke up. "We have people who are with us for many years, during the darkest times when we were fighting the nationalists to turn this country around. Many of our guys spent time in prison. You want us to abandon them?"

"No one's talking about abandoning friends and supporters," Ambassador Lamkin replied. "Elections are highly competitive processes, we understand that. It's a matter of establishing fair rules so the citizens of Vodania can decide who will represent and lead them."

Chilik made no reply. After a moment, Lamkin glanced momentarily at Cauchon before asking, "Could we discuss your border with Pazaria? The demarcation is complete and settled. There's no reason to delay signing and ratifying the agreement."

President Chilik maintained a cool expression. "We will consider it through our normal democratic processes."

High Commissioner Cauchon then launched into an extended narrative about the benefits of international integration, citing as his main example Croatia's progress since joining the European Union. Ambassador Lamkin remained attentive and patient, waiting for the moment to play his trump card.

When Cauchon's sermon after a lengthy journey at last reached its final destination, Lamkin leaned forward.

"I have instructions from Washington," he stated. "My government wants to emphasize its strong desire for closer, more positive relations between our two countries. One of the most important ways we can show this is at the leadership level."

Lamkin straightened his spine and peered with renewed intensity at Chilik.

"I am authorized to offer you, contingent on appropriate progress in the areas we have been discussing this morning, a photo opportunity with the president of the United States."

Lamkin's face shone with pleasure at the image of such a capstone moment.

"Next month, in New York at the General Assembly. This will symbolize a new era in our bilateral relationship."

President Chilik successfully contained any enthusiasm he might have felt. In fact, he noted that he did not normally attend General Assembly meetings, which he pointed out was not a secret. He added that, with the election and the start of a new parliament, he did not plan on taking any trips abroad in the next few months.

"However, if your president wanted to meet with me here, we would provide a full welcome."

Lamkin's triumphant gleam vanished.

Cauchon began another oration, smoothly spinning out further silky eloquence about the election process, the judicial process, the regulatory process, and possibly even the digestive process.

Lamkin endured Cauchon's spiel in silence, a grim frown tightening on his face. He seethed visibly. Evidently, he did not find Cauchon's words soothing.

Finally, as Cauchon seemed to be wrapping up his lecture, Lamkin sat up to his full height and leaned toward Chilik.

"I need to make one further point here. In going forward in its relations with the United States, Vodania has a clear choice to make. And I'm not happy about what happened to my dog."

The arteries in Chilik's neck and temples suddenly protruded in an alarming and possibly medically significant manner.

Ambassador Lamkin and High Commissioner Cauchon walked out of the Presidentorium together, with Gary and Monique trailing. Lamkin and Cauchon stopped in the narrow space between their two idling limos. Both vehicles, pointed in opposite directions, poured gusts of hot carbon compounds into the local atmosphere through their exhaust pipes. A local security man stood next to each limo, holding open the side door for his protectee, deflecting a generous portion of the fumes into the passenger compartments.

"The reference to your dog's misfortune came as somewhat of a surprise," the High Commissioner observed in his soft, pointed fashion. He touched the fingertips of his right hand to the freshly polished trunk of Ambassador Lamkin's limousine.

"I wanted to put him on notice," Lamkin replied.

"You certainly got his attention."

Cauchon looked like he wanted to sigh. He gazed into the distance beyond Lamkin's left shoulder. After a moment, he asked, "What do your people make of the Marko phenomenon?"

"What do you mean?"

"You know, the red goat symbols that have been sprouting up all over. Look, there's one on the side of that trash receptacle." With his left pinkie, Cauchon pointed toward the park.

After indulging his EU counterpart with a cursory glance at the dumpster, Lamkin said, "I think it's fair to say we don't have an official view. Though I personally consider graffiti to be vandalism, period."

"Some people believe Marko to be a kind of social movement, possibly political in nature," resumed Cauchon. "Others think it is the alias of a renegade American soldier who's been living in the Asich Mountains ever since the war."

"That's ridiculous."

With a teasing smile, Cauchon complained, "So you're going to leave me in the dark?"

Lamkin moved toward the door of his limo and replied, "No, I'm going to leave you in this glorious sunshine."

Chapter 14

Tara preferred heat to cold, but she had never experienced such baking dryness. Wednesday afternoon, only halfway through August, and the closest decent beach was probably five hundred miles away. She felt like peeling off her clothes and leaping into the nearest body of water before her skin shriveled in Shizl's furnace. Instead, her top objective for the day was replacing the carpet in the ambassador's bedroom.

Tara arrived at the residence early and passed the time in the shade chatting with the guard on duty at the service entrance. They could see into part of the German ambassador's garden, and Tara noticed a young girl, perhaps five years old, sitting on the grass, singing softly.

"Who's that?" Tara asked.

"The German ambassador's daughter."

"She's in the garden by herself?"

"Sometimes."

Shortly after one-thirty, an Eastern Carpet Kings truck rumbled up the street and lurched to a stop before the residence gate with a painful shriek of brakes. The guard stepped forward to check credentials.

Tara escorted the installer into the respite of the air-conditioned residence. In the master bedroom, the burly installer removed his over-shirt and worked methodically and with what struck Tara as a surprising delicacy. When he finished, the new carpet, combined with a cushiony pad underneath, felt just as pleasant on the feet as did its damaged predecessor. Tara hoped the ambassador's feet, and Lithia's, would agree. While two of her workers returned the large bed and other furnishings to the room, Tara signed the receipt and prepared to walk the installer back to his truck.

"We can take away the old one for a small fee," the installer offered.

"That won't be necessary."

"You are correct, my apologies. We will take it for no charge."

"No, we'll take care of it."

Above the Pazaria-Vodania border, in a clear sky with near-perfect visibility, three U.S. F-16 fighters banked in formation to trace a low flight path above the Asich peaks, whipping southwest to northeast just within the Pazaria side of the line. When they reached the end of the range they turned around, pulling a few g's in the process, and scraped the border going back the other way. For the U.S. Air Force pilots and crews stationed at Camp Stability in northwestern Pazaria, it was a routine perimeter patrol, part of an easy couple of hours to keep their combat flight certifications current.

Three-quarters of the way up Mount Korkit, under the beguiling light of a half-moon, Andy Pulano pulled over to the edge of the road and turned off his engine. Fifteen minutes before midnight. The area was renowned for its magnificent overlooks above Shizl, and even more renowned as a place for couples, or threesomes in this case, to park and enjoy private time together. He had rented a passenger van for the occasion; in case his Range Rover was bugged. In addition, he would not want his diplomatic license plate to be spotted in such a disreputable location.

Reconvening in the laundry room would have been far less embarrassing. But Andy preferred to nudge his partners out of their comfort zones. Besides, hosting Shariz and Farao at his house again would be too risky, what with the guards, neighbors, and nosy passers-by. In Shizl, everyone always seemed to know everything about everyone. So, he insisted they meet along a remote roadside.

Waiting inside the parked van for Shariz and Farao to show up, Andy used the time to compose, in his mind, subtly self-praising emails to various members of his professional network. In particular, he brainstormed about what he would next write to curry favor from his harried and irascible deputy assistant secretary, Vonda Vance. To grab her attention, he needed a fresh supply of Bosnia references. Any mention of personalities or events there needed to be specific enough to gesture in the direction of some sort of meaning, while stopping short of advocating an actual viewpoint. Too risky. Vonda held unshakeable views on everything about Bosnia and heaven help anyone who disagreed.

Three black Land Cruisers roared down from the top of the mountain. Farao's government convoy. They must have had to drive at least an hour out of their way in order to approach from that direction. Probably Farao's guards thought they'd impress their chief with the zealousness of their security consciousness. Andy opened the van's window to ensure the phalanx spotted him. One government vehicle cruised past, another hung back, and the middle one slotted onto the shoulder behind the rental van. No one emerged. Waiting for Shariz. Several minutes passed before Farao's downhill crew flicked their high beams.

Shariz and associates arrived in two silver sedans with gleaming bodies and sparkling chrome. Andy figured they must have come straight from one of the car washes in their extortion portfolio. The Pazaris parked a discreet distance downhill from the van. Andy stepped outside, yanked down on the side latch, and slid open the passenger door. Farao's drivers positioned the two auxiliary Land Cruisers perpendicular across the road, blocking it off from both directions. Farao and Shariz slipped out of their pricey conveyances and walked quickly to the van.

"You'll forgive me if I don't offer tea," said Andy.

Once he made sure they left their electronics in their own vehicles, Andy settled Farao in the far back seat, himself in the middle, and Shariz in the front row. Farao did not conceal his distaste at placing himself and his bespoke suit inside such a shabby compartment. His cologne fumes spiked alarmingly. Shariz, clad only in boxer-briefs that looked freshly removed from their original packaging, unfolded a towel and draped it over his bare shoulders before leaning back comfortably against the van's worn upholstery.

"We can make this fairly quick," said Andy. He looked back and forth at Vodania's alpha security official and at the Pazari kingpin. "My sense is you both have gotten the balance about right so far. Now the story has its own momentum, so you can taper off a bit."

"Maybe there's been too much momentum," Shariz complained. "One of our boys had a tooth knocked out."

"We've had real injuries too," Farao shot back. "Two cops hospitalized."

"That was not our fault."

"Alright," Andy interjected. "There's been a bit of over-zealousness. That's not entirely surprising. We all recognize it's challenging to contain this kind of thing. Let's dial it back."

He paused to hold the gaze of both men in turn, forging a visual contract. He noticed that, apart from the up-swoop of Pazari-style machismo and the down-swoop of Vodanian manliness, Shariz and Farao sported identical mustaches.

"I say we agree there will be no further incidents for the next week," Andy proposed. He refrained from using the word 'eschew', cognizant of the paradox that an excess of verbal precision can diminish clarity. "And while we're here together, let's acknowledge and appreciate that business is picking up, right? It's working. People are paying attention to Vodania."

Shariz and Farao talked through the types of measures they would each take in the final weeks of the campaign to provoke maximum turnout in certain electoral districts while discouraging it in others. And they all agreed on a fresh set of code phrases for texting each other in case of emergency. Business complete, Shariz folded his towel, exited the van, and walked toward his glimmering sedan, his pale blue boxers glowing in the headlights.

As Farao clambered forward toward the van's open doorway, Andy said, "About the border demarcation. We appreciate you guys not overreacting to the recent anomaly."

"What anomaly?"

"Exactly."

In the secure conference room on Thursday morning, Andy rose to his feet along with everyone else when Ambassador Lamkin entered. After the ambassador took his seat, he startled his staff by opening the country team meeting with a vehement harrumph, which was not part of his usual repertoire. He proceeded to describe his session with President Chilik the previous day, quoting himself at length. It was critical to state and restate our positions with utmost clarity, he emphasized. Chilik needed to hear the steps Vodania must take to become a successful democracy and enjoy positive relations with its neighbors and the international community. Reiterating these principles also deprived Chilik of the excuse that he did not fully understand how strongly we felt about such matters.

The ambassador frowned. "We all know what kind of a leader President Chilik is."

Andy could picture Vodania's president sitting stonily as the ambassador's talking points flowed remorselessly, deepening the rift between them.

The ambassador turned to Gary Hambert. "Our cable went out yesterday I presume."

Andy watched to see whether the political counselor understood that the ambassador wanted to know whether Washington had reacted.

"Yes," Gary responded, "but we haven't gotten any feedback yet. We'll ping the desk as soon as they get in."

Andy smiled inwardly. Gary had promise. He had been in the game long enough to know that the State Department would see no reason to reply to a routine write-up of such a meeting. And he was savvy enough to know that even the most level-headed ambassadors were prone to the conceit that their words and actions commanded rapt attention in Washington.

"The DCM has briefed me on our follow-up so far on the Davos poisoning," the ambassador resumed. "I appreciate everyone's efforts and look forward to your conclusions."

The ambassador's gaze circled the table to underscore the point. He stopped at Doug Watanabe. "Have you heard anything?"

Doug shook his head, trying to convey the right blend of apology and exasperation.

"We're not waiting for a smoking gun," the ambassador declared. "The Air Force flew a squadron of F-16s out of Camp Stability yesterday. A border patrol flight conducted to demonstrate U.S. resolve in the face of this type of provocation, and to pressure Chilik and company into ratifying the border deal."

Neither General Elfersen nor anyone else shared how they felt about the maneuver. Andy gave silent thanks to whoever came up with it. Having idiots on your side made it so much easier to prevent problems from getting solved on someone else's watch.

"One more thing before we go around the table," said the ambassador. "Does anyone have any insights about this goat graffiti fad or whatever it is? The EU Commissioner blindsided me about it yesterday."

Blank stares all around the room.

"We'll dig into it," said Andy. Add it to the pile; maybe it'll come in handy.

In the embassy gym, pretending to be interested as management counselor Robert Akes described his plans for defusing the locker crisis,

Andy lifted a hand when the local news came on. He turned his attention to the TV screen mounted on the wall.

Long blond hair, striking physiques tightly wrapped in stylish fabrics, and husky, serious voices. The three indispensable characteristics of newsreaders in Vodania. State Television's afternoon announcer was no exception. She adjusted her posture and watched for the cue.

"Welcome to the four o'clock news," she began, swishing her golden mane sideways with a curt snap of her neck. "We have an important bulletin. According to sources in the Vodanian government and confirmed by the Organization for Security and Cooperation in Europe, there has been an unlawful alteration of our nation's northern border. The Odorian River, which has served as the boundary of Vodania since the earliest pages of our history, has been shifted southward to the detriment of our sovereign territory."

She punctuated this announcement with another decisive swish of hair.

"Authorities are investigating the cause of the change in the river's course, which may have been accomplished by creating a landslide. It is known that our neighbor's border demarcation team was conducting operations in the vicinity shortly before the diversion of the Odorian occurred. From the Presidentorium, there are firm assurances that President Chilik will defend one hundred percent of Vodania."

Credit to Farao. From a tip in the middle of the night to a nationwide broadcast the next afternoon. He was a pleasure to work with.

An hour after sundown, heat still radiating off the cobblestones in Shizl's main plaza, Doug Watanabe and three guests occupied wooden stools inside the chain-link boundary of the Vodania Forever beer garden. Watanabe sat straight, alert. He was on a case.

The way he figured it, the purpose of information is action. It's what makes a cop a cop. He did his best to pound home that lesson during all those years he served as a trainer in the LAPD. But there was a different attitude in Embassy-land. Let the public affairs section, the political section, the station, and even, God help him, the regional security officer, spin their wheels all they wanted collecting information and writing reports about Marko and the significance of the red goat. But the ambassador expected results, solutions. Watanabe made a few phone calls, and now he was sitting with people who could help him do something about the problem. Actual police commanders who planned and conducted actual operations.

Watanabe prided himself on memorizing their elaborate titles. Deputy director of the Operations and Planning Unit. Western district commander. Executive director of the National Police Academy. Basically, these were the guys who ran the show once the higher-ups made a decision. And oftentimes beforehand.

Their waitress brought tall glasses of beer and a large bowl of shredded green cabbage covered with slices of tomato and cucumber.

Watanabe got right to the point. "I'm hearing lots of chatter from the western mountain areas about someone, or maybe an organization, called Marko. Who is this guy?"

The police commanders glanced at each other as they bent forward to suck the upper layers of beer from their topped-off glasses.

The operations and planning guy spoke first, "No one knows."

"Big mystery," added the western district commander.

They both shrugged.

"Is he involved in smuggling? Drugs?" Watanabe pressed.

"Why not? All the Pazaris are," replied the western district commander.

"Sounds like we need to tackle this," Watanabe asserted. "I'll talk to the chief, see if we can get something going."

Every so often, Andy indulged in an early morning walk to sniff around the streets of the capital and gather impressions. Friday morning, he woke at dawn, eager to sense what the day would bring. He went outside in a dark blue short-sleeved shirt, a bit too large, and a pair of baggy cotton trousers, grey. Unobtrusive without being too obvious about it. With the air still relatively fresh, he strolled through residential blocks toward a commercial area.

Half a block from the newsstand, he could read the headline on the display copy of the National Gazette: INVASION! At the newsstand, he purchased three dailies, all competing to provide the most garish claim. 'PAZARI SABOTAGE' was a strong contender, but his favorite was 'THEY ARE STEALING OUR HISTORY!'

Not wanting to call attention to himself, Andy refrained from engaging in conversation with the newspaper seller or any other man-in-the-street representatives of the public mood. But he did linger near the newsstand long enough to listen to snatches of commentary by other customers, grousing about the Pazaris. He partook of similar surreptitious eavesdropping at a nearby café, where he sipped at a scalding demitasse of bitter Turkish-style sludge. He perused the newspapers' vivid, breathless accounts of the causes and consequences of a small rockslide in an Odorian River gorge no one had ever seen.

After he paid for the coffee, he paused to savor the moment. The day would demand utmost seriousness as the embassy lurched into crisis mode. Moves to make, decisions to take, reactions to fake. All the progress toward a border agreement, cultivated over many months of painstaking diplomatic work by the embassy, and by Ambassador Lamkin especially, now lay buried under a worthless pile of rocks. Such a pity. Such an opportunity. Was it wrong, was it so terribly wrong, to take pleasure in the fortuitous calamities that made statecraft such a beguiling enterprise?

Chapter 15

Going through emails in her cubicle on Friday morning, a message from the regional security office caused Tara's spine to stiffen. Unsigned, it read like a summons, directing her to appear in the RSO offices at 10:30 that morning. She approached Chuck about it, but he just shrugged and said she better go.

When the time came, she entered the corridor of embassy sections and agencies that produced and consumed classified information. Except for the two occasions when the DCM called her in about the Davos incident, she never needed to set foot in that part of the building. She felt somehow unwelcome, a sense she did not belong there.

In front of the regional security office suite, she pressed the buzzer. After a moment the lock clicked open. The office assistant, the husband of someone from the station, guided her to Assistant RSO Kerry-Anne Frisker's office. Along the way they passed two full sets of body armor hanging on wall pegs. The only previous time Tara had been inside the RSO space was for her security briefing the day after she arrived in Shizl. She didn't remember any Kevlar on display back then.

Kerry-Anne stood up and came around her desk. "This way please."

Tara followed her deeper into the suite. Kerry-Anne paused in front of Ken Dewitt's office and said, "We'll be in the interview room."

They entered a windowless tank with an airlock seal on the door and sat on opposite sides of a small table.

"We'll wait for Ken."

As they sat in silence, Tara wondered what she might have done wrong. Speeding? Voucher fraud she hadn't caught? She tried to dismiss that line of thinking. This could be anything.

Finally, Ken appeared and took a seat next to Kerry-Anne.

"You have been identified as a possible witness in a terrorism investigation." His tone was grim. "Are you aware of the attack on the ambassador's pet dog?" he continued.

She wasn't sure how to respond. The DCM had been adamant about not discussing her role with anyone, not even the ambassador.

Pink coloration rose up Ken's face and into his scalp. "I have to warn you that withholding relevant information may be considered obstruction of a federal investigation, and may result in the loss of your security clearance, dismissal, and/or criminal prosecution."

Tara blinked. What was he talking about?

"I was at the residence the other day for a carpet replacement," Tara answered, "so yes, I'm aware that Davos got very sick recently. But I don't know anything about what caused it."

"Any special reason for your interest in the case?"

"What do you mean?"

"You're having fences put up, giving advice about leashes."

"Just doing my job."

"Well, it's our job to investigate the incident. Kerry-Anne's going to take you through some questions."

Ken got to his feet and loomed over the table. "Keep in mind what I said."

When the door sealed behind him, Kerry-Anne gave a quarter-smile. Perhaps an apology of a sort.

"Thank you for coming over. I need to ask you about Stimche Chestim."

"Okay.".

"How long has he been employed in the general services office?"

"I don't know exactly. Several years, I think. I can find out."

"That's okay, we can get that from HR. How would you characterize his attitude?"

"Seems normal, I guess. He's a good worker, reliable. I'm fairly certain the job's important to him."

"Could he be a threat?"

"Nothing I've seen or heard suggests that."

"What about the incident with the ambassador's dog, the kick?"

"I didn't see what happened. Robert sent me over afterwards to fix it. I talked to Mrs. Lamkin and verbally reprimanded Stimche and drove him back to the embassy. We had a follow-up discussion about it later. He was irritated that the dog was in their way. But I think he gets it that he needs to be more careful."

"Do you think he believes the dog got him in trouble?"

"Well, he's not in trouble as far as I'm concerned. He made a mistake and we talked about it."

"Did you know his brother-in-law works maintenance for a food-processing company? He handles pest control as part of his duties."

"No. That's news to me."

"Did Mr. Chestim have any work reason to go back to the residence later on that Friday, or over the weekend?" Kerry-Anne looked at her notes. "That would be August the second through the morning of the fifth."

Tara considered the question. "I can't think of any. Did the camera footage show he went back?"

"No. But our system only backs up forty-eight hours. We can't say for sure about Friday."

"What about from the neighbors?"

"Those are focused on their own properties, but there was nothing on either one."

"Just trees and grass all day and all night? That must be fun to watch."

"Tell me about it." Kerry-Anne allowed another smile. "We run them on fast-forward, except where there's any movement. Then we stop to ID who or what it is, make sure there's nothing suspicious, and back to fast-forward. In this case, all that showed up on either tape was a gardener watering trees up on the Alambro side and the German ambassador's little girl skipping around their lawn. So, the review didn't take that long. Not like going over footage from a demonstration, face by face, trying to spot threats."

"Is Stimche a suspect?"

"At this point all I can say is he's a person of interest."

"And me?"

"Not for me to say."

The marble steps of the Presidentorium's ceremonial entrance blazed in the noontime sun. Foreigners suffering through a Shizl summer loved to make comparisons. Pizza oven. Blast furnace. House on fire. As if a shared exaggeration of the city's elevated temperatures made August more tolerable. Most Vodanians didn't take the weather so personally.

From atop the blazing steps, President Chilik addressed his nation. He stood at maximum height behind an ornate lectern that seemed exposed and out of place in the glare of the sunlight. Large electric fans just outside the frame of the television cameras produced a stirring breeze that flared his pelt of salt-and-pepper hair.

"Vodaniaaaaa!" he thundered.

"Our nation must be strong. Throughout our long and glorious history, we have withstood many dangers and many attacks. Including in recent years, when we have endured serious repeated pressures. Economic pressures, political pressures, military pressures. Now this pressure has taken a more brazen form."

Chilik pointed a thick finger northward.

"The Odorian River, the boundary of our ancestral homeland, has been tampered with. Shifted from its natural course to steal part of our lands. While we have been cooperating in an honorable manner to demarcate our true border with our neighbor, other forces, other elements, have played a different game. With rules of their own devising. Can it be coincidence that a so-called survey team undertakes an operation along the far bank of the Odorian, and a few days later there is a big, sudden landslide?"

Chilik glowered in the heat of his righteousness.

"It was an accident, some will say. It is only a small amount of territory, others will say. It is a test, that is what I say!"

Applause erupted from the hastily assembled crowd at the foot of the steps.

"How will we respond?" demanded Chilik. "For true Vodanians, that is a simple question. A very simple question. We will respond how we always respond. We will defend Vodania and Vodanian life."

Sweat glistened on his forehead and trickled down his neck.

"Vodanians, I promise you strength and resolve."

Cheers and whistles from the faithful.

"Vodanians, I promise you; we will take all necessary measures."

More cheering.

Chilik upped the volume. "Vodanians, I promise you! We will not cede even one meter of our territory!"

A throaty, sustained roar of approval from the crowd.

"Vodanians, I promise you."

Behind the closed door of his one-man office, drowsy from a two-beer lunch and three-digit temperatures, Doug Watanabe propped up his head with his left hand and grasped the phone with his right. It was morning in Washington and the DEA lab had just started their workday.

"Case number?" the woman on the other end of the line demanded.

"I don't know. I just mailed it in last week and I want to verify that it's arrived," Watanabe explained.

"I can't check it sir without the case number."

"How do I get the case number?" asked Watanabe.

"The agent in charge is supposed to have that."

"I'm in charge," Watanabe exclaimed.

"So didn't you assign a case number when you launched the investigation?" she asked, more solicitously.

"I must have forgotten."

"Well just make sure you include it when you resubmit the evidence."

"Wait, I can't resubmit! Just hold on to it there and I'll get you a case number."

She hung up before he could finish.

The Mitchell children watched wide-eyed as Stimche Chestim emptied their basement playroom of everything, including the armchair and easel. Then he switched on his portable shop vac to prep the floor and the three children retreated partway up the basement steps, put their hands over their ears, and screamed, "Loud!"

A spider raced along the bottom of the wall. Stimche swatted it with his work gloves and vacuumed up the debris. When he finished with the vac, he carried it up the stairs, brushing past the children. They trailed behind and watched from the front window as he put the machine into the big van outside. Then he disappeared into the van and a cylindrical shape came out through the open back door. It was a long roll of something, and it bent in the middle when Stimche lifted it up and hauled it toward the house.

"It looks like a dragon's neck," said the oldest.

"Eeew," said her brother.

The children scrambled out of the way as Stimche barreled through hefting a rolled-up carpet, his boots clomping on the stairs on the way down. He flopped the carpet face down in the empty basement room and rolled it open.

"It's upside down," the older girl said.

"Mister, the rug has a hole in it," the boy added.

"Two holes," his sister corrected him.

Stimche gave no sign of appreciating any of these observations. With the carpet unrolled, but too large to fit, he marked the excess on the underside with a piece of chalk. He left the playroom and stomped over to his toolbox on the hallway floor. He rummaged around and pulled out the tool he wanted.

The children gasped when he pressed the release to slide out a pointed steel blade. On his hands and knees, Stimche sliced straight lines along the breadth and length of the carpet to tailor it to the room. Before he completed the lengthways edge, he flipped the carpet right side up in order to shape an extension to fit the doorway.

"It's right side up!" the children cheered.

Then he flipped it back over, and the boy said, "Oh no, it's upside down again!"

"Oh no!" echoed the two girls.

Stimche cut two rough squares from the scraps. Twisting and curving his blade he trimmed the pieces to fit the two holes. With strips of duct tape on the underside of the carpet he fixed the plugs in place. When he flipped it over for the last time, it was impossible to see where the holes had been. He finished the job with a rubber threshold cover plate and returned the armchair to its spot in the corner. The children rushed into the room shrieking and tumbling on the golden carpet. Stimche patted each of them on the head and departed up the stairs.

From the front door, Connie Mitchell waved goodbye with an almost spiritual smile glowing on her face, as if she had just been blessed by a saint.

Nearly 7:30 on Friday evening and Gary Hambert still manned his desk in the political section. On paper, his roster consisted of a mid-level deputy, two and a half junior officers, and two local employees. But his new deputy would not arrive for another week, and the j.o. who the political section shared with the consular section was in Atlanta on home leave. The senior local, an ethnic Vodanian, had been with the embassy since soon after Vodania's independence. The other was younger and a Pazari.

Gary assigned Ashley, a second-tour officer with decent language proficiency, to work with the younger local employee to call as many Pazari politicians as they could reach, to urge them to remain calm. They kept a tally sheet on a yellow legal pad.

The senior local was out on the move. He crisscrossed the streets of Shizl, conducting a café-to-café search for gossip and rumors, while working his embassy and personal cell phones in an attempt to arrange a meeting for the ambassador or DCM with someone, anyone, in authority. No one would answer. He told Gary that in all his years as the key link between the Vodanian power structure and successive American ambassadors, he had never been so shut out. Not even his favorite kebab delivery shop would take his call.

Gary asked Jeremiah, his first tour officer, to write a cable summarizing Chilik's televised address and reactions to it. As the evening wore on, Jeremiah, a history major in college, struggled to condense his eight-page draft to fit the two-page limit Gary imposed.

Gary attempted again to reach Chilik's chief of staff Grigor Khalamente. Then he tried the deputy foreign minister responsible for political matters. No luck. He checked in with his senior local again. Nothing.

For the third time that evening, Gary sent the same text message to the ambassador and DCM: *still no rply from prez team. will keep calling and txting.*

As midnight approached, Tara sensed the energy building on the dance floor at Boom Shaka-laka. She felt she and Mads had been pulled to the club by mutual expectation. A half-spoken understanding. Now here they were, at a table filled mostly with other foreigners. Sort of a date, sort of not. Certainly, Mads seemed happy to see her there.

But to what end? There was an attraction, no question, a strong chemistry. And an imminent departure. To avoid thinking about that, and to get away from the platters of pastries that kept showing up on their group's table, Tara stood up. She extended a hand to Mads.

He looked up at her with an amused expression.

"Let's see your moves," she said.

On the dance floor, he managed to look both gangly and stylish. They held their place among the boisterous Vodanians as the lights spun, and the smoke billowed, and the rhythms pulsed. Tara felt herself perspiring with the movement, the heat of the night, the press of bodies.

After a while, Mads took on a wistful look. He leaned close. "I must be going soon."

"Why? It's early. You don't like the band? They're just getting loose."

"I mean from Vodania."

"I know," she projected into his ear. Their cheeks touched. "I mean, I don't want to know." Did she just say that out loud?

This had been coming, of course, but why bring it up now? To make sure she knew, that there was no mistake? To set a clear boundary? She blew a wisp of hair away from her face and spun around and around as if drilling deeper into the moment, anchoring herself to the fleeting present.

Mads caught her in his arms and squeezed her tight. An apology? Or simply affection? She didn't know whether to grab him back or spin away. So she did both.

The main highway running north-by-northeast out of Shizl traversed a broad agricultural valley. On Saturday morning, with the sun still low in the east, most of the fields lay in shadow. Purple thistle flowers swayed in the dry breeze. Meadowlarks clamored in whistling cadences.

A metal pole planted next to the roadside held up a square white sign with the number 80 in black. The speed limit, in kilometers. The zero had been painted over in red, and the letter M added to its center. Further along the road, a large billboard advertising brandy had the outline of a goat sprayed onto its lower left corner.

A long convoy of military vehicles rumbled northward. Artillery pieces trundled along on huge black tires, leaving trails of diesel fumes. Soldiers sweating in their combat gear stared out through the back flaps of troop trucks. Their expressions said it was not an exercise.

Tara worried she would be late for her Saturday class at the Roma school. Not entirely her fault. She had picked up Mads along the way, despite her doubts about bringing him. His eagerness to see the school and see her in action won her over. Not that it took much to convince her to partake of more of his company.

Through the muddy, littered lanes she tried to match his strides, as if they were embarking on a grand expedition. He was hustling, she figured, out of concern he might have made her late. He smiled and she felt an arc of energy linking them. A grey-haired Roma woman lifted her chin and smiled as they passed.

"Can't wait to see what kind of a teacher you really are," said Tara.

"I'm on vacation. I'm just here to observe." He grinned another grin.

When they reached the school room, a dozen kids chanted, demanding apricots. "Kai-she! Kai-she! Kai-she!"

Mads stepped to the front and center position and stood still, capturing the children's attention without opening his mouth. Then he broke the silence, saying, "I have something better."

He reached into his pocket and took out four smooth stones, displaying the collection to the curious kids. He started to juggle, with two, then three, then all four stones whirling up toward the blue plastic tarp overhead and back down to his hands in a blur of motion. After a minute of this, he amused the students by thrusting his head forward into the middle of the spinning ellipse of stones, pretending to try to catch them in his mouth. In mid-performance he took a bow, letting the stones bounce off his back and clatter to the cement floor.

Tara led the applause and then said, "It's time for math."

Mads withdrew to the side. Midway through the hour, he slipped out. Before the class ended, he returned with two plump loaves of raisin walnut bread.

Late Sunday morning, deep in a rural district north of the capital, the town of Pritzi was having its moment in the sun. The mayor and assorted luminaries stood before a cluster of reporters and photographers, encircled by a wider gathering of curious citizens who blocked the main street.

At the center of attention, High Commissioner Cauchon gave requisite thanks to all involved in the EU-funded pedestrian crosswalk repainting project he had come out to commemorate. After extolling the economic and civic benefits of enhanced traffic safety, and with only minimal prompting from the assembled representatives of the media, he expounded his views on the events of the day, in particular regarding the border disagreement between Vodania and Pazaria.

"Perhaps the most effective way to address this issue," he opined, "would be via an international conference, to help de-escalate matters and promote dialogue. If all the parties were amenable, the European Union would be pleased to host such a conference here in Vodania."

Soon after the ceremony broke up, with a few citizens still lingering to admire the dazzling new crosswalks, a line of twenty dull green vehicles led by an armored personnel carrier caravanned up Highway 5 toward town. At each intersection along Pritzi's main street, thin plastic stanchions, linked to each other with strips of ribbon, protected the fresh paint on the roadway. The convoy kept coming.

The heavy treads of the lead APC crushed the stanchions and tore loose the ribbons and trampled two wide swaths through the fresh nite-glo white paint. The rest of the convoy smeared the paint into ghostly northbound streaks.

Tara figured it must be around noon. Up where they were, she and Mads, somewhere in the eastern range of the Asich Mountains, eight thousand feet above sea level, a fresh breeze blew. She shouldn't have been surprised that his idea of a Sunday hike would be pretty intense. Not following any trail, they scrambled over rocky outcrops and climbed through clusters of beech trees and skirted stands of pine. Upward and upward. They hadn't seen anyone for a couple of hours. Just the two of them in the world.

A world aglow with Mads. His thoughts and observations felt fresh and authentic, and he seemed to know when it was okay to let the silence linger. And when to flash that killer smile. In thinking about him, as it seemed she had been doing every chance she could since spilling his beer at the Locust Bar not quite two weeks prior, she considered the logic of protecting her heart. Of drawing a line. But how? She had never felt pulled to anyone so powerfully. Still, he was just passing through, and she didn't see herself as a just-passing-through kind of girl.

That all made sense, but she had no control over what she wanted. His love. Their paths had crossed, by luck or fate, and they had connected. Tara found herself looking back at the hike from some vantage in the future. Lamenting the loss of a doomed romance. Or lamenting the turning away from it. She shook her head. Don't overthink. Just live.

"What are you meditating about?" he asked, his voice sweet in her ears.

"You," she said, her breath coming out a little labored as they ascended into a clearing. Prepare to meet your doom.

"Me?" He pretended to be surprised.

"I've seen you dance but haven't heard you sing yet."

He laughed, the corners of his eyes crinkling, and kept walking.

"How about a Danish number?" she suggested. "How about your national anthem?"

Mads shook his head. "What do you think this is, the Olympics?"

"Sing it!"

"What for?"

"I want to hear what it sounds like. Please."

Tara stopped and faced Mads in the secluded meadow. With the grasses and ferns stirring around their legs, she reached for his left biceps and gave it a firm squeeze. She cocked her head to look into his eyes and watch him read her. From the flickers of his smile, she knew he understood she was teasing and earnest all at once. And that she was thriving on him, on their connection.

He raised his eyebrows. You sure?

She nodded several times.

He filled his lungs with mountain air, and his lips curved open, and out poured the soaring lyrics of Denmark's national anthem. His teeth glinted when he tipped his head back to strain for notes above his normal register.

Tara listened with her hands clasped in front of her. When he finished, she applauded and leaned forward to kiss his cheek.

"Lovely."

Mads shrugged. "You really need to hear the strings."

Tara stepped close and put her hands on his hips. "I really need to hear your heart."

She pressed her ear to his chest and held it there. "It sounds strong. Nice beat."

He put an arm around her. A little tentatively, maybe. Was he uncomfortable? Hesitant? She snuggled closer, feeling his warmth and his strength. She traced her fingertips up the sides of his ribcage, one ridge at a time. She wiggled her hands underneath the straps of his day pack and slipped it off his shoulders. Their bodies pressed together, and she could feel both their hearts thumping. Her doubts and her fears dissolved, she wanted no lines or boundaries.

Tara straightened, and tilted her face up. His lips touched hers. She closed her eyes as they kissed. A gust swirled her hair around their faces. His mouth felt soft, and warm with need. His fingers stroked her back and dipped inside the top of her waistband. A liquid quiver coursed through her.

Their kissing intensified. Mads reached down to grip the backs of her thighs, giving her more quivers. She hopped up to wrap her legs around his hips and he supported her with both hands. He lunged forward step by step, kissing her throat. She flung her head back and let the sensations wash over her.

He carried her to a level area next to a stand of junipers, and knelt slowly to lower her onto a bed of tall grasses. Behind a screen of meadow flowers, they rolled back and forth as they kissed. Making out in the open air gave Tara an extra charge, her sense of daring rising up over the instinct for privacy. Her skin tingled and her blood pulsed at the feel of Mads' body against hers, his breath, his low moans. She lifted the bottom of his shirt to kiss the flatness of his belly, savoring his scent.

They hastily helped each other out of their clothes and kicked their boots aside. His warmth blanketed her against the breeze. Birdsong and the chirping of insects rose up all around them. She had never made love in the open air in broad daylight. She felt wild and natural and delightfully scandalous.

After, glistening and groggy with well-being, Tara lay on top of him, chest to chest, her thighs balancing on his, her toes splayed open around the lower reaches of his shinbones. Under the cool sky she basked in the warmth rising from Mads and the sunlight bathing her skin.

In a little while, she put her hands on his shoulders and raised her torso into cobra pose, tilting her face up to the sun. When she opened her eyes, she loved the way Mads looked at her in that moment. So open. She lowered again and they held each other, breathing in sync, cheeks pressed together, lips touching at the edges. She listened to birds calling out from different parts of the meadow.

"I'm starting to get this mountain thing of yours," Tara purred into his ear.

"Mmm, good. You know, I'm thinking I should better stay in Vodania a little while longer."

"Yes, I think you better. There are a lot of mountains around here."

A thumping percussive noise arose, growing rapidly louder. Tara and Mads raised their heads, swiveling for the sound. The roar came from over the ridge behind them. They twisted to see two army helicopters grinding northward, rotors thwacking the mountain air.

Chapter 16

The embassy's section and agency heads sat alert in grim silence, aware this was not going to be a typical Monday morning staff meeting. For once, Andy did not need to feign concern. When he tipped off Farao about the landslide, he had expected fiery rhetoric from President Chilik and a disruption of the momentum toward signing a border agreement. But not large-scale troop deployments. From a career perspective, perhaps the only thing worse than starting a civil war would be instigating an attack on a U.S. ally.

When the ambassador arrived in the secure conference room, he came straight to the point.

"It has become abundantly clear why Chilik and company evaded all contact with us over the past several days. He has brought Vodania to a very dangerous place."

"Which increases our threat levels," Ken Dewitt, the regional security officer, jumped in.

"We can all do the math," the ambassador replied. "If war breaks out, the U.S. is going to side with Pazaria. So will thirty-five to forty percent of this country. War plus civil war equals big trouble for this embassy."

Andy grimaced. He hoped Chilik was just taking bluster to a new level. But maybe other calculations had come into play. The loudest thought screaming in Andy's head was, how much time do I have? How long before, whether by accident or design, catastrophe crashed down onto his delicate plans? The mayhem of war would demolish all opportunities to shape events and position himself for advancement. And could easily expose him and his career to an ignominious end.

The ambassador looked around at the worried faces of his country team. "So, yes. Reduce burn times and send out notifications and all the usual drill. And keep your people resilient."

Resilience, whatever that was supposed to mean, would not be enough, Andy knew. At least not for him.

Inside the State Department on Monday evening, a profound hush permeated the office of the assistant secretary for European and Eurasian Affairs, evoking layers of dignity and decorum built up over generations. The suite's sixth-floor vantage, situated one floor below the office of the secretary of state, afforded timeless views over the Lincoln Memorial and across the Potomac. From this powerful, storied position, successive giants of diplomacy have directed America's relations with its closest allies and most implacable adversaries, who were often one and the same. In presiding over EUR, the largest and most venerable of State's geographic bureaus, the assistant secretary was charged with carrying forward these proud traditions of statecraft. The role carried deeply embedded expectations of managing events across much of the globe. The responsibilities weighed mightily, the stakes never less than enormous.

Vonda Vance felt the burden as the assistant secretary beamed at her and, in a plummy voice, asked, "What the goddamn fuck is going on in Vodania?"

Vespers. By tradition, the bureau's handful-plus of deputy assistant secretaries gathered every evening in chairs and settees arranged in front of the assistant secretary's desk, there to consider and resolve the pressing problems of the day. In this inner circle, a somber, tight-knit family atmosphere prevailed. With the spotlights trained on Vonda, the other elders could relax and savor the moment.

"Over the weekend, Chilik sent troops to the border with Pazaria," Vonda began, "with more en route today. They're taking up positions on the ridges. Now the Pazarians are doing the same."

"Last week we were talking about a border deal and a signing ceremony. W, T, F?"

"There was a minor rockslide or something which very slightly altered the course of the Odorian up in a remote section of the border. It's unclear how anyone even noticed it, since the gorge there is so deep and narrow you can't even see the river except from directly overhead. But Chilik is just like a Bosniak or a Serb, so obsessed with fragments of territory. This is exactly the kind of move you'd expect from someone like—"

"Jesus FUCK." The assistant secretary cut off the comparison. "Need I remind all that the secretary explicitly directed that we NOT shit all over August with another crisis this year. For a change."

Eyes brimming with empathy, the assistant secretary spoke to Vonda in a soothing tone that somehow reinforced the sense of implacable determination with which EUR addressed all challenges. "Do I fucking need to call fucking Chil and Pris and rip them both a new one?"

Principal deputy assistant secretary Geoff Bentwood smiled and nodded in support. Vonda knew that if he were ever to repeat the line, he would amend it to rip them *each* a new one.

"The NSC is hosting an interagency tomorrow to consider next steps. A U.S.-Pazaria military exercise is one option," Vonda noted.

Vonda braced herself. Everyone knew the assistant secretary indulged in a family beach week in North Carolina every August, detached for the most part from the relentless struggle for status and advancement in Washington. Vonda pictured that pleasant interlude in ruins due to the actions of countries she was supposed to be managing. Not fucking good.

The assistant secretary blinked once, very slowly. "We gotta unfuck this cock-up and get those assholes back in line." With a benevolent smile, the assistant secretary emphasized the gravity of the situation by adding, "And the photo op with POTUS is off the goddamn fucking table."

After sunrise on Tuesday, a desolate, semi-arid wilderness devoid of habitation teemed with bizarre human activity, as if Burning Man had moved to the Asich Mountains. Along a thirty-kilometer stretch near the tops of the cliffs and peaks south of the Odorian River, Vodania's troops did their best to set up encampments on the flattest areas they could find. At ten to twelve thousand feet, the stony, treeless terrain did not welcome tents and other structures. The Vodanian army placed observation and sniper teams up on the ridges on their side of the gorge, and the Pazarian army mirrored their positions. Clusters of soldiers moved around, working on their projects. But there was very little music to be heard, and no dancing.

In the mountains approaching the border area, Vodanian field artillery units struggled heroically to drag howitzers and towed-rifled mortars to high ground. They improvised, chaining together multiple four-wheel drive trucks to tug the weapons uphill. Motors whined and tires spun, and the slopes resisted.

A reserve platoon, fifty-two strong, drew the assignment of placing a mortar on an especially steep mountaintop. Most of the group stood, cigarettes clamped between their lips, watching smoke pour from the engine block of an all-terrain vehicle locked in an unfair fight with gravity. A young corporal couldn't refrain from stating the obvious.

"These weapons are not for the mountains."

"Orders."

"Yes, okay," another corporal spoke up. "But even if we do get this gun up there, somehow, those next peaks are blocking our trajectory. We'll have to aim almost vertical, with a big loss of accuracy."

The platoon leader spun around. "Just because it's stupid doesn't mean it doesn't make sense."

Doug Watanabe reminded himself that Director Stavroski, the head of Vodania's National Police Agency, was not an unfriendly man. He just acted that way.

After a suitable power-wait in the outer reception area, an aide escorted Doug into the director's office. In Stavroski's lair, the leather furniture gleamed in burnished splendor. Plaques and group photos from police conferences and graduation ceremonies crowded the wall. On all available surfaces of the coffee table, desk, and end tables, an assemblage of commemorative medallions and tchotchkes signified fraternal relations with the police of many lands.

After enduring Stavroski's semi-cordial pleasantries, Doug made the pitch for going after Marko. Stavroski puckered his mouth and listened, then reflected for a few moments before replying.

"This might not be the time. We have resource shortages, and Marko has not yet done anything to make himself a priority. And now the military situation with Pazaria. A lot of tension."

"You think there's going to be a war?" Doug asked.

"I think there is going to be an election." Stavroski ground out a sort of a smile. "Our people need to be everywhere, except where we're not supposed to be."

"I get it," Doug nodded. "Been there. We used to face the same thing in Los Angeles."

After the conversation meandered around about training programs and an Interpol delegation that planned to visit Vodania in the fall, Doug came back to Marko.

"I'm thinking there's a good argument for this being the time. Before Marko grows too big, too powerful, and damages the reputation of Vodania, the investment climate, all that. We start small, a probe. A controlled buy to establish a relationship with someone on the inside, who we can then work. We get a better sense of what we're dealing with. Then, after the election, think about making a bigger move."

Stavroski started to respond, presumably to object, but Doug held up his hand and said, "Before you answer, let me put one more thing out there. You mentioned resources, and I get that. And I want to help. I'm confident I can come up with two more vehicles for your force, for undercover work. But I need to show my headquarters that we have active cooperation underway."

Stavroski frowned in silence, his lips pursed. Wavering. Doug had one more card to play, his ace in the hole. The trip dangle.

"While you're thinking about it, let me raise one other issue," Doug ventured. "The Justice Department is planning to host a major international law enforcement conference in Washington next spring. They'll be starting to put together the invite list fairly soon."

He paused to gauge Stavroski's response to the enticement of an all-expenses-paid trip to America. "At some point," Doug resumed his pitch, "I'm going to want to check on your potential availability and get your advice as to who else we should include from Vodania."

Stavroski's pupils dilated for a split second. "Sure, I can help you with that."

Midmorning in the general services office on Tuesday, Tara sat uncomfortably in one of Chuck's chairs. The faces of the three spouses in front of his desk glowed red with righteous indignation.

"It's like, HELLO! We have preschool kids too."

"No one seems to be able to tell us if we're going to be evacuated or not. But if we're not, our kids deserve protective flooring in our playrooms."

"It's only fair."

Tara listened politely to the women, who all stood a rung or two above her on life's ladder.

Chuck looked like he wanted to rip the carpet out of the Mitchells' basement with his own hands and burn it. For a prolonged moment he fixed his glare on Tara, as if to say problems like these can never be solved. They can only be prevented.

To the spousal delegation he repeated, "Please understand that right now our first priority has to be evacuation preparation." He uncrossed his legs and crossed them the other way. "That's why we sent out the readiness reminder to the whole community yesterday. Passports, medical records, key documents, and valuables that can all fit in a carry-on item. We don't know how this stand-off is going to develop or devolve."

"Chuck, we get that. We really do," said the spouse of a USAID officer. "But there needs to be a degree of transparency and basic interagency equality in how families get treated in this mission."

"If I may," Tara ventured after an awkward silence. "We were not aware that others had the same concern. Now that we know, we'll keep alert to possible ways we might be able to help."

"Consistent with the housing standards and budget resources," Chuck hastened to add.

Both sides repeated their points again for several cycles, until the spouses finally departed with the understanding that they would all grapple with the matter further if they didn't need to flee for their lives in the face of war and interethnic conflagration. Tara lingered behind.

"I hope you're pleased with yourself, problem-solver," Chuck muttered, swiveling to glower into his computer screen.

As Tara stepped out of Chuck's office, Robert beckoned to her from down the corridor. She pivoted and headed toward the management counselor's office, trying not to look angry or resentful.

"Let me tell ya something, Tara. Come on, sit down for a sec."

Tara seated herself in one of the ergonomic armchairs in front of Robert's desk. He moved to the side of the desk and settled his right buttock on a clear spot on the edge, allowing his right foot to swing like a pendulum as he talked. His left foot remained planted on the carpeting. Tara supposed he intended this positioning to signal that the conversation was less formal and hierarchical than one taking place across the surface of a desk.

"If you're going to be successful in the management cone, you need to realize what it is we're actually managing," he began, smiling reassuringly. "It's not what people think. It's not resources or personnel or property."

Tara looked at Robert and wondered why his neckties were always too long. Trying to cover something?

"Think about a tennis racquet," Robert urged. "You can't have some strings too tight and others too loose, right?"

"Isn't it all the same string?"

"That's precisely the point!" Robert beamed.

"What do we manage, really?" he continued. "We manage happiness. And in principle it's pretty simple. An ambassador can never have too much happiness. Same for a DCM, except that the DCM can't be in any way happier than the ambassador. For everyone else, we have to manage it. You see, happiness is relative and finite. Providing happiness to one necessarily means taking happiness from another. It's our job to maintain the proper balance."

Hal Passer, the executive assistant to DEA division chief Ellis Caffrey, put his phone on speaker so he could stir the morning's second cup of coffee. For this he used a brass letter-opener he found in the desk drawer when he got the job a couple years back. The tarnished, mottled implement had probably resided in the same drawer in the same office on the same olive-green Drug Enforcement Agency hallway since the 1980s. He stopped stirring and spoke toward the phone.

"Has Watanabe asked you for a case number yet?"

"What for?" came the distant voice of DEA special agent Giardis, eight hours ahead in Embassy Zagovor. It sounded like he was pacing around a conference room, also with the phone on speaker. Maybe it was a DEA thing.

"He hasn't told you? His ambassador's dog puke?" Passer replied.

"You gotta be shittin' me," said Giardis with a dry laugh.

The exec went on to tell Giardis about Ambassador Lamkin's sick dog, presumably poisoned, and how Watanabe wanted to test the vomit for controlled substances.

"What a doofus," Giardis snorted. "And in case you're wondering, I'm not giving him a goddamn case number."

The sound of pacing stopped. "Listen," said Giardis, his mouth closer to the phone, "there is a promising development, though, that I need you to pass to Caffrey. He will definitely be interested."

Passer could picture Giardis scowling, arms folded, legs planted wide, as if he didn't appreciate having to go through the proper channels. A lot of the field agents had that attitude, feeling they deserved more face time with the division chief. As if the exec was just, what, a concierge?

"We're picking up indications of a new outfit in the Asich Mountains," Giardis explained. "The group, or the leader, is named Marko. Very shadowy. No traceable electronic communications. This may be the major pipeline we've been concerned about. Operating on both sides of the border."

"Cool. I'll let him know you're on it."

"Thanks man. Hey, I gotta run, my ambassador needs this room for a call at 5:30. Tell Caffrey I'm going after Marko aggressively."

A couple minutes after the scheduled start of the three-way call, 9:30 a.m. Washington time, 5:30 p.m. in Shizl and Zagovor, the assistant secretary's voice purred from the speakers in each embassy's secure conference room.

"Lamkin, Kunninger, how are you guys?"

"We're having a grand time in Zagovor," ventured Nancy Kunninger, U.S. ambassador to Pazaria. "Maybe you could send us another co-del. More congressional visitors would only add to the fun."

"Wouldn't that be the fucking shit," the assistant secretary chortled. "Let me see what I can do. Lamkin, how are you and yours holding up?"

"Challenging times. But we're all about the resiliency," Ambassador Lamkin responded, peering into the microphone on the conference table in front of him.

"Alright, fuckin'-A. Where do we go from here?"

"With all due respect, we gotta rein in that nut-job in Shizl," Ambassador Kunninger asserted. "He's really destabilizing this region."

"Chilik is a Vodanian through and through, no question about that," Ambassador Lamkin responded. "To get him back on the reservation we're going to need a nuanced, two-track policy. Maybe three."

"Go on," encouraged the assistant secretary.

"Well, military deterrence certainly, to make sure he understands the full consequences of crossing the border. But we also need to recognize the significant complexities in the fabric of power here, with the elections coming up and the nationalists ready to pounce on any whiff of weakness. To get the border dispute straightened out, we may need to pull a few levers with Prime Minister Prismar."

"Pris is not the one who started this shit storm," the assistant secretary replied. "We gotta grab Chil by the balls and squeeze like holy fucking hell."

Inside Embassy Shizl's secure conference room, Gary Hambert suddenly sneezed with shocking force. General Elfersen, startled, dropped his pen, and while it was still clattering around, he grabbed for it and accidentally slapped it across the table into the microphone.

Ambassador Lamkin glared furiously.

"Well squeeze my dick and suck my tits," the assistant secretary exclaimed. "Jesus H. Christ it sounds like the whole fucking congregation is in on this call. It's supposed to be principals only." The assistant secretary winked at Geoff and Vonda, seated across the table in the EUR conference room, and spoke in a voice of liquid velvet, "Hello there, welcome every-fucking-one."

On a drowsy Tuesday afternoon at the Defense Intelligence Agency, Lt. Col. Marvin 'Marvy' Grafter, who ran the procurement office of DIA's center for combating terrorism, looked around his auxiliary briefing room at a dozen or so office directors and budget honchos. Mostly middle-aged guys like himself.

"Anyone catch any of the Winston-Salem Open last weekend? Some great matches in men's singles."

Marvy read somewhere that it was optimal management practice to open any meeting on a lighter, more social note. According to the experts, it was almost as important as distributing an agenda in advance.

"More and more players are using it as a tune-up for the U.S. Open," Marvy continued.

Still, no one responded.

"I know, tennis is such a civilian sport. But football hasn't started yet so whaddya gonna do?" Marvy grinned and swept his eyes around, looking for a positive reaction. Or any reaction.

Marvy put both palms flat on the table and said, "Alright, let's get down to business. Our goal today is pretty straightforward. We just need to spend twelve million to close out the ops account. Leadership directed that we top off our accounts early this year to avoid an unseemly, news-making rush in September."

"Sir." A stocky man in a severely pressed uniform put up his hand. "A lot of folks are on leave this week and next. Gonna make it hard to push things through, especially with regards to concurrences."

"Thank you for bringing that up, Major. We have a week tops, so there will be a premium on projects that are ready to go, that don't need permission slips from half the Pentagon, or Lord help us, from CIA or State."

Marvy paused in case there were any other questions. "Okay, let's go around the table. Tell me what you got in the pipeline that we can push through. We need projects that can start within the month of August."

When his turn came, Lt. Col. Hensrath offered, "I got a short turnaround requirements analysis underway that I sole-sourced with one of my regular vendors. It'll burn fifty K."

Someone snorted, prompting Marvy to say, "Every little bit helps."

"It comes with a phase two for implementation, which is currently set up as a separate decision process," Hensrath continued. "But if we combine both phases into one tasking order it'll bring the cost up to one point two million."

"Sounds great, if your vendor can launch by August 31," said Marvy. "What about approvals?"

"It's a non-lethal, covert CT intel op. We can fast-track it without interagency review."

"Perfect. Put it in."

Chapter 17

On Wednesday morning Doug Watanabe drove out of the city, drumming his fingers on the steering wheel, windows down to catch the last of the morning freshness. About time he sank his teeth into a real case again. Approaching the checkpoint at the entrance to the police training compound, he spotted a red goat symbol spray-painted on the perimeter wall.

"Marko, your days are numbered," Doug said out loud. "You got LAPD on your trail. Your ass is mine."

Inside an austere classroom, the executive director of the police academy introduced Doug to a group of officers working the Pazari-dominated parts of the country.

Doug outlined his approach. "We need to structure this as a counternarcotics training exercise, to fit within my legal and bureaucratic mandate. You know how that goes. But it still has to be real. You need to bring local police on board, work your informants. Offer reward money. My government can put up five hundred dollars for good info."

"Plus, the cars. The chief mentioned that," the academy director added.

"Correct," Doug confirmed. "If we're successfully cooperating, I can arrange for two undercover vehicles for you guys."

"At this stage we're investigating, we're probing," Doug continued his presentation. "Once we establish contact with someone in the organization, we set up a sting, a controlled buy. Then you make the bust, and we flip him. With an informant on the inside, we map out the organization and go from there."

"One problem," said the western district commander, who struck Doug as not too eager to take this on when they first discussed it at Vodania Forever the previous week. "Assuming we find someone to run a sting against, who's our buyer? Our undercover guys are all busy these days."

"I'll be the buyer," Doug replied without hesitation. How long since he'd done something like that? "I'll be Turkish. I'll say I have a pipeline through Turkey, with room for more product."

Going after Marko gave Doug an uplift, a surge of inner vitality. That energy carried him through an afternoon of expenditure paperwork and impact measurement write-ups. Strong, fit, on top of his game. Until it was time to call the DEA lab.

"If it arrives without a case number, we're sending it back. Normally we'd destroy it," said the assistant manager of the lab.

"What if I get someone from headquarters to call you?" Doug pleaded.

"Long's they're calling with a case number. We gotta know what account to charge the testing to."

The art of sitting. By observing the retired colonels and generals who landed at Harrimore Services for their follow-on careers, Travis had learned how to occupy a chair in his military clients' offices. With practice, he came to excel at calibrating the proper point along the continuum from rigid to at-ease. The idea was to display respect and then evolve into warmth and collaboration. The exact posture depended on the relationship and the context.

In Lt. Col. Hensrath's DIA office late Wednesday morning, Travis reclined on the couch almost like he was about to watch a movie on the flat screen in his basement. But he didn't put his feet up on the coffee table.

"Good news, buddy," Hensrath said. "On the requirements analysis for Shizl?"

Travis nodded noncommittally.

"We're going to fast track it. Combine the assessment and phase two, the implementation. Can you deliver?"

"Harrimore always delivers."

"Alright, here's the thing. How much time do you need to neutralize a dog? Can your team move out next week? Reason being, we gotta have it launched by the end of August, so it doesn't look like year-end padding."

"Understood. Remind me of the price point for phase two," Travis requested.

"It totals one point two mil. The fifty K for the assessment you're already doing is part of that."

"One point two mil," Travis repeated. "Meaning one point one five for the implementation. Whatever. Can do, sir."

Tara escaped from the office before six on Thursday and raced her Wrangler toward Shizl's central plaza. She had seen Mads only once since their glorious hike on Sunday. A lovely late-evening rendezvous, but it wasn't enough. Embassy craziness, reflecting the Vodania-Pazaria craziness, kept things stressed all week. No one knew what would happen. But Tara's emergency plans were planned, and her preparations were prepped. She deserved an outdoor café, a glass of wine, and her man. And really didn't much care what her supervisor Chuck or anyone else thought about her daring to do something other than hovering nervously in her cubicle.

The central plaza, the city's heart, pumped life and human energy from one converging artery to another. Even more frenetically than usual, Tara thought. In a green space along the western edge, at the base of the massive ancient fortress, she found an unoccupied bench under the shade of a broad-leafed linden. With the abusive afternoon swelter receding a degree or two, the city's pulse increased, measurable in the rhythm of footsteps, the swirling streams of youths on summer leave from school desks, and the jumble of workers newly freed from their shops and cubicles. Tara gazed past the crowds on the plaza and up the narrow street she expected Mads to arrive from.

She inhaled her momentary feeling of liberty as well. At least here there was little chance of the DCM staring question marks at her, panting like a dog in heat for any scrap of news or rumor about the Davos poisoning. In the cafeteria, at the motor pool, rounding a corridor, she never knew when he would suddenly appear. It felt like some kind of creepy game. How does the DCM expect me to figure out who poisoned the ambassador's dog, Tara wondered? Maybe he doesn't. Maybe he did it himself.

She was just about to open a new paperback she'd received in the latest mail shipment, when a commotion on the plaza caught her attention. A group of Vodanians surrounded four Pazari teenagers. They had knocked their hats to the ground and were kicking them back and forth like soccer balls. It took the Pazaris a minute or two of furious scrambling to retrieve their head coverings and escape the taunting throng. The four youths hustled away from the plaza along the path toward Tara's shade tree, seething with adrenaline.

On the grass near Tara's bench, a Roma man played with two toddlers while his wife laid out their dinner on a piece of cloth. As the Pazaris approached, they yelled something Tara couldn't understand. The woman seized the two children and clutched them to her chest. One of the teenagers picked up a fallen tree limb the size of a baseball bat. The group advanced on the family. The Roma man, still seated, folded his arms over his head.

Tara jumped up and hurried toward the teenagers. "Excuse me!" she demanded in a touristy voice. "Where's the ancient fortress?" She held open her novel as if it were a guidebook.

The youths paused to regard her.

"I'm looking for the ancient fortress," she repeated, frowning into her book.

After a moment, one of the young men pointed to the enormous rampart that loomed above the plaza and said, "It's right behind you."

Tara glanced at the hulking stone structure and replied, "I mean the big one."

They stared at her in silence.

"It's the biggest fort in Wodania!" said the youth with the large stick. "Probably the biggest in this whole area."

Tara looked at the fortress again. She noticed a red goat spray-painted high up on the sheer wall. She smiled back at the group as if she knew they were kidding her.

"Really? Okay," Tara responded. She started to walk away. "Maybe I'll ask somebody else."

"You're crazy. It's the biggest!" exclaimed the stick wielder.

"Where are you from?" demanded another.

Tara stopped and turned. "America."

"America, our friend," one of them responded, in reflexive Pazari fashion.

Tara stepped closer and fist-bumped each of them.

The stick holder asked, "What about the forts in America?"

"We don't have anything as old as this," Tara replied. "But we have some very big military bases."

"How big?"

"Some of them are bigger than Vodania."

By now the Roma family had gathered up their food and moved away from the scene. Tara spotted Mads striding across the plaza and she waved.

The teenagers turned to look and Tara said, "Would you like to show my friend and me the fortress?"

They shook their heads. One of them added, "It's just old stone walls."

Over the course of the week since Chilik sent his troops to the border, the embassy's secure conference room had transformed into a command center. Computer workstations and secure phones crowded the main table. Large topographical maps covered the walls, competing with whiteboards filled with tasking reminders and key phone numbers. Affixed high on the wall opposite the ambassador's seat was a clock set to Washington time.

With DCM Andy Pulano in the role of conductor, the embassy staff had established a rhythm of election updates, press summaries, twice-daily situation-reports to Washington, conference calls with Embassy Zagovor morning, noon, and night. Security environment assessments, evacuation planning. In the hallway outside, the cleaning crew added oversized trash receptacles to handle the outflow of pizza boxes and kebab containers and a mountain of caffeinated soda cans.

On Saturday morning, with a decisive thrust of the airlock door, the ambassador appeared in his customary weekend attire: slacks, blazer, no tie. The staff on duty started to rise, but the ambassador waved them down while striding briskly to his place at the table.

"Stay on task everyone. Good morning! Pleasant out today." He picked up the sit-rep waiting for his approval and scanned it, reading select phrases aloud.

"Campaign posters defaced or removed in Pritzi, Harabad, and several locations in Shizl. Military deployment and configuration unchanged, no hostilities reported, supply pipeline improving, limited troop rotations. Media decry Prime Minister Prismar's 'aggressive' speech. Foreign ministry delegation departs for UN meeting in New York."

The ambassador swiveled a few degrees toward Andy and clapped him lightly on the shoulder. "Nice work, send it."

Like he was rewarding an obedient pet.

That evening, in the national stadium, music thundered from stacks of loudspeakers. A sinking orange sun lit up the massive flags lined up in formation around the entire top of the stadium. Vodania's national banner depicted a brown falcon gripping a red rat in its talons, centered on a muted green background. Outsiders to the region often confused it with Pazaria's flag, which had an identical muted green background. But Pazaria's emblem showed a red wolf eating a brown sparrow.

On stage, the Krushers, a popular Shizl band, blasted a volcano of amped up traditional folk melodies laced with indignant raps. Ethnic Vodanians, many bused in from towns and villages in the eastern part of the country, filled the stadium close to capacity. Most of those present waved smaller versions of the flag, handed out by volunteers at the entrances. When President Chilik strode onto the stage, they all stood and took their cigarettes out of their mouths and shouted, "Vodaniaaaa!"

"Vodania!" responded Chilik.

The crowd cheered again, "Vodaniaaaaaa!"

"VO-DA-NI-AAAAAAA!" chanted Chilik, gripping the microphone with both hands.

"Vodaniaaaaaa!"

"VO-DA-NI-AAAAAAA!"

The cycle continued for several more rounds until Chilik screamed "VO!" and pointed the mic at the seating section in front of him.

"VO!" they repeated.

Chilik pivoted to his right, roared "DA," and pointed to that section.

"DA!" came roaring back.

"NI!" to the seats behind him.

"NI!" from thousands of voices.

"AAA!" Chilik hollered to his left.

"AAAAAAA!" they responded.

Chilik put one hand over his heart and with the other pointed the microphone at the seats in front of him.

"VO!" they screamed.

At a deliberate pace, he pointed at each of the other sections in turn, and they obliged with "DA!" "NI!" "AAA!"

Chilik repeated the exercise, a little faster. And another round, a little faster. VO-DA-NI-AAA, VO-DA-NI-AAA, VO-DA-NI-AAA! And again, and again, until the convulsions of foot-stomping, throat-ripping chants threatened to collapse the stadium. At the crescendo, Chilik waved his uplifted arms to signify all-together-now, and the exhilarated partisans combined their voices, doing their utmost to project "VODANIA!" over the mountains and all the way to Zagovor.

As the crowd settled and caught its breath, Chilik assumed a more formal posture and began his remarks.

"Citizens of Vodania, we are united. As united as we have ever been," he opened. "And we need to be. We face intense, choking pressure. Pressure from powerful nations who do not know what it means to be Vodanian."

Cheers from the stadium.

"They want to smother us. But we will make ourselves heard."

He pointed the microphone at the audience, who summoned up another collective "VO-DA-NI-AAA!"

In an upper row of the stadium, Tara turned to Mads. "Heard enough?"

"You promised there'd be fireworks," Mads teased.

"There will be," she answered, raking her fingers down his torso.

Chapter 18

Shortly after dawn on Monday of the last week of August, a mid-level Harrimore ops coordinator made a left turn into an unmarked gravel lane twelve miles northwest of the crossroads hamlet of Wild Oaks, on the Virginia side of the Shenandoahs. He drove uphill for a quarter mile through scrubby pines, whose silhouettes against the sunrise created a strobe effect as he sped through. Around a sharp bend, the security checkpoint came into view, a standard-issue, fortified two-man post. The company tended to save the fancy stuff for its clients.

The ops coordinator lowered his window and handed his Harrimore credential through a narrow slot. The middle-aged woman in the booth checked it against a list and then pressed a button to lower the hydraulic barrier. The ops coordinator drove on up through another stretch of woods to a broad, level parking lot. A dozen rectangular one-story buildings formed a boxy campus. In the vicinity of Building G, he switched off the ignition. From the front seat he gathered his laptop and a packet of forms and briefing materials. He straightened his spine and strode through the clear mountain air. So much more invigorating than the swampiness of D.C. He had a mission to run.

Going through the parking lot he smiled at the sight of a pickup truck with two cases of empties and a bunch of fly rods and rubber waders strewn around the back. Good ole Darrell made it on time, despite all the bitching and moaning about having to cut short his fishing expedition. He needed the work. Ten thousand for a job lasting a week or so, plus completion bonus. Not bad.

Inside the briefing room, the ops coordinator allowed thirty minutes for coffee and in-processing, plenty for a six-person crew. He sized up the group as he distributed the paperwork, aware they were sizing each other up too. The crew showed the alertness and the energy expected when prepping an operation. After making sure he had all the waivers and contracts signed, the ops coordinator stepped to the side of the room, where a grouping of metal folding chairs formed a semicircle.

"Team," he announced. "Let's get started."

They shifted over and sat. The ops coordinator pulled a chair into the gap in the semicircle. He indicated the man on his left, said, "Chris Braxton here is your platoon leader. But this is a covert mission and we're not using names. Alright, let's count off."

He glanced to his left, and after a pause the woman to Braxton's left said "One."

The tall man next to her followed, "Two."

"Wait, hold up right there," the ops coordinator interjected. "The count starts here." He put his hand on Braxton's shoulder. "Go."

"One," said Braxton.

"Two," said the woman.

"Three," said the tall guy.

"Four," said the man wearing fishing gear.

The next guy said nothing but lifted one hand with his fingers and thumb spread apart.

"Guess that makes me six," said the last man.

Not a bad mix. All fairly recent combat veterans, they each had completed at least three operations for Harrimore Services. They looked fit.

One and Three had been Rangers, and Five was a Seal. Two served as an Army medic, and Four was a decorated Marine Corps sniper. Six's background was classified above the ops coordinator's level.

"I am so looking forward to a dose of Puccini," the ambassador sighed after another long day of fruitless diplomacy.

Seated upright in the center of their bed, still wearing his suit and tie, Ambassador Lamkin eased his shoulders against the headboard and allowed his eyelids to slide closed. He had removed his wingtips and lined them up on the carpet, perpendicular to the bed and facing outward. The ambassador's legs extended straight in front of him. He wiggled his toes inside their black socks.

Lithia sat on the edge of the bed, her feet on the floor with Davos sprawled on top of them.

She bent to stroke the dog's head. "Vienna will be wonderful. I just wish we could take this big boy with us and not put him in that place."

"It's just for two nights. He'll be okay."

"I know but it's smelly in there."

"Well, yes. Kennel, dogs."

"Davos deserves better."

Later that evening, in the town of Kharbam in western Vodania, a meeting got underway in a back room at the Camel Club. Everybody was angry. Always angry. That was the world Shariz operated in.

One of his favorite leadership techniques was to be the angriest guy in the room. In his realm of shadowy enterprises, with conflicting and overlapping rivalries and alliances, there were few clear rules. Staying on top required keeping rivals off-balance. Shariz often found he could best advance his interests by fiercely adopting others' grievances as his own, or by introducing counteraccusations to raise the stakes. He found his temper could often be a more effective tool than a gun, a bribe, or a subordinate.

Sprawled on black leather couches, half a dozen men smoked intently. They were upset because police agents from both Pazaria and Wodania, as they pronounced it, had recently started nosing around about Marko. Shariz became more upset.

"What is this Marko shit?" Shariz demanded. "Who ever heard of him? He is nobody!" Shariz spat on the floor of his own clubhouse.

"You know what this is?" Shariz demanded. "An excuse to move in on our territory, to interfere with our businesses!"

"We need to make it painful for them," a man in the corner said.

"Yes, we do," Shariz answered. "And not so painful for us."

"We should take a few shots at these cops," said a man sitting on a couch with his arms crossed.

"I don't want more cops and more soldiers in my territory!" Shariz screamed. "They're all over the eastern mountains and getting closer. I don't like it. Do you?" He glared around the dim room and snapped the waistband on his red compression shorts.

"We start shooting at cops and we give the armies of both sides a good reason to move in here with us," Shariz asserted. "I don't want to share my bed with any stinking soldier and his lice."

This produced a few snorts from around the room.

"Here is my question for all of you," Shariz continued. "What happens when a controlled buy meets a controlled sell?"

This silenced the room for half a minute, until one of the couch men said, "You don't think they'll talk to each other, figure it out?"

"Does it look like they're talking to each other now?" Shariz retorted, rising up from his seat. "You guys think about it, talk about it. I'm going to take a piss," he announced, and walked out the door.

Wearing a dark blue sleeveless workout shirt that partially covered his form-fitting underpants, Shariz strolled through his establishment. He checked in with the gambling manager, pawed the exposed buttocks of a couple of his dancers, chatted with the bartenders. When he returned to the back room, a lively discussion was underway.

Shariz stretched his hip joint by standing with one foot on the floor and raising his other leg perpendicular to rest his toes on the arm of a couch. Tilting forward at a forty-five-degree angle, he looked at the group and said "What do you think?"

"We can try it, to embarrass the cops and make them ashamed to come here," said one of the older men present. "We can tell them both they can meet Marko, but only on the border."

"Good," Shariz replied. "Where were you thinking?"

"We talked about Mount Korat or Bijar Peak, or one of the high passes, like Tonguebite or Sheeptooth."

"A pass is better, keep them off the high slopes," Shariz decided. "I like Tonguebite, it's farther from here. Can we agree?"

The standard pre-mission drill continued at the Wild Oaks site. Harrimore trainers sent the Shizl team on a warm-up jaunt through part of the obstacle course, back to campus for physicals, over to the range to get recertified on their weapons. After chow, the squad walked from the cafeteria over to the briefing room in Building G.

The ops coordinator opened with an intel brief on President Chilik that Harrimore analysts cobbled together from DIA materials and public sources. It focused primarily on the compound and guard force. The ops coordinator clicked through a series of satellite images. Various angles, different resolutions.

"The mission objective is to tranquilize the guard dog inside the compound, with complete stealth, leaving absolutely no evidence of your presence."

No one on the team was green enough to ask why.

The ops coordinator beamed his laser pointer at the map projected onto the side wall. "You'll fly commercial into Zagovor on Wednesday afternoon, arriving Thursday morning. You will be escorted to special isolation housing on Camp Stability. Our aviation contractor has access to base flight ops, and on Saturday night they'll fly you fixed-wing to the border, twenty-five minutes away."

The ops coordinator continued blasting at the map with his laser pointer. "Your infiltration drop point is here, just on the other side of the mountains. The advance will position vehicles for you here and here. The borders are fairly porous, and exfiltration will be overland. The primary exit is here, and alternatives are here, here, and over here in the west. If necessary, we'll send in a helo."

Most of the team members nodded to show they got it.

"What kinda tranquilizer we using?" asked Six.

"You'll have long-range dart rifles, pistols, blow pipes, and a hand-held syringe option, all fitted with two types of medication. After this brief, the equipment folks will walk you through all that."

"Not a problem," Six replied.

On Tuesday morning, the DIA operations support officer glanced at a global time zone map before tapping in the digits for a secure call to the defense attaché office in Embassy Shizl. It would still be before five there.

Gen. Elfersen's deputy picked up. "DAO Shizl, this is Mesko."

"Hello sir, ops support here. We got that capabilities assessment you been waiting for."

"Hoo-aah!"

"The contractor came up with three options. The minimal requirements are assessed at six special forces personnel, possessing advanced training, tactics, and equipment. They worked up a whole list, you'll see it. The high option would put three teams on the ground and one in the air. The middle option came out, you know, somewhere in the middle. Word we got, the low option was the most plausible scenario. I'm sending you the electrons now but wanted to call first to give a heads-up and make sure this is what you're looking for."

"Good to go. Appreciate the quick turn around," Mesko said.

"Got your back."

Along the main drag in Pritzi, in western Vodania, a man named Hamun strutted through harsh late afternoon sunlight. He pushed through a door into the High Street Lounge like he'd been there before. And he probably had. Whether from personal preference or professional duty, he was acquainted with most of the skuzzier spots in this part of the country. He may not have been proud of his work as a stringer for the police, exactly, but he'd always had a talent for mixing it up with anyone and everyone. Why not get paid a little for it? And after almost five years inside on robbery and drug charges, he wasn't swamped with great options. Plus, if he got into any trouble along the way, it could be brushed off as part of maintaining his cover.

Music videos from Russia and Turkey flickered on the dusty screen, the volume one notch above annoying. Through the welcoming haze of smoke, Hamun spotted his guy, a jumpy-looking young man worrying over his angles on the still-playable pool table in the back. His informant. His sub-contractor, to use the government terminology. Hamun approached the bar and ordered a glass of the local pear brandy. There were only three other patrons in the place, and they didn't raise any concerns.

After savoring the top half of the drink in a single smooth gulp, Hamun swiveled his head to look around the room. He got up, glass in hand, and sauntered to the back. His informant looked up from across the pool table.

"Anything moving?" Hamun asked.

"Quiet mostly. They're still fighting about the council seats."

"Think there'll be action?"

"I don't know, Uncle. So far, it's threats and preparations."

"Keep an eye on it."

The informant nodded as he lined up his next shot.

After the billiard balls finished clacking and bumping around the worn felt, Hamun asked, "What about my friend?"

"Who?"

"The one I asked you about last week."

"No one wants to talk about him." He took his next shot and sank the nine-ball. "Or no one knows anything."

"You were supposed to make that a priority."

"Yeah, well, there's nothing. I been listening, bringing him up in conversations."

"Can't believe there's nothing. I see red goats painted all over this town, all over these hills. And you got nothing?"

The informant shook his head. "Closest was one old guy who supposedly knows somebody who knows somebody. You know, one of those."

"Shit," Hamun responded dismissively.

The informant shrugged, studying the table.

"Gotta start somewhere, right?" Hamun complained. "Where can I find this old guy?"

"Afternoons he's usually fishing."

"I like fishing."

The informant finished clearing the table and followed Hamun to his car around the corner. Hamun drove up into the bluffs west of town to a spot where the river flattens, but the old guy wasn't there. They got back in the car and careened downhill to a crumbling bridge on the other side of Pritzi.

"That's him," the informant said, pointing to a man wearing a hat the color of dried barley stalks.

Hamun switched off the engine, opened his door, and said, "You coming?"

"I'm okay waiting up here."

"No, you're not. Come and introduce me, you idiot."

Hamun and his informant slipped and skidded through loose rocks and litter down the embankment to the river's edge. They approached the old man, who nodded an acknowledgement to the informant and cast his line back into the water.

"Any luck today, Uncle?"

"It's early," the angler replied.

After a few attempts at casual chatter, the informant got to the point.

"My friend Hamun wants to ask you something."

"Me?"

"You know Marko?" Hamun asked.

With an effort, the old man twisted his neck to peer up at Hamun for a moment. "Heard of him."

"Got a client who'd like to meet him."

"Who's that?"

"A potential customer, let's put it like that."

"Does he have to buy from Marko?"

"This guy thinks Marko's got the best and the most reliable supply," Hamun explained.

The angler scowled, and removed his hat to scratch a spot on his scalp. "Could be, I wouldn't know. I could ask someone."

"Alright, I appreciate it."

"Gonna need money for a ride to his village."

"Where's that at?" Hamun asked.

"Over that way."

At the end of the work day on Tuesday, Andy trooped along behind the ambassador to the secure conference room, where General Elfersen and Colonel Mesko, their shoes and decorations gleaming smartly in the businesslike lighting of the secure conference room, stood erect. The military, at the ready, prepared to give their assessment, three weeks after the poisoning incident. Not exactly light speed, but not bad for a bureaucracy that size. The only troubling thing was the fact that their analytical process had not generated any gossip and snickering around Washington, as far as Andy could detect. On the contrary, with the threat of war looming between Vodania and Pazaria, the ambassador's stature and standing had only grown. It occurred to Andy he might be running out of cards to play.

"Sir," General Elfersen began after all four men took their seats. "We have completed our capabilities assessment with regards to the attack on your dog. Thank you for agreeing to receive this brief on short notice. And we also appreciate your patience while we ran our analysis. We knew it was important to get this right."

"Indeed," the ambassador agreed.

"Bottom line up front. We assess that a very advanced level of skill sets and training was required for this attack. Vodania does have the capabilities, as well as home field advantage."

"However—" General Elfersen glanced at his briefing notes and nudged them aside before drawing a deep breath. "We have no indication or chatter among our contacts to indicate whether they did it, one way or the other. But if it wasn't the Vodanians, it almost certainly means that someone else penetrated this area with highly trained commando-type operatives. We can assess with high confidence it was special forces. Either Vodania's or someone else's, take your pick."

"It was clearly a trial balloon, a prelude to the aggressive actions Chilik has taken since," said the ambassador. "Some of us saw that clearly at the time."

Andy tried not to react to the implied reproach. Loyalty first.

The ambassador frowned before returning his attention to General Elfersen. "Your job is to stay joined at the hip with the chod," he commanded, using mil-speak to refer to Vodania's chief of defense. "We've got a war to stop."

Command mode suited the ambassador, Andy had to admit. He would have said the same thing if he were in charge.

Chapter 19

The window sheers luffed in a gentle breeze, and soft morning light seeped into Tara's bedroom. Under a cotton sheet she stirred, coming back into her body. She writhed and shifted under the gentle wrap of Mads' right arm and right leg. She stretched her limbs and spine luxuriously and twisted around to kiss his cheek.

"Good morning, Hiker Boy."

"Good morning," he responded, in Vodanian. Or did his sly grin suggest the Pazari meaning of the phrase?

Tara pressed against his body to find out. "Mmmm, you do," she murmured, "Let's do something extra fun with it."

Midway through the morning on Wednesday, Rhonda Bout, the vice president's national security advisor, entered the White House situation room and strode briskly toward the head of the table.

"Alright, hit me with your dopest, real-deal Iran pressure tactics strategies!"

She did enjoy making a splash when commandeering a meeting.

"This is the Pazaria-Vodania border crisis group," respectfully replied NSC director Winston Bryce, who had been chairing the interagency gathering.

"My bad. Iran pressure tactics is at eleven."

Rhonda kept coming, and Winston stood up to cede his place to her.

"What, we got a river out of alignment, am I right?" asked Rhonda, dropping her derriere onto the smoothly worn fabric of the seat Winston relinquished. "That's what shot my vay-cay?"

After tight nods and half-smiles, the DIA rep spoke up. "Our analysts are picking up indications the Vodanians had been planning this move for a while."

"The way the vice president sees it, we gotta deter the Vodanians. Then we broker a deal." Rhonda stated. "We don't want to have to get involved in another war there."

"State concurs," replied Vonda Vance. "My assistant secretary asked the legal advisor's office to examine international law precedents and come up with creative options for unwinding this. There are six possibilities, which I'll just run through real quick. Traditional use theory. Fixed point territorial integrity. Go with the flow—which means a variable border as the river shifts around. Fudge it—you know, find a way to—"

"We all know what fudge it means," Rhonda interrupted.

"The last two may be promising," Vonda continued. "Joint sovereignty over the disputed zone, or international jurisdiction, to be administered by the OSCE or UN."

"What's to administer?" Rhonda objected. "It's a small mound of rocks at the bottom of a gorge. No one lives there or even goes there. There's not enough sunlight to grow moss."

Vonda offered no reply, and Rhonda capped her slap-down with, "What about when the river's twenty feet higher in the spring? This might not be on the curriculum at Yale Law, but what everybody needs to understand is that what we have here is a good old-fashioned pissing contest."

A low grumble of static came out of the multidirectional speaker in the center of the table. Participating remotely from Embassy Shizl, Ambassador Lamkin said, "Two hours ago the military in Pazaria announced a joint training exercise with the U.S. That's not going to calm the waters in Vodania."

"Did we authorize that?" Winston Bryce asked.

"The exercise has been on the books for a while," replied deputy assistant secretary of defense Bill Padden, deploying his most baritone meeting voice. "But it's not taking place until next April."

"Not helpful to announce it now," Rhonda commented.

"We can't un-announce it," Ambassador Kunninger's voice jumped in, on speaker from Embassy Zagovor. "Don't be mad at the Pazarians. Chilik is the one who ruined everyone's vay-cay."

Aiming to look unnoticeable in the American male business traveler uniform of dark blue blazers, khaki trousers, and monochrome button-downs with no neckties, Four, Five, and Six clustered companionably together in the waiting area in front of boarding gate D-14 at Dulles International Airport. Per standard procedure, Harrimore had divided up the team for travel purposes. One, Two, and Three took an earlier flight through a different connecting city. All the gear went across on a military cargo plane. The team would regroup in Pazaria, at Camp Stability.

"I'm humping up to Dunkin' D for coffee," offered Four. "Any takers?"

Five pursed his lips and shook his head.

"You're schlepping to Double D for coffee? There's a Starbucks right here," Six pointed out.

Five nodded and pointed at Six.

"I like Dunkin' D," Four declared.

"You're some kinda revolutionary, challenging the caffeine supremacy of Starbucks," Six said. "But the deeper question is, what do you want coffee for? Don't you want to sleep on the flight?"

"I hear they've got great movies," Four replied.

"Like you haven't seen 'em all fifty times already," said Six.

Pumped! On Thursday afternoon, Doug Watanabe swaggered through the hallways of the main building of the police agency like he ran the place, arms swinging and shoulders rolling. The text message that brought him there, from an assistant to the operations and planning guy, said there was a development in the case. Nothing further, no elaboration. Which was good. It had to refer to Marko, and Doug sensed it must be something solid. He marched into a tactical command room, where the western district commander and the deputy director of the operations and planning unit stood among a dozen uniformed and plainclothes police.

"Whadda we got?" Doug demanded, softening his brusqueness with a smile.

A core group gathered around the briefing table. "We're set up for a controlled buy. Saturday night," the western district commander said.

"Fantastic. "We're confident this is with Marko?"

"Fully," replied the western district commander.

"Marko insisted on doing the initial exchange on the border," added the operations and planning deputy.

"On the border?" Doug repeated.

"It's a very remote area. But our guys know it well," said the western district commander.

"Where exactly?"

The commander showed him on the map. "It's a narrow pass, up in this part of the mountains."

"What's it called?"

"It has a lot of different names, depending on who you ask."

"Most of the locals call it Tonguebite Pass," one of the plainclothes guys added.

"What size is the deal?"

"Just a sample, a quarter kilo of kone."

"Price?"

"Eight hundred."

"Eight hundred? Did you negotiate?" Doug asked, smiling again.

The police commanders and officers, with the American DEA rep in the thick of it, spent the next hour and a half mapping out and working through their plan to arrest the Marko operative and then try to flip him. When they were satisfied they had everything figured out, the western district commander got to his feet and asked, "Anything else for tonight?"

The operations and planning deputy turned to Doug. "What kind of cars you getting us?"

Over the course of the week, Andy Pulano had been monitoring the likelihood that the ambassador and Mrs. would go ahead with their plans to fly to Vienna on Sunday for a few days' break. Sensing that the call of the opera would prove irresistible, he saw an opportunity for a bold move. Vodania's military faceoff with Pazaria was doing more harm than good. True, it had denied the ambassador the glory of a border agreement. But he was basking in the crisis atmosphere, his stature growing by the day. Andy knew the time had come to pull the plug on the conflict and step into the limelight himself.

That decision brought him to a filling station on the western edge of Shizl shortly before ten thirty on Friday night. After topping off his tank and paying with cash, he climbed back in behind the wheel, but didn't turn the ignition switch. Where westbound National Boulevard compressed into two lanes, he watched a stream of boxy sedans and smoke-belching lorries flowing out of the capital. Noisy motor-scooters buzzed and weaved through the flow of traffic. He scoffed at the row of newly planted saplings on the boulevard's raised median. No doubt another EU accomplishment.

Facing toward his right, Pulano waited until multiple brake lights turned the westbound lanes into a long line of red glare. When the traffic ground almost to a standstill and the symphony of horns commenced, Pulano started his engine, turned up the volume on the local pop music station, and rolled forward to the edge of National Boulevard. He waited until a slight opening appeared in front of a silver Mercedes SUV. He rolled partway into the lane, forcing the Mercedes to brake sharply, accompanied by two horn blasts. The Mercedes then forced its way into the left lane and pulled up close alongside the Range Rover. Then closer. When the SUV's side mirror almost touched the Range Rover's, Pulano lowered his window.

"It's an ugly shitty mess," snarled a voice from inside the back of the Mercedes. "Wodanians with guns all over the place. It makes people nervous and very upset. This is not what we discussed with your stinky friend!"

Mmmm, I thought you'd never ask, Andy cooed to himself. The timing had become rather tight. To Shariz he said, "I can get rid of the soldiers, but I need your help."

"My help? If our guys help there will be a civil war."

"Not with guns. Shovels."

"You think this is a big joke?" Shariz exploded. "Something to laugh about? It is an invasion! They are all over the place, in our villages, on our mountains. The situation is very dangerous. For everyone." He glared at the American diplomat in an openly threatening manner.

Horns blared, seemingly from all directions. The radio inside the Range Rover contributed a headachy anthem heavy on the electric accordion. Both vehicles eased forward half a car length.

Andy, facing forward, shook his head in evident sadness. "Perhaps I overestimated you, Shariz. I thought you were a man of vision, someone who knew how to solve problems. And with the influence and organizational skills to act decisively."

Shariz stared at Andy in an extended, angry silence. Finally, in a controlled voice, he said, "What?"

"It's a simple chore, really, but carrying it out might be challenging. The timing is critical. Actually, we are almost out of time."

"I still don't know what you are talking about."

"Can you get a small team into the Odorian River gorge? Tomorrow night?"

"What part of the gorge?"

"East of Kundamir. Where the troops are concentrated on both sides."

"And what are my guys supposed to do there, with two armies straight above them on top of the cliffs?"

"You heard about the landslide that started this crisis?"

Shariz got the idea. Andy turned his face toward the Mercedes to watch the shifting expressions that flickered over the Pazari kingpin's face as he worked through the various pieces of the problem.

"It's important that it be tomorrow night?" Shariz asked.

"Crucial. They are very, very close to war. Any delay and . . . if something starts, I can't tell you how long the troops will be up there, charging around on both sides of the border. Most likely it will be for an extremely long time."

Shariz craned his neck to peer up through the window at the nearly full moon. "You are lucky."

As the rear window on the Mercedes started sliding up, Shariz lifted his phone to his mouth.

"Move your cars."

In less than a minute, the traffic jam eased, and Andy headed for home.

The open-air produce market in Tara's neighborhood was busy on Saturday morning. The last day of the month. The official end of summer. And the end of Mads' sojourn in Vodania. Best not to dwell on that. As if she could stop herself.

"This is so much fruit!" Mads pretended to complain. "He's not going to invite the whole city."

He acted like he could barely hold up the canvas shopping bag filled with the melons, plums, apricots, and pears that Tara had bought.

"Just a handful of berries for color and we're done," Tara promised. "I can't show up without bringing something."

After Tara paid for the berries, Mads put his free arm around her and squeezed her shoulder. Wordlessly, they navigated the maze of market stalls and turned in the direction of her apartment. In a deeper sense, Tara didn't know where she and Mads were headed. She felt they were hurtling around a blind curve skirting the edge of a cliff. With no brakes, minimal steering, and an unknown amount of gas. But the scenery was undeniably spectacular and Mads had so many ways of bringing out her smile.

In his office on Saturday morning, Andy read through the draft speech that the political and public affairs sections produced for his delivery at the EU-sponsored peace conference on Tuesday. It said absolutely nothing.

Andy nodded his appreciation and set the paper aside. I have trained them well, he mused. For solid, logical reasons, the United States generally did not take positions on other countries' border squabbles. Also constraining any comments Embassy Shizl might make about this particular spat was the highly inconvenient fact of the U.S. alliance with Pazaria. So, the embassy staff filled several pages with lofty principles, benevolent intentions, and inspiring aspirations.

In the ambassador's absence, it would become the DCM's task to read this confection aloud, in a confident and authoritative voice, to the assembled notables. Andy knew that if he performed his role as scripted, he would receive respectable applause at the event and fifteen seconds of coverage on most of the evening news broadcasts in Vodania. End of story.

He switched his computer on and zipped off a few emails to get the rhetorical juices flowing. Then he went to the printer and pulled out two sheets of blank paper. Bracing his elbows on the desk, he uncapped his trusty Montblanc Boheme Marron. Eyebrows leaping like baby goats, he began to compose what he would actually say at the conference, assuming Shariz's guys came through. He tested various phrasings, moving his lips soundlessly. He took great care with the money quote, the line that would make headlines and, with any luck, go viral. It had to sound spontaneous and unanticipated. And should it ever occur to anyone to check, his computer would show no trace of any advance preparation of his startling announcement.

At a street café in Kharbam, not far from the Camel Club, Shariz planted a farewell kiss on the last three centimeters of his cigarette and dropped the smoldering fragment onto the pavement. He saw no reason to stub out his butts and deprive the world of their remaining curls of smoke. Lounging at an outdoor table in a pair of striped boxers and a red Liverpool Football Club jersey with the sleeves chopped off, Shariz ignored the expressionless subordinate by his side. Every so often Shariz flicked his eyes at his watch and tugged up his mustache tips.

At the explosive clatter of an approaching motorcycle, Shariz frowned. It was Munit, one of his lieutenants, arriving close enough to on-time. Barely. Pushing his luck again.

"What did my friend say?" Shariz demanded, before Munit had a chance to dismount.

"He's got seven kayaks," Munit responded.

"We need more than that," Shariz pointed out.

"He said the rest have been rented out to tourists. And two were stolen."

Munit still straddled his bike. It looked pretty. Italian. Shariz jerked his head toward the nearest empty chair and waited while Munit lowered himself into the seat.

"Right, I heard about that," said Shariz. "Damn jerk-off Curly and his lice-ridden mother." He turned toward the aide seated to his left. "Go over to Curly's after lunch. We need those kayaks."

To Munit he asked, "How many guys you have lined up?

"Twelve."

"Plus, you."

"Plus, me." Munit stared at Shariz.

"What's your problem?" demanded Shariz.

"We've noticed the Americans want us to do this the same night as the Marko set-up."

"We?"

"Some of us were talking last night. The timing is interesting, you have to admit."

"What are you trying to say, Munit?"

"This could be a diversion to keep us away from Tonguebite."

Shariz stood up and bent his scowling face close to Munit's. "Understand me clearly. We're doing this for our own reasons. Are the Americans using us?"

Shariz answered his own question by nodding vigorously in the affirmative, his chin almost striking Munit's forehead.

"Are we using the Americans?"

Shariz waited for Munit to nod.

"It's what they call a partnership," Shariz lectured. "As for Tonguebite, why would we want to go anywhere near there tonight?"

Munit stayed silent.

"Let me tell you something about the Americans," said Shariz. "They are useful but extremely dangerous. You know why? Because sometimes they know everything, sometimes they know nothing."

After preparing his surprise announcement for the EU peace conference, Andy attended a luncheon the ambassador hosted for representatives of election monitoring organizations. Over chicken breast cutlets and wild mushrooms, the monitors, both local and international, expressed all the pieties about procedural safeguards, while barely concealing their excitement as the tense, hard-fought campaign entered its final days. They could thank him for the heightened drama, Andy congratulated himself, though they would condemn him if they knew.

The election monitoring delegations departed, and Andy lingered in the foyer next to the guest book stand. Ambassador Lamkin stood beside him. In the background the housekeepers cleared dishes from the tables in the living room.

The ambassador rested a hand on Andy's shoulder. "Our flight is first thing tomorrow. Think you can hold the fort for two days?" He sounded almost paternal.

Andy nodded. "Don't worry, it'll stay quiet. Quiet being a relative term of course," he added with a smile.

The ambassador semi-smiled back. "When we return on Tuesday, it'll still be Labor Day weekend in Washington. I wouldn't expect any trouble from that quarter."

"I wouldn't think so. We can feed them an update when you're back."

"Yes. Including on Cauchon's conference, such as it is. Sorry to stick you with that. Please convey my sincerest regrets et cetera."

"Certainly," Andy agreed.

The ambassador certainly was not sorry to stick him with the conference, though that would change. Andy glanced out the door and then back to the ambassador. On an odd impulse, Andy put out his hand and the two men shook, grips firm.

"Enjoy Vienna."

Makeup artists are strangely sexy, thought Doug Watanabe, perched on a stool in a windowless room at the National Police Agency on Saturday afternoon. This one had dark brown hair piled high on her head, and she stood as close as possible without their bodies touching. He enjoyed the feeling of her fingertips spreading glue above his upper lip and on his chin. She pressed the mustache and goatee into place and held them there with both hands for a full minute, her green eyes gazing at his face.

By around three thirty everything was ready. A convoy of five vehicles lined up in the shade alongside the boxy annex building that housed police locker rooms, weapons, equipment, and a block of detention cells. Doug, as keyed up as he had been in years, took his place in the back seat of a Ford Explorer, sliding in next to the district commander. A patrol car led the way out of the compound, followed by the Explorer, another patrol car, and two unmarked sedans. In Doug's eyes, the familiar scenery took on a dramatic look, befitting the launch of a glorious expedition.

Doug patted his woolen Turkish vest to reconfirm the money was inside. He rehearsed his opening line, in a Turkish accent, "Are you Marko?"

The district commander provided the expected reply, "We are all Marko."

"Then I'm gonna flash my cash," Doug continued in his Turkish voice. "And he's gonna unwrap that sweet kone, purest quality, so I can test it."

The district commander nodded confirmation. "And then you take cover in the gap on the right when our guys move in to make the bust."

Moonlight and a hint of cool breeze greeted Tara as she and Mads reached the roof deck on Stefano's apartment building. Off to the east was an impressive view of the Presidentorium bathed in floodlights. Late night city noises filtered up from the streets, transforming from clanging irritations into an intriguing soundscape. It was a dramatic, festive setting for a party.

Tara found space on a table to set down the big bowl of fruit salad she and Mads prepared. Walking arm-in-arm, she reached her free hand across to hang onto Mads' biceps. With a half-smile, she glanced around the rooftop gathering, wishing it wasn't happening.

She recognized a couple of Stefano's cousins. Her friends Monique and Karolina stood talking with two designers and an actor near the front edge of the deck. The rooftop space was thick with ex-pats. Even Lotte Wuyts was there, husband in tow. Tara overheard her say, "At least the humans can do something to defend their rights, not like the animals." Several dozen members of the chic Shizl crowd danced and smoked to the sultry rhythms emanating from Stefano's band. The evening's host managed to look both self-absorbed and engaging as he and his bandmates worked their instruments in the far corner of the deck.

"The guest of honor is here," Stefano announced into the microphone. "Finally, we can celebrate his departure from Vodania."

The laughter and cheers felt thoughtless, almost cruel, as Tara smiled to project a bravery she did not feel at all.

She put her lips to Mads' ear. "Are you really leaving? I was starting to get used to having you around."

On the airfield at Camp Stability in northwestern Pazaria, the minutes ticked toward midnight.

"Equipment check!" One shouted over the bone-shaking roar of noise blasting out of the C-130's turbines.

Inside the dark metal cavern of the plane's interior, the members of the unit examined their packs and weapons one final time.

"Good to go?"

Two through Five all nodded, and Six said "Right on."

One grabbed the headset dangling from the ceiling and spoke to the pilot, "All set."

The ramp raised up to seal the opening, and the aircraft taxied to Camp Stability's auxiliary runway. The turbines revved and the C-130 clattered over the bumpy tarmac and lifted into smoothness and started climbing fast. The operatives crouched in jump order.

Part IV

One Fall Day

Chapter 20

Silhouetted against the full moon, the C-130 banked to the right when it got above the Asich Mountains. The transport maintained a southwest heading tracing the border on the Pazaria side. As the aircraft approached the drop zone, the rear ramp opened with a rush of cool air. One stood and positioned himself on the edge. The C-130 descended and leveled off just above the peaks and One unhooked his harness from the safety line.

Muzzle flashes burst from the terrain below. Something hit the fuselage with a loud bang. The C-130 swerved and thrust upward and One spilled out into the darkness.

Small arms fire erupted from both sides of the river. Two grabbed the headset and shouted, "Incoming! Pull up, turn around!"

Six called out into the open air, "Thank you for your service!"

Operation Tonguebite! Caffrey is gonna love this, Doug Watanabe thought, scuffing one foot in front of the other on the final trudge up toward the mountain pass, just after midnight. He could picture the broad beaming grin on the division chief's face back at DEA headquarters. Doug perspired from the climb, more than two hours up a steep rocky trail with treacherous footing. His fez felt heavy and hot.

Ahead was the opening to Tonguebite Pass. Its jagged rock walls closed in tighter as the path ascended to the rendezvous point. Doug glanced around at the members of the Vodanian tactical squad taking their positions. He looked over at the district commander and got the nod. Doug adjusted his fez and patted his woolen vest and proceeded into the narrowing stone passageway, heart pounding, all senses alert.

Near the high point of the pass a burly-looking man wrapped in a Mexican serape leaned his back against the cliff face. He braced one cowboy boot against the wall. A sombrero kept the man's features in shadow.

"Are you Marko?" Doug asked in his imitation Turkish accent.

"We are all Marko," came the reply, in a voice that registered somewhere in Doug's memory.

One plummeted. He hoped the C-130 would continue to draw the attention of the forces below. Not wanting to become an easy floating target, he gripped his pilot chute to his chest, delaying release as long as he dared. When the jagged mountain ridges lunged up at him like a shark's teeth, he flung it above his head.

The pilot chute popped open right in front of a recon team traversing a crest on the Vodanian side. He glimpsed their startled reactions as he hurtled past. The main chute inflated just as he cleared the lip of a gorge.

Into the chasm One dropped, focusing on the nearly vertical cliffs on both sides, doing his best to steer between them. An updraft slowed his descent. He could not yet see the Odorian but he knew there was a river at the bottom of this deep split in the earth.

With the C-130 still climbing, Four hollered above the engine din, "We gotta re-improvise the plan!"

He tore the headset from Two's grip and spoke to the pilot, "Stay on course. We're gonna drop further along the border."

Four listened for two seconds, then turned to the other operatives. "How much further? Thirty klicks, okay?"

"Make it forty," said Three.

"Forty's good," Two confirmed.

"Forty," Four declared into the headset. "Find a good clear spot."

Moonlight bathed the crags and rock faces on one side of the pass. Darkness covered the other. The Vodanian police, crouching on the shadow side, watched like leopards ready to strike.

Doug glanced around for his exit route while keeping an eye on the sombrero guy. "You brought a taste for me?" he asked, sounding even more Turkish.

The sombrero nodded once, and the man reached inside his serape. "Let's see your money," he demanded in that strangely familiar voice.

Doug pulled out his handful of hundreds and waited for the suspect to produce the heroin sample.

"Pure kone," said the sombrero guy, pulling out a ziplock bag of white powder.

As they were about to make the exchange, noise from a low-flying aircraft rumbled and swelled toward them from the northeast sky. In the middle of Tonguebite Pass, both men froze, looking up as a C-130 shot into view low over the adjacent peaks.

"Keep it tight!" Two commanded.

The Harrimore team packed together near the edge of the open ramp, bracing against the swirling blast of air. Three and Six cradled M4 carbines.

Two released and jumped, followed by Three, Four, Five, and Six at two-second intervals. Their chutes opened in the same sequence, forming a neat line floating down toward the Vodanian side of the border.

As soon as his chute set, Three's head began swiveling, searching for potential threats. He spotted gunmen on the slopes to his left and laid down a burst of suppressive fire.

Doug heard the gunfire and dropped to the ground. There was shouting and the sound of panicky footsteps. He crawled to a boulder and squatted behind it, listening. Then he ran, bent low, deeper into the shelter of the pass. More gunshots exploded, seemingly from behind him and in front. He spotted a crevice in the rock and squeezed into it. Somewhere along the way he lost his fez.

At the sound of the initial gunshots, the sombrero guy spun away from the wall and clambered over a car-sized chunk of granite that jutted into the pass. He banged his left knee in the process and came down hard on the other side.

Almost as soon as the gunfire from the paratroopers ceased, four strong hands hauled him to his feet and hustled him down the slope away from the pass as shots exploded from different directions. After half a minute they ducked behind a sharp-edged promontory, where there were more men in black uniforms. One of them fired a pistol into the pass.

The men who escorted him to safety still held him tightly. Then they yanked his arms backward and fussed with the serape and clicked a set of metal cuffs around his wrists. With a grip on each elbow, they hustled him further downhill. His knee throbbed and he did not notice that the sombrero had come off and now dangled by the chin cord, swinging and bouncing between his shoulder blades with every step.

After One dropped quite a way down into the narrow canyon, the river finally came into view. But it was not getting any closer. One swayed forward and backward in the breeze, swiveling his head as he realized he was no longer descending. He estimated the water to be sixty to eighty feet below. The canopy of his main chute must have snagged on both sides of the crevasse. Initial sit-rep: not a superior location.

One breathed deeply, searching for calm. He heard the river below and the distant echoing shouts of soldiers way up at the top of the cliff. The oddly stretched fabric of the canopy blocked his view above, but looking down he could see that the gorge widened again below him. He tried to swing sideways but the cliff walls were too far apart for him to reach. He needed a better plan, fast.

Two firefights, our leader lost, and we haven't even hit the ground yet. There's always a right way and a wrong way. And then there's the Harrimore way, Three thought, floating down past the slopes on the Vodanian side of the border mountains. He searched for a safe landing spot and maintained alertness for more hostiles on the ground. He kept his teammates in view, except for Six, who must have been too far back. The wind carried them eastward over a jagged mountain landscape.

The tree line came into view and Three was dropping fast. He spotted a flattish area clogged with brush and aimed for that. Knees flexed, he plunged down and hit the slope at an angle. He took two staggering steps through the low bushes, fell, and shoulder-rolled to a stop. He wiggled out of his harness and bunched up the chute, walking towards its limp folds to avoid getting it any more snared in the thicket. He stuffed the loose bundle of nylon under a shrub and covered the protruding edges with rocks and handfuls of dust. He heard Two's whistle and he responded with three quick chirps on his own.

They regrouped toward the midpoint of their line.

"I'll take Three and Four," said Two. "Five and Six, you keep pace two hundred meters to our right. Use lasers to maintain periodic visual contact."

"Whoa, hold on there, Doc," Six objected.

"Got a problem with the plan?" Two responded. "Each team will have one of the M4s."

"The plan's fine for now. I'm just wondering what gives you the notion you're in charge of this fandango."

"In case you hadn't noticed, One is out of the game. I'm Two, next in line."

"Two is your code-name, not your rank," Six rejoined. "We just counted off in the briefing room."

"You got a better system?" Three asked. "You wanna organize an election or something?"

"Let's move out," Four added. "Before the fire department gets here."

"I don't think it's the fire department we need to worry about," Two commented, starting downhill.

"Take a look over there," Four advised.

A few hundred meters above and to the side of their position, an arc of flame lit up the slope. The wind pushed the burn line forward and downward, lofting a broad cloud of smoke across the mountainside.

"That ain't good," said Three.

"Don't sweat it, kids," said Six. "Just destroying the evidence. Standard op-sec."

"You burned your chute?" exclaimed Two. "Did you listen to any of the briefings? This whole country is drier'n a Baptist picnic. How is a brush fire going to help us?"

Six just smirked, and the two groups began descending the mountain at a quick trot.

The district commander held up his hand and the Vodanian police team stopped their downhill march. He nodded at one of the men, who reached into his pocket for a disposable latex glove, which he stretched over his right hand with a decisive snap. He turned to the captive.

In half a minute the glove guy had the bag of white powder, the suspect's weapon, holster, phone, and both granola bars. Each item went into its own separate plastic bag.

For the first time, the captive seemed to notice the uniforms, the tactical formations, the procedures.

"You guys are cops!"

"Another criminal genius," the district commander commented, in Vodanian. To the suspect he said, "You made a bad mistake. Your gang kidnapped an American agent."

"It's not a gang, it's the Pazaria police."

"Same thing."

"Wait, what American agent? I'm the American agent."

The police looked at each other and laughed. "A comedian," one of them said.

"My name is Paul Giardis. I'm a special agent with the United States Drug Enforcement Agency."

"The only thing special about you is your hat," replied the district commander, relieving Giardis of his sombrero.

"That's genuine," Giardis asserted. "I got it during my tour in Matamoros."

One dangled in the gorge, fuming.

Point one: no one said anything about armed units on the border. Deployed on both sides, and trigger-happy. Point two: we shouldn't be dropping anywhere near this kind of land formation anyways. It's like the rims of the Grand Canyon got pressed together, with the Rocky Mountains piled on top. Point three: help is not on the way.

One peered at the sheer walls, searching for an escape route. Impossible to descend without climbing gear. Plus, advanced rock-climbing skills. Scratch that idea off the option list. One gazed between his boots at the rocks and water below, trying again to gauge the distance. Plans are overrated. What he needed was a longer rope.

Twisting around, One counted the parachute cords above him and estimated their usable lengths. Stretching and reaching upward, he yanked on various of the lines that crisscrossed upward from his harness, to figure out which ones connected with the parts of the canopy that were snagged. Almost all of them felt load bearing. He pulled one of the looser lines as far down as it would go and cut it as high as he could reach. He tied the cut end to his belt as a safety.

He drew a deep breath. Time for Russian roulette, but with a knife.

One loosened his straps. Reaching up to grip a pair of lines in each fist, he hoisted his body upward to extricate himself from the confinement of the harness. Then he climbed, hooking and unhooking his boots around the cords as he proceeded. When he got as high as his safety rope allowed, he tugged on each of the three lines within reach, and selected the one he judged least likely to be crucial. He touched his blade to the outer fibers, preparing to plummet if he had chosen wrong and the remaining lines didn't hold.

A hard slash, and he watched the loose line drop. The connection to the harness arrested its fall, and it jerked and twisted, an angry captured snake.

One climbed back down, and then up a different line, and cut again, like a spider dismantling a web. Or half a spider, since the work would have gone much easier with eight limbs. After five nerve-straining cuts, he wasn't certain he had collected enough line. But he didn't want to push his luck any further.

He eased himself back into the harness, aware that, however long his parachute had originally been destined to hang in the gorge, his actions had likely shortened the timeframe. He groped around in his pack for a roll of duct tape, silently thanking Sickman Hickman, his platoon commander during his rookie year in the Rangers. Sickman's one inflexible rule: Never go on a mission without duct tape. Because shit goes wrong. Ain't that the truth, One thought, as he started fashioning a rope from the severed lines.

Cutting, twisting, tying, taping. It felt like a rainy-day Cub Scout craft project.

Five's peripheral vision caught a sparkle of moonlight reflecting off a windshield. He put a hand on Six's arm and motioned for him to stay silent, then pointed at the vehicle, below and off to the right. The two operatives crept closer. They saw a Ford Explorer, two police cars, and two unmarked compact sedans, all parked pointing downhill.

"Dibs on the Explorer!" Six exclaimed.

Five flashed his laser at the rest of the team, who trudged across the slope to join him and Six. The team conferred in heated, rasping whispers, then fanned out, weapons poised, to check for guards. They spotted only one, occupying the driver's seat of the Explorer at the back of the line. Three and Four, masks in place, approached the vehicle from behind, keeping low and silent. The Explorer's door suddenly opened. Four, across the road on the driver's side, dropped to the ground and flattened in a gulley. Three aimed his M4.

A man in a black police uniform emerged from the Explorer and bent his spine backward in a long, luxurious stretch. He reached his arms up and outward, fists clenched. After holding the pose a moment, he took a few steps downhill and stopped in front of a dry pothole. Four and Three watched from behind as he reached for his fly. Four stalked closer, Three covering with the carbine. When the urine slowed to a trickle, Four pinned the policeman's arms in an immobilization hold. The officer staggered and spun, drizzling the last drops onto his own pant legs and boots. He stopped struggling as soon as he saw Three and his weapon.

"Cuff him," Four ordered.

"Let the man finish his business," Three answered, removing the officer's sidearm. "Less you wanna repack his parachute yourself."

Two and Five checked the other vehicles while Six remained concealed, with his M4 at the ready.

After the police officer was handcuffed and blindfolded face down in the road, the entire group assembled.

Two said, "We'll take both unmarked sedans."

"I already called the Explorer," Six declared. "Five here heard me."

Five nodded his confirmation.

"Too conspicuous. We'll take two sedans, in case one becomes disabled," Two insisted.

"If that happens one compact's too small to take six of us to the cotillion," Six responded.

"We're only five now, remember?" Two rejoined.

"Don't forget Four's date here," Six replied. "Or did you have a different plan?" he asked, pointing his M4 at the prisoner.

Six and Four pulled the police officer to his feet and marched him to the Explorer. They maneuvered him into the back seat, bound his ankles to the underside of the driver's seat and clicked a seatbelt around him, his hands still cuffed. All the vehicles had their keys in the ignition, poised for rapid departure. Two, Three, and Five removed the patrol cars' batteries and loaded them in the trunk of one of the compacts.

Four braced himself in the back seat with the prisoner while Six banged the Explorer madly down the mountain. Five jumped into the front compact and took off after them. Three strode toward the driver's side of the other car.

Two reached for the driver's door at the same moment.

Three held his position, looking down into her eyes. "You have tactical cert?"

After a short staring contest, Two stepped back. "Okay, just try to drive inconspicuously."

Three scoffed. "Driving while black, I can't promise you inconspicuous. Can't even do that in my own neighborhood. But don't worry, I got this."

The Explorer led the way down the rutted lane, spraying gravel and raising a storm of brown dust. Suddenly, music swelled from the prisoner's pants. Beethoven's Ode to Joy.

"What the fuck is that?" Six yelled from behind the wheel.

"Handel's Messiah, ain't it?" Four replied. "And we're nowheres near Christmas."

"No, it most certainly ain't. That's what's-his-wagon. Brahms," said Six.

As the piece built toward its full symphonic glory, Four dug the cell phone out of the Vodanian officer's pocket and hurled it out the window, muttering, "Have some respect for the holidays."

In the moonlight the Odorian River resembled a silver serpent slithering through the mountains. According to legend, the serpent never ate when the moon was full.

Munit and team paddled to the Pazaria side above a noisy channel where the canyon walls squeezed the river into churning, bucking rapids, the most difficult stretch of whitewater they needed to navigate. Their flotilla consisted of two canoes and nine one-man kayaks.

Goran and Jozo, the two best kayakers, stayed in their boats, bracing against the current. Goran looped a long coil of rope through a pulley on the back of Jozo's kayak, and tied both ends to his own kayak. The rest of them got out and traversed the treacherous path alongside the heap of slick rocks at the edge of the rapids. Rotting nooses suspended from iron spikes provided handholds to aid the descent.

After the first of the men reached the base of the rapids, Goran and Jozo stroked out to the center of the river. Goran maintained his position by paddling upstream while Jozo plunged his kayak forward into the roiling current, the rope spooling out. With quick thrusts of his paddle Jozo pivoted, twisting and dodging through the rocks. When he reached the bottom, Munit shouted, and Goran paddled over to the empty kayaks and attached one to the rope, as if it was a chairlift on a ski slope. He returned to the middle of the river and he and Jozo coordinated to guide the empty kayak through the heaving waters.

When the kayak made it to the bottom of the rapids, Jozo towed it to the side where others from the crew grabbed it. A young man in a billed cap hoisted himself into the vessel and paddled out to assist Jozo. Into the madness of the rapids, Goran lowered the empty kayaks one by one. The rope, held taut at both ends, restrained the boats from smashing to pieces on the way down. Once the kayaks were through, Goran launched the first canoe, empty except for shovels and a few items wrapped in plastic, into the whitewater. After all the empty boats went through, Goran released the rope and dove his kayak into the rapids, following the same course as Jozo.

In the flat water at the bottom, the crew reassembled in their formation. They traced a curving line along the center of the current, riding the back of the serpent.

The district commander led the trek down from Tonguebite Pass, careful to avoid building up too much speed. The police had removed the handcuffs from Giardis and replaced them with a chain leash around his neck, the other end gripped by an unarmed officer trailing. Even with his hands freed, Giardis had trouble navigating the dark path in his cowboy boots, and had to more or less constantly guard against slipping. On the occasions when he did fall, he entertained his escorts with explosions of expletives.

As they descended to lower elevations, the group smelled something burning, which raised no concerns. Breathing smoke in Vodania was like finding sand in a desert. The district commander pulled out his phone to try again to reach the officer stationed on guard duty, and was again irritated that he still did not pick up. There would be punishment. The commander did not tolerate napping during special operations.

Ghostly fingers of smoke curled among the trees.

Time to earn another merit badge.

Dangling in the harness, One looped his makeshift rope over his left shoulder to keep it from snarling. It made a decent-sized coil. He tried not to think about it being not quite enough. He wrapped the whole thing around a couple of intact lines for redundancy, prior to preparing to tie the free end to his belt. Then, with a little smile, he remembered that his original safety line was still attached. That would buy him another ten feet, at least. Maybe this plan was actually going to work.

With knots and duct tape, he connected the main coil to the line attached to his belt. He put on his gloves and lowered the whole loop. He scrambled out of the harness and began descending. Hand under hand, boots clamped against the line for extra drag, he clambered down as fast as he could without causing too much dangerous swaying.

The men in Munit's river crew assumed they had seen just about everything the canyon had to offer. Added together, the thirteen of them had racked up more than two centuries of personal experience smuggling over, under, around, and through the Odorian. With eons of ancestral lore besides. Yet here was something new: a human-like shape dancing down through the air in front of them. In silent awe they stopped paddling and withdrew to the dark edges of the river, pressing against the rock walls to hold their positions.

One reached the end of the line. The water was a good twenty feet down, and the current appeared fast but manageable. But he wasn't in the mood for a midnight swim. He looked toward the banks on either side of the river. Or rather, he looked *for* the banks, but could see that the water ran right along the base of the cliff walls. Still, he supposed it would be shallower near the edge. Turning sideways, One kicked his feet forward, drew them back, kicked them forward, again and again, generating a swinging motion, getting closer to each wall with every iteration.

From the shadows upriver Munit and company stared as the figure flew back and forth over the water. Munit removed the plastic wrapping from four semiautomatic pistols and distributed them.

When he reckoned he had maxed out his range, on the next forward swing One gave a final kick, and then released at the peak of the upswing, soaring toward the edge of the river, forgetting that he had tied the end of the rope around his belt. The rope arrested him and he plummeted head-first and backwards, the momentum of his body weight pulling him out of his pants. As the belt and pants shot up toward his ankles, he managed to hook his left knee through the line, saving himself from plunging into the river.

"Son of a bitch!" yelled the twisting squirming human pendulum, swooping back and forth over the water upside down. Pointing up at the moon was One's butt, covered only in camouflage antibacterial underwear.

Chapter 21

Bombing the Explorer down a straightaway through the forest, Six spotted a gap in the trees ahead, a grey space. He slowed. An intersection. With a paved road. He skidded to a stop in front of the crossroads and switched off the ignition.

Six opened his door, then twisted to face Four. "You coming, or you guys want some privacy?"

Both operatives stepped out of the car. Five pulled up behind them.

"Where's the GPS at?" Four asked.

Five held up an index finger. One.

"Right, he would, but who's got the redundancy?" Four followed up.

The other compact braked with a testy spray of gravel, and Three and Two sprang out.

"Why are we stopping?" Two demanded. "We need to put more distance between ourselves and that hot mess up there."

Six turned on her.

"Are you having your monthlies right this minute? We stopped," he explained, "because we either need to form a steering committee or a discussion group to exchange perspectives about where the fuck we are, or we need the goddamn backup GPS."

They pawed through their packs and Four found the spare GPS in an inner pocket, cushioned by packets of dehydrated beef stroganoff.

"Does the committee concur that we start out driving away from Shizl?" Two asked.

No one objected, and she addressed Six and Four. "You want to choose a nice camping spot for your friend along the way? Try to keep him out of sight of the cavalry a little longer?"

They piled back into the vehicles and turned right onto the paved road. After a few up and down kilometers on the curvy two-lane, Six slowed, staring hard at the shoulder of the road. He eased the Explorer into the ditch, rolled up the other side, and rammed it in among a stand of scrubby trees. He cracked open two of the windows and turned around. Four dribbled water from a plastic bottle into the Vodanian police officer's mouth.

"Not too much now," Six cautioned. "You know how that can get him into trouble."

Six left the key in the ignition and he and Four climbed into Five's car. The two sedans drove west and south, Four tracking their progress on the GPS.

After half an hour, Six said, "Wonderful scenery. But let's not try to see all of it on our first visit."

"There's a southbound route coming up. Fifteen klicks," said Four.

While he was still cursing, One heard laughter. First one voice, then several. He stopped struggling to right himself, and instead reached for the weapon inside the pack that swayed from his neck.

Suddenly he had lots of company. He counted six kayaks circling. Seven. Farther upstream, two canoes held steady, the forward man in each pointing a pistol.

"Okay my friend," a man called from one of the kayaks. "We can help you."

Twisting to face skyward, and bending forward at the waist, One succeeded in catching hold of the rope. He pulled himself to an upright position, still swinging a little. A kayaker approached and positioned himself directly under One.

"First, you bag," he demanded, accent thick.

One dropped his pack into the arms of the man waiting below, who paddled away. The gunmen in the canoes passed their weapons to men in the kayaks. The two canoes came forward with their sides touching, the men in the back gripping each other's paddles. In the front, kayakers pressed their vessels in to hold the canoes together and steady. The formation floated into position under One, and the front man in each canoe stood and took hold of One's thighs. A canoer reached up with a folding knife and cut the line. They lowered One into the canoe on the left, and the boats dispersed.

"You are American?" asked the kayaker who took his pack. The leader, presumably.

"Yes sir," One replied.

"Good. We are Pazaris, America is our friend." He extended his hand. One nodded and shook his hand.

"You go with us, okay?"

One didn't really consider it a question, but he responded, "Let's go."

The canoe holding One followed the lead kayak. The others formed up behind, saying nothing as they stroked the water and snaked their way down through the mountains.

The police officers and their captive coughed and squinted in the smoke, now thick as mountain fog. The district commander, walking point, told them they had almost reached the vehicles. After another couple of minutes, he stumbled off the end of the path just above the clearing where they parked, but he could see only the two patrol cars. Which could only mean, hopefully, that the guard had the sense to drive the other three vehicles downhill to safety. The commander could maybe absolve his subordinate for napping if he safeguarded the prized new Explorer.

The police officers hastened down off the trail toward the vehicles. They squeezed six men into each patrol car, with Giardis, now cuffed again, wedged in the back seat of the first car. The remaining members of the tactical squad ran down the road, bent low in search of better air. When neither vehicle would start despite ample cursing, the men in the cars scrambled out and hustled after their colleagues. Giardis got his leash back.

The blaze crunched through the landscape, devouring dry brush and trees. Heat, driving sparks, and a billowing tsunami of smoke surged across from the west. The police and their suspect fled down the road. Along the way they heard two pops in close succession. The patrol cars' gas tanks.

After fifteen minutes, the group staggered to a halt, coughing, perspiring and breathing hard. They had descended far enough to feel sufficiently out of danger. While most of the policemen lit up cigarettes, the commander took out his phone and reported in to headquarters. He requested backup vehicles after briefing on the arrest, the paratroopers' incursion, and the fire.

"Ain't this some safari shit?" Six cackled, bouncing around in the front seat as Five tore across the rolling landscape over a rutted country lane, lights out. Three kept pace a few hundred meters back.

Shooting up over a rise, they noticed a trace of dust hovering over the road ahead. Five pointed out the cause, a truck laboring up an incline in the distance.

Four peered forward from the back seat. "Rustlers."

"You don't know that," said Six.

"Who else is up here in the middle of the night driving a truck around?"

"That is pure conjecture," Six argued.

"Just simple logic," Four insisted.

Six scoffed.

"Care to wager on the matter?" asked Four.

Soft laughter from the front seat, then Six said, "Alright, you're on. A hundred bucks?"

"How about ten percent of our completion bonus?"

"That's gonna be like five to eight hundred bucks."

"If you're not confident in your opinion we can call it off."

"No, it's just, I don't want to take that much of your pay. Don't you have kids and all?"

"Don't you worry none about my family. Just worry about them rustlers up there."

"And I say they ain't." Six swiveled around and extended his right hand back to shake on it.

Five slowed, aiming to keep outside the truck driver's visual range. After another ten minutes the truck braked and turned left, off the road and into a pasture. It rumbled up the slope toward a butte in the distance. Five took his foot off the accelerator and let the car roll to a stop. The car behind did the same. Six and Four got out, careful not to slam their doors, and trotted back to confer with Three and Two.

"What's the problem?" Two demanded.

"Rustlers," Four replied.

"We'll see about that," Six countered. "But in any case, it's getting time to change rides."

"A farm truck?" asked Two, incredulous.

"They won't be looking for that," said Four.

"And there's plenty of room for the whole family," Six added.

"Two men," said Three, peering through his infrared scope.

"What are we waiting for?" asked Four.

Three and Four trekked across the rocky pasture to approach from the left flank. The truck stopped about a kilometer and a half away. Five and Six jogged down the road to approach it from the other side. Two waited in concealment as backup.

Closing in, the Harrimore team saw a sheepfold and could hear the animals' low urgent baaing. The truck had smashed backwards right through the stick fence, and the two men drove the skittish livestock up the rear ramp into the truck's open-air compartment. Three sheep remained in the fold, jumpy and nervous.

Five signaled a question: Let them finish?

Six shook his head, that's enough. He peered through the scope toward Three and Four and gave a thumbs-up. Four mouthed the word rustlers and pretended he was shocked. Five and Six grabbed the top of the fence and vaulted into the muddy pen.

One of the rustlers yelled something in a language that was not English, and the other reached for the pistol in his back waistband. Six and Three both released warning bursts from their carbines and the man raised his arms. Five approached, removed the gun, as well as the man's keys and phone, and shoved him toward the natural rock wall at the back of the pen. Five patted down the other rustler, who looked like a teenager. The kid carried no gun or phone, and Five pointed to tell him to join the older one against the rear wall.

A sheep ran down the ramp back into the pen. Five tossed the keys to Three and raised the ramp and closed one of the latching bolts. Eleven animals huddled together inside the truck bed. Five raised his foot to the bumper and climbed in with them.

Six took two steps backwards toward the truck, his carbine covering the rustlers. Then he changed directions and strode straight toward the man and the teenager. He pointed at their hats. To Six's annoyance, the rustlers were extremely reluctant to part with their headgear. After several rounds of wordless back-and-forth, he persuaded them with an eloquent gesture from the M4.

Three drove the sheep truck over the pasture back to the road and turned right, toward the way they came from.

"Wrong way, cowboy," said Six, handing Three one of the hats.

"Can't leave the cars here. Gotta break the link," Three explained.

"We're gonna be halfway back to Dixie before any of these sheriffs start connecting the dots," Six commented. "But, whatevs."

Two and Four got back into the compacts and followed the truck southward. As the convoy rumbled across the rugged high mesas of western Vodania, the back ramp of the truck in its upright position vibrated in an erratic rhythm. The open latch bolt on the driver's side clattered noisily; the other latch bolt rattled in its housing and vibrated to the truck's rhythm, shifting a fraction one way and then back the other.

Fifteen semi-paved kilometers later, when the road approached Kharbam, they abandoned the cars. Everyone but Five squeezed into the front cab of the truck, with Three at the wheel. He adjusted the angle of his rustler hat several times as he drove into town. They passed rows of low stone houses and metal-shuttered storefronts. The streets were mostly dark and empty, not surprising at two in the morning. Perimeter walls guarded even the most dilapidated structures. At the main intersection at the center of town, a man in a tight-fitting white cap flung his lit cigarette butt at their windshield.

"Friendly place," commented Two.

From the window seat, wearing the other hat, Six saw a string of white lights atop a perimeter wall protecting a nightspot. On the roof of the low building was a lit-up sign in English as well as some other language.

Six stared. "The Camel Club sure looks like a happening spot."

"We got time?" Three asked.

"Maybe we hit it on the way out," replied Six.

Two snorted.

From the bottom of the cliff face a large stony chin thrust into the river. The rubble extended about eight meters out and measured a good ten meters across at its base. The current bubbled in a semicircle around the tip.

The leader divided the men into two shifts to dig a channel and assigned One to one of them. Fifteen minutes hauling rocks, fifteen minutes rest. He made them dig as close to the Pazari side of the river as possible.

Which meant clearing a path through where the landslide piled highest. He directed them to clear out the middle section of the new channel first in order to keep dry. The men labored swiftly, lifting rocks and hauling them far enough to fling into the water past the edge of the obstruction.

One kept tabs on who carried the pistols. They kept themselves out of reach. A bearded guy wearing what looked like a pirate hat positioned himself upstream in front of the kayaks. Inside the third kayak from the front was One's jump pack, with its perfectly shaped pocket containing his 9mm Glock. Which wasn't going to be the answer.

During a shift change, One approached the leader.

"Why are you doing this?"

"It's complicated. Politics."

Hefting a jagged fifty-pound stone, One wished he had packed a few blocks of C-4 to simplify matters.

After more than an hour of steep switchbacks and blind hairpin turns, Three took one hand off the wheel as the road flattened out. Rolling past hamlets and occasional farmhouses, the sheep truck reached the outskirts of Shizl. The road opened up to four lanes and buildings rose up on either side. A taxi and a couple of sedans passed by.

The sharp wail of a siren startled Three. The noise pierced the stillness only for a couple of seconds before cutting out. But flashing lights kept reflecting off signs and parked cars. All four Harrimore team members in the front seat swiveled their necks, seeking the source. About a kilometer back, a line of police cars, flashers blazing, sped along the nearly empty National Boulevard toward the truckload of sheep.

From the truck bed Five rapped on the wall of the cab. Six turned around and hissed "We see 'em."

"Looks like at least five cop cars," Three reported, studying the side mirror. "Correction. There's six of them,"

"I knew we should have avoided this road," said Two.

"Only feasible way in," Four replied. To Three he added, "Keep going. Just drive natural."

"You mean, inconspicuous-like?" Three answered.

"I'd be happy if you kept all the wheels on the pavement."

"Hey, I didn't design the roads in this place."

Up ahead on the right, Three noticed a cluster of shops and apartment towers. He figured that terrain offered the best available evasion prospects. Exploding flashes of blue and red lit up his side mirror like the Fourth of July.

"Get ready for Plan B, people," said Three.

The operatives in the cab took their weapons off safety. When the lead patrol car got within three blocks, Five crouched low behind the sheep. The animals recoiled from the bright lights and crowded into the corners. Blinding blue and red strobes filled the compartment, changing the sheep from one color to the other so rapidly they appeared purple. The police cars raced forward at crazy speed. The road vibrated and percussion waves shook the truck as each one tore past.

Jouncing uncomfortably in the back seat of the third cruiser in the police convoy, Paul Giardis glared out the side window at glimpses of Shizl's urban core streaming past. Blocky concrete buildings, scraggly trees, random piles of trash.

"Impressive place," he muttered. "Looks just like Zagovor, only more so."

The convoy reached the police headquarters compound, and the car carrying Giardis drove directly to the back side of a squat, square structure behind the main building.

They led the prisoner down a semi-dark concrete staircase and through a series of hallways with locked gates and guards. At the end of a tunnel-like passage, they reached an empty cage, smaller than a college dorm room. A heavy-duty steel chain link fence created walls and a low ceiling. The only furniture was a plastic bucket with its handle missing. The police escorts removed Giardis's serape and boots, took off the handcuffs, and locked him in.

Four studied the GPS as they rolled along National Boulevard. "Hang a left in half a klick, onto Khagani Street."

They had reached the thick of the city. As soon as they made the turn onto Khagani, Six said, "Stop here a minute."

Three took his foot off the accelerator and looked over at Six.

"That kebab stand is still open," Six explained.

"Don't be an ass," said Two.

"We can't come all the way to Shizl and not sample the cuisine. They're famous for their lamb kebabs."

"I could eat," said Four.

"Are you all crazy?" Two exploded. "I'm pulling rank. Keep driving," she ordered Three.

Three continued another two blocks and pulled over in front of a row of darkened shops. Six grinned at him, and Three said, "No onions."

Six and Four climbed down out of the cab. Several of the sheep made inquisitive, are-we-there-yet bleats. Down the street, young people dribbled in and out of a dance club. Four and Six strolled back toward the intersection with the kebab stand. After a block, Four peeled off for surveillance and backup, and Six put in his earbuds and plopped his rustler hat back on.

Six approached the stand, bobbing his head and swaying to his pretend music. He got in line behind a tall young man and a very smiley young woman who had their hands all over each other. She reminded him of a Bollywood dancer. He also noticed they were speaking English.

"I can't believe you're still hungry," she said, laughingly rubbing the guy's abdomen.

"It's going to be a long bus trip," he answered.

When his turn came, Six pointed and gestured to order a dozen kebabs. He glanced at the laminated menu, guessed at the total, and handed over three bills of Vodanian money that he figured would cover it. The vendor made change, which Six accepted with a nod and shoved into his pocket.

When Four and Six climbed back into the truck, Three drove uphill through steep, twisting residential roads before easing into a quiet nook sheltered by overhanging tree branches. While the men ate kebabs, Two opened a dried meal from her pack.

"Street food, seriously?" she said. "You're all going to be sick as dogs tomorrow. In addition to compromising the mission today."

Three rolled down his window and dropped a wedge of roasted onion onto the street.

After the chow break, Three maneuvered the truck farther uphill, into Shizl's swankiest precincts. He pulled over next to a small park, and all five of the Harrimore team gathered behind a wooden gazebo to review their plan and assemble their gear. They ignored the persistent baaing of the sheep.

"Maybe it's a little late now," Four admitted. "But did they have cold beers at that kebab stand?"

"Switch," the leader ordered, looking at his watch. Five men leaned their shovels against the sides of the ditch and climbed out, and five others, including One, jumped in. The trench, about two meters deep and four meters wide, extended nearly the full length of the rock pile. Water seeped through the remaining half-meter of wall on the upstream side. They cleared away the barrier on the downstream side and water poured in and began rising. Working as fast as they could, three of the men broke down the remaining impediment and the river gushed into the trench.

Everyone got back into the boats, with One again seated in the center of one of the canoes. Two kayakers paddled upstream, returning the way they came. That leaves eleven guards, One noted. The main body of the group floated through the channel they just cleared, and continued downstream. The men worked their paddles with easy strokes, letting the river pull them along.

After it dropped down out of the high peaks, the Odorian broadened and flattened. The men passed around a bottle of homemade-looking liquor. One put the bottle to his lips and pretended to swig. The squad chattered and joked as they cruised along. The leader appeared relaxed and did not translate any of the banter for One.

After an hour or so the floating party pulled over to the Pazaria side of the river, where a rocky beach spread out below a high overhanging cliff.

"We stop here," the leader told One.

Three of the Pazaris stayed in their boats, one in each of the canoes and one in a kayak. The six empty kayaks got tied in lines behind the canoes. The consolidated flotilla, with the free kayak in the lead, pushed off to drift downstream, leaving One with eight men on the riverbank. My odds keep improving, he thought.

The leader lined them up, putting One in fourth position, between two unarmed men. They filed to the downstream end of the beach and continued along a narrow ledge that gradually climbed to about two stories above the water. On the way up, One considered leaping off and seeing if he could outswim this bunch. He probably could, but he couldn't outpace a kayak, much less a bullet. The line stopped and now there were only two men ahead of him. The foremost of them got to his hands and knees and crawled into a crevice. The man in front of One did the same. One looked down at the water. Anything would be better than a cave.

One turned around. He could start throwing guys off the ledge. But he couldn't see how that led anywhere except to his own swift death. The man behind him smiled and gestured encouragingly.

One dropped to his knees and peered into the crevice. Weak white light jiggled around inside, from the flashlight of someone ahead of him. One crawled in. The passage was too low to stand up in and One duck-walked forward over jagged rock. He came to a wall. Someone fifteen feet above pointed the beam so he could see the finger and toeholds gouged into its surface. At the top of the wall, he could stand upright for two steps. The flashlight swiveled to reveal a pair of shoes vanishing into a hole not much bigger than a pet door. One took a deep breath, and another. The only thing worse than a cave was a tunnel. The man with the flashlight growled something in Pazari, and One got the gist. He squatted down and forced his head into the hole.

Harrimore does not pay anywhere near enough for this shit, One muttered, pulling himself along on his forearms, dragging his legs behind. In the pure darkness he heard the men ahead of him scraping forward. Their odors filled the narrow space. The tunnel seemed to slope upwards and curve to the left. His shoulders touched both sides at once. His heart thumped erratically. It became difficult to breathe. He couldn't turn around and the tube was getting tighter. One squeezed his eyes shut. Remember your training. Focus on the mission. Keep it together, Braxton.

Time stopped as tides of panic rose up and washed over and through him. When the waves eventually subsided, Braxton felt someone pushing the bottoms of his boots, and he began to move forward again. At the end of the tunnel, scraped up and trembling, Braxton found himself in a small chamber. Light came from above. Braxton could tell it was the bottom of a circular shaft. An iron ladder ran up one side. He reached for the rungs and climbed, regaining strength and composure with each step up.

At the top, four men seized him and bound his ankles and wrists with duct tape. They cut off one of his pant legs at the knee to make a blindfold and a gag. Braxton felt himself hoisted up and carried headfirst like a battering ram. He smelled the open air and an earthy scent. The men jostled along a bit further, then they lifted him higher and flopped him face down on the back of a mule, a donkey, something, and tied him on, feet hanging off one flank, head and hands dangling from the other.

In the shadows behind the gazebo in the tidy, well-trimmed park, the Harrimore team huddled in ninja suits and light-absorbing face paint. Four, back from recon, faced Two, Three, and Six.

"Woods, five-meter high primary fence, ten-meter clear zone, secondary fence electrified," Four briefed. "Guards in the clear zone between the fences, dogs behind the secondary."

"Wait," Two stopped him. "Dogs? As in, plural?"

"Yeah, we counted six. Nasty-looking things, almost like Rottweilers."

"How do we know which one's our target?" Three asked.

After a moment, Two answered, "We don't have enough identifying data to make a positive ID. We have to do 'em all. Is Five in position?"

"Working his way in," Four replied.

They commenced the operation shortly after four a.m. local. Three, holding one of the tranquilizer rifles, climbed back in the truck. Four sprinted up toward the woods surrounding the compound, the other tranquilizer rifle slung on his back.

Two and Six proceeded at a more measured pace through the quiet streets of the wealthy neighborhood, carrying a small drone and its controller. They turned off the main road that led up to the entrance of the Presidential compound and snuck along a side street with a smooth curve up the ridge. They pivoted for a moment to watch the sheep truck creep up the slope of the main road, no headlights.

Two and Six darted forward from shadow to shadow, peering into the yards and gardens for the best spot to set up. Two spun at the sound of a growl behind her. Three dogs rushed at them from across the street. Two and Six scrambled onto a parked car and the dogs surrounded them, barking and leaping in angry excitement. A couple more dogs joined the fray by the time Six drew his tranquilizer pistol. With two pops he put darts into the throats of the largest pair in the pack. They yelped and fled, drawing all but one of the rest. Six popped it as well, and he and Two hurried up the street.

They spotted a large modern house with no sign of security cameras. They scaled its high stone perimeter wall, mindful of the embedded shards of broken glass festooning the top. In the back garden they found a concrete shed. Atop its flat tiled roof, they set up the controller and powered it up. Two prepped the drone and synced it to the controller. She started its engines, and on her nod, Six tossed it aloft. The drone shot up at a nearly vertical trajectory.

With night vision goggles wrapped around his face, Four crept through the woods. Steady, soundless. On a rise thirty meters before the primary fence, he selected his tree and began climbing.

Along a dark section of the back side of the property, Five lay motionless in a shallow trench adjacent to the outer fence. His careful observation confirmed their tactical briefing that the inner fence was electrified, but only across the top. He watched, ready to make his move.

Six crouched behind Two so he could view the monitor. She positioned the drone five hundred meters above the compound and scanned the grounds with the main camera. The dogs gathered at the fence line at the front of the property, still agitated by the earlier barking from the neighborhood below. Two lowered the drone to a point just above the roof of the main building. Staring at the monitor, she followed the security camera wiring, got the drone into position on the edge of the eave, and skunked the camera. The spray from the drone coated the lens, blinding it temporarily. Two estimated that in this dryness it would only take about twenty minutes for the spray to evaporate. She maneuvered the drone along the roof line, looking for the next camera.

From twenty meters up in his birch, Four watched the drone at work. When it finished skunking the cameras facing his side, he raised his rifle and sighted through the scope on the nearest dog. He had a clear line over the fences. He pulled the trigger and the dog jumped back and growled, twisting and shimmying. Four fired off another round and plugged another animal before the pack retreated to the area between the main house and what looked to be an oversized garage. The dogs were no longer in sight from Four's vantage.

With the dogs providing a distraction, Five stood up to grip the vertical bars with his gloves. He leaned back and elevated both feet to brace against the bars, folding his body into a crouch. He reached higher with his hands, then kicked upward, again and again, frog-hopping his way to the top. He affixed a line, rappelled down, and sprinted across the gap to the inner fence.

On top of the garden shed, Two and Six peered into the drone monitor. They spotted a guard emerge from his command post at the right front corner of the property. The guard looked around, facing toward the spot the dogs had been.

"What's in his hand?" Six asked.

Two lowered the drone and zoomed the camera to focus on the phone in the guard's left hand.

"Movie night!" said Six. "What's on?"

Two got the drone closer, and on the phone screen they could make out an image of a naked woman bent forward over a chair, a naked man thrusting vigorously behind her, his large hands gripping her hips.

"Yowza!" exclaimed Six. "Zoom in!"

Two half-turned and punched Six on the thigh. She elevated the drone to resume its coverage of the whole compound. Two of the dogs lay prone in the grass next to the garage; the other four milled about in a state of uncertainty. Several minutes passed. The Harrimore team found itself in a similar state. They all knew the operation should be completed by now. They should be on their way home.

"Alright, I've got something," Six said to Two, pulling a kebab from his pocket.

"Not interested," Two replied.

"It's not for you. Bring back the drone."

"What for?"

"We need to lure those dogs to the back fence so Hiawatha can let fly his arrows."

"You're not tying a meat-stick to my drone," Two hissed.

Three was growing impatient. He figured, we have a truck, might as well put it to use. From the top of the cab, he should be able to establish line of sight into the compound and put those dogs to sleep. He started the ignition and began backing the truck very slowly uphill.

"I am so reporting this," Two declared. She attached a thin nylon line to the undercarriage of the drone. Six pressed the tip of his tranquilizer pistol into the side of her right buttock.

"It's mission-critical," he replied.

When it was ready, Six held the drone aloft again, his pistol still pointed at Two's backside. They launched the drone and its payload high into the sky, the moon now obscured by cloud cover. Two eased the drone down above the dogs and began circling. When they noticed the kebab, she led them toward the rear perimeter, keeping the bait just out of jumping range. She knew Five's approximate position from the overhead view she had earlier, but he was impossible to spot against the dark backdrop of the woods.

Up in the birch, Four snapped alert when the dogs ran into view, barking and cavorting toward the back fence. He drew on the hindmost of the four, and got the dart in its flank, above its hind leg.

Five, by now leaning back in a safety harness clipped to the inner fence just below the electrified cables, pressed the soles of his shoes against the bars for stability. He peered forward, hands free. As the dogs passed below and in front of him, he steadied the tube and expelled his breath in a forceful puff. Needle to the neck of the leader. The drone led the pack further along the perimeter fence, then doubled back toward his position, now only two dogs following. His blow tube was loaded. At the two corners of the property visible from his position, security guards stepped out of their booths.

Just a little further, Three calculated. The truck rumbled backward up the empty road, the entrance to the presidential compound coming into view in the side mirror. On the passenger side, the rear tire dropped into a steep pothole. The truck shuddered, jarring open the latch bolt. The rear ramp swung down and clanged onto the road, scraping noisily as the truck kept reversing further up the hill. Three stomped on the brake, tumbling the sheep toward the back of the truck. A ewe trotted down the ramp and away from the truck. The ten others followed, baaing to each other.

On the grounds of the compound, the two undrugged dogs heard the clatter from the truck and the baaing of the sheep. They raced toward the front of the property. Four fired at the streaking dogs and missed. Three adjusted his night vision goggles, reached for his rifle, and pointed it through the driver's window. Guards ran forward, weapons drawn. The two guard dogs launched a frenzy of barking, their ferocious muzzles poking through the inner fence. Five retreated across the gap and climbed back over the outer fence. Floodlights flashed on. Four took aim again. The sheep became agitated, running in different directions. Two raised the drone and flew it over the fences. She buzzed behind the sheep, harrying them toward the vehicle entrance checkpoint below the front of the property. Four fired at the guard dogs and connected this time. Three turned his head to see a pack of stray dogs bounding up the road, rushing past him toward the sheep. Four checked his clip: one dart left. Inside the compound, one target left. Three swiveled back to face the compound. He took aim and fired his tranquilizer rifle. As Four readied his shot, the dog jerked and sprang back, yelping. Must be Three joining the fight, Four figured. Four sent another dart in anyway and began climbing down the tree. The herd of sheep, panicking at the sound of the street dogs charging up the hill, stampeded toward the compound checkpoint. Three shifted the truck into first gear and gunned it downhill, trailing a comet of sparks from the metal ramp dragging along the street. At the checkpoint, sheep dashed under the horizontal blocking arm and leaped over the hydraulic vehicle barrier.

Six holstered his pistol and leaned forward next to Two's ear. "Having fun yet?"

Chapter 22

At Shizl's main bus station before sunrise on Sunday, exhaust billowed up and merged with the grey clouds pressing down from the north. For Tara, diesel fumes invoked the discomforts and adventures of travel. But she wasn't going anywhere. She and Mads stood with Stefano in the gloom.

The bus to the southeast border crossing was scheduled to depart at five, and the driver was anxious to get underway. Jittery passengers shoved parcels and luggage into the open compartment at the base of the bus.

After a night of dancing, feasting, and partying Shizl-style on Stefano's roof, and dreamlike pre-dawn lovemaking back at her apartment, Tara felt disoriented. A jetlaggy sort of buzz jammed all her circuits.

Mads wore a dazed look. "I will write," he repeated, in a faraway voice.

"When will I see you?"

"Before too long."

She raised an eyebrow.

"You're right, it will be after too long."

She grabbed him and they kissed, long and lingering.

When they paused for air, Tara said, "You still taste like a kebab."

The embassy's newest Chevy Trailblazer idled in the driveway of the ambassador's residence, quietly puffing fumes into the surrounding darkness. The regular chauffeur hefted a pair of large designer suitcases into the rear cargo compartment. At the front door of the residence, the taller housekeeper clipped a leash on Davos and led him out to the vehicle. He peed on both rear tires before allowing himself to be stowed in the cargo compartment. In the front seat, stifling a yawn, the Vodanian police officer on escort duty waited.

When all was in readiness, the ambassador and Lithia stepped outside and down the path to the driveway. After they got settled in the middle passenger compartment, the chauffeur shifted into drive and nodded to the guard booth to open the gate.

The Blazer pulled onto the street and Lithia reached around back to scratch Davos' head.

"You poor thing. Off to prison on trumped-up charges."

The ambassador laughed amiably and patted Lithia's knee twice. "It is decent of them to open up early for us."

"You always find the positive side, don't you," said Lithia.

The ambassador bumped his shoulder against hers. She smiled for a moment, until she noticed he was tilting against her to get a better view out the windshield.

"Why are you going this way, we have to go to the kennel," the ambassador admonished the chauffeur.

"Yes sir, but there's a block in the road. A problem with a farm truck that tipped over."

At barely six o'clock Sunday morning, President Chilik glowered out his third-story window. At this hour, he couldn't be expected to decide which was more upsetting, the defense minister's agitated voice squawking from the phone in his left hand, or the flock of sheep outside devouring his flowers and shrubbery.

Chilik heard the minister say, "air and small-arms attack from Pazaria overnight." With his right-hand Chilik picked up his private phone and pressed the speed-dial for Uncle Farao.

Wearing only the rumpled top half of a set of sky-blue cotton pajamas, Chilik ambled down the corridor, past the closed door of his wife's bedroom, and stepped outside onto the back balcony. Invigorating morning air swirled around his exposed presidential areas. A phone in each hand, he marched to his favorite vantage point against the balustrade. He inhaled a lungful and gazed out at the spectacular view of Vodania extending north to the glorious Asich Mountains. As usual, the sight stirred up feelings of patriotism. A change of perspective, the view from on top. So important to decisive decision-making. Then a muttered curse caused him to look straight down.

Chilik's mouth opened in a silent scream as he watched the custodian drag the body of one of the guard dogs toward the service area at the rear of the property. Four inert dogs lay heaped on the ground next to the dumpsters, and the custodian dropped the next one onto the pile.

A disembodied voice came out of the phone in his left hand. The defense minister saying, "Thanks to our preparations and training, there were no casualties on our side."

Farao finally picked up.

"They killed all my dogs and replaced them with sheep," Chilik blurted.

"Who did?" Farao demanded.

"What's that, sir?" asked the defense minister. "I repeat, no casualties on our side."

"They're destroying the garden," Chilik complained.

"Are you in danger right now?" asked Farao.

"We will defend Vodania to the utmost," the defense minister pledged.

"No, but I think we should close the airport and seal the borders, don't you?" Chilik asked.

"I don't understand what in shit you're talking about," Farao snapped. "Meet me in the Presidentorium at seven."

Chilik could smell his uncle's cologne right through the phone line.

"Yes sir, those could be prudent security measures," the defense minister replied. "I can convey that to Minister Farao."

Chilik heard the defense minister say *Farao*. He pulled the phone away from his left ear, glared at it, and flung it vaguely in the direction of the dumpsters. Now he had to go put on his leadership pants.

Andy Pulano congratulated himself for his discipline in sleeping in on Sunday rather than getting up at dawn to peek under the proverbial Christmas tree. But, with sunlight trickling in around the edges of his drapes, he could wait no longer. He reached for his phone to make sure Santa delivered.

The first text he read informed him that the ambassador went wheels-up at 6:45. Which meant he had been chargé d'affaires ad interim for nearly an hour. Lying on his back under a light blanket, Andy indulged in a celebratory shoulder-shimmy. He could feel authority coursing through his veins. The power. Then he shook his head. Humility and service, he reminded himself. Don't tip your hand.

He sat up to scroll through his incoming messages, searching for the main present. He found a text from an unknown number, which read in its entirety: *It flows right.*

Translation: *Feliz Navidad!*

Tara slumped on the couch in her living room all afternoon. A chilly grey rain lashed the windows.

She sipped tentatively at a steaming cup of tea. She stared in silence as time passed. Or didn't pass. Both her hands wrapped around the cup and pressed it to her navel. Her back and shoulders rounded forward, and she folded her legs toward her torso. As if she were trying to curl her entire body around the warmth of her teacup.

"He's gone," she said aloud. "And he took summer with him."

Part V

The Succeeding Daze

Chapter 23

At daybreak Monday morning, Tara drove up toward the northern bluff above the capital. She had the Wrangler's top down to let her hair swirl in the early morning chill. She figured she would get her laps in before half the embassy community flocked to the residence to take advantage of the Labor Day holiday and the ambassador's absence. The last thing she wanted was company.

Sunlight slanted into Shizl's swankiest precincts. The road grew steeper, and Tara downshifted. For the Vodanians, even the most privileged, it was a regular workday. Tara smelled boiling barley along with itchy tendrils of cigarette smoke. She pushed aside her hunger pangs and her emptiness and focused on driving. Rounding a curve under a leafy canopy, she braked to avoid a sheep. Without a glance, it ambled across the street and onto an unprotected strip of lawn.

At the residence, she said good morning to the guard and stepped straight to the pool gate. The water looked cold. Good. At poolside, she re-read the text that came in from Mads overnight.

Hi Sweet! Bumpy bus rides, made it to Turkey finally after dark. Nutty crossing out of Vodania. They were closing the border, then a toy airplane was flying around, the police started shooting at it. Hope you're ok? I miss you!

Tara put away her phone. His message only highlighted the distance. She stripped down to her swimsuit and walked around the edge to the deep end. She flexed her knees, then froze at a sound behind her. A rustling. She turned to see the German ambassador's daughter crouching half-hidden in the bushes on the other side of the fence that separated the properties. Tara smiled and waved at her. The girl scrambled to her feet and dashed away, out of sight.

Before diving in, Tara heard a man's voice calling, "Sabrina!"

The weekend events jolted the embassy staff back into crisis mode. On Monday morning, the command center in the secure conference room again thrummed with purpose and urgency. The DCM, now chargé d'affaires until the ambassador's return, entered wearing a regular business suit and tie. To forestall any ambassadorial-type deference, he sidled over to General Elfersen, put a hand on his shoulder, and thanked him for the military updates throughout the weekend. He conducted a similar ritual with station chief Phyllis Snicklehimer for the intel briefings, and with political counselor Gary Hambert for the latest election campaign developments. He circled the room, bestowing an encouraging word on all the staffers present, before taking his customary seat next to the ambassador's empty one.

Andy picked up the draft sit-rep waiting for his approval and began scanning its paragraphs. He looked up with a puzzled smile, then read aloud, "Nationalist tabloid runs front page photo of sheep grazing on the president's compound, under banner headline: VODANIA'S PRESIDENCY TAKEN OVER BY SHEEP."

Andy smirked at Brian Mitchell, the assistant public affairs officer, and asked "Where do they come up with this material?"

He continued reading from the sit-rep, "Vodania's government spokesman cited a litany of dangerous provocations and escalations over the weekend, including fires, hostage-takings, assaults on military, police, and ordinary citizens, livestock stealing, and a raid on the president's compound."

Andy ran a hand over his smooth dome. "What a plague of mischief. Sounds almost biblical."

"We knew there'd be a lot of election stunts in the final days," Gary Hambert responded. "With the airports and borders now closed, what we don't know is if the main body of election observers will be able to get in. Not good."

"On that point," Andy interjected. "The ambassador and I spoke again this morning. He is very anxious to return, and we need to vigorously pursue all options for getting him here. Let's circle back to that after we finish the round-up."

Andy planned to pressure the Vodanians through a variety of official channels as well as via press leaks and public statements. Under his direction, the embassy would visibly do its utmost to enable Ambassador Lamkin to return. With any luck, these aggressive tactics would irritate the Vodanians enough to enable him to remain chargé during the most crucial days of the crisis, while he figured out who had done what. The chaos was beautiful except that he did not have enough clarity to know whether he could make his big announcement at tomorrow's EU conference.

Andy turned to General Elfersen for the latest on the military situation.

The general squared his shoulders and declared, "The Vodanian ministry of defense accused Pazaria of conducting an aerial assault with paratroopers around midnight Saturday night into the early hours of Sunday morning. These are the first known hostilities of this conflict. No casualties reported so far. Our DAO in Zagovor reports that Pazarian paratroopers did not deploy over the weekend. They were not called up, and there were no flights out of the military side of the airport in Zag."

"They say you just can't make this stuff up," Phyllis cracked, "but maybe you can."

Andy laughed companionably and said to her, "I'm going to want the latest border imagery, with troop positions and all, tomorrow morning before I go over to the EU peace shindig."

Victor Manchego dabbed a bit more tanning lotion on his chest and arms, keeping alert as to whether any of the single women at the ambassador's pool noticed his muscles flexing. It was a pretty good crowd enjoying Labor Day afternoon, despite the absence of the elusive Tara. He wanted to tell her she turns Shizl into Sizzle. He smirked and leaned back in his lounge chair, scoping the pool ladies through his wrap-around shades.

The exuberant chorus of 'Livin' la Vida Loca' burst forth from Victor's phone, shattering his reverie and interrupting his enjoyment of the visual feast. He lifted the phone to look at the incoming number. At least it wasn't Mei-Lin calling to see if he could pick up something on the way back. Her crafty way of asking when he was coming home.

"Hello?"

"Hello Victor? This is Ray from USAID. I got embassy duty this weekend. The police called, they say they arrested someone who claims to be an American, but he has no passport or ID. Do I have to go visit him?"

Victor, feeling magnanimous, replied, "Great . . . no passport or ID, fantastic. We'll look into it tomorrow. Visiting the next business day is within the regs. Do you have a name?"

"I told you, it's Ray from USAID."

Mid-morning on Tuesday, U.S. Chargé d'Affaires Andy Pulano entered Hotel Apex's Magnolia Room through a side door several minutes before his scheduled speaking slot. He stood watching EU High Commissioner Cauchon bustling, beaming, bursting with relevance as he pirouetted nimbly among the dignitaries and panelists. Andy scanned the room as many in the audience craned their necks at his arrival. He did not see any especially high-ranking Vodanian officials. It looked like mostly academics, think-tankers, and journalists, bolstered by cadres of university students, occupying the rows and rows of folding chairs that filled the large event room. He did not feel badly that the EU's solo diplomatic gambit failed to draw any significant politicians, who would presumably be out campaigning this close to the election, but part of him regretted that there would not be a more distinguished group of witnesses to his surprise announcement. But they would all see it on the news.

Jeremiah, one of the junior officers in the embassy's political section, hastened to Andy's side.

"Have the proceedings gone about as we discussed?" Andy asked, his voice barely above a whisper.

"Almost word for word."

"Anything noteworthy? Anything—stand out?"

"High Commissioner Cauchon was pretty eloquent."

"Lengthy?" Andy asked, with a twinkle.

"That too."

When Cauchon noticed Andy, his face ignited in welcome. Of course, he would have preferred the ambassador, Andy well knew, but having the stand-in nevertheless bestowed vital validation onto this European Union initiative. At least until he broke his news.

Cauchon hurried over. He gathered Pulano in a warm embrace and escorted him to the stage.

Andy fixed a demure smile on his face throughout Cauchon's effusive introduction. When he got his turn at the microphone, he opened by conveying Ambassador Lamkin's personal greetings and deepest regrets at not being able to attend.

Having discharged that duty, Andy said, "Let me also add my own appreciation to that expressed by the previous speakers, for all those who worked to create this conference. Particularly the European Union diplomats under the very capable direction of High Commissioner Cauchon."

During the requisite applause that followed, Andy picked up the sheaf of papers containing his prepared remarks, folded the pages in half lengthwise, and slipped them into the inside pocket of his suit jacket.

He placed his hands on the sides of the lectern and leaned forward.

"Several of this morning's speakers have highlighted the timeliness and relevance of this conference. And most of us in this room would naturally be inclined to agree with that view. Indeed, I accepted the high commissioner's kind invitation to speak here today because I shared a similar opinion."

Andy smiled at Cauchon again before resuming.

"Now, in no way do I wish to detract from the righteous intentions and excellent preparatory work that went into convening this gathering of distinguished leaders and concerned citizens from Vodania and Pazaria. Nor do I mean to impugn the vital roles and contributions of all in attendance. Nevertheless—"

Andy raised his palms toward the audience.

"—as a consequence of fresh information I received this morning, I will tell you that this conference is not timely. Nor is it relevant."

He paused to sip water from the crystal goblet on the lectern, relishing the reaction to his attack. He snuck a quick peek at Cauchon's affronted countenance.

"I see that my bluntness discomfits many of you. I promise you will feel much better when you hear what I have to share. Perhaps you may even believe that God has spoken, Nature has triumphed, History has prevailed. All I can tell you, quite simply, is that the Odorian River has returned to its original course."

Silence descended, then a wave of gasps and exclamations.

"Yes, the Odorian River has returned to its original course," Andy repeated. "In the area of the recent landslide, the area of contention, the river has found its way again. Thus, there is no cause and no grounds for any territorial dispute between Vodania and Pazaria."

Andy smiled around at the audience.

"This is a plain fact. The two governments concerned can confirm the truth of it with the most recent satellite images."

The attendees began to perk up at the implications.

"As for me, I'm going back to my office."

Andy focused his gaze on the television cameras.

"What else is there to say or do? No conflict, no compromise."

After a late lunch on Tuesday, Victor Manchego went to the police agency's detention center to meet the arrested Amcit. He was escorted two levels underground, through a dank corridor to a steel cage cell. The prisoner, wearing a cowboy shirt and what almost looked like mariachi pants, glared at him.

"Good morning, my name is Victor Manchego. I am a consular officer from the U.S. Embassy in Shizl."

"It's about damn time. What took ya?" the prisoner demanded.

"Our normal practice is to visit arrest cases on the first business day after notification."

From a casual-looking black satchel slung over his shoulder, Victor pulled out a manila folder and a spiral steno notebook.

"Let's get started, shall we?" He smiled.

The man glared harder.

"Your name please."

"Paul Giardis."

"Let me make sure I have the spelling correct."

"G, I, A, R, D, I, S."

"And your nationality?"

"Jesus Christ, I'm American!"

"Date and place of birth?"

Giardis answered and Victor inscribed the information onto the steno pad.

"Do you have a passport, driver's license, birth certificate, other ID?" Victor asked.

"Not on me. My passport's at home and my wallet and badge are in the police locker room in Zagovor."

"So, you've been arrested in Pazaria also?"

"What?"

"Was that also on drug charges?"

"You don't get it. I'm DEA. I work out of the embassy in Zagovor. Call them right now."

"Sir, we will follow up on your statements and provide all appropriate assistance. In order to contact your family or anyone else you may designate, I'll need you to sign this Privacy Act waiver authorizing the State Department to share information about your arrest case."

"Or you could call Doug Wannabe, I mean, Watanabe, from your embassy."

"Can do. Go ahead and include him in your list on the Privacy Act waiver. And I won't be dilatory."

The EUR conference room was nearly full by the time Vonda Vance arrived on Tuesday morning, a little before the eight-thirty start time. The Labor Day weekend had not been much of a break for her, given all the turmoil in her part of the world. But finally, things seemed to have taken a turn for the better.

The assistant secretary's twice-weekly meeting with the bureau's multitude of deputy assistant secretaries and office directors was part ritual, part functional. The deputies took their customary spots flanking the assistant secretary, filling one long side of the conference table. The rest of the senior cadre, its numbers commensurate with the vastness and weightiness of EUR's responsibilities, occupied the remaining seats at the table and a second row against the walls. Late-comers and others of lower status found places to stand in the corners. By common understanding, and in keeping with the bureau's hierarchical distinctions, the chairs facing the assistant secretary belonged to the more senior office directors, the ones who headed the largest or most important offices.

When her turn to speak arrived, Deputy Assistant Secretary Vonda Vance straightened up. "We have potential good news out of Vodania for a change. The DCM announced at a conference this morning that the Odorian River has reverted back to its original course."

"I fucking know," the assistant secretary beamed. "I watched the goddamn GIF on my phone. No conflict, no compromise. Fucking spank-ass brilliant."

Smiles all around the table.

"But why's the goddamn DCM announcing this?" the assistant secretary asked. "Where's Lamkin?"

"He's on a quick trip to Vienna with his wife, scheduled to be back at post today, but the airports and borders are still closed. The embassy's working hard to find a way back in for him."

The assistant secretary pouted at Vonda and spoke in a sugary tone. "Mucus! Mucus, mucus, mucus. Thick ropey strands of green snot and pus. Not a good fucking time to be away. Just please don't tell me there was any opera involved."

Vonda bit her lip and said nothing.

Everyone froze, knowing the optics were dreadful. The spectacle of an ambassador away at the opera while major developments occurred at his post would mar the reputation of the State Department. And of EUR in particular.

A faint frown scrunched up the face of the assistant secretary, whose shoulders had hunched and stiffened.

After a strained moment of silence, the assistant secretary, in a soft melodic voice, relieved the tension by emitting a torrent of expletives, swear words, imaginatively violent curses, and unprintably foul language.

Throughout the extended symphony of cussing, principal deputy Geoff Bentwood nodded in loyal support.

After bursting the bounds of propriety, credulity, and anatomy, the assistant secretary paused for breath. Then, with a sweet smile for all assembled, finished with, "If you'll pardon my goddamn fucking French."

In the Hotel Apex gym early on Wednesday morning, Tara felt fire in her thighs. She had the elliptical set to level seven. Just keep moving, she told herself. No moping.

Her sluggishness slinked away. She leaned into her left leg. New experiences! Right leg. Fresh start! Left leg. New experiences! Right leg. Fresh start!

The Apex gym attracted few patrons at that hour. But there was Vlado, the Olympian. He was working in the free weights area with a male client. They took no notice of Tara in her form-fitting workout attire. Not that I want to be Katie Nichols, the belle of their A-100 class, she thought. But if I were, they'd be all over me, asking about my routine, giving advice, offering a spot whether I needed one or not. Tara finished with the elliptical, exhaled, and sat on an incline bench. Time for crunches.

The client, a tallish European-looking guy, fit and forty-something, held a barbell in his left hand, elbow tucked in against his hip. Through a double reflection in the mirrors along the walls, Tara watched Vlado standing next to him, his left hand guiding the barbell motion. Tara tried not to grunt too audibly as she raised and lowered her head and torso. On the next crunch, Tara witnessed Vlado slide his right hand down the man's lower back and slip it inside his waistband. A flagrant butt-grab. Each time the client raised the barbell, Vlado's hand squeezed the man's left buttock.

When they finished their session, the men walked past Tara. Midway through a sweaty set of squats, she had apparently become invisible. She heard the client speak in a German accent, "Until Monday morning then."

"I'll bring something sweet," Vlado replied.

"I know you will."

Chargé d'Affaires Andy Pulano aimed to arrive ten minutes late for the summons issued by President Chilik's office on Wednesday morning. He figured that was about the right amount of insouciance for his first meeting with Chilik in this capacity.

From the embassy to the Presidentorium was a short drive along distressed roads. Vineyards and barley fields gave way to recently constructed apartment complexes as they descended toward the city center. Andy insisted on riding in one of the regular sedans, rather than the ambassador's limo. But he agreed to allow the local police bodyguards who normally protected the ambassador to lend their weight to the entourage, in addition to that of his political counselor, Gary Hambert.

Inside the president's office, Chilik got right to the point. "I was not amused by your stunt yesterday. It was embarrassing to me."

A perplexed look clouded Andy's face, as he evidently struggled to comprehend the thinking behind such a statement. "Why should you be embarrassed? You won. You stood up for Vodania's territorial integrity and you won."

"The manner of the announcement was unseemly, coming from the Americans. This is our information, our news."

"It's not your fault the United States has such effective satellites," Andy parried. "And those are the same satellites that revealed the problem in the first place."

Chilik grunted.

Now for the pivot. "Ultimately," said Andy, "what's important is not who reports a story, it's who takes action. If you don't like the news I made, you have the power to replace it with your own. Bring your troops home in triumph. Throw 'em a parade. I'm not a politician, but in my country, voters love a victory. You should be happy the river is back where it belongs."

"How can I withdraw our soldiers when we've just been attacked? They will say I'm weak."

"If you don't take this opportunity now, what's going to change in the future? What reason will you give then, when you want to pull your soldiers back? If you don't act now your guys are stuck up there indefinitely. You don't want them up in the mountains when it gets cold. They'll be unhappy, they'll grow resentful. It costs you a lot of money. The

Pazari-Vodanians become upset and restless. You want to put the country back into success and prosperity after the election. Do you want a stalemate—or a victory?"

"It's risky to leave the border exposed," Chilik pointed out.

"I'll be completely honest with you," Andy responded, lowering his voice. "I don't know what happened with the incident on the border last weekend. I don't think anybody really does. But I can promise you that Vodania will not be attacked from Pazaria."

"You guarantee it?"

"I guarantee it."

Andy made a mental note to make sure Gary understood not to include that in the reporting cable.

Catalogues, magazines, bills, and letters spilled off the countertops onto the concrete floor of the embassy mailroom. But the main action for the two local employees was sorting a small mountain of packages, the weekly harvest from the American employees' online shopping.

The mail pouch usually arrived in country every Saturday. After the completion of certain procedures and formalities, including a snort or two of Kentucky bourbon, the Vodanian customs authorities normally released the shipments to the embassy on Tuesday. The embassy's Labor Day holiday delayed the current delivery by a day, and Vodania's ongoing airport and border closures raised an anxious upswelling of uncertainty about when the next shipment would come in. Through the shuttered customer-service window, the mailroom employees could feel the laser-hot stares of the American staff and their spouses, eager to claim their new tennis shoes, their children's favorite peanut butter, their winter jackets and their wine-pulls and their spy novels and their Oreos.

The mailroom guys knew from hard experience that certain sections of the embassy tended to pay exceptionally close attention to when their mail was ready for pick up. So, they disassembled the mountain looking for packages addressed to employees from those sections. As a routine precaution they wore protective gloves, and so did not feel the sticky dampness that soaked through the cardboard on the bottom of one small box. But that was not the only indicator of a problem.

"Ugh!" exclaimed the older of the two, wrinkling his nose and glaring at his co-worker. "What did you have for breakfast, a horse stuffed with rotten cabbage?"

"It's not me, the air's fine over here." He walked toward the older man, sniffing. "Oy! That is not human," he cried, backing away rapidly.

From opposite corners of the room their eyes scanned the packages.

"That one," said the younger man, pointing to a small cardboard box stained dark brown along one side.

The handwritten address was to the DEA Forensics Laboratory in Washington, but a bright orange sticker proclaimed 'UNAUTHORIZED. RETURN TO SENDER'. In the upper left corner, also handwritten, was the name Doug Watanabe and the address for U.S. Embassy Shizl.

The younger mailroom guy called Watanabe's office. His assistant answered and said he wasn't there; she wasn't sure when he'd be in. She offered to take a message. The older guy decided to call the security office.

Ken Dewitt got on the line. "Exit the mailroom immediately," he directed, "close the door and hold in the corridor. We'll be right there."

Ken and Kerry-Anne donned their white hazmat protective suits and checked each other's breathers and triple-layered gloves. They strode briskly through the embassy corridors, crossed the atrium in front of the cafeteria, and arrived at the entrance to the mailroom to find Chuck from GSO plus two USAID officers and their spouses surrounding the mailroom guys like a press scrum, peppering them with questions about the delay.

Chuck noticed the security officers. "Ghostbusters, right? Isn't it a little early for Halloween?"

Ken disabled the alarm on the exterior door and ordered everyone outside. "This is a security incident. We need you to hold next to the outer wall while we assess the situation," Ken commanded, as he moved into position to stand watch.

Inside the mailroom, Kerry-Anne x-rayed the package. Two thick discs, irregularly shaped, and two ziplock bags of combined liquid and solid material. No wires or detonators. She photographed each side of the package, sealed it in a thick plastic bag, and carried it outside.

"Possible chem-bio hazard," she told Ken. "I'm taking it to the incinerator."

"You heard her, folks. Possible chem-bio. We need to activate countermeasures."

He grasped the pre-positioned garden hose and gave the spigot a decisive turn.

"You can set your cell phones and wallets on that table before we start spraying."

"Have a seat, Victor," said Consul General Barbara Hertz, her voice flat.

She kept her lips pursed as her subordinate lowered himself into the nearer of the two chairs in front of her desk.

For a long moment Barbara regarded Victor, the way a district attorney considers a defendant. Or the way someone with a freshly soiled carpet looks at her pet.

"I read the draft arrest report you sent just now. Quite fascinating. I couldn't put it down. And even more interesting, if you can imagine such a thing, I just got a phone call from Embassy Zagovor. It turns out Doug Watanabe is under arrest up there, and the Pazarian police say Paul Giardis—does that name ring a bell?—the DEA guy from Embassy Zagovor, went missing in the same operation." She stabbed her finger at the printout of the arrest report lying on her desk and glared at Victor. "So, it appears we have a U.S. official in jail in Vodania and you don't think to mention this to me?"

Victor didn't blink. "I was trying to reach Doug to get confirmation of the alleged Amcit's identity. Now we know why he wasn't answering his phone or checking his email. Pretty good reason, you have to admit."

Outside Room 314 of the Eisenhower Executive Office Building shortly before eleven thirty on Wednesday, Winston Bryce, senior director for Europe on the national security council staff, studied the screen of his cell phone like a detective looking for a clue, ignoring the arrivals of the various attendees. When the room filled, he deposited the phone in the cubby across the corridor and took his place at the head of the table.

"Welcome to the Pazaria-Vodania crisis group," he proclaimed. "We have several new faces today. Let's go around and everyone introduce themselves and tell us why you're here."

"Ellis Caffrey, division chief, DEA. Here to figure out how we get our agents out of detention ASAP."

"Lieutenant Colonel Marvy Grafter, counterterrorism procurement office director, DIA, and I'm here to celebrate the awesome start to Penn State's football season."

No one laughed. Or smiled. Winston Bryce shifted his gaze one to the left.

"Geoff Bentwood, principal deputy assistant secretary of state for European and Eurasian affairs."

"Vonda Vance, deputy assistant secretary of state, also EUR bureau."

"Bill Padden, deputy assistant secretary of defense."

A lieutenant colonel from the Joint Chiefs of Staff stated her name and rank and said, "Here in listening mode."

Winston Bryce added, "We also have with us on speaker phone Ambassador Nancy Kunninger in Zagovor and DCM Andy Pulano in Shizl. A virtual welcome to you both. Any thoughts on how we proceed?"

"Once we get Doug Watanabe back here," Andy began, "it'll help convince the police to drop the charges against Giardis. But they do want their four cars."

"Wait, the Vodanians are demanding four cars to release an American official?" asked Winston.

"They say Doug promised them two vehicles for their cooperation, and then they lost two patrol cars during the operation, due to a wildfire."

"That is nothing short of outrageous," sputtered Ambassador Kunninger.

"Agreed, and welcome to my world," Andy replied. "But my understanding is that DEA is willing to provide that support."

"Correct," said Caffrey.

"Can we expect to see Doug later today, Ambassador?" Andy asked.

"It's not that simple, Andy. The Pazarians want to make sure Paul gets released and understandably they don't want to lose their leverage."

"Folks," Geoff Bentwood intervened, "I suggest we don't get too into the weeds here, and instead focus on using our leverage to lay the foundation for linking our efforts to our goals. Let's roll up our sleeves and connect the dots on the ground so we can turn the page to a constructive outcome."

"Thanks Geoff. Can you break that down for us? What it means operationally?" asked Winston.

"I can get my assistant secretary to call in their ambassadors."

Andy spotted two flaws in that approach. A cluster of f-bombs from the assistant secretary could harden attitudes at a sensitive moment. More importantly, if the move succeeded it would steal problem-solving glory that rightfully belonged to himself.

"I recommend working this in capitals," Andy suggested. "Where we have better access to the leadership than their own foreign ministers do. Wouldn't you agree, Ambassador Kunninger?"

"With all due respect," Bill Padden interrupted, "I think State should be able to handle this without a lot of interagency back-stopping. The immediate crisis here is we got a man down behind enemy lines."

"What are you talking about?" asked Winston.

"There's a DoD special-ops contractor missing in Vodania."

"Perfect," said Vonda. "What's a special-ops contractor doing in Vodania?"

"We're not able to brief on that," Lt. Col. Marvy Grafter responded. "The information is restricted."

"Did the embassy approve the operation?" Vonda demanded.

"Non-lethal counterterrorism programs don't need State Department blessing," Marvy stated.

"As far as I know the White House is also not aware of any special-ops program in Vodania," said Winston.

Bill spoke to Marvy, "We can give a redacted version."

Marvy frowned.

"If I could offer a field perspective," Andy interjected, "it'd be helpful to redact in the name and description of the missing person and where he was last seen."

Winston stared at Marvy, who eventually coughed up, "In a nutshell, the mission objective was to temporarily neutralize President Chilik's guard dog."

"President Chilik's dog is a terrorist?" asked Vonda.

"You don't get it, that's not what he's saying," Bill responded. "But I respect your question, because civilians are not well-equipped to understand these types of programs."

"Aren't you a civilian?" asked Vonda. "I mean, last time you checked?"

"Yes, and I'm not claiming to fully understand the program. But I do give it my unqualified support."

Chapter 24

As much as Andy enjoyed serving as chargé d'affaires while the border closure kept the ambassador away, there was one significant drawback. The bodyguards. Their protective hovering certainly cramped his style. Accompanied by a police security detail, it just wasn't possible to move around discreetly. He needed to find another way to conduct his most delicate business.

Early on Thursday morning, as on any weekday morning, the daily queue of visa-seekers at the U.S. embassy's consular entrance stretched far along the fence line, a procession of supplicants. This humiliating procedure had long since become part of the visual fabric of the ramshackle neighborhood on the outskirts of Shizl. One by one they trickled through a security screening checkpoint and traversed a footpath up to the consular waiting room.

Inside, six rows of molded fiberglass seats accommodated the clientele as they waited to be summoned to the next available processing window. For their edification, the reception area offered a trove of fact sheets and brochures documenting, in several languages, America's many contributions to Vodania's well-being. A gauzy layer of dust atop each stack of paper indicated how seldom anyone availed themselves of the opportunity to peruse this occasionally updated information.

A tall scowling man slouched in the back row. His hat was pulled low, its rim almost pressed against the upper tips of his flourishing mustache. After a suitable interval, he was called to the receptionist and directed to Window 3, reserved for special cases. Walled-in booths on both sides of the plexiglass shielded Window 3 from the view and hearing of anyone within the consular section as well as the waiting area. After the mustachioed visitor took a seat on his side of the window, Chargé d'Affaires Andy Pulano entered the interior booth and nodded at the indignant-looking man facing him.

"I appreciate you coming in on short notice," said Andy, pressing his own hands together since the security glass prevented a handshake.

Shariz grimaced and said, "It is my great honor."

"Help me understand something," Andy requested. "In the past few weeks there's been all this buzz about the emergence of Marko. Who or what is he, exactly?"

"He's exactly nothing."

"There is no Marko?"

"We've been doing this for hundreds of years. We'd know if someone new came in."

"I believe you. Speaking of new arrivals, I believe you have one of ours."

"I do?" asked Shariz.

"Christopher Braxton. He landed near the border by parachute on the night you were fixing the river."

"You refer to our guest."

"Yes."

"He is in the car outside. You want me to bring him in? You don't even have to give me a visa right away. Just lift the travel ban."

Andy put his fingertips together. "I can't do that." The crisis was not nearly ripe enough yet.

"You know, I put on pants for this meeting." Shariz stood to display a pair of grey cotton sweats.

"Don't think I don't appreciate it," replied Andy.

"You probably know the Wodanians are strongly interested in Mr. Braxton," said Shariz. "I'm getting very interesting offers from your friend Farao."

"Really."

"Two more seats in parliament."

"That is a nice offer. I'm so happy you two are becoming such close friends."

"Yes, it is fair. But I don't think our guest will enjoy the same level of hospitality with the police. And therefore, I want to make sure you Americans won't become angry with me."

Andy pretended to mull this point for a moment. "We do feel the Pazari-Vodanians should have appropriate representation in parliament. That will be beneficial for Vodania in the long term."

"What about our guest? You want him to stay in Wodania for the long term?"

"Shariz, I do appreciate your concern. Trust me, I can handle our business. Tell me when you will deliver him."

"After the election results are official." Shariz blocked a smile. "I also know my business."

Later that morning, Andy prepared himself for what had become a daily telephone conversation with Ambassador Kunninger in Pazaria. Many, including Ambassador Lamkin, found her hard-edged style grating, even insufferable. But Andy sensed that behind the power-play exterior was a flexibility he could work with when the moment arrived, after paying sufficient deference.

"Finally, some good news to report," she announced as soon as she came on the line. "The troops are returning to barracks. It's about time. I've been pushing Prismar like crazy."

"Wonderful!" Andy replied, feet up on his desk, wingtips resting on a stack of award nominations. But actually, it was terrible. The end of the military confrontation would hasten the reopening of Vodania's borders.

"Congratulations on getting the Pazarians to listen to reason," he gushed.

He refrained from noting that they were simply reciprocating the Vodanians' withdrawal. A withdrawal he had convinced Chilik to make. Humble service, Andy reminded himself. This was no time to claim credit.

"Now if we could just get them to see the light regarding our DEA colleagues," he said.

Andy listened patiently as Ambassador Kunninger explained in fervent detail all the reasons Prime Minister Prismar could not possibly make the first move. The substance of her points matched what the Vodanians had been telling him in insisting they could not be the ones to give in.

"I know you're hampered by the lack of ambassadorial status," Ambassador Kunninger conceded, "but this is the time to man up and find a way to get Chilik to unconditionally release our law enforcement officer."

"Thank you, Ambassador," Andy responded in his warmest confidential voice. "I certainly appreciate your sympathy regarding my handicap. In deference to your experience and your intelligence, I won't recite the arguments the Vodanians make, but you would find them very familiar, I assure you."

"I recognize you're doing the best you can with that wing-ding," Kunninger responded.

"It's a stare down," Andy noted.

Time was running out before the ambassador returned, and Andy had no concrete accomplishments he could call his own.

"This is what I'm going to do," he told her. "I'm calling President Chilik's office to let them know the Pazarians have agreed to release Watanabe and bring him to the crossing at four o'clock tomorrow afternoon."

"They've agreed to no such thing."

"Of course, I'll tell Chilik they'll deny it if asked. Not that the Vodanians are talking to the Pazarians as far as I'm aware. And you may inform Prime Minister Prismar that the Vodanians have agreed to the same with respect to Giardis. And that they have made an exception to the border closure for this purpose."

"Have they?"

"Ambassador, we have to blink for them."

After a pause, she said, "You're a dangerous man, Andy."

One of the USAID carpet-craving ladies was back in GSO, inside Chuck's office. Chuck cupped his chin in his hands, elbows resting on the edge of his desk. Tara occupied the spare seat next to Chuck. She knew he was storing up more irritation and resentment, like an alligator soaking up heat from the sun. Her fault for taking action.

"It is truly astonishing how conditions and discrimination at this post continue to get worse," declared the embassy family member. "Yesterday, at the embassy, I suffered the severe discomfort, and the humiliation, of being hosed down in public like some kind of protestor."

Tara allowed her thoughts to wander. Her musings pinged back and forth between Mads and anything but Mads.

"I hear you," said Chuck, summoning a sympathetic look. "I was first in line."

"Maybe so, but a disproportionate number of the victims were from USAID."

"That water was cold for all of us," Chuck replied. "Believe me, I would very much like to know who's responsible for causing the incident."

"It's clear we're not being evacuated any time soon, since the border's closed," the woman resumed. "Thus, I want a rug to protect my children, just like the one you gave the Mitchells."

"We're short on spare rugs at the moment," Chuck explained again.

"What about the ones in Doug Watanabe's apartment? Might as well put them to use while he's away."

"You realize Doug is in jail in Pazaria?"

"Well at least he's not stuck in this miserable little country."

Chuck turned to Tara. "What do you think?"

Tara blinked, and rotated her neck to face Chuck. She had been wondering why the DCM hadn't been hounding her about the Davos poisoning lately. Too busy with the crisis? Or had he given up on her? Chuck waited for an answer.

"In the warehouse we have extra safety goggles," Tara said. "Also, reflective tape."

"How are goggles and tape going to help at all?" demanded the irate spouse. "I'll take two of each."

Shortly after four o'clock on Friday, on the Vodanian side of a two-lane bridge that spanned the Odorian River where the mountains tapered off, assistant security officer Kerry-Anne Frisker waited with a phalanx of heavily armed police and a still-handcuffed Giardis.

She glanced at her watch and recalled the chargé's very specific instructions. She raised her binoculars again and scanned the vehicles and uniformed men on the far side. Still no sign of Watanabe.

"That's him. Let's go," she declared, and began walking onto the bridge. The chargé had told her, repeatedly, that the police would follow if she acted decisively. She turned and motioned to the men next to Giardis. They looked at their commander, who shrugged. After a moment, they followed her.

A gusty wind scoured the river valley. The surface of the bridge had numerous cracks and potholes, and the guardrails looked flimsy. Through the seams between sections of concrete Kerry-Anne could see the river flowing some two hundred feet below. She kept to the center of the bridge, careful with her footing, and tried to proceed in a steady, dignified manner.

After a full minute of nothing, the Pazarians began to move. A vehicle door opened. A group formed and began walking toward them. Kerry-Anne kept her pace deliberate, aiming not to reach the midpoint too early. The two groups closed to within fifty meters of each other. Kerry-Anne nodded to the police and they removed the handcuffs.

"Raise your arms," she told Giardis, walking forward with him.

From the opposite side, Watanabe also raised his arms and came forward, escorted by a security officer from the embassy in Zagovor. The distance closed, step by step.

As they neared the white boundary line painted across the midsection of the bridge, the two drug-fighters rushed toward each other. The wind blew back their hair and billowed Watanabe's Turkish pantaloons and Giardis's serape. They came together and Giardis reached his arms forward and shoved Watanabe hard in the chest.

"You've got some explaining to do!" Giardis yelled. "You put those mountain monkeys up to this." His jaw jutted out like a weapon.

Watanabe shoved him in return and said, "Tell your goons I want my eight hundred dollars back."

"Tell yours I want my sombrero."

Starlight sprinkled onto the crowd in the open courtyard of the ruins of Shizl's ancient caravansary on Friday night. Tara pictured bygone generations of weary merchants lodging at the inn, with their strings of camels and donkeys filling the grounds, munching dry fodder after long journeys under heavy loads, under the same stars.

She sipped pomegranate juice mixed with honey wine. A jazz trio played in a roofless stone chamber. Hip members of Vodania's elite swayed and danced. In the distance, fireworks lit up the sky over the national stadium, where the military victory parade must have culminated.

Tara noticed a tall man pass beneath one of the decorative torches. The guy from the gym, Vlado's client. He stopped to study the band. She approached.

"You enjoy jazz," she said.

The man glanced at her with the briefest of smiles. "I do," he agreed. "It inspires my work."

"You're a musician?"

"A photographer. I seek mood and spontaneity, just like in jazz."

She pursed her lips and nodded, then smiled at him. "My name is Tara Zadani, I'm here with the American embassy."

He put out his hand. "Dieter Schmidt. I'm here with the German embassy, in a way. My wife is the ambassador."

Not what Tara would have guessed. She tried not to show any surprise or judgment. Not her marriage. But something about the revelation did not sit easily with her. It caused an itch in her brain. She moved on, circulating among the guests, trying to put the brief encounter out of mind. She found her friend Karolina dancing with two painters who were also waiters. Or the other way around. She chatted for a while with one of Stefano's cousins. She danced. A perfect Shizl party. Except.

In the courtyard, Tara looked up to admire the stars and feel insignificant and alone and wonder what Mads was doing in that instant. He felt unfathomably far away.

On the way out, passing under the caravansary's broad stone archway, she spied a young woman wearing an oversized black t-shirt, the excess material knotted above her waist, exposing her midriff. Bold red lines on the front of the shirt formed the outline of a goat with the letter M on its flank.

"Love it," Tara commented, placing a hand on the woman's shoulder. She twirled her around to read the words on the back, embossed in the same blazing shade of red: *I am Marko, said Marko. I am too cool.*

On Sunday, September 8, election day in Vodania, celebratory gunfire began at dawn and continued throughout the day. Warning shots and accidental discharges added to the ruckus. Democracy, Vodania-style.

In Shizl, in Harabad, in Pritzi, in Ratovich, in towns, villages, and hamlets across the country, party activists, many with mustaches too new and sparse to curl upward or downward, raced around in convoys, brandishing weapons and hooting slogans.

U.S. embassy and EU mission staffers, together with the few international election monitors who made it in before the border closed, spent the day racing from polling place to polling place, interviewing officials, watching a few voters cast their ballots, and phoning in their observations to colleagues back in Shizl.

At the end of the day the observers compiled and compared their impressions, cross-checking with trusted Vodanian civil society organizations. The official tallying, everyone knew, would last deep into the morning hours. Then the hard bargaining would commence, with all the political parties using the ballot data among many other considerations as they competed for seats.

Just before midnight, the Vodanian government announced the reopening of its airports and borders.

Tara wheeled her Wrangler into a spot behind her building and switched off the ignition. Still keyed up after a day of monitoring the voting process in a swath of southern Vodania, she inhaled the night air through her open window. She sat still, not wanting to interrupt the thread of thought unspooling in her mind.

Davos's distress occurred early on a Monday morning, a curious time for skullduggery. Tara wondered about a couple of other things she had noticed taking place on Mondays. Possible connections emerged, and then a hypothesis.

Tara's father liked to say a hypothesis without facts is like a house with a beautiful roof but no walls holding it up. Could you live in such a house, he would ask? Once when she was five or six, and with no clear idea of what a hypothesis was, Tara said you could if the roof was hanging by ropes from the branches of a great tree. You are going to be trouble, her father predicted.

To gather the necessary facts, she rose out of bed early the following morning, a Monday, skipped coffee, and drove up the northern bluff that loomed over downtown Shizl.

She parked, top up, in a shaded spot with a view of the German ambassador's front door. A solid-looking black sedan waited in the driveway, pointing toward the street. Eventually, a driver emerged and opened the sedan's right rear door. Ambassador Basch came out of the house and slipped into the back seat. The driver closed the door behind her, got behind the wheel, and drove off. Fact pattern one.

About twenty minutes later came fact pattern two. In the rearview mirror a motorcycle rushed toward her, mounted by a rider with packs of muscle barely contained by a black leather bodysuit. He buzzed past, leaned hard as he took the corner, and dismounted in front of the German ambassador's residence. He pulled off his helmet to shake loose flowing locks. Vlado.

After Vlado vanished into the house, Tara drove down the block and parked across the street from the side entrance of the U.S. ambassador's residence. Towel and tote bag in hand, she greeted the guard and went to the pool. She sat on a lounge chair facing the fence and took her time pulling out sunscreen, a magazine, goggles. In a few minutes, the back door of the German ambassador's residence opened, and the young daughter came out, holding something in her hand. Rectangular, lavender colored. More facts, very solid.

Tara dove into the pool and for thirty minutes she swam her laps and focused on her body and her breathing. When she hoisted herself up out of the water onto the deck, she pretended not to notice the girl hidden in the bushes on the other side of the fence. Tara bent forward to lower her hair and wrap it in a towel. In the process, she saw the girl grasp an edge of the lavender wrapping paper between her thumb and index finger and carefully peel it back a little bit further. Tara finished toweling off, and while repacking her tote she glimpsed the girl nibble at her treat.

"Sabrina!" called a man's voice from the back side of the German ambassador's residence. "Sabrina, komm!"

The girl lingered, moving a piece of chocolate from one side of her mouth to the other while regarding Tara. Then the girl folded the paper over the remainder of her candy bar and scrambled out from under the hedge.

Tara walked around the pool, passed through the safety gate into the lawn, and continued to the back of the pool house. She clambered over the new anti-Davos fence and pressed against the shrubbery as she lowered to a squat. On her belly she struggled to wriggle and crawl underneath the bottom branches to the corner of the property, a dark cranny with the retaining wall on one side, the pool house on the other. Pike fencing divided the grounds of the U.S. and German ambassadorial residences, and a thick hedge on the German side reinforced the boundary.

In the dim shade, Tara looked for the final, tangible, irrefutable fact. She searched carefully but didn't see what she was looking for. Then she extended her body around the corner as far as she could into the tight space between the pool house and the German garden. Something lay on the ground under the hedge, but out of her reach.

She tore a branch from the bush behind her and stripped away everything but the main shaft. She extended the stick into the Germans' garden between the farthest fence pikes she could reach, and gingerly speared a piece of paper. It looked fairly recent, albeit dried and slightly faded from the summer heat. She put it to her nose, but it carried no smell. Definitely not from that morning's treat.

Tara crawled back the way she went in. She stood up ready to hoist herself over the new fence into the yard.

She recoiled at a sudden loud bark. From across the lawn Davos rushed toward her. The ambassador's wife, standing near the side door of the residence, stiffened, her mouth involuntarily dropping open.

Tara pulled back as Davos jumped against the fence and said, "Hi Lithia, it's me, Tara."

"Oh my god. What are you doing?"

"I just figured out what happened to Davos."

Tara stood beaming and proud, crammed in between the fence and the bush, her hair wet and disheveled, mud and debris stuck all over the front of her body, clutching a lavender-colored candy wrapper.

"Wait, let me catch David before he goes," Lithia requested.

Tara scaled the fence, pulled a towel around her shoulders and brushed dirt from her forearms and legs.

Lithia came back and led her in through the kitchen to the foyer, where the ambassador stood in evident impatience. Davos cavorted and jumped, racing into the living room and back to the foyer, his tail whipping like a helicopter rotor.

Tara stood up straight and tried to forget she was wearing only a bathing suit. "I retrieved this from the German ambassador's garden, just the other side of the fence."

She read from the wrapper, "Sixty-two percent cacao."

The ambassador frowned with distaste at the scrap she held out to him and shot her a puzzled look.

"Vlado, the trainer, the former Olympian, comes over to work out with Dieter early on Monday mornings," Tara explained. She opted not to mention the love angle, sensing that would be too much for the ambassador to process.

"They give candy to Sabrina, the daughter, and send her into the garden to keep her out of the way. I think Davos liked to go back behind the pool house before we put up the new fence, and Sabrina probably doesn't know dogs get sick if they eat chocolate."

"You big beggar," Lithia scolded Davos.

"You have a piece of litter and a fanciful story," the ambassador observed. "Why do you know all this, about the trainer and the schedule and everything?"

"The DCM asked me to look into the matter and figure out what happened."

"Did he ask you to spy on our friends and neighbors?"

Tara didn't reply, and the ambassador reached for the door handle.

"What you've described is a completely circumstantial case."

Striding briskly toward his limousine, hot to resume command after a week's mostly involuntary hiatus, the ambassador considered that, far-fetched as this explanation was, it might help explain the bizarre death-sentence lab report Monika Basch gave him. Why else would the Germans want to throw him off the scent?

As soon as Andy learned the ambassador would return on the first flight in on Monday morning, he asked Charlene to assemble the senior staff in the secure conference room for a country team meeting starting at nine or whenever the ambassador arrived. When the time came, Andy, once more part of the everyone else, sat waiting with his colleagues in the conference room. He shared their uncertain, watchful mood. Despite all the recent drama, culminating with the previous day's election, interactions around the table were muted and terse, then fizzled out. A restrained professional hush pervaded the room, as if it would be disloyal to start a conversation before the ambassador arrived.

Andy assumed his standing with the ambassador had become severely frayed. He tried to rank-order the various grounds for ambassadorial ire and fine-tune his defenses. The charge of failing to negotiate an exception to the border closure for the ambassador should be easy enough to turn into an opportunity for flattery. The Vodanian government feared Ambassador Lamkin, et cetera, would not dare defy the international community if he had been present. But Andy of course realized that it was his successes, not his failures, that posed the greatest risk. Finagling the releases of the DEA guys, ending the border crisis (and popping the EU's balloon as a bonus).

No ambassador wanted to be outshone by an understudy, and Andy had always previously avoided the limelight.

When the door opened with a powerful whoosh and the ambassador marched in, the members of the country team shot to their feet. Robert Akes, the management counselor, started a round of applause, which the ambassador quashed with a single word, "Please."

The ambassador took his seat and waited, tight-lipped, for the staff to do the same.

"Good morning, everyone," he began. "We have a lot to catch up on. For one thing, with all the chits and relations we've built up over the years it's still not entirely clear to me why we were able to get a diplomatic exception to the border closure at the staff level but not at the ambassadorial level. That's going to require follow-up."

The ambassador, solemn as a judge, looked from Andy to Robert and back again, full of purpose. Icy needles of alarm coursed up Andy's spine and vibrated in the survival and promotion node of his brain stem. He decided to hold off on the flattery for the moment, so as not to impede the ambassador from moving to his next point. The ambassador's posture told Andy he intended to preside over a lengthy, thorough meeting.

Andy half-listened as the ambassador absorbed Gary Hambert's extended description of ballot stuffing, ballot stealing, family-group voting, intimidation, premature poll closings, and other common 'irregularities'. Gary concluded his report with, "But no one got killed, and the Pazari parties did a bit better than everyone expected, so all in all not a terrible outcome from our standpoint."

If the ambassador ever found out how the Pazaris got their extra seats, and that Braxton could have been on his way home instead of becoming the focal point of another crisis, it would take about two and a half seconds for Andy's career to splatter on the rocks.

Doug Watanabe, looking chastised and subdued, diminished even, apologized for Operation Tonguebite and expressed appreciation for everyone's efforts to get him and his DEA colleague released as quickly as possible. He asked if he could provide the ambassador a more detailed operational briefing in executive session, to which the ambassador agreed with a curt nod. Watanabe would make it, Andy figured. He was a survivor.

RSO Ken Dewitt brought up the mailroom incident and noted that his follow-up investigation concluded with high confidence that this was not an external attack. And that there had been minimal exposure to health risk among the mailroom employees and those in the immediate vicinity. "RSO and Management will issue an all-staff reminder about mail regulations," he concluded, with a glance at Watanabe.

"Speaking of external attacks," the ambassador interrupted. "Anything new to report on the poisoning of my dog?"

Ken shook his head, and the ambassador shifted his glare to Andy.

Andy could feel his eyebrows tensing. Was this just another opportunity to put his uppity deputy more firmly in his place? Or was there something else behind the question?

General Elfersen attempted to frame his presentation favorably by opening with a summary of the end of the armed face-off in the Asich Mountains and the status and verification of the withdrawal of forces. He noted, almost as an afterthought, that DIA headquarters and the Pentagon were conducting an after-action review to determine how the Harrimore Services operation got launched without embassy knowledge.

"An awful lot can go wrong in two days," the ambassador commented. The acid in his voice stung.

"Yes sir. The Pentagon's main concern at this point, sir, is the missing contractor."

"We still have a leg to stand on as long as they don't capture him," the ambassador stated.

Someone better trip up that standing leg before the ambassador regained his footing.

"He's former special forces, sir," General Elfersen declared. "If he survived the fall, he could live off the land indefinitely. And he would be exceptionally difficult to capture."

Very true, Andy thought. Until the election results got certified. Braxton would be in Vodanian custody by sundown. Then the tripping could begin.

At the conclusion of the meeting, Ambassador Lamkin dismissed everyone except the DCM.

After the room emptied, the ambassador said, "Your management of this crisis leaves something to be desired, to say the least. I'm afraid I may have misjudged your competence. It is nothing short of preposterous that DIA contracted to have President Chilik's guard dogs tranquilized. And all the while you knew nothing about it."

"Sir, I fully share your view of the outrageousness of the operation, and had I received any hint of it—"

"It's a matter of being proactive," the ambassador cut him off. "Send Elfersen home, loss of confidence. Can you handle that? Get him out of here before the Vodanians PNG him."

Andy nodded.

"Do you know who was the first person I saw this morning after returning from my needlessly prolonged absence?"

Andy shook his head.

"Tara Zadani. Crawling around behind my pool house to retrieve a piece of litter. She claims you asked her to investigate the attack on Davos. And now she's developed the nifty idea that it was Monika Basch's daughter feeding him a chocolate bar supplied by a personal trainer."

The periphery of the room suddenly turned grey and fuzzy. Andy Pulano felt his entire career flash before his eyes. The years of striving and conniving that had carried him to the brink of the summit. He had climbed so high. The ambassadorial peak was just a few steps away. Now, instead of a glorious new dawn on the horizon, his prospects plunged into a fathomless abyss. Because of the overzealousness of one disobedient junior officer, Ambassador Lamkin knew something that he didn't. Something critical.

Tara's explanation could well be true. He would find out, if he survived. This was the worst possible time to resolve the Davos poisoning mystery, just when tensions between the ambassador and Chilik throbbed on the brink of climax. The ambassador had been on track to tumble into the trap Andy had dug, layer by layer, and concealed so expertly. But Tara just handed the ambassador a map with a big X marking the danger. Should the ambassador use the knowledge he now possessed, and abandon his faith that Chilik ordered an attack on his dog, events could veer uncontrollably. And most unfavorably. The ambassador could apologize and reconcile with Chilik. In discussing recent events, Chilik could become curious about whether the ambassador authorized his deputy's covert deal-making. Andy Pulano had never tasted peril this massive and imminent. He had to save himself. Punishing Tara could wait.

"As part of my overall approach to the attack on Davos," Andy explained, "I enlisted Tara to keep alert to possible sources of toxins or poisons that the RSO and the defense attaché and others might not encounter. Pool chemicals, fertilizer, pest control, maintenance supplies. There were a number of areas, I felt, where a GSO insight could prove helpful."

The ambassador did not respond, and Andy continued, "Evidently Tara has not yet had a chance to brief me on her findings. But it's a relief she has apparently succeeded in discovering information needed to protect Davos."

"Findings?" the ambassador glowered. "She has a crackerjack theory and a candy wrapper. And even if her hypothesis happened to be true, it would still not fundamentally change our understanding of the ultimate source of the attack. This personal trainer fellow is a close associate of Chilik's."

Ambassador Lamkin stood and moved toward the door. Andy followed. The ambassador stopped, spun around, and said, "There are going to be some big changes around here."

Andy nodded. Count on it.

Chapter 25

In the afternoon of the ambassador's return, Andy paced inside his office, feeling caged. He checked his disposable cell phone for the twentieth time since texting the emergency signal to Farao's special number: clothes dryer.

He had sent the urgent meeting request in the morning, as soon as he got out from under the ambassador's blistering glare. Then, to display normalcy, he went to the cafeteria for his usual taste of coffee and local employee gossip. As he waited back in his office, Andy considered his predicament. Tara Zadani's mundane conclusion about what actually happened to that annoying dog threatened to puncture the ambassador's deluded certainty that President Chilik was responsible.

Andy clapped his palms to his temples. In all of diplomacy, there is nothing, absolutely nothing, worse than a headstrong, disobedient junior officer. Thanks to Tara, the ambassador was now in a position to turn a new page with Chilik. He could apologize. He could save himself.

Andy's career trembled in the crosshairs of the ambassador's wrath. Time was slipping rapidly away, but Andy held one more card. An ace. He had wanted to keep it in reserve in case he got nominated for an ambassadorship and needed help slithering through the Senate confirmation process. Getting to that point was what he had dreamed of ever since passing the foreign service entrance exam as a graduate student. Ambassador Pulano. It sounded so right, so natural. It just rolled off the tongue.

But no one would ever address him as Ambassador Pulano if he got dismissed from his post in Vodania in disgrace. Gone. It would all be for naught. Years of networking. Nonstop managing up. Deft, measured ingratiation. All the posturing, the pleasantries. Everything he had ever done.

He took out his phone and accessed the email account he had set up for this purpose. It contained a single draft message addressed to the *Scorcher* columnists. With attachment. He took a breath and tapped send.

Late in the afternoon, Ambassador Lamkin, summoned to an urgent meeting with President Chilik, sat alone in the back seat of his limo. He decided to go without staff in light of the sensitivity of the occasion.

At the gate of the Presidentorium, the guard laboriously went through the list of approved visitors, and at last found Ambassador Lamkin's name. He requested the IDs of everyone in the car, and dutifully carried the credentials back to the security booth to run them through the system.

"Must be a new guard," the ambassador commented toward the front seat.

"No sir," the chauffeur replied, tightening his grip on the wheel. "He's always here."

The police escort in the front seat nodded confirmation.

When the ambassador at last got through security and reached the waiting area outside the president's office, no one offered tea. After a wait of nearly twenty-five minutes, an aide opened the door to Chilik's office and beckoned.

Ambassador Lamkin entered to find President Chilik seated behind his desk.

"Many funny things happened on the morning you left," Chilik began. "Maybe you find them funny. A very professional operation against me, at my home. Damage to my security cameras, all my guard dogs drugged, and a herd of sheep released into my garden. The presidential garden. Do you know what sheep means in Vodania? Coward."

The ambassador opened his mouth to speak, but Chilik waved him off. "This cost me votes, seats in parliament. It was a hostile act, and Vodania will demand compensation."

"Mr. President, I condemn the actions you describe. I assure you I have no knowledge of them, and I have no information indicating any U.S. government involvement. But I do take your concerns seriously, and I will report them to Washington and ask my government to look into the matter promptly."

President Chilik glared and said nothing.

Ambassador Lamkin continued, "And if there was, without my knowledge, an American role, I will do everything in my power to find out how such a thing could have occurred and to make absolutely certain nothing like it ever happens again. As a leader, I'm sure you occasionally have subordinates who take misguided actions. If that is the case in my embassy, I will swiftly take appropriate actions."

President Chilik took out a cell phone and stabbed at its keys with his index finger.

While Chilik focused on his phone, Lamkin said, "May I add, as a pet owner myself, that I am very glad to hear your dogs have recovered from this unfortunate incident."

"You think your house dog can beat any of mine?" Chilik demanded. "Maybe we should put it to a test."

Ambassador Lamkin decided not to bring up the international community's concerns about election irregularities.

With the ambassador safely out of the way at the Presidentorium, and most of the staff gone for the day, Andy opted for a stroll around the embassy grounds. Precisely the type of impromptu inspection a good leader conducts from time to time.

He pointed his steps toward the maintenance building on the far side of the property. Along the way he reached into his suit jacket pocket for the disposable phone he used only for communications requiring the utmost discretion. The phone that still had no reply from Farao, the phone he replaced every Sunday while browsing through one or another of Shizl's outdoor markets.

He dialed the number in Washington and glanced at his watch. It was almost ten in the morning there. Even gossip columnists had to be at work by now.

"Hello, *Scorcher* fan," said a cheery male voice. "What do you know?"

Speaking with an exaggerated Vodanian accent, Pulano said, "I send you photograph earlier. Did you see? Senator and ambassador with dog?"

"Awesome, yeah, let me check."

After a minute, a different, deeper voice came on. "Thank you for the picture. Wonderful, very newsworthy. Senator Mifton, right? And who's the other gentleman?"

"He is you ambassador here in Vodania, Mr. Lamkin."

"Can you tell me about the circumstances?"

"It was party at ambassador's house. They making speeches then started, what you say, fooling with the dog. Nobody knew what is happening. Then they tried to delete all pictures. But, you can see, one survived."

"How can we verify this?"

"Ask anybody! Everybody know about it in Vodania. Or call you embassy, they had many staffs there."

"Who tried to delete the pictures?"

"The embassy staffs. At the door, checking everybody phones."

"We'll need to cross-check this, get confirmation from other witnesses. Can you give me names of people who were there?"

"You want name? Wait please one minute."

Andy reached into his shirt pocket for the printout of his daily schedule that Charlene unfailingly supplied, and rattled it near the phone.

"Here is other name I have." Pretending to read awkwardly in his Vodanian voice, Andy pronounced the words *"Huffington Post."*

"That won't be necessary, we'll figure it out. Thank you, concerned citizen!"

Follow the rooster.

Andy wondered if it was a colloquial idiom he was not familiar with. The message said to wait on the Market Bridge at eleven p.m. and follow the rooster. He looked around again. No roosters, nocturnal or otherwise. No hens, no chickens, no eggs. No fowl of any kind, except three lackadaisical ducks on the water below, paddling around the shadows with no apparent purpose.

The ancient stone footbridge spanned the river in a gentle arc. Andy loitered near the midpoint. He braced his forearms on the top of the wall to gaze down onto the black surface of the Druzhba sliding past. To his left lay the dark streets of old Shizl, where a fair number of people still bustled about. On the other side, the historic fortress loomed over the central plaza and the brightly-lit cafés. Andy tried to keep his face averted while keeping an eye on the pedestrians who trickled in twos and threes across the bridge from both directions. Any of these passersby could recognize him and gum things up further.

An old man on an even older bicycle labored up the slope of the bridge, moving forward just fast enough to keep his balance. He passed within arm's length, and surprised Andy with a wink. Andy recoiled. Pretty sure I could do better, he smirked to himself, but thanks all the same. He glanced at the departing backside of the old man, at his thin legs working the pedals, and noticed on the rack above the rear wheel a wire cage with a chicken inside. He couldn't swear it was a rooster. Was he expected to identify the gender of a captive chicken in the dark?

Andy followed the cyclist as he rolled through the twisting alleys of the ancient market area. Corrugated metal shutters, secured with padlocks at ground level, covered the storefronts of dressmakers and jewelers and sweetshops. The cobblestone passageways lay dark, and became more and more empty further in. An underfed dog peered from behind a torn-open bag of trash. Andy kept the old cyclist in sight as he passed several bars and cafés, small oases of commerce and festivity amid the gloom. The goose chase, if that was what it turned out to be, led to the side entrance of a restaurant that appeared closed. The old man's bicycle leaned against the wall, its wire cage still in place. Andy peered closer. It probably was a rooster.

The door was not locked. Andy entered. A waiter approached and guided him across a dining room with exceptionally subdued lighting. A few patrons lingered. From the narrow corridor on the other side, Andy detected a pungent scent. Unmistakable.

In a private room in the back, Farao sat with three associates, who departed at the American's arrival. Farao, unsmiling, gestured toward a vacated chair.

Andy remained standing, his eyebrows like coiled vipers.

"You captured Braxton. This is quite serious. I realize you are not experienced in diplomatic protocol. You should inform us promptly. Officially."

The eyebrows lunged forward, as if they intended to strangle Farao.

"And," he continued, "not that I expect anything of the kind, but you will be held accountable for any mistreatment."

The way Andy said it made clear the 'you' was singular.

Farao looked a bit taken aback. He was not accustomed to being on the receiving end of a threat.

"I get it," he replied. "Please, sit. We are very unhappy about this attack on the president's dogs, and the bringing in of the sheep. Some kind of weird revenge I guess?"

Andy yanked back a chair and sat. He stared into Farao's unblinking eyes.

"I didn't know about it," Andy told him. "If I had, I would have advised against it. Strongly. But I wasn't the ambassador. And it wasn't my dog."

"We can't work with him anymore. He should go home."

"I can't tell that to Washington."

"Who can?" Farao asked.

"You. Your ambassador in Washington needs to go see Vonda Vance in the State Department."

Jeremiah, the lowest-ranking officer in the political section, waited inside the security screening area at the U.S. embassy's main gate shortly before ten a.m. Tuesday. The metal detectors and bag-scanning machines hummed. Local traffic streamed past. Eventually, a black sedan with foreign ministry plates swung off the road and stopped in front of the hydraulic barrier at the end of the driveway.

A young functionary in a dark suit and stylish heels materialized from the back seat. When the vehicle barrier clattered down, she sashayed up the middle of the driveway. The sedan didn't move.

Jeremiah pushed open the door and walked toward her in the sunshine.

"Mr. Jeremiah?" she said.

Her left thumb and index finger pinched the corner of a manuscript-sized envelope. A breeze fluttered her hair.

"Yes, welcome," he replied.

"For Ambassador Lamkin. Please sign here."

Jeremiah accepted the envelope and signed the receipt. She pivoted back toward the sedan.

"Thank you. I hope we can work together again sometime," Jeremiah offered.

The official did not break stride in parading down the driveway.

Jeremiah brought the envelope to the ambassador's secretary, who knocked once on the inner office door and carried it in.

After his secretary departed and pulled the door closed, Ambassador Lamkin broke the seal on the back of the envelope. The official note was written in Vodanian, and he turned to the page containing the courtesy translation.

He blanched as he read, 'The Ministry of Foreign Affairs of the Republic of Vodania wishes to inform the Embassy of the United States of America of the capture and detention of Mr. Christopher Braxton, a citizen of the United States of America and an employee of the Department of Defense of the United States of America. Mr. Braxton will be charged with . . .'

The ambassador scanned the rest of the letter. Terms such as 'hostile act' and 'prisoner of war' and 'compensation' popped off the page. He sagged back in his ergonomically correct chair and exhaled, his chest collapsing like a hot-air balloon at the end of the ride.

On Wednesday afternoon, Vonda Vance had to bring yet another piece of the Vodania mess to her boss, conscious that the stench of unpleasant events might start to cling to her. As she approached the inner sanctum, she heard the assistant secretary's jocular voice.

"Fuck my horse. Ain't that a pisser."

The assistant secretary, on the phone, waved Vonda in and gestured toward the couch.

"Always appreciate the chance to get your advice, Senator."

Hanging up, the assistant secretary swiveled to face Vonda with a friendly smile.

"Fart-breath shit eaters from the Hill. That's the third fucking one today, demanding military force to free the 'hostage' in Shizl. What the fuck you got for me?"

"Well, related topic," Vonda replied. "Vodania's ambassador came in to see me this morning. They don't want to cause unnecessary offense, but she made it clear that President Chilik no longer has any trust in Ambassador Lamkin. He's convinced David ordered the attack on his guard dogs, and refuses to consider any other explanation."

"Turdballs. Have you checked in with the DCM, what the fuck's his name, Pulano?"

"Andy's loyal to David, and was reluctant to say much. But he acknowledged that an initial misunderstanding between the president and the ambassador has grown into a rift. He implied that it's probably irreparable."

"Fucking Chil. Ball buster."

Vonda nodded. "Plus, they've got living proof, the so-called hostage."

"Fuckum, we brazen it out. We can't let any of these porta potties tell us whose butt we can put on the embassy throne."

"There is one other development," Vonda confessed.

"I don't like the fucking sound of that."

She handed the assistant secretary a photograph of Senator Mifton on his knees, a glass of wine in his left hand. A dog was straddling him from behind, and Ambassador Lamkin was straddling the dog.

The assistant secretary, for once, was speechless, and could only gape at Vonda for explanation.

"The *Scorcher* is going to run this in their column tomorrow, under the caption, 'Who's that party animal?' We're giving Senator Mifton's office a heads-up."

"God fuck it to hell, Lamkin's damaged goods, ain't he?"

Vonda nodded.

"Say it."

"He's damaged goods."

"The whole fucking thing," the assistant secretary gently encouraged.

Vonda blinked and swallowed. "God fuck it to hell, Lamkin's damaged goods, ain't he?" she echoed.

"Yes, he certainly fucking is," the assistant secretary agreed, with a sorrowful shake of the head. "I do fucking hate to throw him under the bus. But he's a package that fell off the goddamn delivery truck, got run over and split open. Then half the fucking dogs in the neighborhood pissed on the broken pieces. Return to sender," the assistant secretary said, with considerable sympathy.

"Recall for consultations?" Vonda asked.

"Bring-your-family-and-pets consultations. Fuckin' A."

On Thursday afternoon, Tara and her crew scrambled to prepare for an embassy all-hands meeting that had only been announced during lunchtime. In Unity Hall, the designation for the empty expanse that divided the classified portions of the embassy from the less sensitive work areas, they erected a two-foot-high portable stage. Stimche and a co-worker hoisted a wooden lectern up onto it and positioned it front and center.

The voices of the IT guys echoed through the enclosed atrium as they tested the mic and speakers. One of the GSO office assistants clipped black bunting around the edges of the platform. Neither Chuck nor Robert had been able to tell Tara the purpose of the town hall gathering, so she opted for the neutral, formal bunting rather than the festive red-white-and-blue.

As four o'clock approached, the GSO crew hustled to get the remaining folding chairs set up. Early arrivals from other sections pitched in. Tara looked around, satisfying herself that all the preparations were in place. But for what? The sudden departure of General Elfersen and family and the reports of a former U.S. Army Ranger being held by the Vodanian government set off waves of rumors about staff firings, the embassy closing, plans for a covert rescue operation, massive government-organized protests.

The hum and buzz of voices rose as Unity Hall filled with curious and apprehensive staff.

Just before four, Andy emerged from the secure wing into Unity Hall. He stood next to the stage, facing the assembly with a controlled expression. The space was loaded. He scanned the gathering. Most of the American personnel were on hand, concentrated in the front third of the seats. He noticed the absence of several faces from USAID, which prompted him to consider various ways to manage and exploit the rift between that agency and the rest of the embassy.

After several more minutes of anticipation, the ambassador flung open the door from the secure wing and strode into Unity Hall, followed by Lithia and Davos. The buzz ceased, replaced by the scrape of chair legs and the rustle of fabric as everyone got to their feet.

Davos stopped to pee on a potted tree. The sides of the earthenware container were too high, so none of the urine reached the tree trunk or roots. Instead, it puddled on the floor.

Nice try, thought Andy, as he mounted the stage. Though the dog's gesture had a certain flair and poignancy. But enough. Andy approached the microphone and said, "Colleagues, please welcome Ambassador David Lamkin."

The audience applauded as the ambassador climbed the steps. After the clapping petered out and the staff sat back down, the ambassador leaned toward the mic.

"I want to begin by saying thank you. Thank you all for the tremendous work you do every day for the American people. And for the building of close ties between the United States of America and the Republic of Vodania. Together during the past nearly two years, we have made marked progress. Areas for improvement remain, to be sure, and this crucial work will continue with your dedicated efforts."

"I also want to share a word of appreciation about this embassy's election monitoring effort, under the able coordination of Gary Hambert. I am proud of the involvement of our whole team, and deeply regret that I was unfortunately prevented from participating in the culminating phase. This parliamentary election, despite significant flaws, marks another important milestone along Vodania's path to democracy and prosperity. Investors and citizens alike want rule of law and that remains a formidable challenge for the way forward."

Talking points talking points talking points, Andy muttered to himself.

The ambassador continued with his statement. "Today it is with decidedly mixed feelings that I announce to you that, for vital foreign policy requirements, I have been summoned urgently back to Washington. At this stage I am not at liberty to say what future diplomatic task the president and the secretary of state may have in mind for me. That will become clear in good time. I look forward to contributing in a new role. The downside is that, unfortunately, it appears unlikely that I will be able to continue serving in my capacity as the president's personal representative in Vodania."

It was the natural spin to put on the situation. But that face-saving veneer would wear off within hours, Andy figured. Soon it would be obvious to everyone that David Lamkin would never get another important assignment.

"Lithia and I, and Davos too of course, have deeply appreciated the support of this embassy and the warm hospitality of Vodania's citizens from all groups and walks of life. We take with us many wonderful friendships and memories, and Vodania will remain in our hearts."

He paused and turned toward Andy. With evident effort, his face contorted into something resembling a smile. "Until the ambassadorial post is once again occupied, you will be left in the sufficiently competent hands of the DCM."

Andy kept his hands folded in front of him and responded with the slightest of nods.

In the hushed comfort of the special departure lounge just after dawn on Friday, Tara and the expediter finished finalizing details with the airline employees and airport personnel. They got all the paperwork signed for the dog crate and the extra luggage. Tara stepped outside to wait.

After a few minutes, the ambassador's distinctive black limousine zoomed into view, American flags snapping smartly from their posts on either side of the hood. The limo approached the VIP gate and eased to a stop.

The chauffeur stepped out and walked around the front of the vehicle to open the ambassador's door. The two men shook hands in farewell. Tara stepped forward to greet Lithia Lamkin, but found she had nothing fitting to say. The ambassador's wife acknowledged her with a brief smile. Side by side, Tara and Lithia walked toward the airport building. Davos strained at his leash, pulling Lithia forward. Her husband trailed two paces behind.

The expediter supervised a pair of porters as they transferred the luggage onto trolleys. The chauffeur stepped to the front of the limo and removed the two flags. He rolled them up and slid them into protective leather storage tubes.

After Davos had been confined in his large crate and rolled away, and all the other details re-checked and re-confirmed among the ambassador and Lithia and Tara and the expeditor, as much to make conversation as any other reason, the time came to walk onto the tarmac.

Outside, David Lamkin grasped Tara's right hand. He raised his voice above the engine noise. "You have a bright future in the foreign service. Please get in touch if I can ever be of assistance."

Lithia moved in close, after first pausing to wipe away tears that started to spill from both eyes.

"Thank you, Tara, for everything. You are one of the good ones." She reached her arms around Tara in a fierce hug.

Another goodbye. Foreign service life seemed to be full of them. When the plane lifted off fifteen minutes later, Tara texted Robert with the exact time of departure.

She went outside through the regular exit. The limo idled at the curb, the chauffeur standing nearby. He offered her a ride back to the embassy, and Tara accepted. She pulled open the heavy passenger door and slid onto the roomy, slithery leather upholstery of the back seat. The police escort was still riding shotgun.

The chauffeur shifted into drive and slipped the vehicle into the traffic flow. Tara had never ridden in an ambassador's limousine. She extended her legs and stretched out her arms and nodded once.

"How's your family?" she asked the chauffeur.

"Thank you. They are fine. My son turned sixteen and got his first job."

"Nice!" Tara replied.

"In the car business," the chauffeur said with distinct pride. "He works at a rental company."

"What does he do?"

"You know they get the new cars in and at first, they smell like something plastic, like a factory? My son's job is to make them smell good."

"How does he do that?"

The chauffeur glanced at Tara in the rearview mirror and pantomimed smoking a cigarette.

"How much does he smoke?"

"To season a new car takes three, four cigarettes. Some special problems take more. About a month ago a van came back full of men's cologne, a very bad one. It took two whole packs before they could rent it out again."

Andy Pulano, chargé d'affaires, took it as a positive sign that President Chilik promptly agreed to see him. At the meeting, which took place on the Monday after Ambassador Lamkin's abrupt departure, Andy reciprocated with one of the most thorough and passionate effusions of flattery he had ever performed.

"A fresh start. I believe that's what we're talking about, Mr. President," said Andy, as the meeting had just about run its course. He grinned at Chilik, who looked absolutely stuffed with compliments.

"Let's hope so," replied Chilik. "I will think about your recommendations." He glanced at the sheet of paper Andy had presented earlier. "Procedural reforms for the next election, and improving relations with our neighbor to the north, and so forth."

Andy summoned another smile. "Mr. President, I'll get out of your way. But before I go, could we have a moment alone? I have a confidential matter to share with you."

Chilik nodded and the aides in attendance stood up. Gary Hambert pushed back his chair and straightened his spine one vertebra at a time, appealing with his eyes to the chargé. But Andy did not meet his gaze, instead focusing on the president.

When the doors had closed, Chilik folded his hands across his stomach.

This was it, Andy knew. The last task to boost his reputation in Washington and open the way for bigger and better things. Chilik was very dug in, for a whole range of personal and political reasons. And Andy had only one round in the chamber, so to speak. He had to make it count.

Andy flexed his eyebrows at President Chilik. "It's about our misguided contractor, Christopher Braxton, now held prisoner here."

Chilik stiffened. "He was the leader of a military incursion, a hostile act. You are familiar, I am certain, with the long list of offenses and damages committed during that attack."

"Your Excellency, we need a clean slate. Mr. Braxton is a burden for you and a strain on our relationship. We both know you don't want to keep him in Vodania."

Andy paused to lock in eye contact. His eyebrows pulsed as he continued, "And as you can probably well appreciate, it would be to my credit in Washington if his release were to take place promptly."

"Well, you know this is a matter for the courts to decide."

"Prolonging the outcome is not going to be to your benefit, I can promise you, Mr. President. As the revered leader of Vodania, you need to act decisively, as you have on so many other matters. What I can offer you in gratitude, not officially of course, is private information about someone close to you who had a role in precipitating this entire incident."

"I find that very unlikely."

"Believe me, you will much prefer hearing this from me, so you have time to shape events. Rather than having to react to unseemly reports on television."

"If you think my wife has been unfaithful with that nationalist poseur, you are very mistaken."

Andy waved his hand. "Not your wife."

The president glared.

"I want to help you," said Andy, "but I can't say more until Braxton is freed."

Another extended pause ensued. The president sipped his tea. Wriggling on the hook. Andy's eyebrows settled into a resting position.

After further silence, Andy placed his hands on the leather upholstery of the couch he occupied. "I realize you are very busy."

He began lifting himself to his feet.

"Sit."

Andy dropped back onto the couch, and Chilik scowled. "I have a personal trainer. You have womanly gossip, nothing new. Vodanians want their president to stay strong."

"It's not about you. Not directly."

Chilik frowned for a solid minute. Andy waited for him to decide if the knowledge was worth the price.

Chilik pressed a button on the underside of an end table.

Grigor Khalamente, the president's chief of staff, entered the room. Chilik motioned him over and whispered into his ear. Grigor drew back, checking Chilik's face for confirmation. The president, grimacing, nodded once.

As Grigor retreated toward the door, the president said, "Two brandies. No cinnamon."

The regular departure lounge at Shizl International was pretty scrappy, with not enough chipped and stained laminated plastic seats for everyone, but Christopher Braxton had been in far worse. Passengers sat on the worn linoleum floor like refugees, singly and in family groups, wherever they could find an open space.

Braxton wouldn't have minded standing, but his handlers from the embassy preferred to occupy the row of seats someone had taken the trouble to reserve for his benefit. Barbara Hertz and Robert Akes, the consul general and management counselor, sat on either side of him. Braxton couldn't decide if they were there to protect him or keep him under wraps. He didn't try too hard to puzzle it out, since it was self-evident they couldn't do either one.

He glanced at the date on the airline ticket they gave him. Tuesday, September 17. Nearly three weeks since the start of what was supposed to be a one-and-done mission. Well, Harrimore would owe him serious overtime and captivity compensation. He would be able to pay off the truck, for sure.

He scanned the other passengers. No one seemed willing to make eye contact. The thicket of stubble hanging off the lower half of his face probably didn't help. He rubbed his wrists and stretched his legs. When an airline employee approached to say he could board, he looked around for his pack, then remembered he no longer had one.

He followed the airline employee, and the two officials from the embassy followed him. They each shook his hand at the exit door. Braxton stepped out into the sunshine and onto the tarmac. Thirty meters ahead stood a portable metal staircase leading up into a Lufthansa 737 bound for Frankfurt.

Braxton strode forward. After three paces, he halted at the sight of a police car with flashing lights speeding toward him. Trailed by a black sedan. The vehicles jolted to a stop between Braxton and the plane, blocking his way. Police sprang out of both vehicles. Braxton looked back over his shoulder toward the departure lounge. The two embassy officials reached for their cell phones.

The rear passenger doors of the sedan swung open. After a moment, a distinguished-looking woman in a tailored business suit emerged from the right side. From the other side, a tallish man and a preschool girl. Carrying small suitcases, the three of them made their way up the boarding stairs into the aircraft. The couple looked dazed and sleep-deprived. The child skipped and danced behind them.

When the police cleared out of the way, Braxton took the boarding stairs two at a time, as if the sooner he buckled his seatbelt the sooner the flight would get off the ground. Passing through the first-class cabin he noticed the two specially-escorted parents slumped in their seats. They stared straight ahead while their daughter pressed her face to the window, bouncing and pointing, saying something in German.

On an overcast mid-September afternoon in the borderlands along the western stretch of the Asich Mountains, half a dozen men rode dirt bikes through gullies and up goat trails. They crossed the headwaters of the Odorian on a narrow concrete bridge not built by any government.

Once over the border and into Pazaria, Shariz and associates switched to SUVs for the rest of the drive to Zagovor. When they reached the downtown bustle of Pazaria's capital, they dodged cement trucks, horse carts, and taxi drivers who seemed to be training for Formula One competitions. All the while keeping a wary eye on the construction cranes swinging overhead. Their business appointments were not until evening, but at Shariz's testy insistence they had arrived hours early.

To the puzzlement of the associates, they detoured to the Xanadu Mall, a sparkling stack of glitter owned by a corporation in Turkey which was owned by a corporation in Dubai. The Xanadu was renowned as an excellent source for designer shoes, the latest cell phones, and tobacco products from around the world. Shariz ordered his men to wait outside.

Clad in a dark grey skull cap, a sleeveless LeBron James jersey, and a red bikini Speedo, Shariz marched down the middle of the mall's central passageway, his motorcycle boots resounding on the marble floor. Across from a decorative fountain, he entered a boutique outfitted like a spa and told the young lady at the reception area what he wanted.

She led him to a private room, where he reclined on a plush settee.

Soon an attendant in a clingy sarong entered and knelt on the carpet nearby.

"This I think you will enjoy," she said. "The essence of four rare varieties of orchid, blended with racehorse semen. Only from thoroughbreds. Plus, ripe banana, diesel, and musk from the glands of Burmese oxen."

Shariz did not change his expression.

"And a hint of organic asparagus, for the top notes."

Holding a vaporizer in her slender hand, she smiled. "May I?"

Shariz extended his left arm and she gave the inside of his wrist a delicate spritz. He brought his wrist to his nose, careful to avoid contact with his elevated mustache tips. Letting his eyelids slide closed, he inhaled.

His eyes watered and he was unable to suppress a cough reflex.

"Delightful," he pronounced, his voice inflected with pain and nausea. "But I need something much stronger."

On the living room couch in a leafy residential neighborhood in Fairfax, Virginia, a woman tapped on a laptop.

"Hey, finally, the deposits came through," she called out. "Minus ten percent off your bonus," she added with a frown.

"Woo-hoo!" came her husband's voice from the kitchen. "Oops, don't mean to wake the kiddles."

"I still can't believe you made that bet. That could have been a nice boost to the college fund," she scolded, looking up from the computer screen as her husband approached, drying his hands on the back of his thighs.

"That's exactly what I was thinking when I shook on it with our backwoods buddy. But this still calls for a hootenanny, don't it?" He bent over and tugged at her V-neck. "I have a notion as to why they called you Two."

She tightened her lips and seized his wrist and pushed his hand into his own crotch. "You packing your Six-gun?"

Twilight at the vernal equinox. An inflection point in the seasons. Change. Summer over. Where did that leave a summer romance?

Full of such musings, Tara descended from her apartment to the parking lot behind the building. She toted a small box with a pair of U.S. Embassy Shizl coffee mugs and an envelope stuffed with cash. Her first Roma wedding. She wasn't sure what to expect from the evening, but she appreciated having a diversion from her emptiness and from the embassy routine.

At work things had gotten off-kilter somehow. The DCM, sorry, the chargé d'affaires, always acted courteous and professional, but Tara sensed he was still smarting over how the doggy detective saga concluded. Nearly two weeks after his debriefing, she still felt dissected. The cold, relentless precision with which Andy cross-examined her account of her actions and observations, extracting everything she knew and the order she knew it in, continued to trouble her. Then came a dispiriting spate of unrequested and unappealing ladder-climbing advice from Robert about the importance of managing up. And last week Tara got saddled with organizing the upcoming semi-annual employee awards ceremony, normally an HR responsibility. When Robert tasked her with it, it didn't feel to Tara like it was his idea.

She made her way toward her Wrangler, a bright splash of red in a parking lot of brown and black. Standing just beyond her jeep was a tall guy with his back to her. A bristle of short brown hair. White tuxedo jacket, black jeans, and well-travelled boots. A backpack. Her legs froze in place and one hand rose up to cover her mouth. Everything went completely still.

After a whirling moment of tumult and dizziness, Tara caught her breath and beamed. She placed her parcel on the top of the Wrangler and walked up behind him. "What are you all gussied up for?"

Mads turned to face her. "Going to a wedding."

"Were you invited?"

"You know me. I've always been a glommer." He grinned and reached for her.

They grasped each other. Her thighs, torso, and cheek pressed into his. Mads squeezed as if to ask forgiveness for travelling away, as if he couldn't let go again. A tingle spread through her body, like bursts of atomic particles pulsed from her core, connecting to a cosmic energy. Or maybe, she thought, I'm just horny.

She walked backwards toward her jeep, pulling Mads along. She reclined on the hood, her face pointing skyward, and felt Mads kissing her throat. She grabbed his hip bones and lifted herself against him.

They squirmed and ground together until Tara opened her eyes and said, "Stop. Wait until after the wedding."

Mads groaned and let his forehead clunk against the hood. They stayed like that for a while before clambering into the Wrangler. Tara retrieved the gift mugs and lowered the top and shifted into first. Navigating the streets of Shizl, she kept half an eye on the traffic as she gazed at Mads in wonderment, one hand on the wheel and one hand on him.

The festivities took place in an illegal settlement, a shanty town that had spawned around a municipal dump a mile or two southwest of the edge of Shizl. Weeds and wildflowers pushed up from clumps of mud and trash between uneven clusters of shacks. An aroma of roasting meat mingled with the odors of decay and burning plastic emitted by the massive hills of refuse nearby. A group of older men tended the fire beneath the wedding goat and slowly rotated the spit. On the barbed-wire fence that demarcated the boundary of the dump, the fresh goatskin was stretched taut.

In an open space where two dirt lanes intersected, the villagers and all the visiting relatives and guests packed together in three concentric circles. They moved their feet in an elaborate rhythm in which the second circle moved in the opposite direction of the first and third. Tara and Mads approached, and the outer circle broke open to accommodate them. Tara took the hand of a man in his forties to her left and Mads took the hand of a teenage boy on his right. The tunes, loud and fast, came from a band squeezed onto a platform set up on one of the lanes. One song started as soon as the previous one finished. The steps changed, but the dancing never ceased.

Jovina, the Saturday school organizer, squealed with joy at the sight of Tara and Mads. She hustled them over to meet her brother and his new wife, pulling the ecstatic bride and groom from the inner circle. They're so much younger than we are, Tara noticed.

The wedding festival rolled on. Music and feasting ran deep into the night, an ancient celebration alive in the dark shadows of a garbage mountain ceaselessly smoldering.

Epilogue

Another Day to Rise

Nearly six months later, on a Saturday morning in March, Fernando Oscar Pulano stood alone on the roof of the embassy. He looked down on Shizl and the countryside beyond. The morning shone clear and bright, but a cold biting wind whistled from the snowy crests of the Asich Mountains. It shook the antenna towers and forced low groans from the support brackets for the satellite dishes. Andy, up on top of this concrete-and-steel, flesh-and-blood outpost of the United States of America, felt he deserved a soliloquy. This he delivered silently, with no audience but the sky.

As chargé d'affaires during the months that followed the momentous and often unseemly events that ensued from one dog's copious vomit, I have been rather fortunate to preside over a far more favorable period. One marked by tranquility and relative progress. Yes, it is true that the elevated prominence thrust upon me in this role as interim head of the embassy has imposed a requirement for enhanced discretion in my nocturnal wanderings amidst the more dubious characters in the more obscure corners of this not-entirely-presentable land we call Vodania. But President Chilik and I have gotten along marvelously. Vodania's interethnic hostilities have simmered back down to comfortable levels. And our humble embassy enjoyed the distinct privilege of hosting an absolutely thrilling and quite substantive visit from the vice president of the United States, to commemorate ratification of the border agreement and the historic establishment of diplomatic relations between Vodania and Pazaria.

The bottom line is that Embassy Shizl has functioned exceptionally well despite the tragic ends that befell the careers of former ambassador David Lamkin and former defense attaché General Elfersen. Former German ambassador Monika Basch and her former husband Dieter Schmidt have also been missed acutely in Shizl's diplomatic and artistic circles. And best of all, the EUR assistant secretary has put my fucking name forward for a delightful little starter embassy of my own. These consequential events, set in motion by a young child tempting a dog by inserting a candy bar into a gap between two fence posts, represent a pivotal point in my career. Counting on the support of a senator from Nebraska and his distinguished colleagues, I will soon be known, henceforth and forevermore, as Ambassador Pulano. This colossal, enduring achievement occurred because I took care to develop the skills, the information, and the network necessary to maneuver effectively, and to capitalize on the opportunities I created.

I should feel triumphant. I do feel triumphant. With the title of Ambassador Extraordinary and Plenipotentiary, I will at last attain release from the agony of being ordinary.

The chargé stood erect. He smiled in the sunshine, impervious to the frosty gusts. Yet something troubled him. An insidious feeling of something amiss. Or that he had missed something. Had a detail, a fragment perhaps, eluded his ever-watchful mind?

Yesterday at dinner, his jolly political counselor Gary Hambert told a story about putting on his shoes one recent morning before work. Gary described sitting on the stool in his front hallway, jamming his feet into his dress shoes, and noticing that the leather appeared to have a subtly different design from what he remembered. Also, the laces felt a thread or two thicker and maybe an inch longer. When he stood up and walked outside, the shoes didn't feel right. The angle of wear was wrong. Finally, Gary realized that, while they looked a lot like his shoes, they weren't. He had hosted dinner for a group of opposition politicians the previous night, and he figured one of his well-lubricated guests must have worn similar oxfords and put Gary's on by mistake on his way out. And was now too embarrassed to acknowledge it. Meanwhile, there was Gary standing in front of his house asking himself, who wants to walk in a nationalist's shoes? In Gary's telling, it made for an amusing dessert anecdote, and they got a chuckle over the phenomenon of having all sorts of evidence of something being wrong, yet the mind refuses to accept it. Because it's not what you want to believe.

From his rooftop vantage Andy mulled this over, bracing his legs against the rude shoving of the wind.

The chargé's memory traced further back, to early February and the fortuitous arrival of the notice from the State Department announcing that Embassy Shizl, along with numerous other posts, had to give up an officer for urgent reassignment to Pakistan. Naturally his first impulse was to dispatch Victor Manchego, but he quickly thought the better of it. Victor already had an onward assignment lined up, so he was safely disposed of. Breaking that arrangement would pose an unacceptable risk that Embassy Islamabad could get wind of his outstanding incompetence, and object strenuously. In which case, the unfortunate Victor could end up extending his tour in Shizl by default. Furthermore, Andy wanted no direct association with Victor's future assignments and subsequent screwups. Instead, he determined that the requirement to dispatch an officer to I-bad offered the appropriate occasion to provide Tara Zadani with the dramatic culmination of the invaluable career lessons he had been bestowing on her. She must learn to appreciate that obedience and loyalty to superiors are the supreme virtues. So don't fucking ever fucking fuck with me, as our dear assistant secretary might well put it.

He recalled the whole delicious conversation with Tara. How she entered his office and perched tremulously on the edge of the guest chair in front of his desk. How he kept the discussion absolutely scrupulous. No questions about her personal or family life. No need to anyway, since he had heard through several channels that her strapping boyfriend had gone back to his Nordic lair. Andy congratulated her again for the special commendation she received from the vice president for her exceptionally skillful work in organizing the visit. Andy asked if she was aware of what had transpired in Pakistan and the urgent need to re-staff Embassy Islamabad with qualified officers. Tara attempted to deflect him, pointing out that her first two tours were in hardship posts and she felt she should go somewhere more happening. She mentioned her hopes regarding an upcoming opening in Stockholm. He emphasized the importance of service discipline and said she would find plenty happening in I-bad. She pleaded not to be chosen. Begged. Argued that her Indian heritage would make it difficult for her to be effective there and would expose her to greater dangers. He noted that the assignment to a place like I-bad, where it is especially critical to take supervisors' instructions as law, would provide an important professional challenge for her. He said his decision was well-founded and final. Her left hand flew to cover her mouth, attempting to conceal her consternation and dread. She promptly excused herself and fled from his office.

He inhaled a lungful of cold air and savored the memory. A fitting send-off for a headstrong junior officer. And yet. This was the same young woman who, on the eve of the vice president's visit, stood up to an entire Secret Service advance team and put them soundly in their places. Who pursued the Davos poisoning investigation with, begging pardon, dogged determination. Who, by herself, essentially forced the embassy to take serious action against anti-Roma discrimination. She really wasn't the type to crumple.

A sudden impulse struck the chargé. He climbed back down into the building, pulling the roof hatch shut above him. In the executive suite, empty as usual on a Saturday morning, he unlocked his assistant's safe. He pulled open the drawer where Charlene kept the training reports. It surprised him to notice his hand trembling a little as he removed the cardboard folder for the management section and pulled out a half-inch thick accumulation of papers. Near the top of the pile, he found what he didn't want to find.

On October 2, Tara Zadani registered to study Urdu through the online language school of the Foreign Service Institute. Urdu, the lingua franca of Pakistan. October 2 was four months before he consigned her there. How was that possible? It made no sense. Eyebrows drooping, Andy Pulano stared at the wall in disbelief.

On the same Saturday, from the upper slopes of the Margalla Hills, Pakistan's capital sparkled and glittered in the valley below. Tara and Mads paused to wave at several of his students and their families, lagging a few hundred meters below them on the trail. Mads claimed he could see part of the roof of the school from where they stood. The breeze blew clean and fresh.

Tara and Mads sat shoulder to shoulder on a large, smooth rock. He reached into his day-pack.

"Mangos in the sunshine!" Tara exclaimed.

"That should be the name of a song," said Mads.

Mads peeled a ripe mango, its flesh slick and slippery. He squeezed the ends of the golden fruit with the fingertips of both hands and presented it to Tara. She cupped her hands around his and bit into the tangy, succulent offering. She slurped. And she giggled when a trickle of sweet liquid escaped from her lips.

His eyes fastened on hers and she felt a smile spring from deep within. His face moved closer. Her eyelids slid down. He brought his mouth near to hers and licked from her chin the renegade drop of mango juice.

Author's Note

When I ended my career at the State Department, I had been a foreign service officer for well over half my time on the planet. The customs and folkways of American diplomacy ran deep in my blood. Perhaps as a result, or a remedy, in the months that followed, I wrote *Dog's Breakfast*.

The events and characters in this novel are entirely fictitious, as is the primary location. But the lampooning of the inner workings of the American international affairs bureaucracy, the narrative's cultural ecosystem, is grounded in what I observed and experienced over the years.

The process of refining and polishing the manuscript became a long and almost entirely enjoyable trek. To all who gave aid and comfort along the way, I offer heartfelt appreciation. Priscilla Hoffman-Stowe, freelance editor and former senior State Department official, provided sharp edits and suggestions on the initial draft. Anne Barbaro, the pre-publication reviewer at the State Department who read the manuscript to ensure it contained no classified information, graciously reached out to express her enjoyment of the story and her hope it would see print. My friend Brooke Lea's enthusiasm for an early version sustained me. Writer friends Chris Mills, David Stowe, and Peter Ziv shared good cheer at various stages of the journey. Former diplomatic colleagues Merritt Chesley, James Gibney, Deanna Horton, Gayle von Eckartsberg, Larry Mandel, and Kim McDonald provided helpful comments and encouragement on early drafts. Critique group partners Jim Ball, Shanti Chandrasekhar, Angie Montgomery Hasson, Kenny Reff, Doug Rowland, Norah Vawter, Lauren Woods, and others helped me hone portions of the manuscript. Warm thanks to avid readers and endless fonts of humor Chris Ritter and Amy Maisterra.

This book reached its best and final form thanks to the great care and expertise of my editor, Penny Dowden, whom I thank vociferously.

I will always be grateful to Abby Macenka and the entire team at Between the Lines Publishing for bringing my debut novel into the world.

My son Justin, a high school student at the time, noticed the draft manuscript open on my computer screen, and as a prank typed in: *I am Marko, said Marko. I am too cool.* I kept the line. For my son Luke, as he embarks on his own adventures in international relations, may this book resonate.

Special thanks to Dan Navratil, an accomplished visual artist—and my nephew, for gracing *Dog's Breakfast* with his cover design.

Tom Navratil grew up in Illinois and Wisconsin. He joined the U.S. Foreign Service after graduating from Haverford College, and served in American embassies around the world. He now writes fiction and humor from an undisclosed (because no one ever asks) location near Washington D.C.